CAGED MAGIC

A Wing Slayer Hunter Novel

JENNIFER LYON

CAGED MAGIC: A WING SLAYER HUNTER NOVEL

Copyright © 2015 Jennifer Apodaca
All rights reserved.

Published by JenniferLyonBooks
www.jenniferlyonbooks.com

ISBN: 978-0-9887923-4-0

Cover Design: Patricia Schmitt (Pickyme)
Editor: Sashaknighteditor.com
Formatted by: Author E.M.S.
Proofreader: devilinthedetailsediting.com
Wing Slayer Hunter Logo Design: Jaycee DeLorenzo of Sweet 'N Spicy Designs

Published in the United States of America.

THE WING SLAYER HUNTER SERIES

⇒ 1 ⇐

LINC DILLINGER SWIPED THE BLOOD from his eyes and blinked to clear his vision. Damned cut on his forehead bled like a son of a bitch. It didn't seem to matter how rich he got or how many lives he saved, he kept ending back up in a damned cage fight deathmatch.

Because women are your weakness, dumbass.

Oh yeah, that. Show him a woman in trouble, and he went all witch-hunter-in-shining-armor on the attacker's ass.

Linc eyed the rogue circling him. Damn, he hated the weak-willed bastards for giving in to the bloodlust they all endured, killing innocent witches to harvest the power in their blood. Yeah, their death amounted to justice.

He just hated doing it in a cage. Too many memories...

Movement snapped him out of his thoughts as three hundred pounds of enraged male dropped his shoulder and barreled toward him.

Time to end this. Linc spun and slammed his foot into the flank of the man's knee. Heard the satisfying crack of bone and cartilage, followed by the man's pained bellow as he fell back against the side of the cage.

Linc calculated how to kill this man with the too-smooth face—a side effect of absorbing so much witch blood. He had to cut into the man's heart to make sure he died. Hard to do without a weapon.

Much as he hated rogues, he didn't underestimate them. The power kick from witch blood meant this bastard could probably bench-press a fire truck.

The man lashed out with hammer fists.

Linc ducked and shoved in beneath the blows to wrap his arms around the rogue's waist, planning to get him on the mat and punch through his chest. Messy but effective.

He sensed movement on the other side of the cage, behind the man. Warnings flickered down his spine. Linc jerked back just as a silver blade flashed in the rogue's fist.

Fucking cheaters. His friends had passed him a blade. The same friends who'd kidnapped and beat up a woman to engineer this deathmatch.

"I'm going to cut out your eyes, you—"

Linc snapped his foot out, hitting the rogue's wrist. The knife flew from his grip. Tracking the weapon, Linc leapt into the air, snatched it, and drove the blade deep into the rogue's massive chest.

Blood spurted out as the other man's heart pumped a few more seconds. Ignoring the warm liquid gushing over his bare chest, Linc twisted the blade until he was certain the rogue wouldn't take another breath.

Dropping the body to the mat, Linc stood while gripping the bloody knife. The need to get out of the cage clawed at him. He stormed to the door, ripped it open and stalked out.

Huge men, both witch hunters and rogues, scrambled to get out of his way.

A hand landed on his shoulder.

Linc whirled, the knife up and ready. He lifted his gaze to Baron Frank's light eyes set deep in a haggard face and old rage spewed up. The leader of the witch hunters here in Las Vegas was the last person Linc wanted to see right now. "Don't. I came. I did the job to rescue your girl. Get the fuck away from me."

"Las Vegas is where you belong. This is our town, Dillinger. You need to be here helping us deal with the growing rogue problem. Not in California."

"Hand. Off." Fury and the sick craving for blood had him wired to a hair trigger. Add in the constant need for sexual release, and he was as stable as a live grenade being used as a hockey puck.

Baron raised an eyebrow but moved his hand, causing his leather vest to creak. "Your crew in Cali know what you're doing? Divided loyalties and all?"

His crew, as Baron called them, was a group of witch hunters who had recommitted to their god, Wing Slayer. But Linc wasn't getting into that same old debate with Baron about whether or not Wing Slayer had abandoned the witch hunters more than three decades ago after the demon witches cast a blood and sex curse. Linc had chosen his path, and if that pissed off Baron, tough shit. The man had more or less mentored Linc, but he didn't own him.

Done with the conversation, he slammed into the locker room and heaved the knife against the wall. It ricocheted off, hit the metal lockers, clipped a bench and clattered to the floor. All the noise did nothing to release the ugliness brewing inside him.

Fucking cage fights.

Retrieving the knife, he cleaned it, wrapped it in a towel and heaved it into a locker. After striding to the shower, he turned the water to boiling, stripped and stood beneath the spray, trying to wash his self-disgust away.

But nothing washed away his past. Every time he

went into a cage and heard that door clang shut, it reminded him that he'd spent six years locked in a cage, forced to fight like a dog that had been brutally trained to kill. Physically he'd escaped eleven years ago, but mentally? He slapped his hands against the cool tile, shoving his head into the water. In his mind, that cage was always there. Just like the brand on his back.

Feral.

No matter that his falcon tattoo covered the reviled word, it remained permanently burned into his skin. Into his very essence. Reminding him that in the end, he was an animal. The things he'd been forced to do...

An odd itch on his back cut into his thoughts. It seemed to be in his tat. What the hell? Turning, he let the water cascade over the irritated skin.

Still itched.

It'd been over a year since he'd gotten inked as a symbol of his commitment to Wing Slayer. He hadn't felt a tingle of pain or itching in all that time. It was weird and more annoying than the cuts and bruises from the fight.

Enough. He had to get out of here. After shutting off the shower, he dried and began dressing, pulling on the identity he'd created, the façade of a charming, successful gambler, right down to his Berluti loafers and Rolex watch. The cuts on his face would be healed by the time he hit the clubs. Spoiling a woman, winning her smile then finding relief in her body fed a deep need in him. Soothed the constant haunting guilt of the things he'd been forced to do in captivity.

Reaching for his knife holster, he started to strap it on when the door swung open. Linc whipped around while unsheathing his knife. Friends of the man he'd just killed might be popping in for a little revenge.

Ramsy Virtos strode in. "Cage fights. Deathmatches. This is where you run off to, Dillinger?"

Jesus, he just couldn't get a break. Ever since Linc had been soaked in witch blood by rogues trying to force him to turn rogue, Ram had been up his ass, making sure he didn't cave into the violent need for more witch blood. *Never.* He'd cut out his own heart before he'd hurt a woman, either mortal or witch. Too many memories of women he hadn't been able to help lived in his mind.

"Something wrong with your hearing? Get your bell rung in that cage?" Ram straddled the bench running down the center of twin rows of lockers.

That didn't deserve an answer. Linc holstered his knife and leaned back against the metal cabinets. "When did you turn into a fretting old grandma following me around?"

Ram's eyes narrowed. "Don't make me kick your ass."

"You must not have been watching my fight if you think that's possible."

"I was there. I stayed invisible, but I had your back if something went south. Like when those asswipes handed your opponent a knife. What the hell are you doing getting into a cage with a rogue?"

"Better than getting into a bath of witch blood, don't you think?" Might as well get it out there. All the Wing Slayer Hunters knew Linc was losing the battle against the curse. Rogues had jumped him, chained him up and doused him in witch blood. Jesus, even months later an internal shudder wracked him at the memory of the incredible high that ripped into him. If the hunters hadn't gotten there to rescue him, Linc would have killed a witch to get more of her blood.

"Bullshit." Dogged determination settled over the other man's features. "I was there when the witches used sex magic to bring you back. They overlaid the craving for blood with a need for sex. Since you didn't screw the rogue in the cage—and fuck, I did not need that mental image—you had another reason for that asinine stunt."

Ram knew too damned much. Including that Linc had to constantly feed the sex magic to keep the bloodlust manageable. Unless he wanted to kill the other hunter to shut him up, he might as well tell him. After digging his phone out, he thumbed through the pics and showed him the one Baron had sent him of a woman with a bloody, swollen face.

"Ah." Ram glanced up. "You know her? She a witch? Someone important to you?"

He returned his phone to his pocket. "Not a witch, hookup or close friend, just a woman I've seen around a few times." Didn't matter to Linc. He didn't like women used and hurt, period. "She works for a friend of mine, was taken by rogues, and they demanded a cage fight to get her back alive. Baron—"

"The older guy you were arguing with after the fight?"

He nodded. "He figured they had a ringer and some point to make. So he called me in to do the wetwork." Much as Linc hated cage fights, he didn't lose.

Anger flashed in Ram's gaze. "You got a death wish? What stopped the rogues from an all-out attack?"

"Don't need a lecture, grandma."

"You need my boot up your ass."

"Kinky and violent. Don't want to hurt your feelings, but that's not my thing."

Ram growled, low and frustrated.

The damned tat on Linc's back itched, beginning to feel like a mosquito party let loose in his ink. He rubbed the annoyed skin against the corner of the lockers. Thinking about his irritated tat meant he didn't have to think about Vegas and how much rogues gaining a foothold in this town pissed him off.

"Ease up, dude. The rogues are making a statement, putting Baron and his M.C. on notice by showing they could snatch one of Baron's girls. Power play."

"Motorcycle Club?" Amusement tinged his voice. "A witch-hunter one?"

Linc shrugged. "Why not? We don't fit anywhere else, do we?"

Nothing changed in Ram's face, but his fingers rained blue sparks. "Fitting in gets a little tougher now that I've become a witch-hunter firecracker. Everyone back in California is constantly watching me, waiting for the day this shit ignites and kills me."

Worry gnawed at Linc. Ram was on borrowed time just like him. "That the real reason you decided to follow me? Needed to get away?" Linc got it. Four of their friends had found their mates, *soul mirrors*—the one witch who had the other half of their souls and could break the curse through mating. While he, Ram and another hunter, Eli Stone, struggled every damned day, fighting the sick urge to hunt and kill a witch to absorb the power in her blood.

Ram dropped his hands. "We're not talking about me." A frown drew down his eyebrows. "Why are you rubbing up against the lockers like a cat in heat?" Shit. He'd been razing his back against the corner trying to get relief. "Tat itches."

Ram stilled, suddenly intense. "No shit? When did that start?"

"Noticed it after the fight, I guess."

"Dude, that could be a sign your soul mirror's close by. Your falcon feels her and is waking."

Soul mirror. It twanged through Linc, sparking hope—his one shot at getting rid of the curse and living to do the job he loved, being a Wing Slayer Hunter. But that hope was shadowed with a bone-deep fear he'd never admit to. The soul-mirror couples he'd seen had bonded so profoundly, they could hear each other's thoughts. The hunter's winged tattoo became the witch's familiar, helping her with her high magic. That took trust.

Much as Linc liked women, he didn't trust them, at least not like that. Oh, he'd find his soul mirror, but he planned to offer her a deal, one they'd both benefit from. "So how do I find her?"

Ram opened his mouth to answer when his cell rang. Pulling out the device, he glanced at the screen. "It's Axel."

"Better take it." They didn't ignore calls from the leader of the Wing Slayer Hunters. Linc pushed off the locker to see the phone better.

Ram hit a button, and Axel Locke appeared on the screen, his green eyes troubled. "Axel, Linc's here with me," Ram said. "What's up?"

The man on the screen nodded. "Good. The soul-mirror witches feel something big happening in the ley lines. They've traced it to Vegas. It's some kind of demon magic."

Linc scowled. "From Asmodeus, or is this something his demon witches are doing? The ley lines are the demon's link to his witches, right?"

"Those ley lines are power grids between Earth and the Underworld, so yes."

"It's definitely demon magic and getting stronger." Darcy MacAlister came into view next to Axel. "All of us soul-mirror witches feel it and think Asmodeus is directly involved in some way. We feel the power collecting, getting ready to erupt."

"Shit, that can't be good," Ram said.

Linc rubbed the back of his neck, wishing he could reach that nagging itch in his tattoo. "Do you know where?"

Darcy nodded, concern tightening her face. "The energy is manifesting right down the center of Las Vegas Boulevard."

"The Strip." Ram's gaze snapped to Linc's.

Linc dropped his hand from his neck. "Maybe the demon witches are summoning Asmodeus through the ley lines there." Far as he knew, the demon witches needed a host body to summon the demon into, but they'd done it before.

Axel's grim face filled the phone screen. "Sutton's in the air, on his way to Vegas. He'll be there in less than an hour."

Linc nodded. Of the four mated hunters who had real wings, Sutton flew the fastest. "We're a few blocks away from the Strip. We'll go check it out and report back."

There was no time to screw around. No way was he letting that demon and his witches get a foothold in Vegas.

Risa Faden drove the small rental car down Las Vegas Boulevard. At close to midnight, the Strip glowed with lights from the towering hotels, and people swarmed the sidewalks and spilled into the streets. Sharp laughter and loud voices mixed with throbbing music that bled from the clubs.

It was a stark contrast to the sluggish heaviness in her first four chakras, from her pelvis to her heart. The strange pull in her magic made her uneasy. What was that?

Maybe this is what it feels like when your mind finally breaks and your magic begins to die.

No, God, don't even think that. Risa clamped her jaw, determined to hold on to her sanity and do the right thing.

"Do you think Archer knows we're here?"

Risa glanced in the mirror to meet the eyes of her best friend from childhood, Blythe Fredrick. The woman in the back seat had one hand on the chubby arm of her sleeping baby, Kendall. "I don't know."

Blythe chewed on her lower lip, strain and fatigue adding years to her face. "He intended to kill me last night. I couldn't believe it when he broke in with two armed thugs. If you hadn't been home—"

"But I was," Risa cut her off, unwilling to think about losing her only real friend and Kendall.

"What is he? That's not the same man I dated. He's...something else now."

Squeezing the steering wheel, Risa tried to puzzle it out. "I thought he was mortal, but last night an inhuman oiliness slicked into his aura. I'd say a demon witch, except men can't be witches."

Blythe rubbed her baby's arm. "What about Kendall? He's her father."

Yeah, that worried Risa too. "She appears as mortal as you." But was she? Didn't matter, Kendall totally owned Risa's heart regardless of her heritage.

"None of this makes sense. What kind of creature spawns?"

The last thing Archer had screamed at them before Risa, Blythe and Kendall escaped was, "Once I spawn, you won't be able to run fast or far enough." What did that mean? "Frogs and fish, otherwise..." She didn't know, damn it. But Risa sure as hell didn't want to be around when it happened with Archer.

"God, Risa. I can't guess why he wants Kendall. When I got pregnant, he paid me to keep him off the birth certificate. He wasn't there when she was born."

"I noticed." Of course she had, she'd been there coaching Blythe and saw her goddaughter come into the world. Even though Risa had left Vegas after her father's murder conviction, she'd stayed friends with Blythe. "Whatever Archer wants, it's not what's good for Kendall." If he cared about his child, he wouldn't have had thugs try to kidnap her or allowed them to use weapons in the process. In desperation, Risa had cast her shield around the three of them to escape. But what if she wasn't fast enough next time? They would have killed her and Blythe to get Kendall.

"I don't care what he is, I wouldn't change anything. Kendall's the best thing that ever happened to me. I love her more than I thought possible."

True, Blythe had been a total party girl, but pregnancy transformed her into a responsible young mom, making Risa damned proud.

And a tad jealous. She'd lost her own baby when she'd been four months along in her pregnancy. *Lost? You see her and talk to her when you're alone. That's not normal, crazy girl. People don't see and chat with their dead baby.* Her apprehension ratcheted up, and she rubbed at the ache in her forehead.

"Hey, you okay?" Leaning forward, Blythe put her hand on Risa's shoulder. "This last episode you had was bad. You were out of it for hours."

No, she really wasn't okay. Not with her mind slowly cracking under the weight of the screams from all the souls trapped in her shield magic. It happened every time she used that particular power, getting worse with each episode. Definitely not okay, but Risa had to hold on to her sanity. Blythe and Kendall were counting on her.

Once she got her, Blythe and Kendall to safety, then she could worry about finding a way to free the souls and save herself. Maybe by figuring out how to reach the Ancestors, the souls of witches who'd chosen to no longer reincarnate, but remain in Summerland. Risa had heard of other witches contacting them through their third eye.

"Risa?" Concern dropped Blythe's voice to a whisper.

Blowing out a breath, Risa tried to release some of the tension cramping her neck muscles. "I'm fine."

Squinting against the glaring lights, she added, "We're almost there."

Blythe leaned back. "How long will we be here in Vegas?"

"Only long enough for my contact, Jim, to get us out of the country." She hadn't wanted to come back to Vegas since this was where Archer lived, but Risa trusted her contact. It had been a judgment call. Jim had a room waiting for them under assumed names. "Hopefully we'll be on a plane tomorrow."

Spotting the Mystique Hotel, she guided the car up the driveway to the front. "We're here."

As the car stopped, the baby woke and began fussing. Blythe clicked the release on the car seat.

"Wait." Risa scanned the portico. Too many people milled around. "I'll come to your side of the car." She grabbed her purse and looped the strap over her shoulder, feeling the weight of her gun tucked inside. She'd spent the last few years as a bodyguard for women stalked and harassed by men, and she was damned good at her job. Too bad she hadn't had a clear shot at Archer last night. She might not be able to cause harm with her magic, but she'd have no problem shooting his ass.

"Got it," Blythe answered. "Shh, Kendall, I know, sweetheart." She tried to soothe the cranky baby.

The poor kid had had a rough day, but Risa ignored the urge to comfort her and got out of the car before the valet could open her door.

Surprised, the man stepped back then recovered. "Are you checking in?"

Nodding, she handed off the keys. The heaviness in her chakras increased. Weird. *Tired, yeah that could be it.* All three of them had hit their limit, and Risa had spent several hours early this morning trapped in soul screams. Time to get into a room to rest. She headed around the car just as a valet opened Blythe's door.

Keeping her hands free in case trouble erupted, Risa moved back and let the valet help Blythe and Kendall out. She watched all the people, searching for any sign of danger.

A loud rumble ripped through the night. The ground pitched and undulated. Thrown off balance, she dropped to her knees, a shock of pain cramping straight down her center, like a hand reaching in and ripping out her magic.

What the hell? Her pulse shot up, heart pounding.

The ground rocked again. A thick sulfur scent billowed up. An oily sensation filled her mouth. Elemental fear raced down her spine. Sulfur? Oil? Only one thing she could think of—*demon magic.*

Boom!

An explosion plunged the entire boulevard into total blackness. *Wrong. Unnatural.* Adrenaline surged into her blood, and she jumped to her feet.

Someone slammed into her, shoving Risa into another man. He heaved her away, and her knees crashed into the car bumper. Damn, that stung. Bracing her hands on the vehicle, she jerked her gaze around. Frantic voices shrilled, and people ran in panic.

Another violent wave of shaking hit. Risa gripped the edge of the trunk. From her pelvis to her forehead, harsh pressure tugged and yanked on her magic, draining her power. Stealing it. A demon witch? Or Archer?

Blythe and Kendall! They weren't by the car. Oh God. Pushing off the trunk, she elbowed and shoved until she spotted them by the hotel doors.

On the walkway between the car and the entrance stood a man with his head thrown back, arms outstretched, a bow clutched in one hand, a fistful of arrows in the other. Live flames lashed over his body like whips of lightning, streaking up and down his arms, torso, hips, sliding between his thighs, covering his legs and back. The flames ate away his clothes but left no burns on his skin. Instead, he seemed to be swelling, his muscles bulking up before her eyes.

Risa dragged her gaze to his face and recognized the blond hair and even features—Archer.

Once I spawn, you won't be able to run fast or far enough.

Chill bumps erupted on her skin, and her stomach twisted. What was he? Her entire being tried to cringe away.

Two police officers ran up with a blanket and tossed it on him to smother the flames.

The blanket ignited in a huge blaze, whooshed back and overwhelmed the two officers. Their pain-filled bellows jerked Risa from her shock. She shouldered her way closer as the doors to the hotel burst open and a thick-set, dark-skinned man ran out. Jim, her contact.

"No!" Snapping into action, she mentally reached for her magic, hoping to douse the flames or create a barrier. But before she could get even one chakra open, the blaze engulfed Jim too.

Don't look, oh God, don't look. Nausea churned, bile shoving up her throat. But she couldn't fall apart. Forcing her stare from the burning man, she spotted Blythe trapped behind the fiery Archer by the hotel doors. Crammed in a corner, she had her body curved protectively around the baby.

Go. Get them both away! Risa fought against the streams of stampeding people escaping, while concentrating to pry open her chakras. She had to cast a shield over Blythe and Kendall.

Her chakras cramped and twisted, the pain worsening the closer she got to Archer.

Her magic wouldn't work, but her gun did. Jamming her hand into her purse, she clutched the weapon. The fiery light show engulfing Archer grew brighter. Risa darted past him, a blast of hot wind searing her skin. The smell of sulfur burned her throat, and her eyes watered.

Like being in hell. Every instinct screamed to run away, escape. Find a closet to hide in.

Rage sprang up to drive back her cowardice. Too many times she'd been weak and scared. Pathetic. Hot determination flooded her, and she pushed hard through the terrified throngs.

Reaching Blythe, she turned and took up a protective stance. They would not die on her watch. She raised her gun, then got her first look at Archer's naked back.

Two flaps of *something* protruded from his shoulder blades down to his waist. His muscles rippled, and those things grew larger.

"Wings," she said. He was growing wings. She'd heard of Wing Slayer Hunters getting wings, but Archer wasn't a witch hunter. So what was he? Would her gun kill him?

One way to find out. Risa took aim. All her earlier panic and horror coalesced into extreme concentration.

The licking flames vanished, and Archer spun around. In a blur of motion, he fitted an arrow in the bow and released it.

Risa squeezed the trigger, but the arrow hit the gun and knocked it from her hand before she could get the shot off. Disbelieving, she stared as the gun struck the wall and stayed there, held by the arrow. It had pierced *through the gun* and into the wall. Flames slithered from the arrow, flared and engulfed the gun.

Her calm control shattered. "Run!"

"Take Kendall!" Blythe held out the baby. "You're faster."

Risa snatched the child from Blythe's arms and

clamped her against her chest. With her free arm, she shoved Blythe ahead of her. The other woman broke into a run with Risa on her heels. They headed to the right, past what was left of the smoldering, sickening remains of the incinerated cops and Jim.

"Keep running!" Risa passed Blythe, taking the lead. She didn't have any weapons, her magic was on the fritz, and she had no way to fight that thing Archer had spawned into. The night had turned into a nightmare like nothing she'd ever seen. Voices screamed, and the hiss and crackle of fire punctuated the unnatural darkness and silence of the Strip. No car alarms, no sirens, no hums of any machinery.

They made it to the street. Cars were stopped in place, as if their engines had all died. People milled around, staring at the flames crawling up the Mystique Hotel. Risa headed across the boulevard. Weaving between a brown truck and a Mercedes, she shifted Kendall and glanced back. Blythe kept up with her.

But behind her Archer gained on them, his naked body gleaming in the moonlight, his growing wings flapping.

And then he stopped. Raised his bow with an arrow poised.

"Down!" Risa shouted.

Too late, the arrow hit Blythe in the back.

Blythe stumbled, weaving drunkenly. Her eyes rounded, her mouth dropping open. The gleaming arrow punched into her back, and the head jutted out from between her ribs.

Kendall screamed, thrashing frantically and reaching for her mother.

Clutching the baby, Risa stared at the arrow in utter blankness. An arrow. Through her best friend. Blood. Flickers of flames.

A harsh, pained cry jerked Risa's gaze up to Blythe's sickly pale face. She swayed in ugly slow motion, canting one way then the other. Like a death dance...

No! Reality snapped into place. Blythe couldn't die. Risa couldn't lose her friend. Kendall needed her mom. Fierce love and resolve flooded her veins. *Do something. Anything.* Blocking out everything else, Risa held Kendall tightly and concentrated on summoning her magic. She mentally reached to her first chakra at her pelvic floor.

Only a trickle of power wafted up.

Not enough. Fighting harder, she pulled on every ounce of will to yank out more magic.

Blythe crumpled to the street. Hissing erupted from her as flames snaked out from the arrow and shaft, licking hungrily at her skin.

Horror gripped Risa's throat. She couldn't get enough magic. Desperation burned her eyes, clogged her nose, and she ran to her friend. "No!" She had to stop the flames. *Come on, chakras, open.* Nothing happened.

Blythe raised her head, eyes wild. "Run!" Her face contorted in pain, terror and purpose. "Save Kendall! You swore, Risa! You swore!" She barely got the words out as the flames ignited into an explosion so powerful, the force of it lifted Risa off her feet and threw her through the air.

She tightened her arms around Kendall as she slammed into a car. The impact knocked the wind from her, and she slid down. Landing on her ass, she leaned against the vehicle, holding the screaming baby while fighting to get air into her lungs.

Blythe was dead.

Where was Archer?

Breathe, damn it! She had to breathe and stay conscious. Oh God Blythe, how could she be dead? No, don't think about her now. Survive first, get Kendall safe, then she could feel the loss. Naked calves and feet appeared. Before she could lift her gaze any more, Archer grabbed her long hair.

Her heart stuttered at the up-close view of his crimson eyes and leathery skin. "What are you?" It came out a scraping whisper. Terror had robbed her of her voice.

His lips stretched, revealing white teeth. "The son of Asmodeus."

Shock grayed her vision, and her chakras slammed shut. *Asmodeus, the demon.* "You're a..." What?

"A demon spawn and your worst fucking nightmare."

That pretty much summed it up. He'd killed Blythe. Murdered her. And now her soul had lodged in Risa's magic with all the others. Too many emotions battled in her head—grief, hatred, her own failure. "Why didn't you kill me? Why Blythe?"

"You held my daughter, and my father wants her alive." His eyes took on a glowing red cast. "And what he wants, he gets."

She tried to shake her head, holding Kendall closer. "She's just a baby." She'd sworn she'd protect Kendall, but wavy lines rippled in her vision, and weakness saturated her muscles. *Hold on, don't pass out.*

"If you hadn't pissed me off, I'd just kill you. But now you're going to suffer." He yanked her forward. "Welcome to your nightmare." He slammed her head back against the car.

Her last thought was that she'd failed Blythe and Kendall.

2

LINC RAN UP THE EAST side of the Las Vegas Strip, where throngs of people rushed in the light from the moon and fire. Powerless, abandoned vehicles littered the road, and flames spewed from one of the hotels. He glanced over at the man pacing him. "What caused the blackout? Cars and machinery to just stop?"

"Head toward the flames," Ram said. "That must be the source of whatever is happening."

Linc passed the Cosmopolitan Hotel in a blur, weaving around people and closing in on the Bellagio, when he caught a whiff of witch blood. His skin heated, and that nagging itch between his shoulder blades intensified. Another whiff and his veins swelled in need, *craving*.

Dozens of smells saturated the air—fires, burning rubber, perfumes, sweat, and sulfur—but the warm cinnamon scent compelled him. *Witch blood.* He wanted it. Not demon, but an earth witch with a fragrance that lured him like nothing else.

Turning away from the Bellagio, he ran into the street, skirting stalled cars and panicked people, his focus on getting to the witch.

He passed another fire, one so hot and vile with the

scent of sulfur and cooking flesh that he slowed a few feet away. Pity and anger roiled in him. Tiny flames flickered around the remains of a human burned and discarded in the street. No one should die like that.

"Christ." Ram stopped beside him.

"How did he or she catch on fire?"

"Look."

Linc followed Ram's gaze to the Mystique Hotel, which was covered in black-edged flames. "That's not natural fire." The flames curled then snapped outward like some kind of fire monster. "Has to be demon magic."

"We have to find the source."

Doing a three-sixty, Linc searched through the dark chaos, while fighting the urge to locate the earth witch he'd scented. He didn't see anything until a group of people moved, clearing his sightline.

About fifteen feet away, a woman had collapsed in a sitting position on the street, clutching a baby. Hovering over her was a naked man with wings growing out of his back, holding a bow and arrow. Thin whips of fiery light resembling miniature streaks of lightning snapped across his skin. "Holy fuck, what is that?"

"Jesus," Ram breathed out. "It has to be a demon, although how the hell a demon got here in that form, I don't know. Thought they had to possess a human body."

Linc heard, but his focus zeroed in on the woman. She had a witch shimmer, faint but definitely there, pale blue with red holes indicating pain. The winds shifted, and he caught a faint whiff of the cinnamon-magic scent he'd smelled earlier. Before he could fully process it, he launched into a flat-out run, shouldering people out of his way.

Had to get to her. Whatever that thing was looming

over her, it would kill the witch and the baby she had cradled against her.

A sound to his left jerked his head around just as two huge men tackled him, throwing him into the side of an SUV.

Rogues, judging by the thick smell of copper coming off them.

Linc rolled so fast a knife meant for him embedded in the tire. Shooting to his feet, he yanked his blade out and attacked.

More rogues materialized and surrounded him. Goddammit, he had to get to the witch and baby. The clang of a cage door slamming sounded in his head, igniting his feral side. He plunged his knife into the rogue closest to him. Internal rage boiled as he stabbed his blade into the hearts of two more. *Hurry! Get to her!* He kept going, slashing and killing until no rogue remained in his way.

"Linc." Ram had the last rogue pinned to a car.

With the fury burning in his veins, Linc stalked over and raised his knife to kill the bastard.

"Wait," Ram ordered.

Don't stop. Kill. Get to—Linc snapped his jaw shut and froze his protesting arm and shoulder muscles. The other hunter didn't throw around orders without reason. It took another breath to leash his frenzy. He shot his gaze to where he'd seen the witch and the demon thing.

Gone.

He had to find her and that kid. Now. He took a step, when a bellow spun him around.

Ram had his knife buried in the rogue's gut, and leaned over him, eyes cold. "Talk and I'll make your death quick. What happened tonight?"

Sweat poured off the man's hairless face, his hands clenched in pain, and defiance burned in his brown eyes. "Fuck you."

"Wrong answer." Ram yanked the knife up a couple inches.

The rogue roared and tried to break Ram's grip on the knife.

Linc caught hold of the rogue's upper arms and slammed him flat against the hood of the car. Furious that the rogues had stopped him from rescuing the witch before she'd vanished, he wanted some answers. There's a good chance that demon thing had her and the kid. "Talk or we start carving you up."

The rogue flinched, his body shaking from pain and stress. "The hybrid is spawning."

Like something out of a goddamned comic book, Linc thought.

"What's a hybrid?" Ram questioned the rogue.

"Half-mortal and half-demon. On their thirtieth birthday, they have to choose—human or demon. Archer chose, and Asmodeus pushed enough power through the ley lines to spawn him," he finished in a hoarse whisper.

"How many?" Linc demanded. "Do they all spawn at once?"

He shook his head, the cords on his neck straining. "Don't know. Archer's the first."

"What's with the bow and arrow?" Ram asked.

The man's eyes fluttered open, and he rasped out, "Hellfire."

Cold sweat broke out on Linc's back. All the fires, then the scent of sulfur and flesh.... "He's shooting hellfire? From the Underworld?" That explained the black-edged flames on the Mystique Hotel.

The rogue snapped his mouth closed, his muscles locked in pain, just before a violent seizure ripped through him.

Linc tried to hold him—they needed more information—but the rogue stilled, his eyes going wide, then the blankness of death settled over his gaze.

"Shit," Ram said. "The seizure forced my knife into his heart. He's done."

After releasing the dead rogue, Linc strode to the car where he'd seen the hybrid and the dark-haired witch. The scent grew stronger as he approached the light blue Nissan Maxima. Linc crouched down and eyed the red smear over the front wheel well. The blood browned at the edges as it dried.

Buzzing filled his ears, drowning out the noise of shouts, flames and general mayhem around them. Beneath his torn shirt, his tattoo itched violently. That four-inch smear of blood drew him. Tempted him.

Don't touch it! He knew better. He'd been blooded before. If he touched the blood, even this small amount, it would be enough to send him to full bloodlust.

Want it.

Need her, the witch with the cinnamon-scented blood.

More brown crept in at the edges of the blood smear, eating away at the rich red that held the power of a witch. He vibrated with the compelling urge for that blood.

He lifted his hand.

Can't stop.

Don't want to.

The thin scent still clinging to the blood cells reached deep inside Linc, and he saw the witch in his mind. Long black hair around a face that even unconscious had been tight with wariness. Her lithe body cradling that child. Desire to touch her snapped and burned his muscles. Losing control, he pressed his hand flat to the smear. Felt the metal of the car warmed from the fires and the slight crust on the drier edges of the blood.

But the wet center of it adhered to his palm and locked his hand in place.

Time stopped as that insignificant spot of blood took hold of him. Fire lashed into his brain. His groin throbbed, and the all-too-familiar hunger for witch blood ripped open the pores on his skin. Sweat slicked his chest, arms and neck with the hunger for her blood. The words *find her* thumped in his head.

"Linc." Ram's hand clamped around his wrist. "I smell witch blood."

Shooting to his feet, he shoved the other man back. Vicious fury reddened his brain. *Wait, it's Ram. Stop. Bloodlust.* "Don't." He held up his hand, nearly panting as he fought the dual cravings for witch blood and sex battling in him.

Anger iced Ram's eyes, and he got up in Linc's face. "You fucking moron. You touched witch blood?"

Shame and disgust tangled in an agitated dance in his belly. "Had to. The itch on my back..." He blinked. Even as flames snapped into the hellish night, people rushed in panic, and bloodlust tore through his veins, a fresh sense of wonder and hope eased his chest. "It stopped."

"What?"

"The itching in the falcon tattoo. It went from a one to a ten, and now it's gone. A second or two after I touched the blood, the itch vanished. There's just a feathery sensation." He studied his palm where the smear of blood had vanished. "The bird is waking. This witch, she's my soul mirror." Right? She had to be. Hope surged.

Ram's jaw hardened. "Could be the bloodlust screwing with you. You were batshit crazy when you were blooded."

Could be, except the itch had stopped. "Her blood is too powerful and..." How did he explain it? "There's a connection. Different from other witches' blood. I can feel her magic in the bird." That was what was creating the faint feathery sensation. "She's mine. I have to find her."

Skepticism lowered Ram's brows. "We have bigger shit to deal with. You heard that rogue we killed. The hybrid chose to be a demon. That means he's dangerous as fuck. He's shooting hellfire. Asmodeus didn't give his spawn hellfire to shoot for shits and giggles. This is a demon attack."

All the wonder vanished as reality slammed home. "Exactly. And that spawn took the witch. My witch, and that baby she was holding."

"A baby witch. Fuck, let's go. We'll track them, then wait for Sutton to get here. He's mated. The witch blood won't bother him."

Linc turned, catching the fading scent of the witch's magic, and jogged up the boulevard. He kept seeing the witch and baby in his head. Had to be her kid, right? Hell, that complicated things. What if she was in a relationship with someone else? Dark, possessive rage simmered.

Stop. Just keep your shit together long enough to find her. Then he'd worry about whether or not she was free.

One way or another, she was his.

Risa woke to a sizzling sound. In the next instant fiery pain lashed around her neck, sending streaks of agony through her nerve endings.

When it stopped, she curled on her side. Cold metal pressed into her cheek. Her head pounded, her neck and shoulders cramped, and just breathing hurt. But something nagged at her mind, poking and prodding. It wouldn't let her slide back into the soft darkness. Something important...

Blythe! Oh Ancestors, Blythe had been murdered

and Kendall taken. Forcing her eyes open, Risa slowly pushed herself to a sitting position. Vertigo made the room spin, and she swayed like she was on a rope swing. Swallowing a wave of nausea, she squeezed her eyes shut and willed the movement to stop.

Once it calmed, she looked around carefully to keep from aggravating the nausea.

Oh God. Surrounded by metal bars of a four-by-four cage, Risa swung a good six or eight feet off the ground. Where was she? It only took a second to focus her vision in the low light provided by several lanterns. Below, to her left, stretched a stage with a pole going up to the ceiling.

Strip club.

And she wasn't alone. Metallic fear shot up her throat as the severity of her situation set in. Across the room, a cluster of hulking men gathered around a long, mirrored bar. A couple lanterns revealed eight to ten, all with bulging muscles, too-soft faces and hairless arms.

Rogues. In a strip club.

She'd hit the mother lode of trouble. How had she ended up here all packaged up in a cage like a rogue Happy Meal? Where was Archer? Struggling to climb to her feet, she noticed something heavy around her neck. Reaching up, she touched a collar. A wave of panic curled her fingers around it, desperate to get it off. It didn't budge. Remembering the searing pain that had forced her to consciousness, she guessed what it was—a shock collar.

"It's not coming off, sleeping beauty." A man rose from the shadows. He'd been sitting at the tables spread at the base of the stage. Dark-haired, wearing slacks, no shirt and a gold chain slithering around his thick neck, he held up the remote control. "For the shock collar."

Cold fear dripped down her spine. Blasts of

electricity from the collar would disable her magic. After setting the remote on the table, he leaped up on the stage and crossed to the opposite end by the curtains. Grasping a handle, he rotated the wheel.

Her cage began descending. Risa grabbed the bars, struggling to keep her panic controlled and think. Finally the cage touched down on the end of the stage.

"Seems you really pissed Archer off." The man shook his head. "So he gave you to me, with the stipulation that I make your death long and agonizing."

Her stomach turned over sickeningly, and bile rose in her throat. How the hell would she get out of this? She had to save Kendall from Archer. On top of promising Blythe, Risa couldn't let that baby stay in the hands of a demon madman.

Just thinking Blythe's name made her eyes burn, and thick, harsh grief twisted in her chest. Why even go on? She'd failed her best friend, her only real friend.

Kendall. That's why. You have to find the baby and save her. Focus.

Renewed determination pushed back her grief. Blythe had loved Kendall more than anything. For Blythe, Risa would find a way to survive and rescue Kendall from her demonic father. What Archer had become...no child should be subjected to that. Risa knew what it was like to be raised by a monster, and she couldn't let that happen to Kendall. "Where's the baby?"

"Not your problem. But I am. You can call me Cyrus when you beg for your life."

"Don't kill her before I get my hit of her blood." One of the goons at the bar set down his glass and strode toward the stage.

More followed.

Fear and anger sharpened her senses. Carefully she

looked over the others. Excitement flared their nostrils and dilated their pupils. When she looked lower, many had erections straining their pants.

"Time for the show. Strip and show us what you've got." Cyrus slid a knife from a holster strapped to his thigh. The black handle and curved blade caught the low lantern light. "Make it good, cupcake. Or I'm coming in there to get the real party started."

A wave of dizziness nearly dropped her to her knees. *Breathe and think.* How did she fight these huge men with no gun? She didn't have any other weapons—not even her protective shield, since the shock collar would prevent her from using magic. "You need to remove the shock collar so I can get my shirt off."

Cyrus set the knife down and shoved his pants off, leaving him in black briefs that did nothing to disguise his thick thighs or rock-hard erection. Retrieving his weapon, he arched a brow at her. "Not happening. Archer warned me that you have some special magic you can use as a shield." After punching in a code on the lock, he swung open the door and stepped into her cage, reeking of copper and excitement. The door clanged shut.

Risa retreated until her back hit the bars. Cyrus stood over six feet in height, his eyes dark and soulless.

Panic squeezed her chest. "I'll do what you want. Strip. Get out and I'll—"

Behind her, hands gripped her wrists where she held the bars. Whipping her head around, she got a close-up view of a blond man with light eyes that gleamed in excitement. "You smell good, like a scared little witch ready to beg."

A second later, fire sliced a few inches up her belly. Jerking her gaze back to Cyrus, she bit down on a scream.

Grabbing the edges of her shirt, he ripped it open, shoved it back and slammed his body against hers. A sensual groan spilled from him as he ground against her cut belly. "Oh yeah, the slut's got magic."

"I want my turn, Cyrus."

She thrashed, but her hands pinned against the bars left her helpless. Red pain swam in her mind. Desperately she tried to reach her magic, but nothing happened. God, when would it stop? Five years ago she'd thought she'd escaped, and here she was being used and hurt again.

You deserve it. What about all those you didn't save? Like Blythe?

Cyrus moaned, his beer-scented breath making her recoil. His skin slid against hers, thick cock rubbing over the cut. Too many memories exploded. Other men hurting her. Risa twisted, slamming her head into his jaw.

He jerked back, grabbed a handful of her hair and smashed her skull into the bars.

Pain exploded in a violent starburst. She squeezed her eyes shut as tiny bursts of lights popped against her eyelids. Nausea boiled in her stomach.

"She's a fighter. So fucking good," Cyrus growled, dragging a hand across her cut.

More pain. Risa panted and concentrated on not screaming or begging as she forced her eyes open.

"I paid you," the man behind her gripping her wrists snarled at Cyrus.

Cyrus sighed and pushed back with a smile twitching his mouth. "They all paid me for a hit of you, but in the end, I get the kill."

She glared at him, breathing through the agony, from the cut, fear and the clawing knowledge that Kendall was out there somewhere. She had to live to find that child. *Think!* How could she get out of this?

A man strode into the club. "I want in on this action."

Cyrus spun, his massive shoulders tensing. "Well, now, look who we have here. Linc Dillinger. The man who killed one of my friends earlier tonight."

Risa strained against the hands holding her to see around Cyrus. On the stage stood a man who had to be six-and-a-half-feet tall, over two hundred pounds, brown tousled hair with expensive highlights. He wore a stained and torn silk shirt, dark slacks and shoes that cost more than her trailer.

Who was he?

Staring at him ignited a tingle that rippled through her first four chakras, startling her. She hadn't been able to get to her magic, but one look at him and it tingled? His eyes burned with a gold heat in their brown depths as he ignored the men gathering behind him, blocking his escape.

"That was business, Cyrus. Your rogue cadre issued a challenge, we answered."

"We?" Cyrus opened the cage and walked out to face the newcomer. "So you're part of Baron's club?"

She had no idea what they were talking about. Right now, being a bleeding captive held at knife point took precedence to their reunion, or whatever the hell it was. "Let me go," she demanded.

The bastard squeezed her wrists until she thought her bones would snap.

"Nope." Smooth confidence laced Dillinger's voice. "But he paid me well and I did the job. Business. I'll give you ten K for the witch."

He wanted to buy her?

Cyrus stopped just out of arm's reach of the man. Tilting his head, he said, "What the fuck is your game, Dillinger? You've made a name for yourself as a Wing Slayer Hunter in California rescuing witches. You don't buy them for sport. Or is this your lazy way of rescuing them?"

"What do you care, if you get the ten grand?"

A strange desperation to get closer to the newcomer rippled down her spine, and she yanked on her wrists. To her surprise, the man let go this time. Drawn to the stranger, Risa shuffled across the cage and wrapped her fingers around the bars. She'd heard of Wing Slayer Hunters.

"So, the rumors are true then." Cyrus's voice took on a gleeful note. "You were blooded, and now you're hooked."

Dillinger's gaze cut to her.

The impact took her breath away. His eyes were lighter than she'd first thought, more gold than brown. Yet the color had a depth that pulled her in and made her long to know more about him. The connection vibrated so deeply, her magic fluttered again. Not enough to do any real witchcraft, but still more than she'd felt since she'd woken in the cage. Maybe he was there to rescue her and claiming he wanted to buy her was a ruse? After all, Wing Slayer Hunters had a rep for saving witches.

He broke eye contact and returned his attention to Cyrus. "It's created an unfortunate problem for me. I need a hit of blood now and again."

Laughter spilled out from Cyrus. "You're slinging bullshit." He glanced behind the intruder. "You two, go outside and see if he brought backup with him."

The two men at the back headed out.

"Fifteen thousand, last offer," Linc said. "You have two minutes and I'm out."

Cyrus crossed his arms. "Why her?"

"Convenience. I smelled her blood, tracked her here. I'm finding it tiresome to hunt down witch blood while keeping that particular need quiet from the other Wing Slayer Hunters. I've decided to acquire a blood donor."

Blood donor? Crap. She guessed he didn't mean the Red Cross-approved type of blood donor. Wait, still could be a ruse. Risa knew all about luring people into believing one thing, then killing them, thanks to her bastard father.

"Tell you what. Let's see you strip down to your skivvies and no weapons. Get in that cage and take a hit of her blood. Convince me you're telling the truth, then we'll negotiate."

No. Don't do it, she silently begged. Please, for once in her life, she needed a hero. Not for her, but for Kendall. Risa willed her hope to reach him. *Be a good guy.* Dillinger shifted his stare to her.

The heat of his gaze slid over her face, down her torn shirt, tiny bra and bleeding belly, then pulled away.

"Scared?" Cyrus taunted. "Can't back up your claim?"

The wound on her stomach burned, her head throbbed, and she hung on to the bars to keep upright, but all her energy focused on hope. She'd read endless stories about the hunters who had committed to serving Wing Slayer. Tales of rescuing witches and resisting the curse filled the secret witch gossip sites on the Internet. *Be one of them, be a hero.* She clung to that lifeline.

He turned, met her gaze. "Scared of a witch? Hardly. I just want her blood."

Despair flooded out her hope, and damn, it hurt. Her throat ached, and her nose clogged. *Blythe, oh God, I'm so sorry.*

Save Kendall! You swore, Risa! You swore! Blythe's death plea rang in her head.

Closing her eyes, she laid her forehead against the bars and whispered, "I'm sorry."

So what now? Would she just give up? Oh hell no. Blythe was dead, her soul trapped in Risa's magic. That left only Risa to do something.

Snapping open her eyes, she glared at Linc. If she could reach him, she'd slug him right in his too-handsome face. "You're a disgrace to your god, you son of a bitch."

He flashed her a perfect smile. "Feisty witches have a little extra kick in their blood, don't you think?"

Hatred roiled in her blood. "Bastard."

That smile hardened as he pulled off his shirt and turned away from her to drop it on the stage.

She gripped the bars firmer, ignoring her sore wrists, her gaze riveted on him. His skin was a light bronze, tight and smooth over roped muscles that shifted and undulated with every breath the man took. His shoulders were nearly double the width of hers. His back bunched with restrained power.

But what caught her attention was the tattoo that stood center stage on his upper back and shoulders.

A falcon inked in incredible detail. The bird's abdomen had gray bars across the white background, and the chest had teardrop markings in the same color. His wide, pointed wings were spread open, revealing a glimpse of the intricate gray barring on the underside and the darker solid feathers on the outside. The bird had a distinctive yellow eye ring, along with a mostly yellow beak and feet.

The bird looked right at her, easing the hard knot of terror in her stomach.

Was she hallucinating?

Dillinger turned and stripped off his pants, revealing abs and narrow hips that cradled an impressive bulge. His long, muscled thighs had a dusting of golden-brown hair. After dropping his pants on the stage, he undid the knife holster at his back and set that on top of the pile.

Clad only in black boxer briefs, he embodied male perfection, and everything in her hated him. Hated what he represented. She'd bet her last dollar he made women love him and believe he was a good guy. They fell for his looks and charm, never seeing beneath to the festering ugliness.

Like her father.

Betrayal and fear ripped up her center. "You're worse than the others. At least they don't pretend to be anything else but killers. You're disgusting." The last two words came out thick and harsh. She didn't even know him, yet this felt personal.

His gaze locked on to hers, and he took a step, anger flashing in his eyes. Linc pivoted in blurring speed and slammed the side of his foot into Cyrus's throat.

The man collapsed, gurgling and wheezing.

Linc snatched up the knife from Cyrus's hand and shoved it in his chest.

More men burst into the club, and chaos exploded.

Stunned, Risa stared. Was it possible? Had Linc been bluffing and intending to rescue her all along?

Or take her for a blood donor without paying?

3

THE SMELL OF THE WITCH'S blood had fueled Linc's bloodlust the second he'd walked into the strip club. But what had ripped out his guts was the flicker of hope in her eyes fading into burning hatred and betrayal. She believed he would hurt her.

She'd seen the truth in him. Seen what he really was—an animal.

He shut it down. The witch didn't have to like him. They would come to an understanding. Ram and Sutton West burst into the club and jumped into the fight. Seriously, had the rogues really thought he'd come in here without a plan? Or that he'd let them live to keep killing more witches?

Spotting a man coming up on his side to attack, Linc dove beneath the rogue's arm and slid across the stage to snatch up his knife. After freeing it from the holster, he bounded to his feet and killed the rogue he'd just evaded.

Below the stage, Sutton's blade flashed as he fought three rogues.

At the end of the stage, Ram fought two others.

A high-pitched, pain-filled scream pierced Linc's brain. He wheeled around to see that a rogue had gotten into the cage and thrown the witch against the bars. He sliced her bra off, shifting the blade to slash across the top of her breast.

The sight of her blood welling ignited Linc's rage. Shoving another rogue out of his way, he raced across the stage, ripped the cage door off and threw it. He grabbed a handful of the blond man's shirt, jerked him out of the cage, then picked him up and heaved him off the platform.

The man slammed into a round table and chairs. If he wasn't dead yet, Sutton would end him. Linc focused on the witch, and her cinnamon-scented blood swam into his lungs. Hot, vicious need ripped a hole in his guts.

He stalked toward her then drew to a halt in shock. The woman had tied the ripped sides of the shirt together over her bared breasts and held a knife. Linc guessed the rogue he'd just thrown dropped the blade and she had snatched it up. Dark, shaggy hair hung wild around her too-pale face, and fear-tinged hatred blazed in her eyes. Despite the blood welling from the cuts on her breast and stomach, she assumed a fighting stance with the knife clenched in her hand.

The bird tattoo heated, and something deep in his guts kicked at the sight of her. Linc had expected her to cry and beg, but this witch was primed to fight.

Like some kind of warrior witch.

"Stay back." She edged out of the cage, her gaze darting around.

A buzzing sounded. The witch stumbled, her head thrown back and jaw locked. Her white teeth dug into her lower lip, making it bleed.

His gaze shot to the collar around her neck. Shit. Spinning around, he stalked to Cyrus, searching as that buzzing kept going. Shit, shit, shit! He kicked the body over, but found nothing. Lifting his head, he scanned the bar. "Where the fuck is the remote? It's shocking the witch."

Sutton slammed a rogue onto the bar top and spun around. A second later, he stalked to a round table, yanked a body off and held up a black device. "Got it." Pressing buttons, he added, "Body must have landed on it and set it off." The buzzing stopped. Finally.

Returning his attention to the woman, he dragged in a breath. How the hell was she even standing after all that? She rocked unsteadily but stayed on her feet, knife up and eyes narrowed with determination even as her muscles twitched and spasmed from the repeated shocks.

He moved toward her. "Relax. I'm not going to hurt you."

She checked her grip on the blade. "Damn right. I'm not your *blood donor*. Move. I'm out of here." She took a step and swayed. A second later, her legs buckled, eyes rolled up, and the knife clattered to the floor.

Linc lunged, catching her as unconsciousness took her. He yanked her against his body. The sensation of warm dampness stroked the bare skin of his stomach. One second later, a raging burst of hot power blasted through him. *Witch blood.* He froze, waiting for the blinding rush of need for more.

Instead, he registered the weight of her in his arms, the feel of his skin against hers. He lowered his gaze to her face. Blood welled up on her lip, and she looked so damned young. The need to protect her rose and drowned out any bloodlust.

"Give her to me." Sutton strode up, his shirt soaked with blood and his blue eyes wary.

Hell no. He had her now; she was his to protect. That fear in her eyes, the pain she'd endured, haunted him. "Don't touch her." He heard the growl in his voice but didn't give a shit.

Sutton dropped his hand. "Easy, Linc. You need to hand her over before you lose it."

He shook his head, cradling her against him. "I'm okay. As long as I'm touching her."

Understanding dawned over the bald man's face. "Your soul mirror?"

"I've touched her blood, and now her. She's the one." Gratefulness welled in him. This witch would save him, and in return he'd give her anything in his power...as long as she didn't betray him.

Slight doubt gathered in the man's eyes. "Linc, it could be the bloodlust screwing with you."

"Believe him."

Linc looked over his shoulder to Ram standing behind him, the man's eyes fixed on his back. "What?"

"Your tat. The eyes of your falcon are open." Ram moved up to the three of them, his hands spraying sparks. "I saw your tat when you were in the fight club. The eyes were still closed." Nodding at the witch in Linc's arms, he added, "See if you can get that collar off her. Once she comes to, she can heal her cuts with magic. I'm going outside."

One look at Ram's arms showed veins swollen from bloodlust. "Go."

Returning his attention to the witch, Linc forced himself to gently lay her down. She moaned softly.

Damn it, he should have gotten to her sooner. It'd taken him twenty minutes or longer to track her. Carefully, he brushed her hair back from her clammy skin. *I'm not your blood donor* echoed in his head. Of course she didn't trust him. He'd burst in offering to buy her.

Her sharp intake of breath jerked him out of his thoughts. She moved fast, knocking his hands away. "Don't."

Her eyes were stunningly beautiful, so dark blue as to appear nearly violet, and brimming with distrust.

To make it worse, her pupils were uneven—he'd been in enough fights to recognize the sign of a concussion. *Talk to her, reassure her.* "What's your name?"

"Risa Faden."

"Risa," he echoed. It fit her. "We're going to get you out of here and to safety. I'm sorry I scared you." More sorry than she could know.

"Doesn't matter. I have to find Kendall." She tried to push herself up, but fell back.

Linc threw out his hand, catching her head before she cracked it on the floor. "Kendall?" He thought back quickly. "Saw you on the boulevard. You were holding a baby." Where was the kid?

"Kendall. I have to find her!"

Linc glanced up at Sutton. "You searched the entire building?"

"Yes, but I'll take another look to be sure."

Linc turned back to Risa. Gently he eased his hand from beneath her head. "He'll search, but you need to stay still. You probably have a concussion. I'm going to get that collar off you." Frankly he didn't know how she stayed conscious. Her eyes kept rolling up, sweat coated her and tremors wracked her arms and legs. Sheer will, he guessed.

Risa snatched the knife he'd set next to her. She held it ready.

He didn't bother telling her the knife wouldn't stop him if he wanted to hurt her. Slowly, he slid his fingers along her skin to test the fit of the collar. His tat quivered, as if the bird were touching her. Once he had a solid hold of the collar, he snapped the metal lock. After removing it from around Risa's neck, he tossed it aside.

Still clutching the knife, she sat up, winced and swayed. "I have to find her."

Her anxiety made him uncomfortable with the need to reassure her. "Sit still for a second so you don't pass out again." Linc grabbed his pile of clothes and dropped his shirt by her. "Put this on." Her torn shirt barely covered her. And the blood...

Nope not looking at that. He yanked on his pants, shoved his feet in his shoes and strapped on his knife holster.

Risa stood, his silk shirt falling to her thighs. She looked so damned lost and worried. Laying his hand on her back, he opened his mouth to reassure her when Sutton came striding out of a hallway.

The other hunter looked at Risa. "There's no one here, no sign of a baby anywhere. No bottles or any of that stuff."

Risa jerked, panic filling her face. "He took her. How do I find her?" She took a step, then nearly stumbled.

Linc caught her hand.

Risa whirled on him. "Let go."

He sucked in a breath of patience. "If Sutton says the baby's not here, then she's not. Who took her, Risa? What happened?"

"Archer. He killed my friend Blythe."

A memory filled his head. "I saw you out on the Strip tonight, not far from a burned body. That was your friend?"

Agony darkened her eyes. "Yes. He shot her with an arrow. I had Kendall and tried to run... Oh God, where is she? When I woke, I was in that cage, and she was gone." She pulled her hand free. "I have to find her. I'll use my magic."

The faint scent of spicy cinnamon made his blood burn. Then the aroma faded. "Crap, it's not working," Risa said.

He closed his hand around hers. The skin-to-skin contact eased his bloodlust. They had to find that kid. "More information. Is Kendall your daughter?"

For a split second, she looked utterly stricken.

"Archer's a demon. He told me Asmodeus is his father. That means Kendall..."

Linc leaned into her. "What?" He couldn't follow her thoughts. Maybe the concussion had confused her?

Determination stiffened her shoulders. "...is in danger. Yes, Kendall's mine. A witch. You rescue witches, right? Please, help me find her!" She twisted frantically. "He murdered my best friend. And others...burned them alive. It was hideous. He's evil."

Her hysteria slammed into him. Linc grasped both her arms, forcing her to look at him. "We'll find her. We don't leave babies in the hands of a demon." What the hell was a half-demon spawn doing with a baby witch? Nothing good.

"Risa." Sutton handed her a bar towel. "Hold this on your stomach wound. You need to heal yourself before you can find Kendall. Try to access your magic again."

She closed her eyes and nodded. But after a minute, she growled in frustration. "I can't reach my power."

"Easy." Linc rubbed her arms. "Let's get you someplace safe, and I'll help you."

Suspicion clouded her eyes. "How can you help me?"

He might as well tell her. "I touched your blood tonight. You're my soul mirror."

She opened her mouth, and her eyes rolled up. The witch passed out cold.

For the second time that night, Linc caught her in his arms. Her face relaxed, making her appear young and helpless. So damned vulnerable, it wrenched his chest and unleashed a powerful need to protect and care for her. Get her well and help her find her baby.

In return she'd save him by breaking his curse.

And after that? When they both had what they

wanted? He eyed her covered in his shirt and instinctively tightened his hold.

He didn't know. He'd never tried to keep a woman, hadn't wanted to. The thought of it made him feel trapped, worried that he'd fail her and end up watching another woman get hurt and killed.

Right now, he had to get her someplace safe and figure out their next move.

Risa woke with a low-grade headache making her squint as bright sunlight flooded the unfamiliar room. Her eyelids weighed a ton, while the soft sheets and a thick mattress tugged her back toward sleep. Quiet, dark, safe...she wanted to close her eyes for a few more...

No. Her heart jerked, and she sat up, wincing as the room tilted and her stomach pitched uneasily. Bending her legs, she rested her forehead on her knees. The clean, lightly floral scent of fabric softener filled her lungs.

Where was she? Raising her head, she found herself in a four-poster bed covered in the fragrant sheets and a pale coral comforter. Beige walls led up to a tray ceiling featuring a huge mosaic using numerous shades of coral and spots of blue. Filmy curtains bracketed the huge glass doors, which probably led to a balcony. For sure she wasn't in her two-bedroom, double-wide trailer back in Phoenix.

Slowly the horrible night came back to her, right up to losing consciousness after Linc and his friends rescued her. Then...she squinted, trying to think. Nothing.

After she passed out might be a total blank, but the image of that arrow hitting Blythe, her friend's shock, then the flames, played over and over in her thoughts.

Memories of the laughing girl, her blonde hair, blue eyes and the dimples that Blythe had hated rolled through Risa's head. She had been Risa's only friend. Having been home-schooled, Risa hadn't been around a lot of kids. But Blythe's mom was a live-in housekeeper for one of the homes in the neighborhood, and the two girls met when Risa took out her miniature horse, Shelby, for a walk on the trails. Blythe had fallen in love with Shelby, and soon the two girls were inseparable.

"Mama, don't cry."

Don't look. She's not real, you know that. She's an illusion of your cracking mind. Her daughter had died in her stomach at only four months' gestation. Risa's father had found out she was pregnant and killed the unborn child through a nasty trick. She'd tried to use her shield magic to save her baby, but it had been too late and her child died. Now Nola's soul was trapped with the others in her magic.

"Mama? You don't have to be sad. I'm here. I love you. I won't ever leave you."

Unable to resist the sweet voice, Risa blinked through her tears and looked into violet eyes. Nola had no lashes or eyebrows—her eyes were large and owlish in her face. But the light of her soul was bright and pure. As beautiful as Risa imagined her daughter would have been had she lived.

Don't do this. You have to stop talking to a hallucination. Squeezing her eyes shut, she willed herself to be sane. She never saw the other souls and only heard them in soul screams when they wrenched control of her mind away to force her to relive their murders. No, Nola wasn't real, but an illusion proving she was losing touch with reality. If her mind shattered, her magic would die. And then what would happen to the souls? Could they survive without her magic? Would they know where to go to find their afterlife? Or would they just float into oblivion and die off? She had to hold on and find a way to free them in a way that allowed them to safely go on to their afterlife.

"I make you feel better, right?"

"Yes." *Stop it, don't answer her. Even if it's true.* Risa had first seen Nola in those awful days when she'd brutally miscarried her. At only seventeen years old, she'd had no idea her father had put an abortion potion he'd gotten from a demon witch into Risa's drink. The following seventy-two hours had been hideous. Nola, her baby, died in the first hours, and then while Risa was wracked with pain and shivers, she'd appeared. Telling Risa to hang on, to live and she'd stay with her.

After Risa had recovered, she hadn't seen her again, except when she dreamed. Not until the soul screams started and Risa experienced the terror of slowly losing her mind as the souls took over for longer and longer periods of time. Nola calmed her, made her feel loved, while the other souls hated her so much.

"How about a song? Playing the piano always makes you feel better."

For a second, she longed to be back in her trailer, home after a day of protecting one of her clients, and sitting down to her ancient piano she'd picked up at an estate sale. If she was alone, then Nola loved to listen, hovering above Risa's hands, her huge eyes watching her fingers. But if Kendall or—

A door opened, and the image of her baby vanished. Risa jerked her head around to the right of the bed.

Him. She hadn't imagined Linc Dillinger. He was very real as he filled up the doorway with six-and-a-half feet of pure, masculine beauty in a pair of tan slacks and a dark shirt. His brown hair with the perfect sun streaks fell in a careless wave that probably took time and product to achieve. He had a tray balanced on one arm. Her throat dried up.

"Where am I?" It came out a croak.

"My house here in Vegas. You're safe." He strode into the room and set the tray down. "I brought you some tea and toast. I put herbs in the tea that Carla suggested would help you heal."

"Who's that?" She couldn't get her bearings.

"Carla Fisk. She's one of the soul-mirror witches in California, and mated to Sutton West. You saw him last night in the strip club."

Risa blinked, trying to clear the sluggish fog clogging up her thoughts. "I've heard of them." What witch hadn't? The soul-mirror witches and hunters were romantic legends, and she haunted secret online sites gossiping about them while looking for ways to free the souls trapped in her magic and help her heal her fracturing mind.

The bed dipped.

The sensation of male weight on the mattress tripped more memories. Her heart rate jacked, and Risa rolled to the other side, her bare feet hitting the tile. Standing between the bed and a wall, she gritted her teeth against a wave of vertigo. *Breathe. Ignore it.*

"Risa, Jesus. I'm not going to hurt you." He loomed up on the other side of the bed, holding the mug of tea. "Think. I'm the one who found and saved you last night. You passed out cold in my arms, and I brought you here."

Her heart pounded in her ears while old shame curled low in her belly. "I'm fine." Lifting her chin, she willed her body to back up her claim. "I need to leave, to go find Kendall."

"You're not going out there alone. It's a disaster, with law enforcement and the National Guard covering the city. Power outages everywhere, the

Mystique Hotel burned to the ground, other hotels have major damage, several cars and bodies are burned, and—"

Blythe. Buzzing roared in her ears. Dropping back against the cool plaster wall, she squeezed her eyes closed, desperately trying to shut out that image. If only she could somehow go back and save her. Hot tears pricked.

A warm hand curled around her biceps. "Your friend. Damn it, I didn't think about what I was saying. Come here."

Snapping her eyes open, she stared at him. While on the bed, she'd felt trapped, but right now, his balmy scent of clean shampoo and strong male didn't trip her flight instinct. Instead, she had the urge to lean into him. Weird. "What are you doing?"

"You're crying." He reached up a free hand, swiping away a tear. "If you need a hug..."

She pushed him away. "No hugs." Get it together. She couldn't fall apart now, not with Kendall out there at the mercy of whatever the hell Archer had become. Besides, she didn't do hugs. Not with men anyway. She couldn't bear their touch.

Linc backed up, his face blanking. "I'm trying to help you here." Frustration edged his smooth voice.

Taking a deep breath, she steadied herself. The man had saved her life, and she'd seen him in action. If he wanted to hurt her, she wouldn't be able to stop him. Risa needed to rein in her inner bitch and get control. "I know. Sorry, I'm not good at being touched." Pushing off the wall, she tested her steadiness. Better.

His eyes narrowed, but he didn't comment on her proclamation about not being touched. "Sit in the chair." He gestured to the two chairs grouped in a corner, then headed around the bed to the nightstand. "Try the tea and toast. I know you want to find your daughter, and believe me, we want to find her too. But you need your magic to help us, which means you need to recover. I went out last night after I brought you here and couldn't find any trace of her."

Wanting distance and to pull herself together, Risa settled in the plush chair. "You went out and looked for Kendall?" Really? But she shouldn't be that surprised. The Wing Slayer Hunters had a rep for being relentlessly protective of witches. Make that witch a baby and, yeah, they would find her.

Except that Risa had lied, claiming Kendall was her daughter and a witch. Guilt twinged in her chest, but what else could she do? If she told him the baby was Archer's daughter, a demon's daughter, they weren't going to be as motivated to rescue her.

Linc set the tray on the table between the chairs and handed her the mug. "Yes. Plus we need to find the spawn. But we can't leave a baby witch out there alone with no one to protect her."

Exactly what she had thought—if they believed Kendall a witch, they'd find and rescue her. She sipped the tea, letting the warm, sweet liquid drown out her regret at lying.

"How are you feeling?"

He crouched in front of her, his slacks outlining his powerful thighs. Her gaze traveled up the black shirt covering his ripped abs, to his broad chest and his sculpted face. But when she looked into those light brown eyes that glowed almost gold, her magic did a little bump-and-grind thing.

"Better. No pain aside from a small headache." Her power had healed her knife wounds while she slept. And speaking of her witchcraft. "When you're close, my magic reacts."

"Soul-mirror connection. I feel your magic too. A lot. It smells like cinnamon."

Having him this close, his knees almost touching

hers, and those eyes looking too deep... Too much.

She dropped her gaze to study his hands, which were scarred with thick knuckles, an odd contrast to his pretty face. She sipped more tea, then gathered her courage and asked, "Are we really soul mirrors? What does that mean exactly?" She'd never met anyone who had first-hand exerpience, so her knowledge was limited to what she'd read.

"That we have the two halves of one soul, and once we bond through a sex and blood exchange, the curse breaks. I won't have bloodlust, and you'll be able to access your high magic."

Risa tried to take that in. She'd never been able to reach the magic in her fifth, sixth and seventh chakras. "How? I mean, we need familiars to help control that magic." The curse cast by demon witches three decades ago had broken witch's bonds with their familiar, and that was the reason they couldn't access their high magic.

"The way it's worked so far, our tattoos become the witch's familiar."

"The tattoos are alive?" Oh she'd read all this, but it sounded even more surreal hearing it. Especially since witches and hunters had become enemies since the curse saddled hunters with a craving for the power in witch blood. Although she'd heard that before the curse, witch hunters and earth witches had worked together and were friendly.

Linc shrugged. "It's a part of us that awakens when we find our soul mirror."

"And you're okay with that? That part of you is my familiar?"

He hesitated, his eyes shading with doubt. "I won't lie to you. No, I'm not. The whole thing takes a lot of trust, including that you will use your magic to prevent pregnancy—something I never leave to the woman, I always use a condom. But in this case, to complete the bond I need to come inside you." He took a slow breath. "But I'm so close to losing against this curse, I either figure out a way to trust and bond with you, or I die."

His bluntness rocked her back, sloshing the remains of the tea in her cup and dribbling on her hand. So she was his last choice before death, yay her. He didn't want her, and he certainly didn't want a child tying them together long term; he just wanted freedom from the curse. Grabbing a napkin, she told herself to stop it, she wasn't looking for the big love story, and she sure as hell wouldn't get pregnant. So he wanted to use her? She'd been used before, so she knew how to do that and how to use magic to prevent a pregnancy.

And she'd get her high magic. She might be able to free the souls trapped in her magic then, and maybe even heal her mind. She needed to know more. "How do you know we're soul mirrors?"

He handed her a piece of toast. "Try to eat this." Once she took it, he went on, "Part of how I know is pure animal instinct. I touched your blood and felt the connection. My tattoo started itching last night, getting worse the closer I got to you."

"The falcon one? I saw it." Saw it didn't begin to describe her reaction to the ink. That creature would be her familiar? "It felt like the bird was looking at me." Did the idea sound as crazy to him as it did to her?

"He probably was. I've had the tattoo nearly a year. His eyes were closed...until I touched your blood. The itching stopped almost instantly."

Setting down her toast, she considered that. "How do I know you're my soul mirror? You have all these signs, but..." Risa couldn't get her head around it. All she wanted was to find Kendall, release the souls in her magic and stay sane. This soul mirror connection seemed big and a bit scary.

"Let me touch you." Huskiness thickened his smooth voice.

"Why?"

Linc leaned a fraction closer. "You'll feel the connection in your magic. And..." a grimace cracked his stone-carved face, "...bloodlust." He held up his arms.

The veins bulged in his forearms, pulsing beneath his skin, the lines nearly burgundy in color, and damned angry looking.

"You want my blood." Her heart shot into her throat, and she glanced between him and the door.

His jaw hardened. "I won't hurt you. But it's getting worse, and touching you helps." Linc took a breath and added, "Don't be afraid of me, Risa. I've spent years becoming a man women don't have to be afraid of."

The raw honesty in that statement trembled straight down her center. Over time, she'd honed her instincts in spotting a liar. Linc didn't ring her lying gong. "Just touch?" Risa verified.

"Yes." He held out his hand to her.

She hesitated. Too many times she'd been touched when she didn't want it. Those memories raced in her mind, but Linc hadn't hurt her. He'd saved her, brought her to his home. Her skin tightened, and her stomach twisted.

She eyed the lines bisecting his palm. Lifelines. More proof that he wasn't rogue. *Come on, just do it. No way can you get Kendall away from her demon father by yourself. You need Linc and his friends.* Decision made, Risa's mouth dried as she laid her hand in his.

His long, warm fingers closed around hers, but he kept his hold loose. His bulging, ready-to-crack jaw muscle eased, and he drew in a slow breath. "Better." He stroked his thumb over her hand. "Feel it?"

Her chakras shivered, from her heart straight down to her pelvis. Power rippled in tiny carbonation bubbles flowing through her hand to his. Almost like her magic wanted to touch him. Long seconds had passed when a faint feathery sensation brushed her magic, the part of her no one had touched before. Talking about a connection like that was one thing, but feeling it? It scared her. "I don't like it."

His eyebrows snapped up. "What? My touch?"

His offended tone curved her lips, and for a second, assuaged her. "I bet that would be new for you."

"Hell yeah. When I touch a woman, I make damned sure she likes it."

Her brief amusement vanished. "I'm not most women, Dillinger. And I don't like being touched, or this connection. We barely know each other, yet I feel you in my magic. That's just creepy." She tugged her hand.

He let go, watching her with sharp eyes.

Her chakras pulled tight, as if reacting to releasing his hand.

"Who hurt you?"

Stunned at his too-soft question, she stared at her tingling traitor of a hand. How much had he discovered just by touching her? Could he feel how broken she was? Or how close she was to going totally and irrevocably crazy? Or that she'd failed so badly as a witch, she had souls locked in her shield magic? She didn't want anyone to know those things about her.

Tilting her chin up, she avoided the question. "Wow, you really don't take rejection well."

He didn't move, just watched her with the intensity of a predator. "Was it your baby's father?"

Her baby...oh, he meant Kendall, not her crazy hallucination of Nola. Urgency tightened her muscles. Setting down the mug she still held, she answered, "No, he's not around." Another lie. She must be breaking records today. "It's just me and Kendall, and I have to find her. I'm all she has. I need to try my magic."

"Do you think you're up to it?"

She had to be. "Yes. But you should leave. I'm really not in the mood to get attacked by a blood-crazed witch hunter."

"I'll smell your magic anywhere in the house. It'd be safer if I touch you. And it might help you. Eventually my falcon will become your familiar."

She drew back. "I haven't agreed to this soul-mirror thing."

Linc's gaze softened. "I won't push. It's enough that I've found you for now. Let's take this one step at a time. We'll help you find your child and protect you both. Then we'll see how we can work this out between us."

Yeah? Because what happened when Linc and his friends figured out she'd lied? That Kendall wasn't her child or a witch, and they would essentially kidnap a demon's daughter?

≫ 4 ≪

RISA SPLASHED WATER ON HER face in the bathroom. She'd needed a moment to pull herself together before returning to the conversation with Linc. Drying her cheeks, she steeled her spine. She couldn't worry about the consequences of lying, not with Kendall's safety at stake. That baby, with her huge smile showing off her new tooth pushing through her gum, light blue eyes and shrieking laugh owned Risa's heart. She couldn't leave her in Archer's clutches. What did he want with Kendall?

My father wants her alive. And what he wants, he gets.

Archer's words from last night sent chills down her back. Asmodeus was a scary three-headed demon Risa never wanted to meet. Ever. And she sure as hell didn't want Kendall in his clutches. The baby had demon blood. Did that mean she could be in the Underworld? Oh God, the thought choked her.

"Risa? You okay?"

She jumped at Linc's voice on the other side of the door. Steeling herself, she dropped the towel on the counter and headed out of the bathroom. "Yes."

Skirting around the big man, she sank into the chair. "I'm ready."

Linc crouched in front of her. "You'll let me touch you?"

"Are you sure that just touching will keep you from losing control?" The memory of those rogues in the strip club made her wary.

Rising to his full height, he nodded. "Touching you will keep the bloodlust down. The problem will be when I let go of you. Then it'll hit me with the force of a bullet train."

His unflinching honesty helped her believe he was at least trying not to hurt her. "What do we do?"

Something almost desperate flickered in his gaze. "Don't let go, don't pull away. And if something does happen, don't run. It triggers the predator in me when prey runs."

He considered her prey? Had she lost her freaking mind here? Goose bumps broke out on her skin. *Kendall. You're doing this for Kendall, and for Blythe. You owe them both.* "Tell you what, hunter. I'm not prey, and you don't pull that predator shit on me, or I'll find a gun and shoot your balls off. And believe me, I don't miss." Damn Archer for melting her gun. She'd feel better if she had it.

Linc raised both eyebrows, his lips twitching. "Tough girl, huh?"

"You know it. I'm a trained bodyguard. I protect women from men who don't know the meaning of the word no." Reminding herself of her skills and how hard she'd worked to get strong steadied her.

"Oh, I want to know more about that." He settled into the chair on the other side of the small table. "But right now, I'm going to hold your hand. Then when I let go of you, I have a straight line to the door. I'll leave until the bloodlust calms." He stretched his arm across the table, his palm up.

Don't hesitate, just do it. Find Kendall. For the second time in a few minutes, Risa laid her hand in his.

His warm fingers gently captured hers. "The table is between us, Risa. You don't have to worry about anything except not pulling your hand away and focusing on your magic."

She sank into his gaze over the empty mug of tea and half-eaten toast. Trusting men didn't come easy to her. Hell, it flat out didn't happen. But when she looked into his eyes, she wanted to. He made her long for...something. As if he touched her in a place she hadn't known about. Risa shook it off and turned her gaze to the bed.

Focus.

Drawing in a calming breath, she mentally reached for her magic, starting with her first chakra. It popped open, spilling out a slender stream of power. Her second and third chakras opened with no real effort on her part. Her magic rose and traveled right to Linc's hand wrapped around hers.

Huh. Soul mirror, she thought, then set it aside to concentrate on finding the baby. After a few beats, her magic began gliding up and down her center, until her fourth chakra in the vicinity of her heart opened.

Linc's fingers tightened, and his breath caught.

Risa glanced over, but his face remained impassive. Good enough. If she were doing shield magic, she'd need her hands to weave her power into a magical shield. Instead, she used her magic like a tracking dog and didn't need the hand enveloped in Linc's massive one. She chose one of her favorite memories of Kendall—when she woke up and did the full-body wiggle, her entire face splitting into a grin—and held the picture in her mind. Focusing her magic on the image, she mentally reached for Kendall. Hard.

Her psyche opened up to the universe. The

vulnerability of it unnerved her. Danger could latch on to her magic, especially since she didn't have a familiar to protect her by chasing off anything threatening.

Linc's fingers squeezed her hand, his thumb sliding over her skin. The sensation anchored her, providing at least an illusion of safety.

Distant crying caught her attention. Honing in on that, Risa pushed her magic harder to strengthen the connection. *Kendall?* In answer, misery rolled over her—fear, confusion and loneliness. Oh God, Kendall. Damn it, she wished she had her high magic. With her third eye, she'd be able to see the baby.

All she could do was feel her. She wasn't really hearing her crying. It was more of a vibration in her magic. Pouring out more energy, she struggled to get a sense of where Kendall was. She'd come this far, she had to succeed in locating the baby.

Linc took a moment to study Risa while she concentrated on her witchcraft. Her dark, nearly black hair tumbled around her in curiously uneven lengths ranging from hitting her shoulder blade to almost mid back. Had she grabbed handfuls and chopped it off? That mess of shining locks framed stunning dark blue eyes, apple cheeks and full, sensual lips.

Her butchered hair, no makeup, cracked lips and the fact that she hadn't touched her hair once since he'd come into the room told him she didn't care about her appearance. Yet even swimming in his stained shirt she'd put on last night, her cargo pants and bare feet, she was undeniably gorgeous.

I'm not good at being touched.

Anger simmered in his blood. Someone had hurt this woman, and it infuriated him. She had the signs—

recoiling from touch, defaulting to humor or sarcasm in a form of self-protection. Yeah, she'd been hurt.

She knew how to fight. She had some skills. He'd seen that in the cage last night when she'd held the knife.

Yep, someone had hurt her, and—

His breath caught as Risa's magic rippled in the air and zinged his hand where they touched. Holy shit. That had a kick that penetrated his skin and buzzed his veins. The bird tattoo warmed, and he swore he could feel the feathers quivering. His heart rate escalated like he'd run twelve miles—uphill, in the snow, with a pack of pissed-off hellhounds on his ass. He'd had witch blood dumped on him, and it had been a powerful contact high.

But this? A sexual fire blasted straight into his veins.

Fuck.

His mouth watered, his cock swelled, and his balls ached. Need gripped him so hard, he had to lock his muscles to keep from leaping over the table and tugging Risa to the floor. Once there, he'd strip off her shirt and pants to spread her legs and bury his cock so deep, he'd brand her as his.

Jesus. Crazy much? Not from bloodlust, not as long as he touched her. Nope, what had him by the balls was raw, pulsing, sexual lust, backed by an oversized helping of feral possession.

Only the feel of her hand in his, her soft skin warmed by luscious magic, kept him from totally losing it.

Sweat slicked his back and burned the skin between his shoulder blades.

Wait. That scratching was the bird. Something had upset it. Risa's fingers fisted in his hand, and she gasped. Worry swamped out everything else. "Risa? What is it?"

She turned her head, her eyes wide and haunted. "I felt her." Digging her teeth into her bottom lip, she added, "But something got in my way."

"Could you see where she is?"

She shook her head, frustration defined in the tendons on her neck. "I think I'd need my third eye for that. But I hoped I could get a sense of the location. Like the sound of a train going by, jet flying over her, a feeling of moving if she's in a car. Instead, I hit a block. But I did feel how lost and frightened Kendall is." She blinked, and the stark vulnerability hardened into determination. "Damn it, I have to figure out how to get around that block."

Her protectiveness and aching love for her daughter were so vivid, it stole his breath. He admired her resolve to find her baby. "What kind of block?"

"Magical. It felt oily." She swallowed, her worry transmitting clearly from her hand to his. "Some kind of demon magic, I think."

Not good. Linc stroked her bent fingers and rigid wrist, needing the contact. At least feeling her worry, seeing her frustration about her child, drained off enough lust to think. "We'll talk to the other witches. They can help."

"The witches mated to hunters? Like Carla?"

"Yes, Darcy, Carla, Ailish and Roxy. For sure, they'll want to help find Kendall. I'll set up a video conference." He pulled out his phone and sent off a text with one hand. "They've been using their magic trying to find the spawn, but no luck."

"When can I talk to them? I have to get to Kendall ASAP." Her anxiety clipped her words.

"Soon, I swear. In the meantime, tell me where you live. I'll go gather up things for you and your baby." Sutton would watch over Risa, and that would give Linc a chance to get away once the bloodlust hit.

"Oh. Damn, that's right."

More problems. "What?"

She glanced behind him. He assumed she was looking out the French doors to the balcony. "We live in Phoenix. I don't have a place to stay since we were booked in the Mystique. And my car, it was right in front, so I'm guessing it burned too."

She didn't live in Vegas? Linc spent most of his time in California, which would separate them by almost four hundred miles. How would that work? And why did it bother him so much? He didn't want a permanent mate.

"I don't even know what happened to my purse. I don't have anything with me."

"Hey, breathe." He frowned at just how stranded she must feel. "I'll get you whatever you need."

Her gaze swung to his. "Kendall. She's all I need."

God. This woman twisted him up when she said things like that. "Why were you guys here in Vegas?"

She studied her free hand for a few seconds before she answered. "Blythe needed to close out a bank account here."

"She's from Vegas?"

"We both are, but I moved five years ago. She came out to live with me after she, uh..."

When she trailed off, he realized how hard it was for her to talk about her friend, the one she saw burn to death only a few hours ago. He opened his mouth, but Risa went on.

"She moved in with me about four months ago to help care for Kendall while I worked, and also to do some of the administrative end of my business."

"You're a bodyguard?" She'd mentioned that. An odd career choice for a mom. And where was the dad? Why wasn't he in the picture? He cared more than he liked, already feeling a possessiveness about a baby he'd never met and a woman he'd known only hours.

"Specialized personal protection for women, yes.

Anyway, we came here to finish up a couple things for Blythe."

Hmm. There was more to this story. How the hell did they happen to be exactly where Archer spawned? "Did you come with her as a friend, or protection?"

"Both." Closing her eyes, she grimaced. "It's just so awful. I still can't believe it happened. That Archer killed her."

The way she said it sounded personal. Like he'd targeted Blythe. Risa's obvious grief over the whole thing made him want to pull her into his arms and comfort her. He resisted the urge, settling for stroking her hand as he asked, "Did she know him?"

That panicked, trapped-animal wildness filled her gaze. Then pain. Regret fisted in his chest, but he made himself push her. "Risa? I know it's hard to talk about your friend, but we have to find Archer and figure out what he's doing and how much of a threat he is." Then he went in for the one thing that seemed to motivate her. "And he either has, or knows where, your baby is."

"Blythe and Archer dated briefly well over a year ago. I recognized him, but I don't know what he was doing at the hotel."

So she knew more about the spawn. "You need to tell all of us—"

"Who is us?"

"The hunters and witches. Axel will want in on this conference. This is our first lead. We need as much information on Archer as you can give us."

She bit her lip. "Can I take a shower first?"

A minute ago she'd wanted to talk to the witches right away. But her pale face revealed just how damned exhausted she was. "Yes." He eyed her damaged clothes. "I'll get something for you to wear."

She waved that off. "I can use magic to make these work."

CAGED MAGIC

She looked so damned alone, it made his chest ache. Rising, he rounded the small table to stand over her while clutching her hand, close enough to lose himself in her stunning eyes.

"What are you doing?"

"Trying to let go of you." He wanted to tug her up into his arms and taste her. The need for sex continually ground into him, an unrelenting pressure on his balls that orgasms relieved for five freaking minutes, then it began all over again. A constant need. Sex and bloodlust.

Risa could end all that, but at what cost? She was already getting beneath his skin. Touching places he hadn't allowed any woman to reach.

"Would it help if I kicked you in the balls?"

He blinked, then laughed at the unexpected comment. Damn, she wasn't like the other women he'd dated. Not even close. "No ball kicking."

"Are you always this much of a buzzkill?"

"Absolutely, when it comes to my balls."

"Then I suggest you let go of my hand and leave. Because I'm in a ball-kicking mood."

Amused, he asked, "Do you always threaten the people who save your life?"

"No, just you."

Whoa. Her full lips curved into pure wickedness, flashing straight white teeth. Like he'd taken a punch to the gut, he lost his breath. She was the first woman to knock the breath out of him with just a smile.

That couldn't be good. Once, he'd escaped people who'd thought they owned him. No one would own him again. Ever. Not even the woman who possessed the power to save his soul and drop him to his knees with a smile.

Risa followed the sound of voices down the sweeping staircase with the beautiful wrought-iron railing. The foyer had a massive chandelier hanging from the cathedral ceiling. She ignored the living room and crossed a hallway, her boots clunking on the marble floor.

She really classed up the joint. Growing up, she'd never have worn camo pants and a tank. Her closet had been full of designer clothes she'd adored—until she learned that her father paid for all her luxuries by murdering people as a hired assassin. She'd come to hate all those clothes, shoes, handbags, jewels. The only possession bought by blood money that she'd continued to love was Shelby, her horse.

Shelby had paid a price for Risa's love, like her unborn child...

Stop. None of that helped now. Kendall was what mattered, not the past. She had to lie to find the baby, so she'd do it and deal with the ramifications later.

Her stomach churned, but she ignored it and headed into a huge kitchen and family room. Her gaze went right past the marble floors and countertops, plentiful cherry cabinets and stainless-steel appliances, to the wall of sliding glass doors opened to a covered terrace overlooking hills and a lake.

Breathtaking.

"Risa." Linc walked into the house. "Come on outside. I have the video conference set up. The witches are using some magic to make it easier to see one another on the screen."

Her magic did that shimmy-and-shake thing again, spreading ripples up her center. Damn, had he gotten prettier in the last twenty minutes? His sun-streaked hair tumbled artfully around his chiseled face, framing golden eyes and full, sexy lips.

Wait, when did she start thinking lips were sexy?

Shifting her focus, she eyed his black shirt

stretched across his broad shoulders, the sleeves revealing thick-muscled arms.

"Sugar, you're making me hard checking me out like that."

She yanked her attention up to his face.

One side of his mouth twisted up in a *you're so busted* smirk.

"I was *not* checking you out." Nope, the blame went to pure curiosity about her soul mirror. That was all.

He crossed his arms. "You were staring."

She shrugged, striving for disinterest. "I was trying to figure out how much time it takes you to style your girly hair and squeeze yourself into that too-tight shirt, pretty boy."

His gaze heated and traveled over her face, hovering at her lips for a few seconds.

Don't lick them.

Her neck tingled, and her chest warmed. His stare on her was almost a caress. Even her nipples tightened with sudden awareness. She didn't do attraction or whatever this was. In fact, she cut her own hair, avoided makeup and ordered most of her clothes from cheap online sites because she didn't want any man noticing her.

"That tank you're wearing is tight."

His voice carried the same smooth and decadent quality as the cream inside a Twinkie. Except as much as she loved Twinkies, they never gave her the shivers like Linc did. She needed to redirect this conversation. "Magic shrinkage. Not my fault."

Linc's eyebrows shot up. "What the hell is magic shrinkage?"

Don't laugh. That would tip her hand. "You know how a washing machine shrinks clothes over time? Well, I had to magically repair this shirt—magic shrinkage."

He tilted his head, studying her. "You're lying."

She stared back. "Am I?"

"Not sure yet. But I play poker, and trust me, sugar, I don't lose. I'll learn your tells and figure out when you're lying."

That sucked the air out of her swagger. What the hell was she doing verbally sparring with Linc when she needed to find Kendall? "If you're done flexing, can we get down to business?"

"Sure thing, I'll flex for you later." Closing the distance between them, he settled his large hand on her back. "Come on outside."

Out on the terrace, Risa took in the huge space. Heavy couches and chairs covered in thick cushions faced a fireplace with a big-screen TV over it.

A bald man set aside a laptop and rose from a couch. "Hi, Risa, you look better today. Not sure I introduced myself last night. I'm Sutton West."

A gold eagle earring flashed in one ear, and his gentle eyes softened his otherwise harsh face. The man's build screamed mountain rugged. "Hi, Sutton. Thank you for helping last night."

Nodding, he picked up something from the couch and handed it to her. "New phone. Linc said you lost yours. I've programmed in all our numbers."

Stunned, she automatically reached out to take the phone. Black and sleek, it looked expensive. "Uh, thanks."

"No problem." He shifted his attention toward the big screen. "This is my mate, Carla Fisk. She and the others you'll meet are in Glassbreakers, California."

A woman with white-blonde hair, hazel eyes and a pretty smile filled the screen. "Risa, nice to meet you. We'll help find your daughter any way we can."

Grateful, she released her breath. "Thank you."

"I'm Axel Locke." A big man with raven-black hair, green eyes and an aura of power so strong she could see it on the screen appeared. "And this is Darcy MacAlister."

The camera moved over to the woman next to Axel. She waved her fingers. "Hey, Risa. You have no idea how glad I am to meet you."

Star struck, she wasn't sure what to say. Part of her had been skeptical that these people were real. New hope bubbled in her chest. "Uh, okay. I'm happy to meet you too."

The screen shifted to a dark-haired hunter leaning back in a chair and radiating a *don't fuck with me* attitude. "I'm Phoenix Torq. And this..." he looked up at the woman perched on the arm of his chair, "...is my mate, Ailish Donovan."

The witch turned her head to face the camera.

Risa barely stifled a gasp. Ailish had silvery-blue eyes surrounded by a faint webbing of scars.

"Don't look at me, Phoenix, look at her," Ailish said.

"Right, sorry." Phoenix shifted his gaze to Risa. "Ailish is blind, but she can see through my eyes."

"No shit?" Slapping a hand over her mouth, she grimaced at her crass outburst.

Ailish laughed. "It's true."

Relieved that Ailish didn't seem offended, Risa relaxed. "That's amazing that you can see through your mate." Another sign of the depth of the soul-mirror connection. But she didn't have time to dwell on it.

The camera moved to another couple. The man leaned against a pool table, with blond hair and a surfer-god face. He had his arms around a woman with red hair and green eyes. "Hi, Risa. I'm Kieran DeMicca. Most people call me Key. The beautiful woman here is my mate, Roxy Banfield."

Key's hand rested protectively over Roxy's rounded belly. The witch was pregnant, maybe four to six months along.

That pinged her heart, but Risa forced a smile. "Hi."

Axel reappeared on the screen. "That's everyone here in California, except Eli Stone and his sister, Ginny. You'll meet them another time." The man's eyes moved over the terrace. "Where's Ram?"

"Right here."

Risa turned at the new voice behind her, vaguely recalling the man from last night. Now his sweat-slicked blond hair lay flat, and he had a white shirt looped around the back of his neck. His bare chest bore a bronze thunderbird tattoo with wings spread high as if coming in for a landing. But what fascinated her were the twin streaks of jagged lightning streaking from the partly opened eyes.

Ram reached for his shirt, and Risa jumped back as blue-tinged sparks arced from his fingertips.

The man frowned. "Sorry. I hoped a run would drain off some of it."

"What causes that?" She'd never seen anything like it. Oh sure, static electricity could cause a spark of two, but not this. "Is it magic?"

"Electrical buildup. It's nothing." Ram yanked on his shirt, ignoring the dozens of tiny scorch marks where he touched the cotton.

Didn't appear to be nothing to her. He sparked like a downed power line. How did it happen?

"Let's get started." Axel's voice commanded attention. "I checked in with Wing Slayer. He said no hybrid has ever successfully spawned on earth and survived, that he knows of."

Ram moved a few steps away from the group and focused his attention on the screen. "Did he know about Archer?"

"Not until the hybrid spawned."

Linc asked, "So it's been tried before but the spawn didn't survive?"

"Not for the entire process. There's an initial burst of power which can last twelve to twenty-four hours, and that's the period the spawn is in now. Next, he'll go into a hibernation state to finish the transition, and that's when he's most vulnerable. Some don't make it out. They just can't endure the transition. In a few rare cases, witches have found the hibernating spawn and banished it to the Underworld."

Risa sank into a chair as it hit her that Kendall's future would include having to choose between her human or demon side.

"He has protection here. The rogues knew he was spawning." Linc stood by her shoulder, his tone harsh. "I spotted the spawn standing over Risa and her baby, and ran toward her when several rogues attacked me."

"I saw that," Ram added. "We managed to get some information from one rogue. He said the spawn had to choose to be either demon or human on his thirtieth birthday."

Thirty. Okay, she had years to help Kendall make the right choice—if she got her back.

Axel nodded. "Wing Slayer believes the rogues have found a safe place for the spawn to hibernate, feeding him energy from the ley lines and probably witch blood to help the transition. And when he comes out of that, he'll be fully immortal, impossible for us to kill and too dangerous for the witches to get close enough to banish."

"How does Wing Slayer know all this?" Risa's knowledge of the hunters and their god mostly came from the Internet.

Linc answered, "Wing Slayer's half-demon, half-god. His mother is a demon, and he grew up in the Underworld until his mother kicked him out."

A flash of hope bubbled in her. If their god had demon blood, then maybe they'd protect Kendall after all. She started to open her mouth.

Axel jumped in. "Wing Slayer lived on Earth disguised as a human. That's when Asmodeus corrupted witches and got them to banish Wing Slayer. He and Asmodeus have a long-standing feud. Asmodeus wants control of Earth, and Wing Slayer is determined to prevent that. So much so, he invoked his god powers and created Wing Slayer Hunters to help."

Her hope crashed and burned. Kendall's grandfather was the god's enemy. Her fear for the baby ramped up. She didn't dare tell them the truth.

"Risa." Axel looked at her from the screen. "We need any information you have to try and track Archer. I haven't forgotten about your baby either. Archer will have to put her somewhere before he goes into hibernation, probably with a demon witch. But we need to find out more about him to figure it out."

All eyes turned to her.

The weight of her decision pressed in on her, and for a second, she wanted to blurt out the truth. But the risk to Kendall was too grave, so she launched into the story she'd come up with while in the shower. "While still living here in Vegas, Blythe dated Archer briefly over a year ago. She told me about him, and I ran a background check."

"Why?" Sutton asked.

That she could answer truthfully. "Because she's my friend, and I didn't live close enough to check him out personally." Blythe had been a party girl, and Risa had worried that she would get into trouble. "It only lasted a couple dates, but I know Archer is not his real name, it's Gavin Orr. His mother is Petra Orr, the former supermodel and owner of Lustrate Publicity."

Sutton looked up from his computer screen. "Petra Orr. She's the Hollywood publicist who mysteriously vanished four months ago?"

"Yes. That's her."

68

"Oh, damn." Ailish leaned into the camera. "I know that name."

Chills went down Risa's spine, and she sat forward, dropping her elbows on her thighs. "How?"

The witch thinned her mouth, tension radiating from her. "She was a friend of my mother when I was little."

All three men around Risa tensed, which made her pulse stutter. "And?"

"My mother was a demon witch."

Oh God. She shot to her feet, her heart slamming against her ribs, a low roar in her ears. "Could Archer's mother have Kendall? How do we find her?"

5

Risa's distress rubbed his skin like sandpaper, and the smell of her magic fanned his bloodlust, winding him tight enough to explode.

He had to touch her, and laid his hand on her shoulder.

She whipped her head around, her eyes frantic. "What do I do?"

"We'll find her." He turned his gaze to the screen. "Start with Petra's house and office. See if Archer has a home in L.A. too. Rip that town apart."

Axel broke in. "Phoenix, Key, you two go. Find out everything you can."

Sutton's fingers flew over the keyboard of his laptop. "I'm pulling the latest photos of Petra Orr from the company website and media shots. I'll forward them to you guys."

Linc looked down at Risa. "What about Kendall? Can you magically produce a picture of her?"

"Yes." She lifted the phone Sutton had given her and concentrated on the screen.

Her magic rolled up from her shoulder, through his hand and buzzed his veins. Damn. At the same time, a light blue shimmer danced over her skin. She was so beautiful, he couldn't tear his gaze away.

"Here." She held up the phone.

Linc eyed the image of a baby sitting on the floor with her fat little legs stretched out and arms reaching as if wanting to be picked up. She had wisps of blonde hair and light blue eyes very unlike Risa's. "She doesn't look like you. Must take after her father." And didn't that just piss him off. Who was this man who'd left Risa pregnant and alone with a kid? Who had touched her? Hot possession fueled his anger.

Risa stepped away from him. "Does it matter who she looks like? She's only a baby."

Shit. He'd screwed up by opening his big mouth. "No. Of course not. I'm surprised." And a jealous asshole, which was pure bullshit. Linc didn't do jealousy. Returning his attention to the picture, he honed in on the kid's face-splitting grin with a single tooth poking through her gums. The thought of any baby in a demon's clutches, yeah, that wasn't happening. "I'll forward it to the contact list so all of us have a picture of her."

"Risa," Carla jumped in. "Describe what happened when you tried to magically reach Kendall."

Done with sending the picture, Linc listened as Risa described it again. Just the memory of that much of her magic pouring over him tightened his balls. The need for sexual release always rode him, but near Risa, it hit critical levels.

"Sounds like demon magic." Carla frowned and added, "It's dangerous, as the magic can latch on to yours, and you don't have the protection of a familiar. Whoever is using the demon magic can track you too."

"How do I get past it?"

"You need your familiar and high magic to get above the block and see Kendall with your third eye.

Your familiar will keep you safe." Carla's hazel eyes slid to Linc. "It takes time once you seal your bond to gain more magic. The sooner you do it, the better."

Linc stiffened. "She's not ready." He was. Hell, he was desperate. But he'd seen Risa's skittishness. Something had happened to make her mistrustful.

Carla's gaze softened. "We've tried to help from here, but when the demon spawned there in Vegas, it caused a magic drain in that area."

"Along with knocking out all the electrical power on and close to the Strip," Sutton said.

Carla nodded. "I'll come there."

Sutton's head jerked up. "Carly, it's too dangerous here."

The witch's eyes blazed with yellow light. "Exactly. I need to be there in case something happens to you. And I want to help Risa find her baby. I'm coming to Vegas. If I'm there, I'm sure I can connect with Darcy, Roxy and Ailish here to combine our power and assist."

Sutton compressed his lips in a tight line before sighing. "I'll come get you. I want you safe."

"Wait." Axel raised his hand, getting everyone's attention. "How about if I have Eli drive her out? He'll stay there and help with finding Archer. Wing Slayer believes Archer needs to stay within fifty miles of where he spawned, so he's there somewhere. You all work on that, while we tear Petra's life apart here and see if we can find her. She'll have or know where the baby is, and her son."

"Works for me." Linc liked the idea. Risa would have another witch here to help her, make her feel safer.

"I'll be safe with Eli," Carla added.

Sutton set his computer aside, got up and walked to the screen. "Be careful. Please, Carly."

A smile lit up her face. "Promise."

"Okay, that's the plan," Axel said. "Once Carla's there, Risa, she'll help you."

"Back to locating the spawn. I'll set up a grid search." Ram leaned against a far post, working on his phone. "Linc, will your hunter friends here help us search?"

He nodded. "Yeah, I'll contact them." He and Baron had some issues, but Baron cared about Vegas. He'd agree.

"What else can I do to find her? I can't just sit here." Risa glanced up at Linc. "Unless I go out searching, and maybe I can feel her nearby?"

"No." The word snapped out before he could think better of it.

"He's right, Risa." Sutton stopped typing. "The media has descended and are calling what happened a terrorist attack. On top of that, rogues are all over the city, and we don't know where Archer is, or if he's still in his original burst of energy or in hibernation."

Linc rubbed the clenched muscles in Risa's shoulder, trying not to think about how smooth and warm her skin felt. How much he wanted to kiss and lick—*Stop or you're going to have a massive boner.* "You have to stay safe to find Kendall. You're our only link to her."

Frustration hardened her jaw. As Risa turned to the screen, rising desperation drove her to ask, "Carla, is there anything I can do?"

Sympathy filled her gaze. "I know it's quick, but the sooner you and Linc form the soul bond, then you can work on accessing your high magic."

Risa spun around, clutching his arm. "I'll do it. The mating thing, I'll do it."

Heat ripped into his belly, and his cock jumped at the idea. But the desperation in her eyes wrenched out his protectiveness. He opened his mouth, then looked around, remembering they had an audience. Grabbing her hand, he tugged her with him. "We'll talk about this in private."

Once back in the room she'd woken in, Risa's stomach churned and flipped. The door shut softly, and she whirled.

Linc stood there, big, imposing, and taking up way too much space. Unable to catch her breath, she backed up, then caught herself and stopped. "Uh, where do we start?"

"We talk." He sat on the bed and held out his hand.

Don't think about other men, other beds. Block it. She'd gotten to be an expert at blocking things she didn't want to feel. But her magic remained stubbornly active, refusing to send out the blessed numbness that had saved her so many times before. Instead, her chakras quivered with low-grade excitement. She took his hand, perching uneasily on the edge of the mattress.

"Are you sure you want to do this?" Linc's voice softened. "You're emotionally wrung out and desperate."

With his warm hand surrounding hers, the solid presence of him next to her didn't seem so overwhelming. "I need my magic. Kendall's all I have. And you want to break your curse, so we both get what we want."

His gaze grew concerned. "I more than want it. But I don't want to mislead you. I'm always honest with women, Risa. This isn't some big romance for me, and I'm not going to fall in love with you. I need this to break my curse, and I want to help you, but this thing between us isn't a long-term relationship."

She looked away. "I understand that. I don't want it either." The image of Key holding Roxy in front of him with his hand resting protectively on her pregnant belly rose in her mind, tripping a longing. She pushed it away. Her mom had chased a romantic dream into a depraved life of helping Risa's father commit murder. Love wasn't only blind, but stupid and destructive. Risa lived in reality. "This is necessity, not romance."

He tightened his fingers around hers. "It can be more than necessity. It can be pleasure between friends. And once we both have what we want, I'll still be your friend. If you need me to help with your magic, I'll be there."

What man had ever offered to be her friend? The idea appealed to her, but it wasn't smart to want more than she could have. The truth about Kendall would destroy any chance at friendship. Yet she was curious about Linc. "What about you? I understand that you are focused on breaking your curse, but do you ever want what the other mated hunters have?" Wait that sounded like she meant falling in love. "I mean, they have real wings and can fly, right? Do you ever want that?"

He shrugged. "The wings are the witch's familiar and usually come out to help her. That kind of bond is deep. I don't see that happening for us."

That pinged in her chest, touching too close to a place she refused to acknowledge. The part of her that wanted love, that might be a little too like her mom. Not happening. And yet she couldn't resist wondering what Linc would look like with real wings. His falcon tattoo was gorgeous, and she wanted to see and touch it again. What if Linc got real wings, and she could actually touch the feathers? The thought sparked thrills in her belly.

Crap, what was she thinking? He didn't want his wings, and once he found out she'd lied, he'd loathe her. Lifting her chin, she focused on her goal. Only her goal. "Got it. We should stop talking about this and just do it."

"Look at me."

His smooth voice drew her with a nearly magnetic power. Risa looked into his eyes.

He moved slowly, skimming his knuckles down her cheek. "The whole point of sex is pleasure. For both of us."

His words and touch ignited warm tremors in her stomach. She'd never felt that before. Oh, sure, she'd heard about sexual gratification, but in her case, sex had been awful. Most of the time her magic had numbed her, kept her distant from the experience. But now her witchcraft spilled out, chasing his touch, making her skin ultrasensitive. Her nipples tightened. The new feelings robbed her of words.

"We're not going to rush this." He rubbed his thumb over her bottom lip.

Goose bumps broke out on her arms, and she parted her mouth. Her magic shivered and danced, one chakra opening, then another, as power tumbled out and rose in her belly, dashing to any place Linc touched her.

Heat flared in his eyes. "I want to kiss you, to taste your lips. Slow, Risa. Just a kiss." He leaned a fraction closer. "Let me taste your sweet mouth and hot magic."

She shivered, his voice and touch pulling her closer. When had she ever just kissed?

"Say yes. Or no. Do you want me to kiss you?"

He was doing this for her. Taking the time, letting her feel in control. She should tell him that she didn't deserve his gentleness. But for just a moment she wanted to feel what it was like for someone to care a tiny bit. "Yes."

Linc leaned in, and the scent of soap and male rushed into her. He touched his mouth to hers, light and easy, brushing her lips, creating sensation. Heat. Want.

Another chakra opened.

A growl rumbled in his chest. Letting go of her hand, he snapped his arm around her waist and pulled her across his hard thighs.

"I can't get enough of you." Against her hip, his cock throbbed. With his hand in her hair, he tilted her head back and kissed over her jaw, his sexy mouth trailing along the sensitive skin of her throat.

Shivers charged down her body. Magic rippled and rushed.

Linc opened his mouth over her collarbone, licking and sucking at the tender flesh there.

A moan slid from her, and more magic surged out of her chakras. Deep between her legs, she swelled and pulsed.

She liked what Linc was doing. Wanted it.

No. Oh God, no. She couldn't like it. Her heart rate shot up, and fear drenched her.

It was too much, too confusing. Her magic swelled fast and out of control. Concentrating, she called on her witchcraft to help her now as it always had.

In seconds, her magic calmed and cooled, and familiar numbness spread until she felt nothing.

Linc lost himself in the beauty of the woman in his arms. Her warm, silky hair spilling over his fingers sent shock waves right to his cock. The lightest blue witch shimmer danced over the top layer of her skin, so pretty he couldn't look away. When she released a breathy moan of surrender, her eyes growing heavy with desire, lust roared into his blood.

Need her. Want her. More.

He forced air into his lungs that did nothing to

appease his wild hunger. *Go slow*. His instincts screamed that she'd been hurt and scared. But she trusted him for a kiss.

Hot. So damned hot. Her magic rippled everywhere he touched, and when he latched on to her collarbone and sucked gently, the power filled his mouth, slipped over his tongue and spread inside him.

The bird shivered in his tattoo.

More. Jesus he had to have more. Lifting his head, he eyed her lush lips. Leaning into her, he took her mouth, licking and sucking until she parted her lips. Easing his tongue in, he wrapped her tighter against him. She tasted of sweet tea and savory spice. He delved farther into her warm, wet mouth.

Wait, something was wrong. Her magic dimmed, and Risa stilled. She didn't resist him, but she didn't kiss him back either.

He brushed his fingers over her face. "Risa, hey, talk to me."

Her gaze swung to his.

Linc drew back. Her eyes had taken on a vague distance that bugged him. Anger that she pulled her magic back festered and heated. Linc clamped his jaw. *Control it. It's the curse screwing with you.*

"No talking. Let's get this done." She sat up on his thighs, reaching for the hem of her tank.

He fisted his hand in her hair to keep from helping her get that shirt off.

Strip her. Push her on the bed and—

No. Steeling himself against the painful beat in his balls demanding relief—a relief that was getting harder and harder to achieve—he strove for patience. Laying his hand over hers to stop her from stripping off her shirt, he said, "You're not ready for that."

Her eyes narrowed. "I don't need you to tell me what I'm ready for." Releasing her shirt, she glided her hand along the ridge of his dick beneath his pants.

Holy fuck. Her touch sizzled and rocked him right to his bones. Sweat popped out on his back, and sharp claws of sexual need dug into his balls. His cock swelled and hardened to unbearable. Heat suffused him.

Fuck. His control slipped with every stroke of her hand along his aching length. The ball-squeezing compulsion to slam inside her, bury himself deep and get relief took over.

Her fingers found the head of his cock and squeezed. "I want this inside me."

His control shattered. Linc whipped them around, dropped her back to the mattress and covered her body, then sealed his mouth to hers, demanding entrance.

Mine. The word screamed through him. *Mate her, bind her forever.*

He sank his tongue into her mouth, tasting his witch. Risa.

Just a bare trickle of cool magic teased his tongue. He wanted more. It enraged him that she was holding back. Her magic was his, damn it.

Pain sliced between his shoulder blades. The shock of it pierced his possessive lust fog, and Linc pulled his mouth back, panting. The falcon tattoo flamed to life, scratching at his skin. He didn't give a shit about that.

But when he looked down at Risa....

Oh Christ, what was he doing? Ugly disgust at himself damn near choked him. She lay there pale and quiet, her eyes fixed blankly at a point over his shoulder.

Withdrawn. Not there. Not fighting, but not there either.

God. Sliding off her, he laid his hand on her face. "Risa, look at me, sugar." He had to fix this, whatever *this* was. He had the sick feeling she'd done this too many times to count.

She stared at him vacantly. "Why'd you stop?"

Because he didn't want to be a fucking animal. He'd spent years becoming a rich, sophisticated man who charmed and pleasured women, not one who jumped them like a beast in heat. But he didn't dump all that on her. "I—"

A loud shrieking exploded around them.

Risa jerked beneath him, her hip grinding into his cock with the sweetest torment. "What's happening?"

He jumped off the bed. "Trouble. It's the house alarm." Grabbing her hand, he tugged her up. "Come on!"

Ram strode across the yard of Linc's house, needing to get away from Risa's magic.

Envy rolled through him. Inside that house now, Linc would mate with his soul mirror and break his curse. While Ram had gotten stuck with a soul-mirror connection tainted by demon magic that caused an electrical buildup in him. Holding out his hands, he watched the sparks rain down from his fingers.

Fuck.

The sparks were a direct message from the thunderbird inked on his chest that it wanted Ram's soul mirror, Shayla Banfield.

But Ram didn't want her. Nope, he loved another woman, wanted her more than his own soul. Or to live, apparently, because this bird would kill him if he didn't give in, find Shayla and mate with her.

Yeah, it sucked to be him. He needed Shayla to live, but loved Ginny.

His phone vibrated as he reached the end of Linc's property. Standing in the bright sunlight, he pulled it out and held it in his shadow to check the screen. The fire in his veins shifted from bloodlust to a longing so fierce he lost his breath.

Ginny. Her lovely face stared back at him in a face chat. Ram smiled and said, "Angel, I've missed you."

"Ram, I heard about what's happening there. I can't believe it. A demon spawn?"

Her troubled voice made his heart ache. He should be with her, protecting and comforting her. But he'd come to Vegas to talk to Shayla and check on Linc. "There appears to be more than we ever guessed around us."

"You didn't see Shayla, did you?"

Ram leaned his back against a fence post, drawing the warm Vegas air into his lungs. Ginny had pushed him to find Shayla and talk to her. "No. She was gone when I got to the motel where we'd agreed to meet. But she most definitely had been there. I smelled her magic, and the bird reacted." Frustration gnawed at him. "Damn it, she needs to stop playing games and talk to me."

Silence flowed over the line.

"Ginny?"

"What happens when you do see her, Ram? I mean...what if there's more between you than you think? The other soul-mirror couples couldn't stay away from each other. Maybe you need to be with her. She's your soul mirror."

"It's wrong, Ginny. Carla and the other witches could feel the demon magic in the thunderbird, and he's her familiar. Shayla doesn't want the bond, and neither do I. I want you, angel. Nothing is going to change that."

Her silence killed him.

Gripping the phone tighter, he stared into her eyes on the screen and willed her to hear him, believe him. "Ginny, I love you."

"I know. I'm just...I know."

But she feared it wasn't enough. "Trust me, baby. I'm going to talk to her, and Shayla and I will figure out what happened to cause this problem. If we can undo it, there's a good chance this thunderbird in me will die off." And he'd be free to have Ginny. Although her angel sire had other plans for his daughter, but one problem at a time.

"What if I talk to her? She's not letting you too close because she doesn't want her infertility magic, right?"

Ram looked up at the brutally bright sky. "That's what her cousin Roxy says. There's one infertility witch born every generation, again from some kind of demon magic, the same crap that's in this thunderbird." He tapped his chest where the bird was inked beneath his shirt. "Infertility witches are hated and avoided by other witches for fear of infertility. I don't want you anywhere near her."

Sympathy filled her eyes. "Ram, she's not a demon witch. She's a victim of demon magic just like you. Imagine how lonely it is to be her. Maybe she needs a friend."

Damn it, he didn't want to think about that. Yeah, Shayla had been dealt a rough hand too. Ram's friends had his back, but who did Shayla really have? It'd been easier to think of her as the enemy, the woman he didn't want. But his greatest concern still went to Ginny. "I know you want to help, but you can't interfere. Your father might punish you."

She touched the camera in her phone so it looked like she was trying to touch him. "I can endure it, Ram."

"I can't!" Ram would never forget what her father had done to her, never forget the sound of her screams. Hatred for the angel sliced deep and violent. He'd do anything to protect Ginny, but how did he safeguard her from an ancient angel?

She dropped her hand, her eyes filling with resignation. "We're running out of time anyway."

Ram opened his mouth to reply when he heard a whooshing sound. Jerking his head up, he spotted a shape streaking across the sky, right for Linc's house. A sizzling sound grew.

A second later came a flash of unholy light as a fiery arrow hit the roof of the patio.

Flames exploded, and a piercing security alarm shrieked a warning.

"What is it? Ram?"

He glanced at the phone. "The spawn. Archer and his hellfire arrows are here." No time. Ram shoved his phone into his pocket and raced for the house.

⟫ 6 ⟪

LINC PULLED RISA BEHIND HIM as he raced toward the stairs. With his free hand, he yanked his cell phone from his pocket and punched in the code to silence the alarms.

The blaring died.

Violent, furious hissing grew louder until it reached the roar of a freight train. Black-edged flames flooded the first floor.

"Fuck! Hellfire!" It raced across his foyer, stopping him at the top of the stairs.

"Has to be Archer." Risa clutched his hand. "Where is he?"

Linc snapped into survival mode. They had to get out, but first he needed to find his friends. "Sutton! Ram!" Were they still in the house?

Shouts sounded somewhere from the first floor. Shit, that meant at least one of them remained in the house. Fire licked across the floor at the bottom of the stairs. The red-and-black flames paused, then turned to shoot up the stairs.

Damn it. He couldn't leave his friends trapped in hellfire.

"Look!" Rise screamed.

A huge, winged shape rose from behind the flames to hover just beneath his cathedral ceiling in the entrance. Sutton. Before Linc could drag in a breath of relief, the winged hunter dove down and vanished into the growing inferno.

Only one thing would make Sutton do that—Ram had to be trapped. Linc nudged Risa toward the hallway. "Go find a way out." He went down two steps, trying to gauge a way around the red-and-black blaze.

Violent coughing pierced the air. Glancing up, he saw Sutton rise again. His wings beat furiously, the wind he created pushing the flames back. As the man rose higher, Linc caught sight of Ram hanging on to Sutton's hips and coughing. Once high enough, Sutton flew over the flames climbing up the staircase.

Ram yanked his legs up, using sheer strength to hold on to Sutton and away from the fire. At the top of the risers, Ram dropped and landed on his feet. He coughed once more and shouted, "Go."

Linc turned, raced up the last steps, grabbed the stunned Risa, and they hauled ass down the hall toward his bedroom. He had a balcony there.

Halfway to his goal, oily smoke billowed around them in thick plumes, making it impossible to breathe.

"Linc," Ram shouted. "Sutton's wing's on fire."

Linc shoved Risa ahead of him. "My room, straight ahead. Get to the balcony and out." He pivoted, backtracking through the choking smoke and blazing heat a few steps. Oh shit.

Sutton had dropped to one knee in the middle of the hallway. His eagle wings were slightly spread, flames licking the highest tip of the right one, growing quickly.

Ram ripped his shirt off, trying to smother the flames. Behind the two men, raging hellfire crested the stairs.

"He was using his wings to push the flames back," Ram said. "I can't put it out."

No time, no choice. Linc palmed his knife.

"Flames are too close." Thick rivers of sweat streaked through the sooty grime on Sutton's face. "Get out." It came out a pained croak. His shoulders shook, and he snapped his jaw closed, hissing.

And leave him behind to burn to death? "Fuck that." Vicious heat and thicker blooms of smoke rolled over them. Linc could barely see. "Hold still." He grabbed the wing, yanking it lower.

"Shit," Ram said.

Linc glanced back. A wall of flames barreled toward them from less than four feet away.

Sure death racing right for them with no escape.

Risa ran. She had to live to save Kendall. Had to. Drawing a breath burned her nose, then seared down her throat and lungs.

What was she doing? She couldn't leave three men to die. Three men who had saved her.

Skidding to a stop, she pivoted and hurried back. Once close enough, the smell of burnt feathers and flesh sickened her. She blinked tears from her eyes to clear her vision. Fire hissed at the top of Sutton's wing. Linc held a knife in his hand, but behind them an inferno of hellfire threatened. Too damn close.

Only one way to save them.

Going still, she reached deep. Her chakras shivered, then released so fast she almost fell. That had never happened before.

Harness it! No time to worry about why she had more magic. Quickly, power surged from her pelvis, up her stomach, through her heart. Growing stronger. The magic hit her throat chakra and wavered.

"Risa," Linc yelled, "run!"

She threw up her hands, grabbing strands of her magic, and laced them in the air. She had to get every stand of magic in the shield. Remembering the burning wing, she yelled back, "Cut the wing. Throw it!" Brutal, yes, but necessary to live.

Bigger. Faster. She wove the power streaming through her into a shield of magic. Sweat from the exertion, from trying to control the vast magic, made her shake.

"What are you doing?" Linc's shouted demand distracted her.

"Just do it! I'm going to shield us." Hard to talk, both from the smoke and the extreme amount of magic and energy to control it. "Fire can't be inside the shield."

Linc's knife moved in a blur, slicing through the top of the wing.

"Son of a bitch," Sutton roared over the flames. "Motherfucker."

Blood spurted, some of it hitting her face. Odd, she felt a tug of magic in it. Must be from his soul mirror, Carla. *Use it, keep going.* She pulled the threads of the other witch's magic into hers. Weaving stronger, faster, bigger.

"Trying to stop the bleeding," Linc said. "Can't Carla help here?"

Sutton shook his head, his fingers digging into his thigh. "She's helping Risa. And Christ, I don't want her to feel this if she tries to heal me through our bond." He dragged in a harsh breath.

Sympathy edged into Risa concentration then vanished as the wall of hellfire rose higher and began to arc like a killer wave. She had to act now. Using every fiber of her strength, she magically threw her shield. Pain cramped her stomach, and her muscles quivered from the tremendous energy she used.

Time froze as the shield sailed into the air, the pale blue threads that only she could see spreading. The fire roared down the hallway, only inches from Linc.

Work, please work!

Or they'd all die.

Her shield slammed down, snapping into place over the four of them.

One heartbeat later, the wave of hellfire screamed overhead but didn't touch them.

Risa swallowed against the bile and kept her focus razor sharp. She had to feed the shield a constant stream of magic to maintain it.

Linc caught her shoulders as she swayed. "Can we move? Will the shield thing move with us? I can't see it, but I feel it like an invisible bubble around us."

She nodded, totally fixated on feeding the shield magic. "Hurry," she managed.

He swept her into his arms and ran. "Stay tight with us," he told the other two.

Risa barely saw the walls or Linc's massive bed as they raced through what she guessed was his bedroom. He shifted to one leg, then he kicked open the French doors.

They all rushed onto the balcony.

"Shit, in the sky. That's the spawn."

She peered through the smoke to see the creature with leather wings hovering about twenty feet away. He yanked an arrow from the quiver at his back and fitted it to his bow.

It slammed into her shield. Pain exploded in her chakras, and Risa groaned. Her skin pulled tight and stretched as she struggled to keep her magic open, weaving frantically.

"Jump together," Linc issued the order. He took a step and leaped over the railing of the balcony.

She made out the shapes of Sutton on one side, Ram on the other. They all fell through the air. No choice but to trust Linc to hold her. Risa barely felt them land. Somewhere in her mind, she truly grasped his strength. But her thoughts, all her will, focused on her shield. Sweat streamed down her face, between her breasts, and her shirt stuck to her over-sensitized skin.

But the worst was yet to come, when the soul screams would attack her later, after she dropped her magic.

Don't think about it. Just concentrate.

Linc pulled her tight to his chest, his body curled over hers as they ran. "Doing okay?"

She managed a nod before another arrow banged into her shield. Risa had to keep reinforcing spots that were thinning, using her hands to reweave the magic. Every place she plugged took a surge of energy.

"You won't get away, witch!" Archer's bellow rang so loud, it echoed in the shield.

"Bastard wants her dead," Linc said. "Flank Risa in case she loses the shield."

The two men moved in tighter around her as they kept moving.

"Hang on, Risa." Linc's voice rolled over her. "Just another minute."

It felt like hours. Despite her efforts, the shield thinned, getting weaker.

"Here, Ram, open this," Linc said.

The man bent over and pulled something on the ground. "What?" Risa asked.

"Escape tunnel," he told her, then said, "Sutton, you're going to have to fold your wings to get in here."

"Don't worry about me, you just hang on to Risa." Sutton's voice was tight.

"Few more seconds." Linc's face was so close, his breath fanned over her face. "Once we're in the tunnel, you can drop the shield." He turned to the others. "It's a one-story drop to cement. Jump."

She heard the thud as each man landed.

"Our turn. I won't drop you."

Before she could respond, he stepped off into nothingness. Her stomach bottomed out like she was on a roller-coaster ride, but she held on to her magic by the merest thread.

They landed. Linc shifted her to one arm and reached for something. Metal scraped, and darkness closed in on them with a dull thud. He lowered her to her feet, keeping one arm around her shoulders. "We're safe. You can drop the shield thing."

She let it go by lowering her hands. Her magic crashed, leaving her shivering and panting from the exertion.

His arm tightened around her, keeping her steady. "I need to keep touching you."

She didn't argue. Not when she could barely stand and was using all her concentration to hold off the soul screams.

A lantern clicked on. Light flooded the damp space.

"What now?" Sutton asked. The hunter crouched down with Ram standing over him, slowly sliding his hands over the cut edges of Sutton's injured wing, creating little sparks.

Ugh. Ram was using the electrical energy in his hands to cauterize the wound left after Linc had cut away the burning chunk of wing.

Unable to help herself, Risa blurted out, "You were in so much pain, but you were more worried about Carla than yourself." His comment about not wanting Carla to feel his pain hadn't quite registered until now.

Sutton eyed her. "Carly's my everything. Having part of my wing cut off was like having part of her severed from me. It was more than physical. The eagle connects us, is part of our bond. I didn't want her to feel that moment of loss. Like having something precious and vital amputated."

What was that like? Such a personal, soul-deep connection? It seemed like too much, too all-consuming. "Does losing part of the wing change anything between you and Carla?"

He shook his head. "No. It's only a few inches and will heal. But Carly would feel it too deeply. She loves our eagle."

And he loved his Carly. Risa might not understand it, but she respected it.

Linc rubbed his hand up and down her bare arm. "We need to get moving. Got a vehicle stashed. It's a mile though this tunnel. We'll take that to a place I know." He looked down at her. "You saved our asses back there."

"Glad it worked. Last night I couldn't summon enough magic to blow out a candle."

"Probably means the spawn is weakening, needing to go into hibernation." Sutton stood and rolled his shoulders. "One thing's for sure though, he wants you dead, Risa. If we had any doubt that thing is evil, I'm sure of it now."

Ram examined the wing. "It's not pretty, but the bleeding stopped." Holding up his arms, he added, "I'm going to hike on ahead. Bloodlust."

Risa eyed the swollen veins pulsing beneath his skin. "I'm sorry."

"Nothing to be sorry for. Without you we'd be flame-broiled. But I have to get some distance." He turned and jogged down the tunnel, vanishing in the blackness.

She shivered, the lantern light hurting her eyes and exhaustion weighing her down. The souls stirred, creating tiny pops in her mind.

Not yet. Hold it back. Fear shuddered into her. What if this time her mind cracked entirely?

Too late, she couldn't change it. She'd used her shield magic, the souls would launch their screams, and she'd be at their mercy. She just hoped she could get to a private place. Alone. Where no one would see her like that.

7

LINC FOLLOWED THE NEWLY PAVED road through the gates.

"What is L.C. Academy?" Ram asked from the passenger seat of the Suburban.

Passing the sign placed in the drought-resistant vegetation, Linc glanced in the rearview mirror to see Risa holding Sutton's injured wing to keep it from rubbing the ceiling.

Hot, possessive anger blasted him, and he frowned. The sight of Risa touching another man's wings pissed him off. What the hell? This had to be an aftereffect of her magic flooding him when they'd been in her shield. He jerked his gaze away, focusing on answering Ram. "Last Chance Academy. It's a school for kids who have nowhere else to go." That was all he wanted to say on the subject. Instead, he recalled how Risa's magic felt sliding all over him inside that shield.

Fucking awesome.

He'd gotten hard right there in the hallway with the wall of sure death coming at them. Even now, his dick twitched at the memory. Yet when he'd kissed her, it'd started hot until her magic had suddenly pulled back and she'd withdrawn.

What the hell had happened?

"Doesn't look like anyone's here," Ram said. "Appears brand new."

"It's not open yet."

"What's your connection?"

A public parking lot led to the offices, on the left stood the infirmary, and behind that the classrooms. On the right were staff quarters and the dorms. The grounds also held an Olympic-sized swimming pool, athletic field, track and gym. He ran his gaze over it all in satisfaction. "Investment. Best place I could think of to go to ground until we get this shit figured out."

He pulled around the back of the staff quarters into the parking garage and shut off the Suburban. "We're going to the staff residence. We'll use the underground tunnel." Piling out, Linc hit the button to close the bay door. He led them into the fully equipped laundry room that went into a large kitchen, where they were enveloped in the smell of fresh coffee.

Hilary Seyer stood at the industrial stove, spatula in hand, looking slightly rumpled in a pink T-shirt, gray sweatpants and flip-flops.

"You didn't have to come over here." He strode up to her and kissed her cheek. He'd only let her know they'd be here so she wouldn't be alarmed when she arrived in the morning.

"I don't take orders from you, now do I?"

"No, ma'am," Linc answered. Her dark eyes were sharp as ever in her barely wrinkled face. She might be in her fifties, but he suspected age was too intimidated by her to try any of its crap on her.

"Lincoln, do you know that one of your friends appears to have sprouted wings?" She frowned. "Oh dear, one of the wings is injured."

He tilted his head toward the other man. "This is Sutton West. And yes, I'm aware of his wings."

"Hello, Sutton. Do you need anything for that wing?"

"No, ma'am, but thank you."

"That's Risa Faden and Ram Virtos."

"Risa, Ram." Hilary nodded, then turned back to the stove. "The coffee is ready, there's iced tea in the fridge, and I'm making grilled cheese sandwiches." She glanced over then shoved the spatula at Linc.

He took it automatically.

Hilary walked to Risa. "Come, I'll show you to a room where you can rest." Pausing in front of her, she added, "Or do you need a doctor?"

The witch had zero color in her face, her cheeks appeared hollow and her eyes bruised with dark circles. White-knuckled, she held on to a counter. Damn, she didn't look well.

"She doesn't need a doctor," Linc said.

Hilary narrowed her eyes. "I didn't ask you, young man."

The flicker of anger in Hilary's tone shamed him. "She's a witch. A doctor won't be able to help her."

The older woman focused on Risa. "How can I help you?"

"I'm okay. I just need a place to be alone. Anything is fine."

Risa's thin voice pricked his guilt. "Put her in the guest suite on the top floor, far away from the rest of us." The first floor was all communal space, the next three floors staff apartments, and the top floor had four suites for VIP types that might be persuaded to invest in the kids and the school.

"Nice," Hilary muttered. "Come on, Risa, we'll get you settled."

Hell. He'd been thinking of her safety in keeping her far away from Ram and Eli, once the other hunter arrived. "I just meant—"

"Get those sandwiches off the griddle and eat."

Hilary took Risa's arm, led her across the spacious lounge area with the big-screen TV, and into the elevator.

He forced himself to concentrate on the damned sandwiches, or he'd get a lecture on manners and wasting food.

"Why does she act like your mother?" Ram asked, as he searched through cupboards until he found mugs. He filled three of them with coffee and handed them out.

Linc plated a couple sandwiches each and put two more in the oven in case Risa or Hilary were hungry. "She's not my mother, she's my business partner." Hilary was nothing like the woman who birthed him.

He glanced at Sutton, concern for the man's injured wing mixing in with worry about Risa. "How long until Carla gets here?"

"Soon, less than an hour."

If Risa didn't feel better by then, Carla would know what to do. After taking a quick bite of his sandwich, he swigged some coffee and pulled out his phone. "Texting directions to Eli." Done with that, he shoved the phone into his pocket and picked up his plate and coffee. "Follow me."

He led them out of the kitchen, through a large living space and down the shorter of two hallways. They passed a book-lined library with several private cubicles, and into a room that buzzed with electronic equipment.

"Holy fuck," Sutton said, turning to slide his wings through the doorway. His eyes gleamed as he surveyed the room, taking in the wall of monitors showing the entire academy. "Dude, this place is secure."

Damn right. Linc knew how easy it was to grab a kid. The students would be safe here. "This is Vegas, and you never know what some of these kids may have gotten into before we're able to help them." Why was he explaining this? "What I want you to do is code into our system with the thumb and palm prints of you, Carla, Ram, Eli and Risa. Possible?"

Sutton handed Ram his almost empty plate, shoved a chair out of his way to give his wings room, and dropped to his knees. He started typing codes, pulling up menus. "Hell yeah, I have everyone's but Risa's. Scan it into your phone for me, and I can do it. Jesus, I think I have a boner."

Linc laughed. "Carla will be here soon."

Ram ran at inhuman speed, whipping around the mile-long track so fast, the buildings, rocks and vegetation blurred. Electrical sparks flew from his fists as he pushed his body harder. Faster. This was all he knew—harsh training to beat back the sick cravings growing inside him.

Witch blood.

Don't think about the witch in the building he'd just left. The way her power had felt washing over him in waves of cooling bliss when Risa cast her shield. It'd be so easy...

No. The thunderbird tattoo on his chest sizzled around the lightning bolts. Those were new—one for each of the two times he'd made love with Ginny. The bird hated Ginny, would probably kill her if he could.

It wanted Shayla as their mate.

But Ram didn't. He only wanted to find the witch, to see if the two of them could figure out the solution to the thunderbird creating electrical buildup, before it fully awoke and turned him into a pile of ash through what mortals called spontaneous human combustion. They believed the bird had done it generation after generation to whatever person he'd been born into, but they didn't know why.

He needed real answers.

He rounded the end of the track, estimating he'd run seven miles, when his phone vibrated against his hip. Slowing to a jog, he pulled it out and saw the caller.

Unknown.

His blood pressure spiked. Easing into a walk, he put the phone to his ear. "Ram."

"I wanted to make sure you're still alive."

"You keep jerking me around like this, it's not going to end well, Shayla." He needed to be in control when he saw her, or he'd kill her.

"I've never trusted any man, especially a witch hunter."

"I'm not your therapist." He paced around the track, struggling for self-control. "Look." He dragged in a breath of air tainted from the dust kicked up by the speed of his run. "We really don't have much choice here. We're going to have to trust each other. You don't want to mate with me, do you, Shayla?"

She hesitated.

Fuck. "Shayla?"

"I don't want to become an infertility witch."

She'd made that clear, but maybe, deep down, she wanted what her cousin Roxy had—a soul mirror. His head throbbed, while the tattoo rippled in his skin. The bird wanted Shayla.

Ram wanted Ginny.

And Shayla wanted him...if she could find the key to her infertility curse.

Weren't they all just a fucked-up love story?

He looked down at his free hand in the darkness. No sparks. Guess the bird had reined in the electrical pulses for a while. "Shayla, you ran from me right from the start. You never wanted me." She hadn't trusted him.

"I don't know what I want anymore. Every time you

get physically close to me, it creates an ache in my schema and my chest. I don't..." She trailed off and sighed. "My schema is a birthmark where my magic lays dormant. It's on my inner thigh."

"Roxy told me," he said softly, feeling an answering ache in his cock. He clenched his jaw, hating the visceral reaction that wasn't him, but the bird. "She also told me what happened the night you were taken by the rogue." How could he not feel sympathy for her? That bastard had cut off her schema. Shayla should have died, but Roxy got there in time to save her. The pain had to have been vicious. Ram didn't want her hurt, he just wanted to be free.

"My schema healed."

He stopped walking, lifting his gaze to the soft night. "Shayla, you and I, we aren't the real deal. There's something wrong in our soul-mirror connection." What he felt for Ginny? That was as real as it got. "It goes back to this thunderbird. Do you think he was your familiar in a past life?"

"Probably. But there's more. Another missing piece. That's what I'm trying to find."

He froze, every cell of his body tensing. "What piece?"

"I don't know yet. I'm trying to get what I can out of my mother's witch book without actually awakening my infertility magic."

Understanding snapped into place with stunning clarity. "That's why you keep luring me close to you then slipping away. You're triggering just enough magic, maybe getting a power boost from the bird."

"That's not all," she added, her voice gentle. "I think it eases your bird. I'm trying to keep you alive too, Ram." She sucked in a breath. "I'm not the evil bitch you and your friends think I am. I'm just trying to survive and figure this out." Her tone grew heavy. "In some ways, you're my only friend. The only one who understands what it feels like to... Never mind."

"Like if you let your guard down for even one second, evil will take over and win?" He felt it too. Along with surprise that she actually did care about him.

She sighed. "Exactly. The other witches don't want me near them, except Roxy."

Her utter loneliness tore through the anger he'd been holding on to since that day he'd walked into the apartment and unknowingly crossed her path, setting off this whole nightmare. "We can be friends, Shayla. Work together." He shifted his gaze, scanning the area. "What have you found in your mother's witch book?"

"She trusted the wrong people. Talked to witches, and they told rogues where she was, and the rogues killed her."

Anger blasted through him. "Demon witches?"

"No. Earth witches."

Hell, now her fear and refusal to trust anyone except her cousin Roxy made sense. "You won't tell me where you are." How could she? He was close to going rogue himself. So desperate, he'd either kill her, or mate her and unleash the infertility magic she didn't want.

"I can't. But I'll tell you this. I think the piece I'm looking for, it's a man. My mom called him Lasting Man. Not human, not hunter."

"Hybrid?" Or something else?

"Roxy told me what's happening in Vegas with the demon hybrid. I don't know. Maybe. But that's all I know until I can get more from Mom's witch book."

"What about another witch, Roxy, could she read the book?"

"No. Roxy tried, but infertility magic in the witch book somehow blocks anyone else but me."

Shit.

"I'm going to go to New Mexico."

"Why there?"

"My mom searched there, I think. Maybe going there will help me unlock more in her witch book."

"If you'd let me closer to you—"

"I can't. I just...I can't trust myself. Or you."

Ram closed his eyes, knowing exactly what she meant. The pull between them even on the phone was strong. Yet it felt unnatural and forced, not the sweet, aching attraction Ginny ignited in him. "Be careful. And, Shayla?"

"Yeah?"

"I don't think you're a bitch." He had been blaming her in some way for the thunderbird tattoo and the whole mess. Now he realized she was as trapped as him.

"Thanks for that. I'll call you if I find anything." The line disconnected.

Ram put the phone away. The bird was calm, his hands barely tingling. The electricity had eased. Huh, talking to Shayla had soothed the creature.

His thoughts shifted as he heard a car approaching the school. Must be Eli and Carla arriving from California. He raced across the academy grounds to the parking structure. Damn, he missed Ginny so much, he actually wanted to see her brother just to hear any tidbit Eli'd have about her. He had it bad for that girl.

The door to the staff dorms opened, and out spilled Sutton and Linc. The car slid to a halt, and Sutton ran to the passenger side, pulling open the door. He helped Carla out of the car and into his arms.

Ram allowed himself a second of relief. Carla should be able to heal Sutton's wing. Turning his attention back to the car, he sucked in a breath and got a lungful of sun and rain, the scent of an angel. The rear door behind the driver's seat opened, and Ginny Stone stepped out.

JENNIFER LYON

Rage and joy slammed through him. Rage that Ginny was here, right in the same city where a demon had spawned. He held himself perfectly still, locking his muscles in place. And joy...oh fuck, raw, pulsing need and happiness to have her near him.

He couldn't touch her, didn't dare. But he could drink in the sight of her. Ginny's long brown hair flowed around her, and she wore a T-shirt and flowered skirt that revealed her long sexy legs.

The need to touch her clawed through him. The memory of Ginny stripped down to only her skin with the morning sun pouring over her as he kissed and tasted her before sinking his cock balls-deep into her ignited a firestorm inside him. Hot, painful lust seared his body. Ram used discipline and endless physical workouts to keep himself under control. But with Ginny?

His formidable control ruptured, leaving him at her mercy. "Ginny." Her name slid from his mouth.

She lifted her chin. "I'm not leaving."

"It's not safe."

Her aura flared and vanished in an instant.

Eli cleared his throat. "It's not safe for her in Glassbreakers either."

Icy fear shot through Ram. "What happened?"

Ginny glanced around at the others, then back at him. "Later."

It had to be her father, the ancient, powerful angel, Vigilance, who wanted to rip Ginny out of her life here to serve him for eternity. The celestial bastard planned to force Ginny to ascend. But that wasn't all, once Vigilance had Ginny with him, he'd destroy the very heart of her.

Ram couldn't let that happen. She was his angel. He'd do anything to save her from that fate. Including die.

～ 8 ～

SHE ACHED TO BE HELD by him, but Ginny Stone determinedly kept her hands to herself as she followed Ram's stiff back into a long, two-story school building on the academy grounds. Normally she'd be interested in the grounds of the school, but right now?

Ram consumed her. She hated not being able to touch him.

He doesn't belong to you. Not really.

The truth of that shafted straight into her heart and made her hate her father more than ever. He'd manipulated her from the day of her birth, engineering ways to force her to feel every possible emotion.

All because daddy dearest, one of the most ancient and powerful angels in the universe, had gone cold. Time had drained the angel to a frigid beauty, and without the ability to feel, he could no longer empathize with his mortal charges. But the angel had a plan...Ginny. He'd sired her with a human woman, creating a halfling. And once she'd experienced every possible human emotion he required—right up to falling in love with Ram—her father would rip her out of her life and steal her emotions. Then Vigilance

JENNIFER LYON

would possess all the feelings he needed to care for his charges. But Ginny would be an empty shell, as cold as her father was now.

That was one family reunion Ginny had so far refused to attend.

Turned out, Dad didn't take refusal well. She now had a cranky angel sire riding her ass and threatening her loved ones. That she could deal with as long as she had Ram. Ram's touch anchored her to this world.

Too bad her touch also set off electrical energy in the thunderbird that could and would eventually kill him.

Ram stopped, and only her halfling sharp reaction time kept her from crashing into his back. Jeez, she needed to get her head out of self-pity land and pay attention. Ram led her into a room and flipped on the lights.

"A classroom." Ginny eyed the rows of desks facing a bigger teacher's desk, and behind that, a whiteboard.

Ram shut the door. "We won't be disturbed, and the other hunters shouldn't be able to overhear us, since they're in another building."

She strolled around the desks, going back to her own days in classrooms. She'd wanted friends so badly. Her father, however, wanted to play with her emotions. Oh sure, she would have a best friend for a while. He wanted that emotion—the love of a friend, the way a child depends on that friend.

Then he'd find a way to rip it away, leaving Ginny heartbroken and bereft. Feeling lost. He wanted those feelings too.

"Angel, your aura's out."

Ram's low, gruff voice tugged at her insides. He stood with his back to the door, pinning her with his penetrating gaze. His eyes, normally ice blue, flared with a touch of sunset. He was the only one who'd ever looked at her like that, and it instantly warmed her.

104

The air between them crackled with sexual tension and sheer desperation.

Struggling to get control, she tried to concentrate and pull in her aura.

"Don't." Ram shoved off the door and came toward her. "When we're alone, you don't hide from me."

She flushed in pleasure, the realization that she could be herself with him. The real Ginny, part human, part angel, and all woman. Sensual shivers fluttered deep in her belly.

Reaching her, he added softly, "We don't hide from each other."

Emotion boiled up and choked her. Never had anyone made Ginny feel as safe and cared for, as real and important, as Ram. The second he got close enough to touch her aura, hot tingles rippled through her.

"I felt that. Your aura latched on to me." Stepping back, Ram looked down his front. His shirt and skin had tiny bits of her brilliant light clinging to him. As they watched, the lights dimmed and winked out.

He sucked in a breath and turned, moving so fast she could barely track him. One second, he was in front of her, the next, he stood with his back to her at the whiteboard, his shoulders bunched into granite bulges, and his breathing grew ragged.

"Ram?" She heard a sizzle and rushed over.

He had both his hands cupped around, but not touching, the metal tray that ran beneath the whiteboard. Sparks flew from his fingers, and the silver tray began to glow blue, the color racing down the strip of metal.

"Get back. Now, Ginny," he ordered.

She took one step back but kept staring in horror. The skin along the back of his palms turned red, then black. Blisters sprang up.

"Oh God." Her stomach lurched. She had done this to him. Again.

The sizzling slowed, then stopped.

Ram stepped back and shook out his hands.

"That was from my aura touching you?" Immediately, the warm light that had been flowing around her, the part of her that was as normal as breathing, retracted sharply, vanishing. Leaving her feeling more useless than ever.

He whipped around, his gaze slamming into her. "I told you to get back."

His anger didn't intimidate her. Not even a little bit, and besides, she'd brewed up a whole lotta pissed-off disgust at herself. "This isn't working. It's getting worse. I'm destroying you."

Ram took another step toward her.

She backed up. Even with her aura stuffed inside her—something that was getting harder and harder for her to do—she feared hurting him again. "I should have let my father force me to ascend."

Ram kept coming, his movements sliding from ticked-off male to silent predator. His eyes darkened, and even his breathing became measured. Controlled.

She moved back another step, determined to protect him and fighting to keep her aura beneath her skin, until she hit the teacher's desk.

Before she could turn, escape in one direction or another, Ram loomed in front of her, slapping his hands on the desk and caging her between his arms. He shoved his face into hers. "Your father tried to compel you to ascend again? Why didn't you tell me when we talked this morning?"

It was pointless to tell him to step back when he'd gone into hunter mode, completely focused on his goal. "Yes. I fell asleep after we talked. He forced me to dream...showed me how you'll die. I woke up terrified that you were dead." She closed her eyes, the utter despair washing over her again. "You were electrocuted from the bird, cooked from the inside out."

Grief and guilt tangled in her guts. For a long time, she and Ram had been friends, just hanging out in the evenings at the club where she worked. He'd stay late while she closed up, and made sure she got home safe.

Both ignored the sexual attraction between them. Until Ginny had asked him for a kiss.

One kiss. A perfect kiss, even though they both knew it couldn't go further. Ginny had to stay a virgin since her father had demanded she have sex and fall in love before he took her from the Earth realm. Ram had his own reasons.

Until a bit over two months ago when her father blackmailed her into seducing Ram by threatening her brother. Ginny had hated that—Ram meant too much to her to be a pawn in her father's game. She'd been half in love with him already. Her desire for him had been very real, but they'd chosen to ignore the sexual tension between them and remain friends. But then she had no choice but to seduce Ram. When they gave into their desire, all thoughts of her father vanished. All that mattered had been the two of them. The moment he'd pressed deep into her body, their friendship began expanding into a fiery, soul-searing love.

And as she'd known he would, her father had tried to rip her out of her world and into his.

But Ram refused to let her go. When her father's powerful aura had appeared, blazing with angel-fire light and called her to him, Ram leapt across the room, grabbed Ginny and begged her to stay, telling her he loved her.

It worked. Vigilance hadn't been able to force her from the Earth realm to his.

"What happened after the dream? Tell me. Did your father appear?"

Ram's sharp questions brought her back to the present. "Yes. He told me it would be my fault if you died like that. If I just went with him, you'd turn to Shayla and be saved. Then he held out his hand." She couldn't stop tears from welling in her eyes. "I can't let you die like that. I don't want to hurt you." She wanted to love him.

His jaw clenched, and a vein in his forehead throbbed. "What do you think your leaving would do to me? I know what will happen—he'll strip out all your emotions, leaving you barren. I'd rather die in any torturous way than think of you like that."

A single tear rolled down her face. "It's my destiny. I either destroy you or make this sacrifice to save you." After seeing what he'd gone through just now, she hated herself more.

"Fuck destiny, Ginny. We're going to find a way to break your father's hold on you, get rid of this thunderbird and be together."

Why should he want her now? "You don't understand. In my dream, I saw what you'll suffer. Loving you means I should be willing to sacrifice for you. But I panicked at the last second and pulled my hand back."

Fury iced his gaze and made his jaw tick. "Then what happened?"

"He tried to force me, his aura wrapped around me, but I remembered you telling me to fight. I focused on your love for me and fought to stay with you. It was a battle, but in the end I was able to resist and push his aura out of mine."

"How, Ginny? We need to know so we can keep him from compelling you to ascend into his realm."

"You saw my aura tonight, the way it latched on to you? I think..." She trailed off, trying to find the words.

"Last time we made love, I think we bonded tighter than my father expected. And since he doesn't feel anything, hasn't felt in centuries, he doesn't remember how powerful that is."

Ram's eyes lit up. "Sex and blood, it's how our souls bond with our mates."

"But I'm not a witch or your mate. I don't have the other half of your soul." Like Shayla, she thought, bitterness coating her throat.

"True, but it's you I love. That night in your bed, you demanded I concede my control to you, remember?"

She did. He hadn't been able to touch her, just like now. But she could touch him, and she had. Then she'd ordered him on the bed and straddled him.

"When we orgasmed, your aura came out, spilling over me, I remember feeling it, Ginny. That's part of why I didn't notice my hands burning and fusing to the iron headboard. Sex—it bonds us and keeps you here with me." He leaned down, kissing her softly. "Where you belong."

God she wanted that, wanted to belong to his man, and he to her. But while sex helped her, it increased the electrical energy growing in him. She pulled her mouth from his. "We can't. Both times we had sex, you developed another lightning streak on your tattoo and your hands got worse."

"I don't care." His eyes glittered with fierce love. "All that matters to me is you."

Her father was right—she really was destroying him.

Linc climbed the stairs to the guest suite. He'd check on Risa to see if she felt better or needed Carla.

Then he'd leave her alone. Not touch her. *Don't push her. Give her time.* He repeated the refrain over and over. He could hold on for a while longer, let Risa get used to him.

But damn, her spicy, cinnamon-hot magic clung to his skin. While he'd been in that magical shield with her, he'd been desperate to mate her. But once he'd stopped touching her, the curse screamed for her blood, to cut her, bleed her power, make it his.

Christ, he was so fucking close to losing it.

At the top of the stairs, he paused before the door to the first suite. *Just check on her and leave. Give her space to rest and recover from using so much magic.* Determined, he went inside to the spacious living room with the couch and two chairs facing a big TV. Hallways opened on either side, leading to bedrooms with en suite bathrooms. Ahead was a small dining area and kitchen that opened to a balcony.

The sour scent of sweat and sickness jerked him around, and he jogged into the right bedroom. Barely scanning the untouched bed, he honed in on the closed door to the bathroom. Was she ill? She'd used a lot of magic, been so drained she'd scarcely been able to stand.

"Risa?" He knocked on the door.

Nothing. No response. No water running, no splashing. Only the faint sounds of ragged breathing. Biting worry coiled his muscles. Linc tried the door handle. "Risa!"

Locked. No answer. Not even a moan.

Sudden, razor-sharp pain scratched his back. The falcon rippled and clawed, its panic fueling his. He punched a hole through the wood, reached inside and released the lock. Carefully easing open the door, he spotted Risa crumpled on the floor, the toilet at her head, back to the shower, feet to the wall.

He rushed in and crouched at her side. Her eyes

were squeezed shut, her face tracked with dried tears, her bottom lip cracked and bleeding.

Don't touch the blood. "Risa, where are you hurt?" She must have been injured and hadn't said anything. Damn it. It was his job to protect her. "Tell me," he snapped, when she didn't respond fast enough.

She parted her lips, but nothing came out.

Frustrated, scared and pissed that Risa was suffering, he yanked out his phone and sent a quick text to Sutton that Risa was hurt and he needed Carla up here stat. The other witch could help her.

While waiting, he touched her side, trying to look for an injury.

She flinched, curling in tighter, and moaned.

Linc dropped his hand in helpless anger. What the hell had happened? She'd said she was okay when Hilary asked her. The sound of hurried footsteps made him turn.

Carla raced in first, dropping to her knees next to Linc. "Where is she hurt?"

"I don't know. She can't, or won't, tell me." It twisted inside him. He barely knew her, but one thing he was certain of—she was his soul mirror. She would free him from the curse, and in return, he was supposed to protect her. Yet she had been the one who protected them earlier in the day. Maybe been hurt in the process, and he'd been too fucking preoccupied to notice.

The bird rippled across his back in obvious agreement.

"Please, Carla." Linc glanced at Sutton, seeing that his wings were gone. "I know you're probably tired from healing Sutton's wing, but she's suffering. She saved us today."

"I know she did. I felt her magic through Sutton when she cast her shield." She shifted her stare back to Risa.

Carla's magic rose. Because she and Sutton were mated, it rolled over Linc like a soft breeze but didn't incite or aggravate his curse. Her witch shimmer danced in beautiful silvery sparkles over her skin. She laid her fingers on Risa's bare arm.

Linc shifted foot to foot, impatient to know what had happened to Risa.

Carla gasped and jerked her hand away.

Despite his massive size, Sutton moved fast, reaching around Linc to touch Carla. "I feel that, like spikes being driven into your head. What's wrong with her?"

"What is it?" Linc demanded.

"Hang on, I'm going to go to the astral plane." She turned to look at Sutton. "Don't let go of me."

His face tightened, but he merely said, "Never."

Carla unleashed more magic, filling the bathroom with her scent. The hair on Linc's arms shivered as the atmosphere changed around them. The witch glowed with a silvery light, appearing ethereal and not quite there.

Linc didn't fully understand the astral plane, some kind of magical realm where Carla could see more than was readily visible on Earth. He didn't care about the specifics. He just wanted to help Risa.

Finally, Carla's shimmer died off, and she opened her eyes.

"What is it?" he demanded.

"Soul screams. A lot of them, and they're breaking her mind."

Soul what? He stared at her. "What the hell is that?"

Carla's face filled with sympathy. "She's a shield witch. Before the curse, if a witch cast her shield around someone but they died anyway, the familiar would push the soul away from the witch's magic and the soul would go on to its afterlife."

Linc tried to follow this. "What does that have to do with her being sick now?"

"Risa has cast her shield and failed a lot. More than a dozen times, probably in the twenties. All those souls are trapped in her magic. When she uses her shield magic, the souls are disturbed, reliving their deaths over again. It's called soul screams. It's agonizing, and it's breaking her mind and her magic."

He glanced at Risa, who lay like death, emitting an occasional twitch or moan. "So she's hearing screams?"

Carla touched his arm. "She's feeling each and every death, Linc. Experiencing it as if they had happened to her, all the pain, terror and confusion. The screams are like spikes through her head." She paused and lowered her voice. "Every time it happens, she loses more of her control, both of her magic and her mind."

Linc refused to feel useless pity. What they needed were answers. This witch was the key to his survival, so she simply had to live. "Won't my falcon be her familiar? Once we bond our souls, she'll be okay, right?"

"I don't know. Her mind is fraying, beginning to crumble under the weight of so many souls. It's harder and harder for her to wrest control of her magic back from the souls."

Yeah, well, he'd been at the last stop on the crazy train himself when he'd been blooded. It had only been the determination of his friends and Roxy's powerful sex magic that had saved his sorry ass. Linc didn't fold until he was out of options.

He wasn't out of options yet.

"I touched her blood. What if I give her some of my blood, will that help her now? Get her well enough to finish our bond?"

Carla looked dubious. "Probably. But don't you

want to find out first how one witch could be connected to that many deaths? They were all violent deaths, Linc."

"No." He had enough to answer for in his own past.

Sutton pulled Carla to her feet.

She touched Linc's shoulder. "After you give her your blood, you have to try to help her get control of her magic in her chakras. Start with her first chakra in her pelvis and work all the way up to her throat chakra."

"Got it."

"Do you want me to stay with you?"

Linc shook his head. "I'll call you if I need you." Touching Risa in a way that would draw out her magic would require some intimacy. They didn't need an audience for that.

She squeezed his shoulder then Carla and Sutton left.

After taking his knife from the holster, he held up his arm. The veins bulged and writhed, darkening with bloodlust.

Cut her. You felt her power tonight, cut her. She's your witch! Yours to cut and feel her hot blood cooling the burn...

Christ. His fingers tightened around the hilt, and the wicked, sharp silver blade caught the lights. He could see himself doing it, see himself ripping off his clothes, cutting Risa... He remembered how fucking awesome witch blood felt. The power kick as it hit his skin and sank in, the rush of pure strength and bliss.

Weariness and soul-deep loneliness made him wonder just why he fought so hard, resisting the one thing that felt so damned good.

He gazed at the witch. She lay there covered in sweat, her hair sticking to her pale face.

Sharp pain hit his back and ran down his arm. His

hand numbed, and the knife slid from his grasp to clatter on the tile floor.

Damned bird. Touching Risa's blood, kissing her, then being soaked in her magic from the shield, had woken the creature further. "Found my nerves, did you?" Shaking the numbness from his hand, Linc snatched up the knife. "Do that when I'm fighting and we both die." Bringing up his other hand, he sliced his palm and laid it on Risa's arm.

The too-warm, sweat-slicked skin and her shaking gave him an idea of her misery, but he couldn't feel anything. As her soul mirror, he should be able to draw out some of her pain and help her. Come on. Finally, a vague, barely there twinging traveled up his arm, more of an impression of suffering.

A whiff of cinnamon, faint but there, caught his attention. Her magic flickered, responding to his blood. This had to help her. Moving his hand, he watched as the blood he left behind faded, then disappeared.

Soaked into her skin.

He sucked in a breath, the sight of his blood penetrating into her, becoming part of her, tripping something primal in his chest. Needing to feel her against him, he scooped his arms beneath her and cradled her to his chest as he sat back on the floor. Her magic brushed his skin in the faintest shimmer, weak but there, definitely responding to him. Looking down into her face, he desperately wanted her to open her eyes. To see the fiery, determined light that glowed there, the same woman who'd asked him if he needed her to help him let go of her by kicking him in the balls.

His mouth quirked at the memory. Risa had a tough and sweet side. He liked that a hell of a lot and found himself wanting to discover more about her, figure out how her mind worked, what her hopes and dreams were.

What caused her to shut down when he'd kissed her so he could fix it? Protect her from it.

But he couldn't let her break from the soul screams. "Fight, Risa. You need to keep your mind intact. Your baby needs you." And so did Linc. Not forever, of course, but to break his curse. For that alone, he'd give her anything he could.

Except his heart.

⇛ 9 ⇚

RISA'S ENTIRE WORLD NARROWED TO screams and terror. Soaking in horror, she shuddered and bounced from murder to murder, unable to find a way out, trapped, exhausted and hopeless as another piercing scream raked across her mind. Shuddering, she retreated deeper, burrowing in a crack, trying to hide. To stop existing at all and make the pain stop.

Something touched her. Feathery soft and tinged with the faintest trace of magic. It didn't hurt her, didn't scream and force her to relive a murder.

What was it?

As she tried to focus, the screams faded into the background. Slowly the mental image took shape.

A bird looked at her with yellow-ringed eyes. He raised his wings slightly and fluttered his gray-and-white feathers. Staring at him eased her and pulled her away from the angry, hate-filled souls. Risa locked in on the mental image, concentrating on the bird. When he began to float up, she instinctively followed.

The higher they rose, the more clear the image became. She strained until recognition bloomed.

Falcon. The tattoo from Linc's back.

Awareness seeped in. Her first two chakras opened,

sluggish magic inching out and spreading, gaining strength as she and the bird surfaced from the soul screams.

Another chakra opened, and more magic spilled out.

Dumbfounded, Risa couldn't drag her internal gaze from the wings as they gained more definition. They began to sweep up and down, as if in flight. Powerfully majestic, yet they moved with elegance over the landscape of her mind. She followed along, almost as if she and the bird had an invisible tether linking them.

Soul-mirror connection. If Risa had had any doubt, she believed it now. Every sweep of the falcon's wings freed more of her magic and her.

The souls stirred again, tiny flashes of light snapping and popping. The pressure in her head ramped up as she began to feel torn, dragged into two directions.

Toward the falcon.

Trapped by the souls.

One scream began, then more joined in. The pitch stabbed her head like red-hot knitting needles.

No! Oh God, she couldn't do it again.

The snapping, popping lights converged on the wings in a full-on attack. The fierce screech of the bird added to the racket. The wings began to fade.

Her magic slipped away, draining like water between her fingers. She couldn't catch it.

One scream broke away and headed toward her. The piercing sound dug deep into her head until the soul touched her magic. Then it yanked, trying to capture Risa and force her into reliving the memory of its death.

"Fight, Risa. You need to keep your mind intact. Your baby needs you."

Linc's voice, smooth and liquid, pulled at her,

tugging her and the bird free of the souls. She became aware of a strong arm curled around her back and warm, firm fingers sliding over her stomach, dipping low over her panties, then up higher, past her belly button, to the hollow between her ribs. And higher still.

Warm shivers danced and moved with his touch, creating a pleasant sensation. Gentle, swirling caresses softened her muscles, yet tingles rose and skated over her skin. Her breath hitched, then released in odd little sighs.

Honing in on it, she tracked the path of the fingers sweeping over her bra to her chest. The rough fingertips drew easy circles and lightly brushed her throat.

A deep ache throbbed between her thighs. Magic spilled out and flowed toward his touch.

"That's it, Risa. Let me help you."

She recognized Linc's voice. Soothing and coaxing. His breath feathered over her face, causing her to arch slightly, seeking...she wasn't sure.

He pulled her closer, then moved his fingers down, skimming the inside swell of her breasts.

Her nipples tightened and ached. Such a sweet little torment. His caress moved to her stomach, using one finger to rim her belly button.

"I feel you relaxing. The bird's relaxing too." He slipped his hand lower, flirting with the elastic of her panties.

Her thoughts turned thick, languid. The souls quieted, and a gentle touch of wings brushed her chakras.

Was this sanity? Or was she sinking into a world of sensation that wasn't real? Terror began to claw at her. What if she was lost in her mind?

"Risa, open your eyes."

His smooth voice shifted into a sharp command

that she obeyed. Linc's face filled her vision. His light brown eyes were dominated by dark, swollen pupils. Sitting on his lap gave her a view of the flush riding across his cheekbones. His erection throbbed beneath her hip.

Sudden, harsh reality washed through her. She'd been unconscious on the floor, covered in sweat and agony, and she had made him hard?

"What are you doing?" Her voice cracked.

"Hey, easy, I'm helping you."

She glanced down. "I don't have a shirt on."

"I took it off. You were sick. I gave you some of my blood, then traced your chakras, calling out your magic."

She shook her head. "That's not just magic. It's more."

Linc's eyes softened. "It's desire, sugar. That's all."

She frowned at him, but the movement hurt. "I don't like it. Let me up." They were too close. She wasn't in control. Worse, what had she said while trapped in the soul screams?

Sick shame made her need to escape. Hide. Find a way out of her own skin. She'd done awful things by luring people, mostly men, to their murders. Let them use her body, because as her father said, when a man had his dick out, his brain shut off and made him easy to kill.

Linc scooped her up, set her on the edge of the tub where she could rest against the cool wall, and laid his hand on her thigh. "I need to touch you. Bloodlust."

With no strength to argue, she just sat. Breathed. Regrouped. "There's a hole in the door." Fist sized. She kept her gaze on that, anything to avoid the huge man sitting on the floor at her feet, hand resting on her leg. The contact confused her. It should scare her. She should hate it. Why didn't she hate him touching her?

"Hey. Can you look at me?"

Could. Didn't want to, but that made her a coward, and she hated enough about herself. She shifted her gaze to the concern in his eyes.

He stroked his thumb over her thigh. "The door was locked, and when you didn't answer, I punched it to get in here. You were unconscious or close to it, so I got Carla in here—"

"Carla's here? She saw me?"

"Yes."

It took everything she had to hold his gaze. "You know about the soul screams?"

"Carla used magic to see what was happening to you."

She dropped her stare to his hand spread on her thigh. Yep, add coward to her list. Now she'd add begging. The irony didn't escape her—begging for the one thing she hated, sex. *Kendall. Think of Kendall.* "We only have to have sex once to complete the bond. You were hard when I came out of the screams. Men don't care about a woman's past when they just want to have sex, right?" So what if he was revolted now that he knew she had souls in her magic. He'd still get off, and the curse would break for him.

His fingers tightened on her leg. "What are you talking about?"

"The soul-mirror thing. It'll break your curse. Come on, Dillinger, now's not the time to be picky about who you have sex with." Oh nice. That kind of sarcasm would get him right in the mood.

Silence.

Crap. "We both know this isn't a romance. You don't have to like me to, uh, make use of my body. Other men have done it." Desperation spilled out of her. "Please. I don't know how else to find Kendall."

"Risa."

She took a breath. No tears, she wouldn't cry. "What?"

His biceps flexed and rippled. "I've had sex with a lot of women, but not one of them was just a body to me. They were women sharing themselves with me so I could get through another day, another hour, another fucking five minutes without the curse frying my veins and pickling my brain. And in return, I made sure they enjoyed it too."

His passion, the way he talked about those women, made her magic retreat deeper into her chakras. She wasn't going to be any kind of memory for him, she'd just be...

A woman whose body he made use of.

Didn't matter. She couldn't let it matter. Needing distance, she jumped up. Woozy, she slapped her hand against the wall to steady herself. "I'm not other women."

His hand closed around her arm, and he turned and pressed her shoulders to the plaster. Towering over her, he glared down at her. Fury pumped off him in hot waves.

She lifted her chin, refusing to show fear.

"Who hurt you, Risa? What men used your body? Tell me, damn it."

Exhausted, barely able to stand, even leaning against the wall seemed like an effort, she sighed. "What does it matter?"

His gaze bored into hers. "It matters. I'm going to find them and kill them." His fingers bracketed her arm gently, in sharp contrast to his fierce glower.

"They're dead. Even my father."

His body tightened until the cords in his neck stood out. "Your father raped you?"

"No." She looked away, the sheer intimacy along with her fatigue cracking her normal barriers. She closed her eyes, admitting a deeper truth. Linc's kindness, the way he touched her, cared for her—Risa had never experienced this with a man.

He released her biceps, laying his forearm on the wall alongside her head, the other hand gently catching her face. "What did your father do to you? We have a deal. Nothing you tell me is going make me turn away from you." He caressed her cheek with his thumb. "We need each other. Why not be friends while we're at it?"

Friends. With Linc. He offered her so much and in the end, she would destroy it. Too tired to resist, she told him the truth. "My father was an assassin."

Linc's thumb froze on her face, and long seconds ticked by. Then he said, "Your last name, Faden. Christ, I never connected it." He seemed to refocus on her. "Vic Faden was your father?"

"You knew him?" That couldn't be good. How would Linc have known him?

He shoved away and turned as if he couldn't bear to look at her one more second. "All those souls in your magic..."

His back bunched and twisted. Aware he'd evaded her question about knowing her dad, she stated the facts. "They are his kills. The ones I tried to protect." And failed.

He whipped around, staring at her. "He took you with him on his jobs?"

"My mom used to shill for him, lure his targets to where he needed them. Distract them, and then he'd kill them. But Mom was murdered." Risa couldn't stop the words spilling out of her. Part of her wanted this connection with Linc. The other part of her wanted the truth to drive him away. Keep the distance between them.

Sucking in a breath, she went on. "I was fourteen when she died. Everything changed. We were wealthy. I thought my parents were *consultants*. I had closets filled with beautiful clothes, a miniature horse...but once my mom died, my father needed a new shill."

Linc reached across the bathroom, catching her hand. His warm, firm fingers anchored her. Startled, she lifted her gaze to him.

"Come here, Risa."

She started to shake her head, but pain pierced her skull. She hadn't recovered yet. It would take hours of sleep to regain some strength.

"Here's the thing. If you want your high magic, you're going to have to learn my touch is not like the others. I am not *just making use of your body*." He squeezed her hand reassuringly. "Not while I still have a soul. We clear?"

She resisted for a second longer, searching over him with her gaze. When he showed her this kindness, acting as if he cared enough to get to know and understand her, it opened her up, left her too vulnerable.

"Take the first step. That's all you have to do." His voice flowed smoothly to wrap around her like a silky ribbon. Her chakras relaxed, and her muscles unlocked.

She took the step.

And won a smile from him. His face softened, a dent forming in his chin while his eyes crinkled. This wasn't Linc's charming smile, the one he tossed off with his fast and glib comebacks. That smile had polish.

This one was real, sexy, and made her feel like smiling back. Unsure what to do, she just stood there, staring at the amazing grin on his face.

He reached out, caught her waist and tugged her between his thighs. He tucked her beneath one arm, surrounding her with his body heat.

"Do we have to be so close?"

He looked down, serious again. "Yes. You're safe. You know it or you wouldn't have taken that step. I would bet my balls you've developed finely honed, self-protective instincts. Now finish the story. Your mom died, your father needed a new shill. You were appointed with no say in the matter, I take it?"

Risa let out her breath as some of her tension eased. "I was a beautiful girl, everyone said so. I was so vain. I thought it made me special. I grew up on compliments." It made her sick now. Disgusted. "He used that, made me dress in clothes to show me off and lure men to places he could kill them." She shivered in spite of the heat radiating from him, partly from the horror of her memories, partly the aftereffects of the soul screams. "If the guy made use of me before my father got there, well, he didn't worry, as long as they didn't damage my looks."

He pulled her in tighter, rubbing her back. "You were raped."

The three words came out harsh, in sharp contrast to his gentle touch. "After the first time, I learned to not feel it much anymore."

"Your magic protected you. That's why you went cold when I kissed you."

She stared at the floor. "Yeah, but I couldn't protect the ones he killed. Not all of his marks hurt me. Some were even nice, and a few were women." The need to explain welled up. "I was just learning about my magic then, and figuring out what I could do with it. I tried to protect his marks with magic, but my father knew how to hurt me to disable my shield. The souls in there are all the ones I failed. I was so weak. Eventually, though, I found another way. I went to the police, testified against him and got him convicted of murder. He went to prison, where he later was killed in some kind of fight."

A beat of time passed, and his hand on her back slowed the caress.

Nothing changed in his expression, and yet she

sensed an odd tension in him. Unable to read him, she filled the silence. "I tried to do something better with my life and magic and became a bodyguard. Witch karma prevents me from causing harm with my magic, but I can shield, and I know how to use a gun."

Linc searched her face. "How did you manage to have a baby while being a bodyguard?"

Pure panic gripped her—of course a bodyguard couldn't exactly drag a baby around on jobs with her. *Think!* "That's why Blythe moved in to help me." She changed the subject. "How did you know who my father was?"

Linc stilled. Too still. "I hear things."

"So this friends-and-trust thing, it only goes one way." Time to pull herself together. She shoved out of his arms. Dizziness spun and tilted the suddenly too-hot bathroom. Risa grabbed on to the edge of the counter.

Linc's hands wrapped around her shoulders. "Let go, I've got you." He swept her up into his arms and strode out to the bedroom.

She opened her mouth to protest, but he cut her off.

"It goes both ways." After shifting her to one arm, he pulled back the thick blue satin comforter and settled her on the cool sheets. Releasing her, he stood and stripped off his pants. "Scoot. I sleep closest to the door."

"Sleep?" Or sex? She moved to the other side.

"Sleep." Linc slid into the bed, reached out and pulled her back to his front. "You need rest. I need to touch you to keep the curse calm." His chest expanded in another breath, and he added, "And to make sure you're okay."

Her chest tightened. He was taking care of her. Again. No one had done that since her mom died, and it confused her. Made her want it, and at the same time fear becoming attached. "I need to focus on Kendall."

"Can you use your magic after a bout of soul screams?"

Curling her fingers around the sheets, Risa sighed. "No. I have to sleep first."

"If you relax, I'll tell you how I know your father."

"Blackmail," she muttered, but settled back against him. He didn't lock his arms around her, thereby trapping her. Instead his right arm pillowed her head, and his other hand rested on her waist. He soothed her with soft strokes of his thumb. It felt good. Some weakass part of her drank in the sensation like she was starving for affection.

Unnerved by her reaction to him, she pushed him to fulfill his part of his blackmail bargain. "Pay up, Dillinger."

"Your dad was sent to collect my mother's drug debt. But she didn't have the money."

All her muscles strained tight. "He killed her?" That had been his job, far as she knew. But maybe he did debt collection too, or some variation of that.

"No. Mom negotiated a deal instead." His voice was too flat.

"What?"

"Me. She sold me to him to settle her debt."

Linc felt the threads of fear and suspicion rising off Risa. But his own memory surged up and overtook him.

Three men, led by Vic, had stormed into his bedroom, jerked him out of bed and beat him bloody with fists and clubs before he'd had a chance to defend himself.

He'd been thirteen. Vic Faden had known what he was. A witch hunter, stronger, faster and more dangerous than any human.

Once they had him writhing on the floor, a mass of

pain and blood, they'd chained him up. He could still feel the collar snapping around his neck, then more hardware around his wrists and ankles. After that, they dragged him out into the shithole living room. His mother scratched at her arms and legs, and muttered, *Had to. Need my fix, baby. Had to sell you.*

His mom had sold him for her coke fix. Evidently his price bought off her debt, with enough left over for more drugs. The old anger, sense of confused betrayal, the realization that he was less important to her than her drugs poured over him.

"Linc?"

Risa's voice pulled him from the memories drowning him. "What?"

"Are you planning some kind of revenge? Use me to break your curse then kill me for being the daughter of the man who took you?" She shifted, twisting her head to look up at him.

Linc stared into her eyes and realized how screwed up the two of them were. She was in his arms, he wore an aching hard-on that didn't care Risa was sick from the soul screams, and she'd calmly asked him if he planned to kill her.

Nope. Why would he? Linc had already killed her father, but she didn't know that. Jesus, the two of them were a fucked-up pair. "I don't blame you," Linc said. Shit, she was a victim of her father, just as he'd been a victim of his crack-addicted mother and Risa's father. "We're survivors. We both know better than to trust love."

Risa slowly relaxed. He wasn't sure if she believed him or if she was too tired and sick to fight.

"What did my father do with you?"

He smoothed down the ragged ends of her hair, surprised by the silky texture. Stroking her soothed the feral beast inside him, making it easier to talk about his past. "He took me to the man who'd hired him. I was caged and trained to be feral. For deathmatches. My owner got rich, and Vic got a cut for procuring me."

"Oh God. My father did that. I knew he was evil, but I keep finding out he was even worse." She curled in on herself, away from him. "The things I had, all the pretty clothes and possessions, some of them were paid for by your suffering."

Linc wasn't having it. He wrapped his body around hers. "Risa, you were a child. How could you know?"

She shuddered.

"Shh, baby, it's okay. We both got out. We both made ourselves strong. And by bonding our souls, we can be stronger still."

She turned her face to him. "How? How can you touch me when you know my true ugliness? You have to see it."

The agony in her eyes cut him. No tears, just endless dry pain. "I see a woman afraid of her own beauty." And her sexuality. But he wasn't going there tonight. Risa needed time to recover from the soul screams. Shifting his thoughts from that, he added, "I see a woman willing to fight for her child." That drew him like nothing else. How could it not?

She turned her eyes away. "I have to find her."

It was all he could do not to leap out of bed, drag on his clothes and start ripping Vegas apart until he found the baby for her. But with that spawn out there, he needed to be smart. "Sleep," he said softly. "You have to regain your strength. In the meantime, Ram and Eli are going out to look for her tonight."

"Eli?"

"Another hunter who arrived earlier tonight. He and Ram have her picture and are seeing if they can turn up any leads in Vegas. I'll head out early in the morning. Then when you wake and I get back, we'll work on sealing our bond and using your high magic."

Once Risa dropped off to sleep, Linc moved away from her but kept his hand on her waist.

The contact eased the bloodlust to a low buzzing. But raw and harsh sexual lust pounded in his ears, heated his blood and kept his cock rigid. Just a brush of her hip spiked his lust to unbearable.

He ignored it, forcibly slowing his respiration, trying to cool the need.

He did not have sex with women who didn't want him. He knew exactly how awful it was to be forced, coerced or trapped into unwanted sex.

The feral animal in him remembered it all. The times he'd been raped, the times he'd been forced to have sex with a terrorized woman who didn't want him. Oh he'd fought it, refused to have sex with whatever unfortunate woman they brought him at first. Beating him hadn't worked to get him to perform for the pricks who owned him.

But they'd found his weakness. They always did. Hurt the woman, and Linc agreed to anything they wanted. He never knew if the women put through it ever understood he tried not to hurt them. That he was trying to save them from worse. But that was just sugarcoating the truth.

Nothing ever made it okay. Nothing. No soft words or gentle touches mitigated the violation.

Once he'd escaped, making damn sure he killed all his owners, trainers and the assorted scum, Linc had refused to hurt another woman again. Ever.

What worried him was Risa somehow reached past the man he'd become to remember the abused animal he'd been. All this time, he'd never told anyone about those years he'd been chained and owned.

Was it a weakness, another sign he was getting closer to going rogue?

≈ 10 ≈

"MAMA, I COULDN'T SEE YOU when you slept."

Risa hung up the towel she'd dried her hair with, picked up Linc's comb and began working out the tangles. As she did that, she looked into the mirror at her daughter floating in the steamy bathroom. "You only come out when I'm alone." *Don't do this, she's not real.*

"I wish I had hair like you."

Her hand froze mid-stroke. "When did you get eyelashes? And eyebrows?"

The baby blinked. "They seemed to grow when you were fighting the other souls."

Sucking in a breath, Risa dropped the comb and clutched the edge of the counter with both hands. The cool stone pressed against her palms but didn't dim the hot fear racing through her.

She was losing her mind. She never saw a physical form of the other souls in her magic. Just Nola. It was crazy to see and talk to her baby.

"Mama, don't you like my eyelashes? They aren't as long as yours, but they'll grow, right?"

Oh Ancestors. It was so unfair that Nola had gotten trapped in her shield magic. "Nola, you're beautiful. With or without eyelashes." Releasing the counter, she

131

stood straight, digging for strength. She had to stop believing she was seeing Nola. "I'm going to get my high magic. Then I should be able to release the souls. Until then, you should just rest."

Her daughter's face crumpled. "No. I don't want to leave you. I can't. Please, I'll be good."

Her heart wrenched, and tears burned her eyes. Nola looked so real to her, felt real. "Baby, you'll go to Summerland. It's beautiful there, and the Ancestors will love you so much. Then when you're ready, you'll be reborn." She had to believe that. Had to.

"But you won't be my mama." Her tiny bottom lip quivered.

Her chest ached with the old grief. "You'll have a better mom, Nola. One who will protect you so you can be born and live. Not die—" *murdered!* "—in my stomach and remain trapped in my magic." Her throat tightened so painfully, her voice cracked.

Nola began to fade, her solid form going fuzzy at the edges.

Panic squeezed Risa's lungs. "Nola, I love you, baby. I just want what's best for you."

"Then don't make me leave you. Please."

It stunned her to see two big fat tears rolling down the fading image of her baby's face. Now she had tears, real tears.

"Swear, Mama. Swear you won't make me leave until I want to go."

She wasn't strong enough. She could do nothing but nod and agree. When Nola pressed close to her, Risa swore she felt the faintest touch, soft yet brimming with love.

Crazy. She's not real.

But she drank in the feeling. Somewhere inside of her, the need for touch and affection had been unlocked. "I love you, Nola. I will always love you. I won't make you go."

Nola grew more solid and smiled.

The sound of the door unlocking in the suite warned her someone was coming.

Nola vanished. Bereft loneliness settled over Risa as she headed to the living room.

Hilary stood there surrounded by a sea of bags. "Clothes and essentials."

Risa took in the bounty, confused. "Uh, where'd these come from?"

"Linc's personal shopper sent them over for you. Linc told her to get things she surmised you'd need since everything you had burned in his house."

Her stuff actually burned in her car before she met Linc, but Risa hadn't given a thought to what Linc lost in the fire. "He lost everything?"

Hilary waved a hand. "The boy can buy whatever he wants."

"Boy?" Jeez, could she sound more like a dimwit? This woman's confident, assertive manner intimidated her.

Hilary's smile softened her formidable lines. "I met Lincoln when he was little more than a boy. Nineteen, if I remember correctly. Body of a man, mind of a very angry boy."

How long had Linc been chained? Tortured? Risa frowned, not liking the slew of uncomfortable feelings swirling around in her. Pity, admiration, respect. "How'd you meet him?" She didn't understand how Linc would have come across this stern and prim-looking woman.

Hilary leaned her hip against the arm of the couch. "I caught him stealing my dinner out of my oven."

Risa gasped. "In your house?"

"Enchiladas. He stood there holding that sizzling pan with no potholders. I could smell his skin burning and see the hunger in his eyes. Ratty boy, long, snarled hair, filthy clothes, and reeked like he hadn't seen soap and water in a month." She shook her head. "Told that boy to put dinner down and go take a shower. When he was clean, we'd eat."

"But..." She was pretty sure Hilary was mortal, couldn't feel any magic around her. "Weren't you scared he'd hurt you?"

She shrugged. "If he'd wanted to hurt me, he would have attacked when I first discovered him in my kitchen. All that kid wanted was the food. I saw him debating. He could have run with the enchiladas, and I'd never have caught him."

Risa stood there, absolutely riveted, trying to fathom Linc as an unkempt young man. "So what did Linc do?"

"Took a shower. I found him some clothes, a razor, toothbrush and comb. Then we had dinner."

"That's how you became friends?" Hunger to know more about her soul mirror, to understand him, consumed her.

Hilary eyed her carefully. "What do you think?"

A probing question. As if this woman wanted to know how Risa's mind worked. Risa didn't want to let her down and considered what she knew about Linc. "No. He wouldn't trust that easily. He couldn't." Not after his own mother had sold him. "You would've had to earn Linc's trust."

She nodded once. "And he had to earn his dinner. Each afternoon, he came by the house, showered and cleaned up, then I required an hour of math before we ate, and an hour of reading afterward. If he wanted dessert, he had to turn in homework assignments."

A deal. They'd made a deal. Like Linc had made a deal with her. That was how Linc operated, what he trusted. He was clearly intelligent and articulate. But at thirteen he'd been ripped out of whatever sorry life he'd had with his mother. Caged and enslaved, he wouldn't have gone to school at that point. "Could he read?"

"He could. Probably about a sixth-grade level. But it was his math ability that astounded me. He could calculate things in his head that has impressed every math professor I have shown."

It finally hit her how strange this all was. "Why are you telling me this?"

"Because that boy saved me. I'd given up on everything, my marriage, my career as an educator. I didn't care anymore. Until Linc showed up and gave me a reason to care again. Someone who needed me." She lowered her chin slightly, and fierceness took hold. "I couldn't love him more if he were my own blood child. But I'm losing him. I know what he is, what you are. You can save him, Risa. You're the only one who can. I just wanted you to understand. Lincoln is special."

"I understand."

"Do you?" Hilary stared at her. "This school was built with his money. Do you know what the L.C. in L.C. Academy stands for?"

She thought back to Linc telling them when they arrived. "Last Chance."

"For all the kids out there who are out of chances, out of hope. He built this place for them. Linc made most of his money off gambling, which I don't approve of. He's brilliant, could have been anything he wanted. But he uses his money for projects like this school." She turned, walked back to the door and looked at her. "Save him, Risa."

Linc stopped in front of the Baron's tower located not far off the Strip. The high-rise building had heat sensors and cameras. Whoever was on security detail had already spotted him. He lifted his face to the cameras and said, "Tell Baron that Dillinger is here."

While waiting, he studied the block that Baron owned. Across the street loomed Baron's Custom Rides, where he restored motorcycles.

The door buzzed and swung open. Linc strode in, ignoring the bikers sprawled around the clubhouse. Most wore cuts with Baron M.C. patches.

Vice unfolded from a couch, his eyes hard on Linc. His massive arms crossed, legs spread, in total enforcer mode. "You know where to go."

Yeah, no love lost there. Vice hadn't liked being Baron's second choice for VP of the club. Baron had groomed Linc, but the motorcycle club life didn't appeal to him, and he fucking hated the strip clubs and high-class call girls the MC ran. Oh they protected their girls, but women weren't a commodity. However he had zero concern about turning his back on the VP.

If Vice thought the time had come to settle a score, he'd bring it to Linc's face, not his back.

Linc nodded, headed into the elevator and came out in the penthouse done in black marble and silver.

Baron had his long, blond hair tied back, revealing his sharp features. The man was tall and fast, his arms popping muscles and ink, including a hawk with an American flag flying from its wings. Sitting on a couch, he clicked off the TV. "You're here about the spawn."

Linc dropped down on a chair. Of course Baron knew—Archer hadn't exactly been subtle. And Baron had spies everywhere. "It's war, Baron. We can't let Asmodeus, his half-breed spawn or the traitor witch hunters that turned rogue take over Vegas."

Baron turned slowly, fixing his gaze on him. "Is Vegas your town or not?"

"Not the time to argue about my choices." They'd met after Linc started winning too many hands at poker and Baron heard about him. Baron figured out two things—that Linc was a witch hunter and he was counting cards. After that, the witch-hunter biker had bankrolled Linc into high-stakes poker games. It'd been Baron who cleaned him up, putting him in designer clothes to look the part. But he hadn't owned Linc.

No one owned him.

"We need more men," Linc said. "Are you and your crew on board to fight this battle?"

"We'll fight, but we're not going to be answering to Axel Locke and his crew. Your leader isn't going to be flying into my town and setting up shop. I run the hunters in Vegas."

Which Linc had refused to join, then headed to California to join Axel's group. Sitting there, he let quiet settle as he considered the problem. Finally, he said, "What do you want, Baron? Let the spawn take over Vegas while we fight each other for power?"

"Don't be a moron, Dillinger. I'll run my own men, we'll consult, and we'll kick that hellfire half-breed right back to his demon daddy in the Underworld." He leaned forward. "But make no mistake, Vegas is my town."

That plan worked for Linc. He had no idea what Axel would think, but they needed men they could trust. Baron and his men were solid. "Then let's get to work. How many hunters do you have?"

"Twenty that are committed to the club and keeping their souls."

"Impressive. What info do you have about what's happening so far?"

"Rogues are protecting the spawn while he hibernates. And they are sweeping through Vegas, gathering up witch hunters and forcing them to choose—kill a witch and go rogue, or die."

Linc nodded. "Same info we have. But our witches have an emergency system set up. If a witch is near her phone when she's taken, and has the chance, she can alert us. Once the witch triggers the alarm, the GPS on her phone will send us her location information, and we have a chance of rescuing her."

"Add us in. But once we rescue them, we need a place to take them. I don't want my men exposed to witches longer than necessary."

"Bloodlust is a bitch," Linc said. "If the witch is unhurt, she can go wherever she wants. If she's injured, Sutton's here, he's mated and has wings. He can meet the hunter and take the witch. We'll establish a place at the academy for them. Carla's there, she can help them heal." They could put them in one of the other buildings, away from Ram, Eli and himself. Then move them out as soon as it was safe.

Baron agreed. "I propose we combine our training. I have plenty of room here to bring in more hunters who want to fight against the spawn."

Linc nodded. "Our hunter in charge of recruits, Ram, oversees our training. And our tech guy will arrange a communications system for all of us so we can stay in contact, both to prep and while fighting."

Baron clearly measured that idea as he rose and paced around. Finally, he looked up. "That works. We'll meet here tonight, combine intel and make a plan of attack."

"One more thing," Linc said. "And this is business. Worth twenty-five Gs."

Baron snapped up straight. "What?"

"Archer kidnapped a baby. A witch named Kendall. If you or one of your men find her location and it pans out, I'll pay for it."

"What's the baby to you?"

Nothing. But she was everything to Risa, and Linc intended to keep his end of the bargain with her. "That's not relevant. If you want the money, find the kid."

"I'll put the word out."

Linc nodded once and left, anxious to get home to Risa. To the witch he needed to teach to trust his touch.

≥ 11 ≤

RISA DIDN'T FIND ANY FOOD in the suite kitchen. Not surprising since she, Linc and the rest had shown up unexpectedly. She made her way down to the first-floor kitchen, threw together a quick sandwich and went looking for Linc while eating. They needed to seal their bond so she could find Kendall.

Her chest ached with longing. She missed the baby's one-tooth smile, full-body laugh, the way she wiggled and bounced when she was happy. But what Risa missed most of all were Kendall's hugs and touches. Before she met Blythe and Kendall, she hated being touched. Reminded her too much of the things she'd done, the men she'd let touch her...

Ugh, she couldn't think of those men in the same headspace as Kendall.

Hearing soft voices, she followed them to a library with floor-to-ceiling bookcases. There were plenty of areas to sit and read, or nooks with desks, or a few larger tables to work quietly on projects. One entire wall opened to a courtyard about the size of a big master bedroom. A stacked stone water feature splashed into a small pond surrounded by desert plants, thickly cushioned furniture and a teak bar all set on a cool stone floor. Overhead, sunlight poured through some kind of mesh material that filtered the harsh rays.

Two women sat on a stone bench by the water feature. They had their heads close together and were talking. She recognized the one with the long white-blonde hair as Carla, but not the one with the dark hair.

Deciding to ask them about Linc, she set her partially eaten sandwich down and walked out to the patio.

"Risa, you're up." The blonde rose and walked toward her. "I'm Carla, we met on video conference."

"Sutton's mate, I remember. Nice to see you in person." Steeling herself, she added, "Linc said you tried to help last night, thank you."

"I want to help. That's why I'm here."

That gentle kindness helped her relax. "Thanks." She glanced around. "I'm looking for Linc."

"He and the other hunters went out. Linc is gathering up more hunters to help, and Ram and Sutton are checking out anything to do with Archer—the last place he lived, clubs, work, friends, anything. They're all spreading the word that your daughter has been kidnapped." She took a breath and added, "Phoenix and Key are searching every lead in L.A. for Archer's mother, Petra, and the possible whereabouts of your baby."

"Has anyone found a lead?"

She shook her head. "Not yet. Petra's house hasn't been lived in for a while. There's no payments going to any mental health or rehab facilities, no money moving out of her account beyond previously set up automatic withdrawals."

"Could she be dead?" If so, then where was Kendall?

"I wish I knew. She's a demon witch, so we can't track her magically either."

140

Crap. "Thanks, Carla. If you see Linc before I do, can you tell him I'm looking for him?"

Carla moved closer. "We can try to circle our magic, and if you can get close to Kendall, I might be able to use my third eye to see her."

She stared at the woman's uncanny hazel eyes outlined in a thin blue ring. The colors seemed alive, and power danced on Carla's skin. It caused Risa's magic to stir and bubble. "Oh, is that possible?"

"Maybe if I can feel Kendall through you. It usually has to be a personal connection for us to reach someone with our third eye. But let's try. Even if I can't, there's a good chance we'll learn something valuable. Like, does Kendall feel close by or far away?"

Grateful, she said, "I'd appreciate any help."

The other woman rose and joined them. "Hi, I'm Ginny. I'll get out of your way so you two can work."

Turning to the dark-haired girl with muddy-hazel eyes, Risa thought she would have been almost plain except for the way she moved with a lithe grace. The closest thing she could liken it to was a ballet dancer's ability to glide. "I'm Risa."

"Ginny is Eli Stone's sister," Carla filled in. "He, Ginny and I arrived last night. You'll meet him later."

Right, Linc had told her that, and Axel had mentioned Eli and Ginny in the video conference. "Good to meet you, Ginny." Her curiosity grew at the vibration coming off Ginny—not chakra magic, but something Risa couldn't identify. "So your brother's a witch hunter, but you're not?"

The woman grinned. "How sexist is that? Only letting men be Wing Slayer Hunters. You can tell their god is a man."

That surprised a laugh from her. "About as sexist as only women being witches, I guess."

Ginny's eyes dimmed. "I'm going to go look into those gloves, Carla. Thanks for listening."

Carla laid her hand on Ginny's arm. "Ram loves you. I know it's hard, but I really think his love for you is helping him fight against the thunderbird."

A flash of pain radiated off Ginny, stirring Risa's shield magic with the urge to protect the woman. But the conversation didn't make sense. Ginny was mortal. Ram had to find his witch, his soul mirror.

"I just hope this is the right thing for him." Ginny turned and walked inside.

Risa watched her go, the emotional pain flowing from the woman lessening the farther away she got. "She's in danger."

"Yes."

Dragging her gaze back to Carla, Risa struggled to shed the lingering need to bring out her shield magic. "From Ram?"

"That's part of it. It's a complicated story, and I don't know all of it. Let's go sit down." Carla turned and walked to the plush charcoal-gray top to the stone bench.

Risa followed and sat. "Doesn't Ram need to find his soul mirror?"

"He has found her. Her name's Shayla Banfield, and she's on the run from him because their mating will bring out magic she doesn't want." Carla sighed heavily. "The bird is driving him to find Shayla and will kill him with electrical energy if he doesn't, but his heart belongs to Ginny."

Risa had seen the blue sparks coming from the man's fingertips. Love had caused Risa's mom to make bad decisions, and now it looked like it was causing Ram and Ginny to do the same thing. "Then he needs to forget Ginny and convince Shayla."

"He won't. What he and Ginny have..." Carla shrugged in a helpless gesture. "He's willing to die for it."

Risa studied the shadows stretching out over the

patio that reminded her of the souls trapped within her, looming bigger and longer each day. Marking her. She wasn't someone a man would love. Nor did she want to fall in love and give anyone that kind of power over her. Her mother had been weak, becoming a monster to please the man she loved.

Reining in her thoughts, she said, "Ginny's in danger. Maybe it's from Ram, but it feels bigger than that." She hated this, worrying about someone she'd barely even met. "Just wanted to warn you since you seem to be friends."

Carla watched her. "How do you know? Are you an empath?"

Risa pulled her mouth tight. "No, but when I'm around someone who feels threatened, it triggers a compulsion in my magic."

"That must be hard, especially given how risky it is for you to shield."

Failure was hard, and the guilt? Unbearable. "I can usually control it. I don't shield unless I want to."

"Like when you shielded the men from the hellfire in Linc's house. Even knowing what you'd suffer after." Carla's eyes clouded with yellow. "Thank you, Risa. Sutton's immortal, but it's possible that hellfire could have killed him."

Risa shrugged it off, uncomfortable with Carla's gratitude. "Thanks for trying to help me last night. I know you were shocked."

"Concerned," the witch answered. "I just...Linc is..."

"Special." Sensing a theme here, she clarified for Carla, "I get why you're worried." After all, Carla had witnessed the soul screams. "But I'm not going to be in his life permanently. We both know we're not right for each other long term. I can't be the witch you'd wish for Linc, but I can be the witch who frees him of the bloodlust." That had to mean something. She wanted to be more in Linc's memory than just another woman he slept with.

Carla tilted her head. "You'll need him to help you funnel your magic. The soul-mirror bond, it's not some piece of engineering where you follow three steps and it's done. It's a living entity and must be kept alive, or you'll lose your familiar, the bird in Linc, and your high magic."

Concern rippled over Risa. "What about him? What happens to Linc if I'm gone? The curse won't come back, will it?" Anxiety ate at her guts.

"No. But the wings will die off. He'll just be a very strong witch hunter."

Relief calmed her. Getting control of her emotions, she looked at the other witch. "Will you still help me try to find Kendall?"

Carla caught Risa's hand. "Of course."

Shock coursed through her body at the contact. She stiffened but didn't pull away.

"Go ahead and summon your magic," Carla instructed. "Then I'll begin adding mine."

Risa shut out the feeling of the other woman's hand around hers, opened her first chakra and the next three quickly followed. Power streamed out, looping through her chakras and gaining strength. Magic swelled, creating an adrenaline rush and making her body feel alive and vital. Tingles raced along her skin, and her breasts tightened.

The same thing happened when Linc touched her. Desire. But Linc wasn't here, so she shouldn't feel it now. Shame rose. What would Carla think? Uneasy, she called her magic back.

At that second, a new power surged into her, fast and strong, weaving with her magic. Thickening and pulsing.

She couldn't get a hold of her witchcraft. Instead, the sensation filled her. Everything engorged until her breasts ached and belly fluttered. The caress of a soft breeze made her shiver and almost moan. She clenched her jaw against the onslaught of vivid sensations, as if a dormant part of her was awakening. It was too much.

"Risa, you're pushing out my magic. What's wrong?"

"I..." She jerked her hand from Carla, unable to bear the touch. Chills broke out on her skin. Tingles of awareness. She willed her magic to calm and cool.

Detach.

But it kept pulsing until everything throbbed, even between her legs.

Desire. Too much, too sexual. It was *in* her magic and rushing, racing, desperate for...

Linc.

His image appeared in her mind, the way he'd looked as he'd touched her face, then brushed his mouth over hers, trailed kisses down her jaw, the tender skin of her throat. That moment when he'd opened his mouth and licked her collarbone. Sucked.

The throb between her legs bloomed hotter, heavier.

Everything hurt. Need clawed at her.

The need for Linc.

Linc pulled into the garage, got out and waited for the SUV holding Sutton and Ram. Once they arrived a few minutes later and jumped out, he said, "Find any sign?" He'd wanted to be out there with the two men searching the Strip for Archer and Kendall, but he'd needed to secure Baron's cooperation.

"It's a goddamned disaster." Sutton shut the car door. "Fires still burning, power out, debris in the streets."

"No sign of the spawn or baby." Ram started heading out of the garage.

Linc took a step, and a wave of powerful magic slammed into him. He stumbled at the impact. Catching himself, he snapped his head up. "Risa."

"Jesus, Dillinger." Ram bent over, his hands on his thighs, panting beneath the bloodlust. "Go mate her before she destroys us."

Linc fought down a wave of possessive anger. No one talked about Risa like she was a dog to be bred. But the rational part of his brain recognized Ram was right. The witch was in extreme danger. Any one of the three of them—Ram, Eli or him—could snap and kill her. That propelled him into action. He raced for the door, going through the tunnel into the laundry room, when he heard Carla's voice.

"Trust me, and I can help."

Sutton's mate meant well, but asking Risa to trust in someone? He knew better than anyone she couldn't do that. Judging by the strain in Carla's tone, Risa had hit some trouble. He raced through the kitchen, dining room and into the library, where he spotted a partially eaten sandwich resting on a plate atop the worktables.

Turning his gaze to the patio, he sucked in a breath. Risa had dropped to her knees, bent over with her arms wrapped around herself. Her hair fell forward, shielding her face, but he could see her normally silver-blue witch shimmer had threads of red and yellow. Her scent carried the too-sweet bite of pain.

Linc leapt forward, rushing out to his witch.

Carla, hunched down beside Risa, looked up. Her hazel eyes swirled. "Her magic is out of control, and I can't get past it to help her. The blood you gave her last night must have opened the soul-mirror connection more, and it's too much for her to handle."

Damn it, he shouldn't have left her. She needed his falcon. Needed him. He resisted his first impulse to lift

Risa and hold her tight. Using every shred of self-control he had, he said, "Move back, Carla."

Without a word, the witch got up and went to stand by the sliding glass door to the library.

He walked to the front of Risa, sat down on the stones and stretched his legs out so that she was on his left.

She shuddered violently.

Her power slapped at him in undisciplined waves. He could only imagine what it was doing to her. "Risa, I'm here, love. All you have to do is let me help you. The bird's here too. Do you feel him? He wants to help you get your magic under control."

"Can't."

God, he had to touch her to make this better. "Come here, baby. We can do it together."

She desperately shook her head.

He gently stroked the fingers wrapped tightly around her arm. "It's okay."

She looked up.

Linc's breath caught at the sight of her huge, haunted eyes. The bird tugged and pulled on Linc's back, trying to get to Risa.

"It's not just magic. It's hot need leaking through." Her voice cracked. "Something broke."

Drumbeats of rage exploded in his mind while the bird shrieked in fury. He got it. She felt desire, something he was given to understand was normal and natural for witches when summoning their magic. But Risa had seen too much of the dark side of sexuality.

The bird shifted, his entire being telegraphing that he wanted to wrap around her, protect her from what she had suffered.

Risa, strong and resilient, had found a way to protect herself by having her magic numb her sexuality. And now by beginning their bond with the blood exchange, he'd ripped away her only coping mechanism, revealing the festering wounds beneath.

His entire world narrowed in that moment. Nothing else mattered, not the shredding of his veins by her magic, not the pounding in his dick, not even the threat of losing his soul.

Nothing mattered but this witch.

Glancing up at Carla, he was grateful when she got the message, nodded once and went inside the library. He heard the door close, leaving them alone. No one would disturb them in this private time between him and Risa.

Turning back to his soul mirror, he stroked her fingers again, using the tiny contact to keep the bloodlust controlled. With his other hand, he cupped her jaw lightly, just enough to keep her with him. Appealing to her tough side, he asked, "Risa, do you want to control your magic and desire, or do you want them to control you?"

She panted but managed to shove her shoulders back and raise her chin. "I want to be in control."

"Then come here." He held out his hand.

She stared for a long second.

"You're in control," he reminded her. "You want me to get up and leave, say the word." Fucking liar. He couldn't leave her, was incapable of it. And if he tried it, the bird would probably sever his spinal cord. But he had to give her the space to make the decision and hope like hell she didn't test him.

She unclenched her fingers from around her arms, rose on her knees and shuffled closer until her leg touched his thigh. Her magic heated his skin at contact and pulsed through him, taking his breath away. Her fragile trust held him perfectly still, waiting to see what she'd do.

Would she believe in him? Give him a chance to prove he'd help her? Not hurt her?

Finally, she settled her hand in his.

The bird preened and pranced in his skin, his feathers spreading out and fluttering. The violent ache in Linc's chest eased. He wrapped his fingers around hers and for a second just held on to her.

Then he tugged her. "Closer."

With jerky movements, she threw her leg over his.

Linc curled his free hand over her hip and drew her down. Her warmth covered his dick.

He hissed. Pain. Pleasure. Hot and cold. He kept his eyes open, his gaze on her, letting her see what she did to him. Letting her know they were both right there in the vortex of need.

Her power streamed straight down, slamming into him.

He arched back, shocked by the hot magic whipping through him. "Shit." He'd underestimated the reaction he'd have, the extreme urge to shred the clothes between them and surge up inside her.

But she trusted him to stay in control.

Damn it.

Grabbing her waist, he shifted her to sit across his lap. He put his arm around her waist and pulled her back enough to see her face. Her shimmer had red pain cracks and flashes of yellow heat. And her eyes— her pupils were dilating.

"Magic is swelling in my first chakra. Too much." She rotated her hips in desperation.

Linc struggled to breathe past the whirlpool of lust sucking them in. He knew how it felt to have a driving need for release, but for Risa, it meant her magic that had protected her all these years was betraying her. And sexual lust? She'd been forced to use men's sexual lust to lure them to places where her father could kill them.

That kind of shit would fuck with anyone's head, but a teenage girl? Anger helped him get another sliver of control. He wanted to care for her, to be the one who helped her see the beauty in her desire. "Desire's part of your magic and part of you, the part you've been repressing. Our bond is bringing it out."

"I've never felt this before."

Oh hell. Being the first man to show her the pleasures of sex. He liked that a hell of a lot and would make damn sure it was good for her. "Because you haven't been with someone you could trust with that part of you. But you are now." And didn't that puff up his chest with pride? She'd crawled right into his arms. Lowering his face to hers, he said softly, "Let me show you the beauty in giving pleasure. I want to watch you own your desire, let it surge through you until you come."

"I don't know what that feels like."

Christ. Every cell in his body fired to show her. Teach her. Watch her surrender to his touch. Linc's heart pounded, and urgency thumped in his blood. "I want to give that to you." Brushing his mouth over hers, he added, "Do you want more? To let me kiss and taste you? Touch you?" But he'd hold back from sealing their bond.

For now.

Risa might be physically ready, but every instinct he had screamed that emotionally she needed time and care, a little space to figure it all out. She'd been forced into sexuality too damned young, abused and betrayed. Trust took time, and Linc would give her as much as they could afford.

This moment wasn't about finding her child or breaking his curse. It belonged to Risa, to them.

Shifting, Risa sat up, snagged the ends of her T-shirt and stripped it off.

Linc's brain stuttered. No coy answers or helpless act. Nope, when Risa committed, she went for it. He freaking loved that. Her dark, untamed hair fell around her shoulders. And shit, no bra. Just fucking perfect tits, with rosy nipples that ignited his hunger. He caught his hand in her silky hair and dragged her close enough to feel the damp heat of her breath.

She closed her eyes as a shudder raced through her. "This is what it feels like to want someone." When she opened her eyes, fear and wonder merged in their depths. Digging her fingers into his arm, she added, "What it feels like to want you."

Her honesty humbled him. He had no more words, and he skimmed his hand up her rib cage and traced over the enticing mounds of her breasts. He brushed his palms across the tips of her nipples.

Her lips parted.

He kissed her, catching her bottom lip with his teeth then soothing it with his tongue. Damn, the taste of her inflamed him. The mere tease of her flavor intoxicated and drew him in deeper. He slid into the heat of her mouth, exploring her.

A hint of magic rushed over his tongue.

More. He needed it, craved it.

With deft fingers, he drew a line down between her breasts, into the dip of her ribs, over the tight muscles of her stomach and spread his hand, feeling the edge of her magic where it swirled and pulsed. So hot, so goddamned amazing, his heart pounded. Her thick moan made him and the bird tremble.

He forced himself to move slower, sliding his fingers right to the edge of her low-riding pants.

Her magic burned there. Throbbed. Oh Christ. He tried to catch it, felt all the swirling power suck at his fingers.

Her pants vanished.

Risa jerked her head back, her eyes wide. "I didn't—"

Linc kissed her, invading her with his tongue, then sucking hers into his mouth. Risa clamped down on his shoulders, her fingers digging in. Finally, he lifted his head. "You are that powerful, love, your need that fierce. You want me to touch you." He brushed his mouth over hers. "No lies between us. Tell me the truth."

She laid her hand over his on her belly. "I want it, *you*, enough to magically strip myself bare for you."

His chest burned at her words and trust. The falcon made embarrassing cooing sounds in his head, but Linc couldn't fault the bird. "Damn, that's hot. Own it, Risa. Show me what your magic feels like."

He looked down her body, to where his hand, covered by her smaller one, rested between her hipbones. Watched as pushed his hand down.

The sight of her guiding his hand to the strip of hair and lower was more erotic then anything he'd experienced.

Fuck. Razor-sharp lust pounded at him, but nothing would stop him from giving her this. He let her stay in control of his touch, guiding him. Owning her desire.

She curled her hand until his fingers dipped between her thighs to her heat.

"Risa." It came out a heated growl. He stroked along her seam, his chest tightening while his cock surged against his pants, desperate to feel this. He parted her folds, right to her most vulnerable flesh. "You're wet and slick. And this..." He dragged the tip of his finger over her clit and circled the swollen nub.

A wave of magic bloomed, rich with her scent. Oh yeah, she liked that. Linc fought a wave of searing need, keeping his touch easy as he rubbed and caressed her clit. "This is temptation begging to be licked." Hunger flooded his mouth, but he held back and let her set the pace.

Her power shimmered, his shirt vanished, and she ran her hands over his shoulders and down his back. "I need to touch Falcon."

Damn, she dragged her palms over his skin, creating a path of crackling magic that lit him up. His heart rate jacked, but he kept his voice calm. "He makes you feel safe?"

"You both do."

He bit off a groan. His balls swelled, cock ached, but the feeling of her hands on him was worth the torture.

"I feel ridges. Beneath the ink." Her fingers began tracing the brand.

Linc didn't want to talk about that ugliness, not when he had her beauty and trust right here. "It's nothing. But you, little witch, you are filling with power. It's blazing over your skin, your scent making my mouth water." Leaning forward, he sucked in a nipple.

She arched. "Please."

Her sweet plea arrowed a burning shaft of hot pleasure through him. He dipped his fingers deeper between her thighs. Damp and hot, another wave rolled over him, need so vital he could barely breathe.

He dragged his gaze back to hers. "Don't hide from it now. You're going to come. Own it. Go after it." He stroked and teased, finding the spots that made her moan. Her magic rushed around his fingers.

"Yes." She canted her hips, a flush on her skin spreading, her fingers digging into his shoulders.

Linc lost it. Moving with hunter speed, he lifted her, got up on his knees and set her on the padded bench. "Lean back on your elbows." His voice was rough. Harsh. Desperate.

If he couldn't slide his cock into her, feeling the very center of this woman, he'd make love to her with his tongue.

Risa leaned back. The waterfall cast a fine spray over her nude body, hundreds of tiny droplets clinging to her shoulders and breasts.

Beautiful.

Linc caught her thighs, spreading them open.

Wet, swollen, pink. Fucking beautiful.

He leaned down and tasted her. Wild magic and pure Risa flowed to him. Through him.

So deep it felt like she marked him.

$$\rightleftharpoons 12 \rightleftharpoons$$

RISA HAD NEVER UNDERSTOOD THE elemental drive to have sex.

Until now. Until this man. Linc, a man who had survived being held captive and tortured, and yet cared enough to help her, give to her.

Not take from her.

The depth of his physical generosity was a new experience. She had only known herself as a tool, something to be used. He showed her that she was so much more.

Her eyes burned and her throat filled as he knelt between her legs, his hand holding her ass as he ran his tongue gently over her clit in an intimate kiss. One that deepened as he licked her. Sucked her.

Her first four chakras threw out continuous magic that pooled and whirled in her pelvis. Every touch of his breath, lips and tongue shot through her in lightning streaks of pleasure.

He groaned and lifted his gaze to hers, light brown eyes darkening to bronze and swirling with something potent and primitive.

Her womb contracted in response, sparking an ache desperate to be filled.

Sliding one hand from her ass, he traced her from her clit down, until he circled her opening.

Arrows of need shot through her. She cried out.

"More, Risa? Tell me you want more."

Delicious tremors raced from his touch, her body coiling, tightening. Fear tried to edge in as she hung on a precipice. Did she jump? Or pull back? Uncertainty hovered.

Until she looked back into his eyes. Pupils swollen, color dark and desperate, need so vivid it echoed in her blood. But he didn't take what he needed.

Instead he gave her what she craved.

Her last threat of hesitation melted beneath his intensity, leaving nothing but trust and hunger. "More. You, Linc. I want you."

Color flooded his face. "You have more of me than I've given anyone else."

Emotion surged into her throat. Despite who her father was, what he'd done to Linc, he trusted her, had told her his past. That opened her until she shuddered and moaned to feel more of him. Get closer.

He slid one finger into her. Filled her.

"Hot, wet and pulsing with magic, so damned honest and sexy, Risa."

His voice trembled through her, pushing her higher, firing a voracious throb she had to satisfy.

"Ride my fingers. Catch it, Risa." He pushed a second finger in, stroking her and seducing her magic.

Sensation built. She pushed against his hand, chasing it, pumping hard and fierce. Every slide of his knuckles fired her nerves into wild hunger. In, out, deeper and never enough.

"More!" Her voice came out a ragged demand.

"Fuck yeah." Still keeping that possessive gaze on her, he lowered his face between her spread thighs until his breath feathered over her swollen, wet folds.

"Argh, God." Sinking her hands in his hair, she held

on as he teased her clit with the edge of his hot tongue. Back and forth, ripping her apart as the yearning built to unbearable. Just when she wanted to beg, he pushed his fingers deeper, hitting a hidden spot that lit her up. At the same second, he caught her clit with his lips and sucked. Hard.

Risa exploded, hot surges of bliss rupturing in wave after wave. When Linc raised his head, she caught a reflection of wings in his bronzed irises, sweeping up and down in a fluid motion. Both man and bird were in powerful unison, owning her as she soared with them. Finally she floated down, her muscles lax and her magic gently burbling.

Linc eased his fingers from her, rose on his knees and pressed his forehead to hers. The wings moved in his eyes.

"I feel that, your wings inside me, gliding with my magic. Up and down, through my chakras." It should be invasive, too intimate. But after her bone-melting orgasm, she couldn't feel anything but a soft glow. "Is this real?" Or had her mind snapped and she'd retreated to a dark hole and hallucinated? "Are you real?"

"As real as it gets." Leaning on one elbow over her, he brushed her hair back. "You took my breath away. So sensual and honest, there's nothing sexier."

Risa touched his face, skimming her fingers along his jaw. The wings in her magic fluttered. "I feel you inside me. I can't decide if it's sexy or scary."

"Baby, when I'm truly inside you, you won't feel fear. Only pleasure. That's the bird. The tattoo is hot with your magic right now."

The ache he'd just satisfied tingled, heat spreading at the thought of him inside her. He'd been patient, seducing her, showing her she could trust him. Time for her to do her part. They both needed to seal the bond. But she'd never forget this moment with him.

Even when he hated her later for lying.

Anxiety edged in, but Risa held on to his gaze and slid her hand over his stomach. Jeez, the ridges of his muscles entranced her. The man felt as cut as he looked.

Focus. She knew how to do this. Reaching his belt, she—

He caught her hand. "Wait."

"Why?"

"You feel the bird, right?"

She nodded. The sensation of the creature winging gently around her magic almost protectively resembled being hugged from the inside.

"He's helping you harness the magic. Let's see if we can find your girl, now. As long as you feel him, he'll keep you safe."

Startled, she stared up into his eyes filled with wings. This man constantly surprised her. "Don't you want to break your curse?"

"Fuck yes. Even more than that, I want you, want to feel you, to take our pleasure together."

"Then..." She tried to understand. Kendall was his ace card, the one he could play to make sure she gave him that. "Why wait?"

"Because more than all that, I want you to be free to choose, Risa. Right now, you'll choose to do this for Kendall. And God, baby, I respect the hell out of that. But it's not what I want."

Confusion spiraled. "What do you want?"

His gaze pierced hers. "For you to do this because you want to, not because you have to."

Hot tears threatened, and her chest ached. Why? Dear God, why did Linc, this man who'd endured being sold by his mother, caged and used in ways that she couldn't fathom, why did he have to be so kind to her?

She didn't deserve it.

Swallowing her tears to put conviction in her voice, she told him the truth. "I want to. You don't have to—"

"Yes, I do. Let's try this, while the bird is in your magic. Do this for me. Use your magic and reach for your daughter."

With no words left, she nodded and did it. Her magic rushed out. Flutters of soft wings joined in, as if the bird chased her power. The bird was helping her. Maybe she could really reach Kendall and find her. Hope inflated.

Yet she couldn't help but think about the lie that would shatter this fragile trust and budding friendship blooming between her and Linc. It loomed up thickly between them, slowing her magic. Her heart chakra squeezed.

The wings in Linc's eyes began to fade as her magic faltered, tripping on her guilt over the necessary lie.

He slid his hand up her waist and brushed his thumb over her nipple. Desire arced up, reigniting her magic. "Now, love. Before I completely lose it here."

Risa focused on the wings in his gaze as they grew bigger and bigger, until they filled her vision. Without thinking, she laid her hand on Linc's face. The connection between her and the bird strengthened, and she could almost feel feathers brushing her fingers. Her power surged and coalesced. Risa projected outward, searching for Kendall.

A thin, distant screech echoed. Her magic paused.

"Risa?" Linc stiffened, hand gripping her waist. "The falcon, he's warning of something."

She opened her mouth, but the harsh drag on her witchcraft cramped her chakras. The bird faded away, and Risa panicked. She couldn't reach her magic. All her power fused into a massive curtain lowering.

Blinding her.

"Risa!"

"No!" Terrified, unable to see anything except

blackness, she couldn't breathe. Couldn't think. She shivered violently as chills attacked her, and her magic lay out of her grasp.

A hand caught her face. "Risa, talk to me. Tell me what's happening."

"I can't see anything! The souls did something to my magic!"

Linc grabbed his shirt and pushed it over her head and arms. Wasting no time, he scooped her up and ran into the house. "Carla!"

"What?" She rushed out of the computer room with Sutton on her heels. Behind them, Ram walked out, his shoulders tense and cords on his neck standing out. Risa's magic was affecting the other hunter, but Linc had no time to worry about that. Going to the couch, Linc sat with Risa on his lap. "Risa can't see. Something's wrong."

Carla sat on the coffee table facing them, with Sutton standing behind her. Ram stayed back, as far from the magic as he could manage without leaving.

Carla took Risa's hand, then frowned. "I feel the souls. They're disturbed. Are they screaming?"

"No."

"Did you use your shield magic?"

She shook her head. "I have to use my hands and weave the magic to shield."

Linc remembered the way her hands had moved when she cast the shield to save them from the hellfire. The entire time, she had kept her hands up.

"The blackness is fading now," Risa said. "I'm seeing shapes."

Relief cascaded over him. Wrapping his arms around her, he slid his cheek across her silky hair and inhaled her scent. "Carla, what happened?"

Gently, the other witch said, "I'm guessing, but I think so much magic and desire at once made the souls feel threatened. You've never allowed sex to feed your magic before?"

"I didn't know that sex and magic could work together like that." Risa rubbed her forehead.

Linc took over. "We're practicing harnessing her desire into her magic." Pride filled him. "As soon as she connected with Falcon she was amazing." Nothing was as gorgeous as Risa, covered in desire and her witch shimmer, working her magic. He'd have given anything to spread her thighs and sink into her as she gave herself to the magic.

Except that he'd hurt her. Pushed her too far, too soon.

Sutton glanced over Carla's head at Linc. "You're throwing pheromones the size of baseballs."

Linc stared back. "Can't be helped."

"You're going to lose it."

"Eventually. When I let go of her." He had no illusions. It was a constant battle between him and the curse, and every day the bloodlust got a little closer to kicking his ass into becoming a rogue.

Risa whipped around, squinting to see him. "Damn it, Linc. You shouldn't have stopped. We have to seal the bond to free you."

She'd been practically blind just minutes earlier, and she was worried about him?

"I don't think that's a good idea. Not now," Carla interjected. "The souls are too restless. Somehow, they got control of enough of your magic to temporarily blind you." She touched Risa's knee then frowned. "I can feel their anxiety. I'm worried they'll interfere with the soul bond."

"Because I'm going insane," Risa said quietly. "And if that happens, Kendall will have no one."

The hopeless tone in her flat voice ignited dark rage

within him. Frustration ground down his control. The craving for witch blood simmered in his veins while sexual lust pounded in his groin. The feel of her ass pressing against his hard-on wasn't helping. Linc could barely think over the buzzing of raw animalistic need for blood and sex.

"Easy." Sutton moved around the back of the couch and laid his huge hand on Linc's shoulder. "Carly, go on."

Carla flicked her gaze up to her mate, then back to Linc and Risa. "When I was on the astral plane last night, I could see the souls were fighting Risa for control of her power. When they are awakened, they're angry, confused and reliving their deaths. They fight Risa for her magic because they instinctively know that magic is keeping them alive. Correct, Risa?"

"Sounds right. But I don't know what would happen to the souls if I died. They've been trapped for a long time. I think they're confused, believing that being in my magic is their afterlife."

Carla nodded. "That's a better explanation. But now they have a new invader who is helping you with your magic."

"Falcon." She sat up on his lap. "It feels weird to me, so yeah, I can understand why they'd see him as not belonging there."

"Right, and as your familiar, the falcon is your protector. He sees the souls hurting you and deems them a threat."

Sighing, she rubbed her palms over her T-shirt-covered thighs. "Well, that's a punch of sucky irony since I need my high magic so I can free the souls, and my high magic requires a familiar."

How did she endure it, always carrying those souls, feeling the responsibility? Respect for his witch notched up. She'd borne this burden for years. A need to care for her thrummed in him. He tugged her back to his chest and looked down at her. "Can you see any better?"

Risa blinked then settled her gaze on him. "It's improving fast, almost normal." She faced Carla. "I feel a thread of your magic."

The other witch nodded. "The souls are starting to recognize me a little bit since we've circled our power a couple times now. I've only been sending a trickle of calming energy, keeping it as nonintrusive as possible so they don't feel threatened." She tilted her head. "What that tells me is the souls can be coaxed into trusting. Linc, you and the falcon need to slow down and build trust with these souls before you finish this bond."

Risa turned to him. "We don't have time. Linc needs to break the curse, and I have to find Kendall."

"If you want to find her, you'll take the time." Carla leaned forward, seriousness radiating from her. "It's a fragile balance—your mind seems to be able to handle the souls in your daily life. But the soul screams are creating too much internal pressure on your psyche. You need to keep the souls calm and get them to accept the falcon to prevent another full on attack or next time, you might break entirely."

For a second, he struggled with the urge to push Risa despite the risk to her. No, damn it, he wouldn't do that to her. Even if they weren't going to do the whole love-story thing, it was his job to protect her. To calm himself, he pulled in a deep breath.

Mistake. The lingering scent of her cinnamon-hot magic and arousal stoked the fires of his lust, ramping up his need to drag her to a room, spread her thighs and bury himself in her. The urge climbed until it pounded in his spine and drowned his brain.

"How long?" It came out a snarl. Shit. His control was slipping with every breath, the need eating into him. Right now it was sexual lust. But the second he let go of Risa, the curse would slam him into madness.

He shifted his gaze to her eyes. "I'm barely hanging on. I've got men out there, hunters, looking for your baby, and I promised them a big reward if they find her. I'm doing my part." *Shut up!* But the craving dug in. Hard. "How fucking long do you need to calm the souls down and do your part?"

Goddammit, he heard himself being an asshole, reverting to the animal he'd been for six years in that cage. Damn near growling at her.

Risa froze.

Apologize before this goes bad.

She exploded off his lap, breaking contact.

"Shit. Don't run." He swallowed, the burn of the curse igniting through his veins. Adrenaline stormed his muscles, making them twitch. Buzzing roared in his head. Linc slapped his forearms on his thighs and fisted his hands. If she ran, it'd unleash the predator in him. He hung on through sheer will. *Wing Slayer, don't let me hurt her.*

Sutton's grip tightened on his shoulder. "Risa, take Carla's hand. Move around the couch. Get behind me."

"No. You stay out of this."

Snapping his head up, Linc got the full force of Risa's defiant eyes as she glared at Sutton then him.

"Let's go, Dillinger. You want this done, we'll do it." She turned and stalked across the room, ignoring the elevator for the stairs. Her long, lithe legs climbed the treads, his T-shirt swishing around her thighs.

His predator instincts surged. Jackknifing off the couch, he went after her. *Have to touch her. Need her.* Ignoring Sutton and Ram yelling at him, he took the stairs three and four at a time, moving so fast even Sutton couldn't catch him.

Just steps ahead of him, Risa rounded the landing to hit the second flight. A dangerous mix coursed in his blood—fury, lust, *madness*. His veins swelled as if injected with acid. Agony seared him. Only witch blood would cool the burn. *No. Don't hurt her. Touch her.* He just had to—

He slammed into her, cushioning her face with his hand before he pressed her into the wall next to the stairs. "Stop." Growing red need roiled inside his mind. Images flashed like a crazed neon sign.

Risa on that bench, her nude body shimmering as he tasted her.

Another image of him chained to a wall, witch blood dumped on him as his body seized with the violent pleasure.

The cage he'd lived in.

Risa's tears.

Wait. What the fuck? A vicious scream ripped through his head, shoving back the madness of bloodlust. Full awareness snapped into place. Two things dominated his attention.

His palm cupping her face was wet with goddamned tears.

And her magic, that beautiful cinnamon-candy magic, had gone cold.

"This what you need, Dillinger? To force me? Put on a show for your friends? You're just like the others." Risa shuddered and added in a choked whisper, "Just like them."

No, he was worse. Risa had begun to trust him, and look what he'd done. Sick regret twisted through him, and yet his cock throbbed against her back. *Animal. You belong in a cage.* Feeling movement behind him, he glanced over his shoulder.

Ram and Sutton closed in on him, both moving silently. Sutton had his blade in his fist, while Ram held a gun.

"Get out of here." Jesus, it was bad enough he'd done this to her. He didn't want the men to see her crying and add to her humiliation.

Sutton's stare pierced him. "Risa? It's up to you."

Her body shuddered beneath his, but her voice came out strong. "Go."

The bald man nodded, and both of them turned and vanished down the stairs.

Silence pulsed around them, just their labored breathing filling the landing that led to the staff apartments. The full contact of her body against his pushed out his craving for witch blood, leaving the deep ache for sexual release. Tough shit. He pressed his face to the wall next to hers. Her eyes... Christ.

Naked pain magnified by unshed tears. Using his thumb, he brushed away the few that had fallen. She'd been so strong and tough for two days—enduring being shocked and tortured by the rogues, casting her shield to save the four of them from the hellfire, the agony of soul screams—but it had been Linc who made her cry. He knew why—she'd let herself be vulnerable with him, trusted him.

"I'm sorry, Risa. I had no right to say that."

"I'm acting like a girl."

He had no idea what to do with that. "You are a girl."

"So was my mom."

"Usually how it works." He wanted to draw her out, get her to talk to him. Anything but crying. He'd rather she hit him or cut him with his own knife.

Her mouth twitched. "Yeah, but Harmony thought that just because my dad gave her orgasms she was in love. Even worse, that he loved her. She turned her back on her heritage as an earth witch to be with a hired assassin. Her family cut her off. The witches shunned her. But she didn't care. All that mattered was my father. My mom refused to see that he used her love to manipulate and control her."

"You're not doing that. It's not the same thing."

"No? One orgasm and I'm suddenly upset because you're telling it like it is? Yeah, not doing that."

Protective anger built in his chest. "You know the

difference between you and your mom?" He didn't give her a chance to answer. "From what you told me, she sold out for a few orgasms and a fantasy of love." For whatever reason, Risa had let him keep his hand on her face. He tunneled his fingers into her silky hair. "While you're demanding respect from the man sharing your body. You called me on my bullshit, and my friends were ready and willing to stand up and protect you. They'd have dragged my ass down those stairs and out of this building if you'd told them to."

Shock widened her eyes.

Linc pushed on. "And you're doing this for your baby. I'm going to help you find her and get enough magic to release the souls so you can take care of her. That's how you're different from your mother. That's not a foolish girl, but a strong woman. You have every right to insist I treat you with the care and respect you deserve."

Hope swam through her eyes then drained as guilt and regret took over. "I don't deserve respect or care. You know that, so don't lie. I'm not backing out because you said what you meant."

Damn it. He had to tell her. "It was the sex magic talking. I've never gone this long without sex, and it's taking control."

A furrow carved between her eyebrows. "I don't understand."

"A few months ago, I was captured by rogues, chained to a wall and doused in blood from witches to force me to turn." Just saying it caused his body to shudder with the memory. "I was so far gone in bloodlust by the time the other hunters got there to rescue me, they had to tranquilize me or I'd have gone after any witch I could find. Axel should have killed me."

She leaned into his fingers massaging her scalp. "He obviously didn't."

Linc lowered his finger to the base of her skull, trying to ease her tension. "No. He took me to the witches. Roxy Banfield, you met her on the video conference. She's a fertility witch with the gift of sex magic. Using her magic, the witches worked together to push enough sex magic into me to shove out some of the curse."

"It worked?"

"Yes. The original curse is based in blood and sex. The witches basically forced the craving for sex over the craving for witch blood. But I have to feed the sex magic to keep it going." He ground his jaw, fighting the burn in his spine and balls, that constant need to ram his dick into a willing woman.

Risa dropped her gaze. "So what do you do if there's no woman around? Take care of it yourself?"

His engorged cock strained against his pants. Grasping her hair, he tugged her head up. "Jacking off used to work. Now it makes it worse. I can't release that way anymore." It was getting harder with a partner, but this was between the two of them. He didn't want to bring any others into the conversation.

"Oh." Color climbed up her neck and spread.

Linc's breath caught. "Are you embarrassed?" The sweet vulnerability in her touched something long dead inside of him.

"A little. Everything feels bigger with you, more vivid and intimate, personal." She sucked in a lungful of air, her nipples pressing against the soft cotton of his shirt.

"And the thought of me masturbating?" He wanted to understand.

Her eyes brightened, and her nostrils flared. "Not just embarrassing." She dug her fingers into the wall they leaned against.

Linc covered her hand with his. "It turns you on."

She glanced down at their hands, then up. "The

thought of it never did before. But you..." She trailed off, visibly swallowing. "Is that wrong?"

As badly as she'd been used and abused, she'd still retained a sexual innocence that tore past all his defenses. But even more, she hadn't questioned anything out on the patio, rather she'd trusted him to help her with her desire. He didn't want her holding back now as he was discovering new feelings and yearnings.

He took a breath, catching the scent of her magic sliding out in a light, fragrant mist. "As long as it's something we both want, nothing is wrong between us. Nothing. Are we clear?"

"Yes."

Heat blasted his nerve endings, and his cock throbbed painfully against his pants. "You want to watch me, baby? See how it looks when I stroke my cock, then fist it and pump?" Jesus, the thought of her eyes on him made him burn.

"But what if you can't, uh..."

A dark laugh spilled out. "Everything is different with you. This connection between us goes both ways. I damn near came when I was on my knees with my mouth between your legs."

Her full lips parted on a soft gasp.

He looked around the hallway. "We're not having this conversation here." Quickly he led her into the elevator, up to his fifth-floor suite. Once there, Linc locked the door for privacy.

Unable to think beyond Risa, he slapped his hands on the closed door, trapping her between his biceps. "Now we're talking about it."

She swallowed, her eyes flaring. "We are?"

Did she know how gorgeous she was, wearing nothing but his shirt and enough trust to let him hold her between his arms? That wasn't fear dilating her eyes and quickening her breath. Fear smelled cloying and sick like a dying flower. This scent? Warm, sexy female desire with traces of cinnamon magic.

Risa needed time for her and the souls to acclimate. No sinking his cock into that sweet heat between her thighs. But they could do other things, very sexy dirty things that made his dick beg.

She'd been vulnerable in front of him, trusted him. He could give her the same thing. "Do you want me to strip naked and stroke my cock until I lose control and come?"

✺ 13 ✺

RISA SUCKED IN HER BREATH at the intensity rolling off
Linc as he loomed over her. His eyes locked on her, his
chiseled face tense, huge shoulders and chest filling
her vision, making her feel small and delicate. She
dropped her gaze down his ripped belly to the massive
bulge in his pants.

Her mouth dried. The idea of him naked and
aroused enticed her.

"With your eyes on me, I'll come. Hard."

His voice flowed over her skin and seeped into her
body. Her magic stirred and buzzed with fizzy
excitement.

"But there's a price."

She jerked her gaze up. "What?"

He lifted her hand to his mouth, his warm lips
sliding over her knuckles. "You'll let me kiss you first.
A deep, owning kiss."

Her heart started to pound. "You want to kiss me?"

"I want to kiss you so hard you'll go to sleep
and wake up with the taste of me. No one else, Risa.
Me."

Intensity. She'd never experienced this pull, this
inability to emotionally distance herself from another

person. He had a magnetic effect, tugging her into him. "Is this the soul bond?"

Bronze shimmered in his eyes. "I don't know. But you're ripping me open, making me need more than sex. I need your touch."

Recognition sounded in her like a gong. *Touch.* They'd both had too much of the wrong kind and not enough of the right. She thought of the way he'd held her last night, even after finding out it had been her father who kidnapped and gave him to the bastards who'd caged him. Yet Linc hadn't seen her ugliness. Instead, he'd held her until she fell asleep.

Safe in his arms.

And now he was unfailingly honest in what he needed. A kiss. Touch. Unable to stop herself, she wrapped her hands around Linc's sides. The powerful muscles twitched beneath her palms.

"Kiss me." She tugged him to her.

Linc curled his palm around her nape and lowered his gaze to her lips.

The air between them thickened. Sizzled. Her lips tingled, and her heart thumped.

He stroked his thumb along the sensitive curve of her throat. Arousal rode her nerve endings, pebbling her nipples and warming her belly. She squeezed her thighs together, vividly aware of her nakedness beneath the shirt.

His mouth touched hers, warm velvety lips gliding over hers with a slow exploration while his thumb lazily caressed her jaw.

No one kissed her like this, as if they needed to learn every secret of her mouth. She tracked her hands over his shoulders, absorbing the warm skin stretched over powerful muscles. Bold hunger flickered, and she licked at his mouth.

A groan rumbled against her palm on his chest. He wrapped his arms around her and lifted her off her feet. Pinning her to the wall, he tilted her chin up and consumed her. His tongue dueled with hers, then darted away, exploring and marking her.

Risa shivered as the taste of him hit her tongue, like dark chocolate mixed with real cream and whipped until irresistible. Greed for more pulled out a moan. She'd never have enough of his flavor or the feel of his mouth moving over hers as if he were as starved for her as she was for him. The kiss devoured her.

Until he stroked her nipple through the shirt. Her senses exploded, firing to razor-sharp need. Magic spilled out, rushing around, chasing every touch.

She had no idea how much time passed before the heat and raging need became unbearable. Squirming, the folds between her legs swollen, her clit throbbing, she tore her mouth away and dropped her head back. "Linc."

"Your magic, hell—" He sucked in air. "More than your magic. You. Your taste, the way you feel in my arms. It all feels so damned good. Hot."

"I want more."

His lips quirked. "Right." He set her down and stripped off his pants.

Linc had a thin line of tawny hair feathering down his ripped stomach and leading to his massive cock. Long and thick, the head dark plum, beaded with a clear drop, made her hands itch to touch.

Linc beat her to it, his hand wrapping around his heavy erection, sliding up, then down, his thumb sweeping over the head.

Mesmerized, it took her a second to process what was happening here. She'd let him kiss her, and now he was fulfilling his end by performing.

Like a trained animal who'd gotten a little kindness.

Linc spread his feet, his hand working his dick, his eyes on her. Desperation built there as he jerked harder, his jaw bulging, tendons nearly snarling in their swollen fury. His cock darkened, his thighs bunched with tension.

He slapped his hand against the wall, his arm brushing against hers, his hips pumping. "Have to touch. Bloodlust." It came out a vicious plea.

I need your touch.

His earlier words echoed in her head and snapped her fog. He needed her touch. Overwhelming tenderness and desire collided in her. Risa laid her hands over his.

He stilled, his muscles twitching and eyes cautious. "Risa?"

"I want you to touch me. I want to help you come, to feel you come." It surprised her how true that was. Her magic opened up, streaming to her hands.

"Jesus." He let go of his cock, snapped an arm around her and lifted her, kissed her, his mouth searing hers as he pumped into her hand. Shifting, he spread her legs and pressed her bare sex down on his bunched thigh.

Every pump of his cock drove his thigh against her sensitized, swollen clit. She dropped her head back. "Oh, oh." The sensations ripped through her, his cock in her hands, the heat of his body, being held by him. Riding his thigh.

Her magic swelling, spilling out.

Linc opened his mouth over the curve of her neck, lapping and sucking.

Risa exploded.

His arm around her back tightened. A feral roar spilled from him, and he came, shooting his release over her belly.

"These are the administrative offices."

Risa tried to focus on the sleek reception area, but

the feel of Linc's hand wrapped around hers dominated her consciousness. In the last hour, they'd seen and touched each other intimately, had both rocketed to orgasms, and yet this felt more personal.

When had anyone just held her hand?

"Lincoln. Risa."

She jerked from her thoughts and found herself in the doorway of another office. Hilary rose from behind an oak desk and strode toward them. "Something up?"

"Nope. I'm taking Risa on a tour of the academy." He turned to her. "Hilary is getting this school, and another of our projects, up and running. She's runs our L.C. Group. The top chain of command reports to her."

"What all do you do with the L.C. Group?" She tried to sound intelligent, but the woman intimidated the hell out of Risa.

Hilary said, "We're working to build schools and other resources to help kids and families who don't have any other options."

"Hilary has accomplished miracles."

The woman snorted. "With your money and charm that beguiles people into donating generously."

His grin rolled out slow and roguish. "Don't forget my poker skills."

Hilary turned her gaze on Risa. "He's a card shark and too proud of that sad fact. Maybe you can convince him to put his brilliance to better use. Boy could have been an engineer, scientist or physicist. Instead he plays cards and takes the money of fools."

Linc leaned in and kissed Hilary's cheek. "You love me just the way I am."

"That's your problem, young man, you're too loveable. Now off with you. I have real work to do. I'm going to shoot you some financials I need you to check over." She patted his arm.

"I'll look at them later."

She nodded. "Risa, I'm contacting everyone I know

to see if they've heard anything about a baby turning up unexpectedly. Linc sent me the JPEG of your daughter. We're spreading her picture everywhere."

Risa's stomach clenched. She wanted to be out there looking. Needed to. "I can't do this."

Linc turned to her. "What?"

"Stand around and do nothing, go on a tour of the school like that's more important than Kendall. I have to go out and find her. Maybe if I drive around, I'll feel her."

Linc's shook his head. "I told you—"

"She's right," Hilary broke in.

Linc swung his gaze between the two women. "It's dangerous out there. We don't know if Archer's still awake or hibernating. Rogues are snatching and killing witches. We need to do what Carla told us. Then you can find Kendall with your magic."

"Don't tell me what I need. I don't care." She ripped her hand from his, so damned sick of everyone telling her what she had to do or not do. Didn't they get it? Kendall was in the hands of a demon, his mother, or someone equally scary. "I don't need your permission. If you won't let me use one of your cars, I'll walk." The thought of the baby out there alone burned her stomach, and anxiety snapped at her spine. She spun around and got one step.

"You can use my car."

Hilary's voice stopped her. Pivoting, she whispered past the grateful lump in her throat, "Thank you."

"I'll take you." Linc caught her hand, stalking out of the office.

Risa had to trot to keep up with his long legs fueled by anger. Ten minutes later, after Linc stopped to pick up his gun, they were in the same SUV they'd arrived in, the tension in the car thick and stealing her breath. She glanced over at Linc's jaw. "You're mad."

"No."

"Liar." The word shot out before she could stop it.

"I'm not mad at you." His fingers white-knuckled the steering wheel. "I'm furious that we haven't found the kid. Not here and not back in Glassbreakers, and believe me, Phoenix and Key are tearing that town apart looking for any sign of Archer's mother in case Kendall is with her." Visibly relaxing, he released his death grip on the steering wheel and took her hand. "And I'm worried about you. This is a long shot, Risa. I've had people scouring the city, checking the hospitals, the convention center that's been turned into a temporary shelter, children's welfare system, and morgues."

Risa gasped. "She's not dead!"

"Fuck, sorry. I know that, it was a matter of covering our bases." He squeezed her hand, regret softening his features. "Can you think of any place Archer would stash the baby? Not the Strip. I have hunters getting past the police blockade to check, so we'd be going over the same territory."

She eyed his hand holding hers. Would he do that if he was mad? "What about the condo Archer had?"

"Ram checked that unit and the entire building."

"I don't know." Tears burned her eyes, but she blinked and fought to steel herself. She couldn't fall apart. "Okay, residential areas outside the Strip? If you drive through neighborhoods and she's nearby, I'll feel her."

"Are you going to use magic? You know what happened earlier."

"No. I mean, it's more of a passive magic." She gazed out the window as they headed through the town toward the Strip, passing military vehicles, police and news crews, but not many civilians. "Kendall's in danger, so if I get close enough, my magic will react with the compulsion to cast my shield." She explained how it happened with Ginny and that it was stronger with Kendall. "It shouldn't trigger the souls or problems." Biting her lip, she added, "Even if this is a long shot, I have to try. She's scared." God, it hurt to think of Kendall distressed and alone. Or what if she was hurt? Hungry? Sick?

"If you feel her, tell me. All I need is her location, then I swear we'll get her for you, Risa. But I can't have you there. If Archer's around, he may feel your witchcraft. We have to be damned careful."

She winced, drawing back in the seat. She'd seen Archer kill Blythe and others, and the destruction he'd caused at Linc's house. "You think I'm taking a foolish risk." But he wouldn't let her do it alone. These hunters protected witches, and on top of that, he needed her to break his curse. She'd put him in a no-win situation.

He turned into a housing track less than a mile from the Strip and close to an industrial area. "What was foolish was trying to convince you to go on a tour of the academy. I wanted to..." He trailed off, the muscles in his forearms knotted.

"What?" Risa leaned toward him as small houses slid by.

After checking the mirrors and guiding the car around a corner, he said, "Spend time with you. Try to make you smile, maybe hear you laugh." He turned back to the road. "I can't even take you out to dinner, treat you like you matter. Instead I'm hiding you in a secure location and waiting for you to get well enough to fuck you." He ground his jaw, a vein in his forehead throbbing. "You're the one woman who can save me, and I don't know what you sound like when you laugh. Or what your dreams are. Hell, I don't know your favorite food or what kind of movies you like."

The disgust and anger in his voice reverberated in the car. Her heart swelled. Searching the granite lines of his profile, she tried to understand. "You were trying to get to know me. And share a part of you by showing me the school." Because he truly wanted to? Or because Carla told them that the souls needed to learn to trust Linc and the bird?

"Pretty damned selfish considering your baby is missing." He rubbed his thumb over the back of her hand, but he checked the mirrors and streets in a constant search for any trouble.

"Twinkies," she blurted out.

"What?"

No man had cared enough to find out these things. "Twinkies are my favorite food. Although I like those Sno Ball things, and some days, I just have to have a Ding Dong. But Twinkies are the best thing ever."

He shoved up his sunglasses, his eyes shining with suspicion. "You're screwing with me, right? Like claiming magic shrinkage made your tank top tight?"

To her surprise, a grin touched her mouth. "Careful, dude. Magical shrinkage is real. I could show you next time you get an erection."

His eyes narrowed. "Next time? Sugar, I've been hard for you since the first time I saw you. There's no magic strong enough to shrink that." He jerked his head around, eyeing a young man walking out of a yellow-trimmed house. When the guy got a backpack out of the car and went back in the house, Linc relaxed. "Twinkies? Seriously? No one actually eats those things."

"I do. Growing up, we had chefs who served fancy gourmet food. It wasn't until recently that I discovered Twinkies." Talking to Linc distracted her from the sinking realization that her shield magic stayed quiet, not a blip of reaction. Kendall wasn't on this street. "She's not here."

He pulled his mouth tight. "We'll keep going as long as we don't run into trouble. But once this is over,

I'm taking you out for real dessert. Since you like cream filling, maybe an eclair or cannoli."

Risa closed her eyes at the longing that swirled up unexpectedly. She could almost picture it, her, Linc and Kendall at a little outdoor café, trying desserts, giving the baby tiny tastes of the creamy center. She had to stop, no fantasies. Getting the conversation off her, she recalled some of what Hilary had said about Linc and asked, "So you're a numbers guy?"

He shrugged. "I didn't have much to do in my cage when I wasn't training or...other things."

Other things? Her stomach clenched as more houses passed by.

Before she could ask, he went on, "My handlers and trainers would talk about bets, odds, statistics of the fighters, and I listened. Eventually I started calculating them for myself. It passed the time. And it made me a better fighter."

"How?"

"Mental acuity, calculating the distance to punch or kick, everything is based on math." He eyed her. "Your turn. What was your favorite subject in school?"

She wrinkled her nose. "I didn't go to school, I had private tutors. It was boring, but I guess music was my favorite subject." She didn't want to talk about herself. "Did you go to regular school? Was math your favorite subject?"

He snorted. "Yeah, I went until I was taken. Liked math, had lots of friends, but I'd say getting into trouble was my favorite subject."

She eyed the next row of houses in the bright sunshine and felt nothing. No sign of Kendall. Quashing her disappointment, she focused on her curiosity about Linc. "Trouble for what?" Risa didn't get into much trouble until her mom died. She'd been spoiled, but she'd been compliant, wanting to please.

"My mouth or fighting."

"You got in fights before..." She trailed off, hating to bring up that dark time in his life.

His mouth tensed. "We were trailer trash, my mom a junkie who did anything for a fix. People talked, kids repeated what they heard, and I defended her. Every damn time."

Bitterness coated his words. The mother he'd obviously loved and defended with his fists hadn't defended her son. No, she'd sold him to monsters. "What happened to your mom? Did you ever see her again?"

He shook his head. "She overdosed not long after I was taken. Hilary found out for me."

Sadness for him filled her. He'd lost so much. "I'm sorry."

"I don't know how you get me to talk about this shit. Usually women are telling me their life stories."

Warmth spread through her, combined with uneasy guilt. Here in the quiet car, just the two of them sharing, it was too intimate. She couldn't hold his gaze and turned to the window. They'd hit the end of the second tract of homes. "Still no sign of Kendall."

A few seconds ticked by with no answer. "Linc?"

His jaw tensed, and his stare locked on to the review mirror. "Trouble."

She opened her mouth to ask when the car shot forward so fast, the seat belt locked. Risa's heart jumped, and her pulse thumped. Frantically, she craned her head.

"We're being followed. Hold on." He spun the wheel, the SUV leaning precariously, wheels squealing. "Get my phone, call Baron. He's on my contact list."

Risa fumbled the phone out of the cup holder, scrolled contacts and hit call.

"Baron." A gruff voice came through the speaker. Risa held it up to Linc's face.

"I've got a tail," he explained. "One car, two men I can see, guns. I need them off my ass. Risa's in the SUV with me."

"Location?"

Linc rattled it off.

Bang!

The back end of the SUV fishtailed.

"Fuck," Linc snarled, straightening out the car. "Taking gunfire."

"On our way," Baron said.

Risa dropped the phone and twisted around to look out the back. "Shit!" A huge man leaned halfway out the passenger window of a black Dodge Charger, firing a handgun. Ripping off her seat belt, she glanced up. Sunroof. Good. "Give me your gun, open the sunroof."

Linc took a corner and shot down a street lined with industrial buildings. "Get your seat belt back on!"

Another shot shattered the back window. No time to argue with Linc. Risa summoned enough magic to pull his gun from his holster, then used her witchcraft to open the sunroof. She scrambled up and anchored one foot on the center console. Not the best stance, but all she could manage. She raised the weapon and sighted the shooter.

"Risa! Jesus Christ, get down!"

The man hanging out the window saw her and aimed.

As she faced off with the gunman, reality ground into slow motion while her thoughts sped up. Did these rogues have Kendall or know where she was? Had they hurt the baby? Cold determination iced her veins. She wouldn't die. She and Linc would live to find Kendall. *Sight, breathe, squeeze the trigger.* The gun boomed in her hand.

The bullet slammed into the man's shoulder, the bullet's impact violently jerking the upper half of his body before he disappeared inside the vehicle. She dropped down to the seat, ears ringing and the smell of burnt gunpowder stinging her nose.

"I hit him." She held the gun on her thigh, trembling.

"Hang on." Linc jerked the SUV around another corner. "A truck just picked up the chase."

She shook her head, trying to dislodge the roaring. Wait, that growl of multiple engines was real and getting louder. Turning, she blinked. A half dozen or more motorcycles bore down on them and the truck. "Linc! More rogues!"

"The guys on motorcycles are friends. The man you called, Baron? That's him and his crew."

As she watched, the men on the choppers fired guns at the rogues. "Kendall. What if they know where she is?"

"Baron knows what to do. They'll try to take one alive to find out about Kendall and Archer. Now get your damned seat belt on."

Numbly, she obeyed. Buildings, signs and the few cars on the road blurred as Linc broke every known traffic law. She eyed the gun in her hand. It shook. Hell, her whole body trembled. "Do you think I killed him?"

He laid his fingers over hers. "You hit him in the shoulder. You have to shred a rogue's heart to kill him."

The warmth bleeding off him made her realize how cold she was. Shock? Fear? Memories of her father killing, the sounds of the gun, the blood and horror, mixed into everything else.

"But you damn near killed me. Don't ever scare me like that again."

His voice chased out the past, while his solid strength and warmth helped calm her. "Told you I could shoot." She'd trained diligently at the gun range.

Linc's eyes glinted shards of gold approval. "Baby,

it was fucking awesome. But you scare me that way again, and I swear to God, I will buy every Twinkie, Sno Ball and Ding Dong in the world and burn them. Then I'll buy the company that makes them and shut down production. Hear me?"

All her fear, terror and nausea boiled up into a near-hysterical laughter. As they left the chaos and danger behind, she laughed harder. Probably not sane, but the release of tension felt pretty damn good. Finally regaining control, she caught her breath and said, "You sure you want to threaten my Twinkies after I just shot a man?"

Linc grinned. "I like to live dangerously."

After dropping Risa off at the school, Linc headed back out to help Baron and his men deal with the rogues. In all they'd killed six, and the two they managed to question first didn't have any helpful information. Arriving back at the academy, Linc tracked Risa down in the infirmary, where she was helping Carla and Ginny get the medical wing set up to treat any injured witches they rescued.

He found her in the six-bed ward, bent over and smoothing a sheet over a twin bed. Damn, she had a sweet ass in those camo pants. The image of her in the SUV, standing up through the sunroof, hair flying as she aimed and shot the rogue filled his head.

Scary as fuck and hot as Hades. Drawn to her, he strode in and wrapped his hands around her hips.

"Oh!" She turned, her hair flying out behind her. "I didn't hear you." Surprise widened her eyes, then concern edged in. "Did you find out anything about Kendall?"

"No." He hated failing her, causing her even one more minute of agony. "We questioned two of them, but they knew nothing about a baby. Or anything new about Archer."

She wilted, dropping her arms and looking lost. "I'm not sorry for trying, but I'm sorry I put you and your friends in danger."

That sucker-punched him. "Baby, I wasn't in danger. If you hadn't been with me, I'd have stopped the car and killed those rogues on the spot. But they're like cockroaches. If two were there, I knew more would be coming. I couldn't risk being involved in a fight and more of them arriving and attempting to snatch you."

"I can defend myself pretty well with a gun."

His mouth curved. "I noticed. You looked like a sizzling-hot warrior witch right out of my erotic dreams. If I hadn't been distracted trying to keep us alive, I'd have dragged you into my arms and kissed you. Long and hard." He sucked in a breath as his groin tightened and need burned low in his guts. He dropped his gaze to her sensual mouth. "Still want to. But I'm not."

"No?"

Color chased out the worried pallor, warming her skin. The pulse at the base of her throat fluttered. Oh she wanted him. Despite all the shit going down, they were building a real connection, one that should help the souls to get used to him and the falcon. Before he could change his mind and kiss her, he said, "You said your favorite subject in school was music, right?"

She raised her eyebrows. "Yeah."

"Come on, then. I want to show you the music rooms." He tugged her hand, leading her out of the infirmary.

"You have a music room here? At the school?" Enthusiasm bubbled over as they went outside, followed a sidewalk curving through grass and plants. Linc led her past the first two-story building. "This is the math and science wing. It has classrooms, labs, computer science rooms. Everything is state of the art." He couldn't keep the note of pride out of his voice.

Risa stopped, tilting her head up. "You really care about this school."

The L.C. Group projects were his passion, his way of making sure kids had options. If he did this and made a difference, then he was more than the feral brand on his back. But what surprised him was how much he wanted Risa to know this about him. He'd never had the urge to share this side of himself before. "I care about the kids."

"What you're doing here, it's important, Linc. You escaped after having your childhood ripped away, got a second chance and did all this. I do this little thing trying to protect women from abusers, but this..." She trailed off, looking around. "You're doing so much more."

Aside from Hilary, no woman's words had ever meant so much. But he had to disagree about one thing. "The work you do is important, Risa. I saw how fierce you are in that car today."

She swung her gaze back to his.

The second her gaze hit his, his chest hollowed with a whoosh. The air between them sizzled, and his heart rate shot up. He didn't have words for this...connection. It was almost too intense.

He turned, breaking the moment by taking her into the second two-story building. Risa showed mild interest as they passed by the English and language departments, visual arts and theater, but perked up as they entered the large music room at the end.

Her eyes sparkled, and she rushed inside to run her fingers over the drum kits and guitars before moving to the piano and dropping onto the bench.

Leaning on the side of it, he watched the way she

caressed the keys. "You play piano? Took lessons with one of your fancy tutors?"

"It's been years."

"Think you can remember anything?"

"Let's see." She struck a few keys with her right hand, and a few more with her left.

"How many years since you actually played?"

"Too long." She flicked her gaze up. "Maybe I should try this later when you're not around."

Yeah, he wasn't buying it. She'd been too excited when she saw this room. Leaning on his forearm, he took in the flush on her face and the fluttering pulse at the base of her throat. Excitement. Little witch couldn't bluff worth shit. He was definitely learning her tells.

"Sugar, I didn't win a fortune in high-stakes poker by letting a pretty face and innocent blue eyes distract me. You're sandbagging, Twinkie girl."

Risa dropped her head back and laughed. The sound bounced off the acoustics in the room and punched him in the chest. Before he could recover, she laid her fingers on the keys.

The notes rose from the piano, the familiar melody beginning softly, then building with restrained power. She commanded the music and him. Helpless against her lure, he moved to stand behind her shoulder.

Her hands flowed over the keys in a graceful dance so compelling and intimate, he felt every touch like a caress.

Cinnamon. The scent of her magic rode the notes, whispering over his skin in perfect time with every beat she played. Even his heart rate shifted to match the pulse of building music. Dual cravings exploded, the need to cut her or fuck her. Lust for her blood seared his veins, and his cock swelled with the drive to slam into her and mark her.

Mine. She's mine. I could—

The bird screeched in his head. A streak of pain ripped down both his arms. The bird went to work chomping on his nerves again. But damned if it didn't snap the feral shit out of his brain.

To calm himself, he laid his hand on her shoulder. The contact sent a shudder through him, quieting the sick hunger for witch blood.

She looked up, her fingers slowing.

"Keep going." Even as the music and magic ruthlessly shredded his emotional defenses and stripped him raw, it also fed the most primitive part of him. Both rousing and soothing the beast in him. It didn't make sense, but he wanted more. "Please."

Her smile lit up his veins. Then her eyes slid closed as she sank back into the power of her playing.

Linc pressed his thighs to her back, feeling her move as the music and magic wove through the room and deep into his very essence.

Finally the last note died away, leaving him with aftershocks.

Looking down into her eyes, he tried to catch his breath and recover his equilibrium. It wasn't just the music. It was the depth of the song, "Bohemian Rhapsody". To Linc, that song represented his mother killing the boy he was, the man he might have become, that day when she chose her life as a druggie over her life as his mother. "How are you that good? Where did you learn?"

"My mother. She was a pianist before she married my father. I played before I walked. I'm not as good as she was, though."

"Your mom was better than that?"

"She came from a family of music witches."

After shifting around the bench, he sat next to her and laid his hand on her thigh to keep his bloodlust down. "What's that?" He wanted to know everything about her.

"It's a little bit vampirish." She flashed him a grin. "Basically, they harness the emotion of their audience, feed it into their music and return it, enhancing the emotion. The bigger the crowd, the more powerful the experience."

"Is that what you did just now? With me?"

"I have a minor ability. But with you..." Her eyes shimmered with vulnerability. "It's more. When you talked about your mom earlier in the car and I could feel your pain, your sense of betrayal...it came out in this song. I don't know how to explain it."

Linc leaned away for a second, needing distance. "Damn." This woman saw too much of him, digging into places he wasn't fully ready to share. "I don't know what you're doing to me."

She dropped her stare to her hands. "I wasn't trying to do anything. It's just what I felt. My mom and I played, and then after she died, it was the only place I could feel her. Even after I understood what she'd done by helping my father assassinate people, she was still my mom. I missed her." Her fingers caressed the keys.

Oh yeah, he understood that.

Shaking that off, she added, "I used to play for Kendall too. She's just old enough to sit on my lap and bang the keys. Or sometimes, when she doesn't feel well, the music soothes her."

The desolation in her voice ached in him. "Hey, we're going to find her. Baron's crew are looking for the baby too. I've offered a twenty-five-thousand-dollar reward for information. We'll find her, Risa."

"Twenty-five..." Her eyes widened. "I can sell my trailer. It's worth more than that. I'll pay you back."

No bluffing now, she meant that. "Forget it. A child doesn't have a price tag. And you aren't going to live in some trailer when this is over. We'll get you a house, a nice place for Kendall to grow up." Somewhere he knew they would be safe. Cared for. With security. And some rogue-eating dogs. Damn it, the thought of her out of his life and protection didn't sit well.

Her back stiffened, and she shook her head while twisting her hands. "Don't, Linc. Just...don't. Once I have Kendall and your curse is broken, whatever you think you're feeling now? It'll be gone."

Pushing her hair back over her shoulder, he studied her profile. She really didn't trust him, and why should she? Hadn't he told her, clearly, they weren't anything more than sex? Had she ever had more than sex? Thinking of Kendall, he had to ask. "Your baby's father, did he leave you?" That thought ticked him off.

"I don't want to talk about him."

Ugly possessiveness rooted in his chest. "Were you in love with him?" *Calm down.* He'd lost it with her earlier today, been a complete fucktard.

"I've never been in love. Not ever doing that. Saw it destroy my mother." She stroked the keys of the piano. "Kendall's father was nobody, just a man I thought I wanted to try to have sex with, be normal. But I'm not, okay? And he wanted nothing to do with us."

Relief coursed through him. Only Linc had made her feel safe enough to experience desire and pleasure.

Turning bleak eyes on him, she added, "Kendall's just a baby. What if she's not eating? Or scared? Cold? She could be teething again, and it makes her cranky and cries. What if they hurt her?" Tears welled in Risa's eyes.

She broke his fucking heart. Wrapping an arm around her, he pulled her into his side and kissed her hair. "Don't forget, everyone in Glassbreakers is looking too. They're ripping apart the lives of Archer and his mother, looking for any clues."

Taking a shuddering breath, she lifted her gaze to his. "The souls are calmer now. I was fine when we fooled around. What if we have sex now? Finish the bond, and try to find her again? Please."

Linc's cock jumped, and need clamped him. But Carla had warned him against it, and he believed her. "We didn't try to harness your magic, and the falcon wasn't helping you control it." Instead the creature had basked in the feel of it, like a cat in a sun spot.

"I don't know what else to do."

Yeah, he'd seen her in action, Risa wasn't one to sit around and wait for others to solve her problems. Something else he liked about her, except he didn't want her in danger. "You're doing it. Plus rogues are snatching witches all over the place—we think they're using their blood to replenish the spawn's power."

Layers of horror filled her eyes. "In his hibernation state?"

He stroked her arm, needing the contact. "There's been nothing from him since he burned my house. So yeah, that's what we think at this point. Tonight we're beginning a grid search, operating on the theory that Archer needs to be close to where he spawned. We're hoping to rescue witches too, and some will be injured. You can help heal them, and ask them if they know or heard anything about Kendall." He wasn't placating her. Witches might not be sure enough of Linc and the other hunters to tell them, but they'd trust another witch who was helping them heal.

"I want to help, and asking the witches you rescue from rogues is a good idea." She tightened her hand on his arm. "But we have to find Kendall before Archer wakes."

Linc could feel her panic building, and so did the bird. The creature flexed his wings in Linc's skin.

"I feel that." Wonder filled her voice. "The bird. His wings are brushing my arms." She pressed between her ribs. "And here, like an internal caress."

He pulled her closer into his side. "And the souls?"

"Uneasy, but he's not harnessing my magic, more like soaring gently above it, his wings barely causing a ripple in the surface."

He opened his mouth, when his phone shrilled urgently.

"What's that?"

"Alarm that a witch has been taken or located." Pulling it out, he glanced at the message. "We have a lead on where witches are being kept. I have to go."

"What about your bloodlust?"

"I can handle it as long as I don't touch their blood. I have to do this, Risa. I have to." Once, he'd been forced to do reprehensible things. Unspeakable things. Saving witches eased his guilt.

Rising, he looked down at her. Every muscle and tendon fought him, trying to resist leaving her. The need to pick her up and take her to his bed pounded in his spine.

No. He wrenched himself back and headed to the door.

≋ 14 ≋

THE SCENT OF COPPER AND sulfur hung on the night air over the Las Vegas Strip. The whole area was on lockdown, patrolled by police and National Guard to prevent looting of the hotels, shops and a nearby mall. Reporters hovered at the crime-scene barriers.

Linc ignored them all, shielding himself to appear invisible. Just like the rogues did to move through the Strip, unbeknownst to the authorities. The rouges had dragged in a few witches too. He and Eli had been searching each hotel, looking for more rogues, rescuing witches if they were alive, and hunting for clues to where the spawn had holed up. Ram was checking out the restaurants and shops, while Baron and his men had spread out to the surrounding areas and known rogue hangouts.

All of them called in Sutton, with his immunity to witch blood, to move any injured witches. He'd been taking them back to the academy infirmary.

"Ground zero," Linc said, staring at the blackened rubble of the Mystique Hotel where Archer's demon side had spawned.

"It burned to the ground." Eli's voice floated from

the vicinity of Linc's left shoulder. "Even the steel beams are obliterated."

"Hellfire. It destroyed my house too."

"From what I hear, you'd be dead if your witch hadn't cast her shield. She must have some powerful magic to stand up against the hellfire that melted the steel beams of this hotel."

Just the memory of her magic made him shudder in a violent combination of pleasure, pride and an ugly craving for her blood that sickened him to his soul. But Eli was right, Risa was extraordinary, and yet so very fragile at the same time. "Ram and I would be for sure. Sutton has as much immortality as Wing Slayer can grant us, but there are things that can kill mated hunters."

"Like the Immortal Death Dagger."

"Exactly. But Quinn Young and his daggers are in Glassbreakers. Our problem is the spawn. Once he wakes, he can exterminate us with that hellfire."

A hand landed on his shoulder. "Get mated, dude. Fast. It's your best chance if we're forced to fight a demon spawn."

He turned toward Eli. "What about you? You need to find your soul mirror."

Silence hung like a ticking bomb before Eli said, "Ginny's father destroyed my connection with my soul mirror. For that alone, I'd kill him if I could. Savi's alone out there. I was her lifeline and...Fuck."

The growl in Eli's voice raised the hairs on Linc's arms. Sutton and Eli were the quietest, but there was a fierce and primal alpha creature in Eli, one they all recognized. "You met your soul mirror?" Linc couldn't quite believe it since he'd never said a word before now.

"When she was six and crawled into my arms in the dream world."

Christ, the raw possessiveness in Eli's voice

vibrated against the shield creating the illusion invisibility. And who the hell was Ginny's father? They'd all been told not to ask, but Ginny was more than human. Since he couldn't inquire about that, he focused on the other part of Eli's revelation. "So you haven't met your soul mirror in person? But in some dream?" How did that work? They had to touch the witch to find out if they were soul mirrors.

"Linc, Eli." Ram's commanding voice came through their Bluetooth, cutting off their conversation.

"Here," Linc answered. "Go."

"We got intel. Group of witches transported from California are being held in the fight club."

Ice-cold rage seared his veins. "The club I fought in a couple days ago? We searched it earlier after seeing Baron. Archer's not hibernating in there."

"Same club. One of Baron's men, Vice, is texting me and Baron from inside. He overheard that these are just a few of the witches rounded up and brought to Vegas."

"They likely took the remaining witches to Archer, wherever that sick fuck is holed up." Sutton's voice came through the earpiece. "We won't get to them in time. We need to rescue the ones we know about."

"Exactly," Ram said. "Meet us at the fight club."

Linc broke into a run for the car, followed by Eli. In less than a minute, Linc peeled out, heading for the fight club.

Ram continued on with the intel. "According to Vice, the witches are chained in the main room, dragged one at a time into the cage for the rogues to fight over. Winner can either kill them in the cage or take them to a private room." Ram took an audible breath. "Three dead witches so far."

A wicked burn simmered in Linc's veins, the craving sparking to life. The thought of all those witches in one place, enough powerful blood to...*No.*

As he rounded a corner, he shook his head to clear the depraved craving. "What's the plan?" Ram always had a plan.

"Baron's going in the front to demand a chance in the cage to win one of the witches. That will help distract the rogue's attention while we get inside to attack."

"How many men in there?" Eli asked.

"Vice counted thirty."

"Against us four," Linc clarified.

"Six," Ram corrected. "Baron and Vice will be there, and Baron has a half dozen more of his hunters on their way."

"Okay, we just arrived. Parking a block away." Once he and Eli were out of the car, Linc outlined the layout of the club from his memory. "The front is a big space with a cage surrounded on one side by tiers of benched seating. The other side is a gym area where I'm assuming the witches are chained up. There's one hallway that leads to the back of the club. Opening off that are smaller training/sparring rooms, bathrooms, lockers rooms and a small kitchen area."

"I'll take the roof access to the locker rooms," Ram said. "Once Baron goes in the front, we need to get in, clean house and get the girls out."

"Agreed." Linc and Eli covered the remaining distance to the club. "I'll take the back door. Eli, use the side window by the gym. That should put you closest to the witches. Can you hold off the rogues?"

"I have my whip, gun, knife and a whole lot of fury. No one hurts a woman, human or witch, on my watch."

Amen. Linc had seen what Eli could do with his whip. Terrifying and beautiful. Also hurt like a bitch, and Eli wasn't shy about using the tail when he was pissed. So yeah, Eli would take care of the girls.

Leaving Linc free to do what he did best—kill. Once

he reached the back of the club, he quietly tested the door. Unlocked. "Everyone in place?"

Several affirmatives assured him they were ready.

"Waiting for a text from Vice." Ram's voice came across the Bluetooth in a bare whisper. Rogues lost their souls when they killed a witch, but they retained their supersized hearing, sight, speed and strength.

Linc scanned the parking lot through the darkness. Even the streetlights were off. A generator hummed relentlessly, providing electricity to the club.

Where was Archer holed up? Had to be someplace they could take witches to him and slaughter them for their blood. Linc knew this town. They'd checked every damned place he could think of. So where?

"Baron's in, go," Ram ordered.

Freeing the blade strapped to one thigh, Linc opened the door to roaring voices, the sounds of flesh hitting flesh, and frightened, crying women. Keeping his shield around him, he focused on the long, dingy hallway, cement floors and a bulky man charging him. Clearly he'd seen the door open.

Letting his shield drop, Linc grabbed the guard, shoved his knife into his heart and twisted. After heaving the dead rogue in a storage closet, he pulled his shield around him again and moved silently down the hallway. The smell of copper and witch blood rode over the cement-deep scent of sweat, adrenaline and dead rodents.

He checked in a kitchen, sparring room, bathroom...Fuck. Blood was splattered over the puke-green tile, and on the floor lay a young witch's body, her face contorted, eyes open and vacant. Too late. The smell of her dying blood seared his nose and throat. Backing out, he closed the door. He couldn't help her. She belonged to her Ancestors in Summerland now. But hopefully he could save the others.

Their soft crying and chanting flowed down the hall like a river of horror and pain. *Block it*. Instead, he honed in on the sounds of fighting and the roars of the frenzied men. They were his target.

A sound froze him. The door to the locker rooms opened and closed. He saw nothing but smelled a tinge of electricity. Ram. "I'm here," Linc whispered.

"Behind you," Ram acknowledged. "Go."

As Linc neared the front, conversations blasted down the hallway.

"I've got two thousand reasons why I'm next in the cage." Baron's voice rose over the din.

"Bullshit. I was here first," another snarled. "I'm next in the cage."

A shot exploded. Women screamed. Men roared. The noise was so loud, the building shook.

Linc materialized and raced out of the hallway into the gym area. He took in a half-dozen witches on their knees, hands cuffed behind them and attached to a thick chain bolted into the wall.

Eli yanked his knife out of a dead man, then spun. His whip lashed out, snapping around the wrist of another man approaching with a gun.

The weapon clattered to the ground.

Ram sprinted over to help guard the witches and kill their kidnappers.

Linc checked the rest of the room. Baron and another man fought a thick group of men, but the raised octagon cage grabbed Linc's attention. Two hunters struggled on the mat, blood gushing out from various wounds. A bleeding witch huddled against the side of the cage.

The smell of her blood hit Linc so hard, he stumbled toward the octagon, gaze fixed on the witch. He didn't care about her straight brown hair, torn clothes, desperate expression. Only the blood flowing from the cuts on her leg, arm and torso. He recognized the crosscuts—one leg, opposite arm and middle. The pain caused most witches to lose their ability to control their magic.

Crosscuts made them prey.

A sudden roar in the crowd jarred his concentration from the witch. The bigger hunter rose as the victor and honed in on the witch.

"No!" She jumped up and tried to run.

The man caught her hair, yanked her back and slashed his knife across her thigh.

Sutton materialized and gripped the cage door. "Locked, damn it!"

Linc fought the fog of craving and rushed forward, killing the two rogues attacking Sutton. The scent of blood and madness choked him. In a fast move, he ripped a couple small, thin knives from his calf holster and threw them dead center into the hearts of two more rogues.

The witch screamed.

Linc's veins throbbed. Bloodlust burned his guts, sizzling his skin. Everything in him strained, desperate for the power-laden witch blood. He inhaled then froze at another scent infiltrating the air.

Sulfur.

That jarred him back to reality. Going utterly cold, he scanned the room. Earth witches didn't smell like sulfur, demons did. Was Archer here after all?

A second later, Sutton snapped the lock on the cage and ripped it open.

But where was the source of the sulfur smell? Linc searched over the crowd, until he reached the highest bleacher.

"Oh fuck."

"Archer?" Sutton asked Linc as he leapt into the cage, dragged the rogue off the witch and killed him.

"Quinn Young." The dark-haired, dark-eyed leader of the rogues back in Glassbreakers. Linc stared at him, trying to process it. Young held the black immortal death dagger that gave him the ability to kill mated hunters. What the hell was he doing in Vegas? Young drew his arm back in a blur.

Sutton jumped down, the witch in his arms. "Shit." He dived, slamming both him and the profusely bleeding witch on top of Linc.

Thrown back, he crashed to the floor. A second later, the fierce and wild power-kick of witch blood blew through him.

Fucking amazing!

Dimly aware that Sutton had gotten up, Linc wrapped his arms around the witch, turning her against the base of the cage.

His.

Chaos exploded around him.

After Linc left with the other hunters, Risa went to the infirmary to help Carla and Ginny. As the night wore on, she ached from exhaustion, and her head throbbed. They had three injured witches, one of them six months pregnant. The woman had lost a lot of blood, and both Risa and Carla were taking turns feeding her magic in the small private room to keep the baby alive while she healed.

Right now, Carla was helping the other two witches in the bigger, six-bed ward. The medical infirmary for the academy was well-equipped, even boasting of sleeping rooms if staff needed to stay in the building.

But witches were very different from mortals. Most had severe allergies to synthetic medications, so traditional medicine hurt more than helped. Risa looked over at the woman's pale face. What was she, maybe thirty? By the time Sutton had brought her in, she'd been unconscious and barely breathing, with cuts everywhere. It'd been hideous. So much blood and horror.

But the baby hung in there.

"Risa."

Jerking from her thoughts, she focused on Ginny. The young woman had been a powerhouse through the last hours, physically moving the injured witches, bringing Risa and Carla supplies, like healing herbs and poultices, before they could even ask. It was uncanny.

"Tea and a sandwich." Ginny set the steaming mug on the table, picked the sandwich up off the plate and held it out. "It's not great, but you can eat it one-handed."

Gratefully, Risa took it without even bothering to look at what it was. The life-sustaining magic she provided for the baby required her to keep her hand on the mother. "Thank you, Ginny. You must be tired too."

The girl sat on the bed. "Nah. I'm pretty strong."

"I noticed. I couldn't lift a six-month-pregnant woman." But Ginny made it look easy. She bit into her sandwich. "Chicken salad?"

"Yep. Protein, calories and some herbs to help your magic and the pain."

"There's not much pain now." Not like when repairing the cuts. Pushing in healing magic forced the pain out of the patient and into Risa. It'd been brutal, feeling every cut. But her chakras had managed to break it down and get rid of it pretty quickly. "She's doing better. Her magic is getting strong enough to work with mine. How are the other two?"

"Awake. Scared. Carla's calming them. They're two friends who went shopping together and were walking to their car when they were snatched."

"Thank God the guys found them." They'd been cut but nowhere near as badly as the pregnant witch.

"One of the girls alerted the Circle Witches emergency system."

"What's that?"

"Circle Witches are an online group that witches belong to," Ginny said. "I don't know a lot, obviously, since I'm not a witch. But Sutton set up an alarm with cell phones, so a witch in trouble can alert the system. Sutton can track their phone through GPS and hopefully find them. Anyway, these women had time to send an emergency alert, and Sutton tracked their phones. The guys caught two rogues on the street transporting them."

Risa dropped her legs, keeping her hand on her patient while leaning forward. "Where were they taking the witches? Maybe Kendall is there."

Ginny touched her arm. "They don't know. Eli, my brother, said the rogues died in the fight. But they're all looking for your baby. Linc is determined to find her."

Her flare of bright hope wilted, and exhaustion returned. Risa took another bite of the sandwich. "Have you known Linc long?"

"For almost a year. I work at Axel of Evil, the nightclub the guys all hang out at back in Glassbreakers. Linc is a handsome charmer on the surface, but beneath that, he's deep and deadly." She shook her head. "But most women don't see that. All they want is the suave, charming gambler to take them on brag-worthy dates." Ginny looked around the small room. "Like this academy. Linc never said a word to any of us about this place. A boarding school for lost kids."

Risa dropped her gaze to her tea. "He deserves more than superficial dates who don't take the time to know him." *Right, and you're so much better. Lying to him, to all of them.*

Ginny smiled. "He has you."

Not wanting her regrets to show, Risa quickly checked the pregnant witch and could feel more of her magic, a very good sign. Shifting back to Ginny, she changed the subject. "So you and Ram? That's complicated."

"It's impossible. I'm not what he needs, but I can't leave him."

The sadness in Ginny's voice tore through Risa. "You love him." Was love worth this?

"I'm going to end up causing his death. He needs his soul-mirror witch, not me." Ginny closed her eyes, her hands fisting. "Maybe that's what he wants. For me to feel that agony of knowing I killed the man I love."

Confused, Risa asked, "Ram? If he loves you, he wouldn't want you to suffer." Right? It wasn't like Risa had a good example of love.

Ginny opened her eyes, and for a second the murky hazel cleared to a blinding jewel green. "No. Not Ram. My sire."

Sire? "Like your father?"

"Yep." She sighed. "I'm forbidden from telling you who, or what, he is."

So she wasn't mortal, or at least not entirely. As much as Risa wanted to know more about this mystery sire, she had to respect Ginny's lines. "How did you and Ram get involved?"

"We were friends. I had learned to keep myself separate from everyone else, except with Eli."

"Why?"

"Because I never knew when they'd be ripped away. My father wanted me to grow up feeling every human emotion possible. He often engineered things. For instance, if I had a best friend in second grade, she would get a new best friend and dump me. Another time, I was excited to get a white little dog, and he got sick and died. Just so I'd feel the loss."

A wave of empathy compelled Risa to set down her tea and touch Ginny's leg. "That's awful. I'm so sorry. But then you met Ram?"

Her face softened. "Yeah. He'd come into the club after hours and we'd talk. Laugh. And I wanted him, desperately, but I knew that was what my father wanted, for me to have sex with a man I cared about."

Risa pulled back. "That's twisted. Almost as twisted as my father. Where are these insanely overprotective fathers everyone talks about? I sure haven't met one."

"Wait until you meet Key. His mate, Roxy, is close to six months pregnant, and believe me, he's going to take insanely protective to a whole new level." Warming to her topic, she went on, "And there's Axel. He has a little sister, Hannah. She must be five or six now. Axel would kill or die for her. Oh, and Joe, he and Morgan have a son—"

Risa laughed, holding up her hand in surrender. "Okay, I get it. So how did you and Ram end up as more than friends?"

"My father threatened my brother—"

"Eli, right?" Trying to keep all the new people in her life straight required a flowchart. She'd seen the man with incredible light green eyes around the academy but hadn't talked to him yet.

"Yep, Eli and I have the same mother, different fathers. Anyway, I had no choice. To protect Eli I seduced Ram. And now he loves me, and that love may kill him."

Sudden sadness stole Risa's breath, and she squeezed her eyes shut. She had no one. No parents; her baby hadn't survived to be born; her one friend, Blythe, was dead; Kendall was in Archer's clutches.

She hated her mix of longing and jealousy that Ginny had love. Real love. Ram was willing to die to be with Ginny.

While she and Linc were using each other to get what they needed.

"Risa?"

Forcing her eyes open, she focused on the woman confiding in her. This wasn't about her, but Ginny and her fight to be with the man she loved. "Just thinking. So the problem with Ram is the electrical energy in the thunderbird tattoo, right?"

"It's going to kill him. It gets worse when we're together."

Recalling the earlier conversation she'd overheard, she asked, "That's why Carla suggested gloves to you?"

"Yes. She wanted to try to infuse them with a magical barrier."

Risa shook her head. "That will backfire. I could shield the gloves for you, but you said the buildup is in Ram, right? Internally?"

"Coming from the thunderbird tattoo, yes."

Risa nodded. "What he needs to do is release it, not block it."

Carla strode into the room, looking as tired as Risa felt. Nodding toward the witch on the bed, she asked, "How's she doing?"

"Better. Her magic is doing most of the work now."

The blonde witch laid her hand over the woman's swollen belly, a soft smile curving her mouth. "Her color is good, and the baby is moving." Taking her hand off, Carla added, "She's doing really well. You can stop feeding her magic."

Relieved, Risa let her chakras close. A deep sense of satisfaction unfurled in her. She'd helped save lives, not lured someone to their murder. It filled an internal emptiness and made her feel like a real earth witch.

Carla pulled up a chair. "I overheard you mention releasing Ram's electrical energy. Like a lightning rod?"

Risa considered that. "That could work. The safest

way would be to bury a rod deep and let the energy go into the earth."

Carla tightened her mouth. "It'll reach the ley lines that way. The electrical energy comes from a demon magic curse."

Good point. "And now with Archer here, sucking energy, that could be a disaster. We could be inadvertently feeding him more magic."

"Exactly."

Ginny dropped her legs and leaned forward. "We have to do something, or the thunderbird will kill him."

Risa's shield magic pushed at her chakras, wanting to help Ginny. Or maybe Ram since she'd already cast her shield over him. And that thought gave her an idea. "I could shield some kind of box to hold the electrical energy Ram expels."

"Is that possible?" Carla asked.

She nodded. "Yes. Like I shielded to keep the hellfire out, but this would take a lot less magic because it's not coming live from the source. This is some kind of curse cast long ago, right?"

"We think so," Carla said cautiously. "I can't find the origin—things like who cast it and if someone is feeding it to keep it active through the years—we just don't know enough to be helpful."

Encouraged by their interest and pleased at being a part of this group, Risa got up and paced the room. "This could work. I'll have to reinforce the shields regularly with more magic, but I know I can do it."

"That would buy us more time to figure out where the curse came from and undo and fix—" Carla froze for a couple seconds, then jumped up. "I have to go." She rushed out the door.

Risa stared after her then shook her head. "Must be more witches coming in." She was slowly getting used to the fact that Carla and Sutton talked to each other in their minds. Sutton had telepathically updated his mate all afternoon and evening.

Ginny rose with fluid grace, crossing to Risa. "Thank you."

"For what?"

"Carla and the other witches have been working hard to help us, but they know and care about Ram and me. You just met us."

Risa held up her hand, uncomfortable with the praise, given how much she had to atone for. "I shielded Ram from the hellfire, Ginny. I need him to survive. If he dies, his soul will get stuck in my magic like the others."

"No," Ginny said. "Wing Slayer is stronger than that. He'd pull it away before it got tangled with your power."

Since Ginny's brother was a Wing Slayer Hunter, Risa assumed she would know, and relief nearly sagged her. One less thing to worry about. But that didn't matter as far as trying to help Ginny and Ram. "I still want to create the shield to hold the electrical energy Ram drains off."

She was so immersed in chatting with Ginny, she had no idea how much time had gone by when the door burst open and Hilary rushed in. "Risa, it's Linc!"

≫ 15 ≪

RISA'S HEART POUNDED AS SHE ran flat out across the
grounds of the school. A half-moon lit her way, but all
she could think about was Linc. Blooded. Crazed. So
out of control, they'd locked him in a room in the
gymnasium.

Could she help him? She had to. He'd saved her
from those rogues, held her when she'd been sick, then
helped her when desire had suddenly unleashed,
flooding her veins and ripping out her old fear. He'd
even told her about being caged, trained.to kill like a
feral animal.

It couldn't end like this.

Blowing past the pool, she headed across the open
field and finally spotted Carla rushing toward her.

"What happened?"

Worry rolled off the other witch. "It's bad, Risa.
Really bad."

"Was it Archer somehow?" Fear slithered around in
her belly. Linc couldn't die. She wouldn't let that
happen.

Carla touched her shoulder. "No, he wasn't there.
But another problem was. Quinn Young."

"Who's that?"

"He runs the rogues back in Glassbreakers, California. Years ago, he made a deal with Asmodeus. The demon gave him the Immortal Death Dagger."

More anxiety twisted her belly. "It can kill immortals?"

"Yes." Carla took her hand and led her toward the huge gymnasium. "The blood of a soul mirror can save them. But it gets worse. Quinn has turned into something more than rogue. He grows these daggers on his body so he has more than one. He could have killed them all tonight."

Her chakras cramped at the thought of Linc dead. "But they're all alive, right? No one died?"

Carla stopped walking outside the door, her eyes filling with tears. "It was your shield that saved them."

She reared back. "How? I have to hold it to keep it active."

"We think it's the soul-mirror bond with Linc. There was enough there with your blood exchange. All of us soul-mirror witches working together were able to use enough magic to reinforce your shield. We couldn't have done it if you hadn't shielded the guys earlier, or if it had been any longer since you cast the shield. Basically your magic clung to Linc and his falcon."

Stunned, Risa lowered her hands from where she'd been twisting her tangled hair. "My shield...lingered?" In the past, once her father had forced her to drop her shield, it had been gone.

"Apparently. I don't think we'd have been able to hold it very long, but more hunters showed up and joined the fight. In the confusion, Young got away."

Risa shook her head. "I still can't believe you were able to do that."

Carla took a breath and squeezed her hand. "Linc's in bad shape. We're hoping you can save him by finishing your bond with sex, but not if it breaks your mind. I swear to you, no one will make you do this. It's a risk for you, and your choice."

There wasn't a choice. She had no chance without Linc. He deserved to live. "I'll do it."

Carla hesitated. "Risa, you'll need to let the falcon in as your familiar. For this to work, you have to accept the bond." Worry weighted the air between them. "You need to understand, Linc isn't himself. He's caught up in blood and sex lust, crazed and violent with it. He might hurt you."

Dread clotted her determination. This wouldn't be the Linc she knew, but a near monster. He wouldn't care about her. He'd just use her or kill her. Part of her wanted to run the other way.

Carla stepped closer. "Risa? You can say no."

She looked up at the witch's troubled gaze. "Then what would happen?"

"Axel is on his way here. There won't be any more options. We've already brought him back from the madness of bloodlust once. Axel will have to kill Linc. Otherwise he'll get away from us, kill a witch and lose his soul forever."

"No!" Oh Ancestors, she wouldn't let that happen. Linc could have finished their bond any time, but he'd held back for her. He'd put her first in that respect. And now he could die because of it.

No more pathetic self-pity. Steely determination rooted in her spine. "Take me to him."

Once inside, Risa's shoes echoed on the wood floors of the vast gym bracketed with basketball hoops, and one side lined with bleachers. They went through doors and into a long hallway. After passing a couple small offices, they came to the end where brooms, mops, buckets and grim-looking men cluttered the hallway.

Sutton had thick, clanking chains thrown over his

massive shoulder. He stepped in front of Risa and Carla before they reached the small window. "Carly, you don't want to see this."

Carla put her hand on Risa's arm. "I'll be right here if you need me."

Nodding once, she walked up to the window where the last hunter, Eli, stood, his shoulders tight and his mouth flat.

The groans emanating from inside the room turned to a moan of agony.

Shifting her gaze to the window, she took in the eight-by-eight room with painted block walls, cement floors and nothing else.

"Storage room." Sutton's voice came from behind her.

That explained all the crap stacked in the hallway. But it was the man in the room who caused her heart to shove up into her throat. Linc stood completely naked, one hand on the bare block wall to her right. The other was jerking over his cock, his hips pumping and his face contorted in sheer agony.

"He can't get off," Eli said.

Risa couldn't look away from the beautiful and terrible sight of Linc. Huge shoulders and chest, the muscles moving as he worked his dick. Tight waist, his ass perfect as he pumped into his fist. Powerful thighs all the way down to his feet, toes digging into the concrete as he fought to orgasm.

I need your touch. That's what he'd told her earlier today. He'd tried to jack off for her but couldn't do it without her touching him. Linc's suffering tore through her.

"Let me in." She clawed at the newly installed deadbolt.

"Stop, Risa."

Ram strode to her, a second set of thick chains looped over his shoulder. "We have to chain him. We hoped he'd be able to jack off, get some relief before you go in there."

"Let me in and get out." She took a step closer. "You want someone watching you like this? Want them to see you at your most desperate moment? Leave us alone."

The hunter's face hardened, and tiny blue sparks snapped from his hands, sizzling as they hit the chains. "He can kill you. Right now the sex magic is fighting the bloodlust. But one smell of your blood and bloodlust will win. Then," Ram said, his voice harsh, "Linc will go rogue, and we'll be forced to kill him."

None of them wanted to do that. They cared about Linc, were willing to fight for him. Well, so was she. "I'm not going to die." She hoped.

The ice in Ram's gaze cracked to protective worry. "I can't let him hurt you, Risa."

She saw it then. This man intended to keep her safe even at the cost of his friend's life. Linc had meant it earlier when he'd said that Sutton and Ram would have dragged him away from her if she'd asked them too. Arguing wouldn't win. Instead she had to divert Ram enough to let her in there without chaining Linc. Every instinct she had told her that if they chained him, it'd make him more feral.

Like her magic had protected her, Linc's feral side protected him.

Decision made, Risa toed off her shoes and yanked off her shirt.

Ram stepped back, surprised. "What the hell?"

After ripping open her pants, she dragged them down her legs and kicked them away, leaving her in a bra and panties. She meant to reduce herself from a woman to an object in Ram's eyes. "Open the door and go away. You want me to save him, I'll do it. But I don't need an audience, and you aren't chaining him." She wouldn't allow it. He'd come to her in her worst moment, and he'd been kind. Gentle. She wasn't going to have him treated like an animal.

"He'd want us to protect you."

"He's not an animal." And neither was Ram. Despite her stripping down to basic underwear, he maintained his protective expression and stance. Sudden humiliation choked her. How much did these men know? That she'd been a whore for her father, luring men to their deaths? That Linc didn't want her beyond sex to break his curse? Earlier today, Linc had snapped at her in front of them that she wasn't doing her part to keep their deal.

Tears threatened, and finally anger. What did it matter what they thought? This was all temporary. "Ram, he needs me. I'm his only chance. If you chain him, he'll fight, and I won't be able to reach him. Please, open the door and leave."

"Do it," Eli said. "Give her the chance."

Ram's jaw bulged, and the veins in his neck pulsed. After an endless second, he released the deadbolt and opened the door.

She rushed into the room before he could change his mind. Quickly, she pulled the door shut.

Linc shoved off the wall and spun around.

His eyes, oh God. Dilated pupils, membranes as swollen and red as his huge, rigid, abused cock.

True fear broke through her cool. She whipped around and reached for the door.

One second later, Linc grabbed her arms from behind, lifted her and pressed her face first against the opposite wall.

"I smell your blood. It's mine."

At that moment the icy truth hit her. He was going to kill her with his bare hands.

The witch was his. He didn't have his knife, but nothing would keep him from her blood. Spicy cinnamon.

Something about that scent tugged at his mind. Reminded him of...he couldn't remember.

Instead, he felt the soft woman against his torturously hard dick. The smooth cotton of her panties covering the hot skin beneath. He pushed his cock deeper and pressed his face to that luscious spot where her neck curved into her shoulder. Groaned as her scent filled and saturated him.

Something nagged him. What was he supposed to remember? His head throbbed as he fought to think.

Blood.

Sex.

They were all he could think about. And the unbearable heat in him.

No knife. Teeth. He could use his teeth. He licked her shoulder, and the taste rippled through him. His cock jerked and pulsed against her panty-covered ass.

An image of her flitted through his mind. The dark-haired beauty trapped in a cage with a collar around her neck. Confusion swirled...there and gone.

Something moved on his back. Whipping his head around, he growled a warning. His witch. He'd kill anything that came in the room.

Nothing there. Yet he felt scraping on his back.

"Linc, I'm here to help you."

Her voice. It made his head hurt more. He turned back, but he didn't want her to talk. He wanted her to bleed. All the powerful blood soaking his skin, cooling his veins. Making the pain stop. Making him stronger. Undefeatable. He'd rip the door off and hunt for more witches.

Gazing down again at her exposed neck, he lowered his head and latched on. Bit down.

A wave of magic rose.

He inhaled just as he tasted her blood. Wild pleasure hit his tongue and jolted through him, so strong his jaw slackened.

A force that smelled like hot candy threw him back. Shoved him. Kept pushing until his back slammed into the opposite wall. Something that felt like feathers snapped around him. When he struggled, the feathers turned hard as steel, refusing to budge.

What the hell?

He watched the witch as she turned, so beautiful with her witch shimmer soaking her skin in silvery-blue sparkles. She wore black panties and a bra, and walked softly toward him. "I'm going to help you."

He winced at her voice. It made him want to remember. Need to remember. Made his cock throb too much. Forcing his gaze up to her face, he met her eyes.

Dark blue. Intense. Determined. Familiar enough to create a tug in his gut. "Your magic won't save you, witch." How had she bound him? He didn't understand.

"The falcon tattoo on your back is helping me." She stopped in front of him. "He's my familiar, remember?"

He measured her, ready to kick when she got close enough. Pain would snap her magic. But her voice. It tore through his mind, shoving back the burning fog. The insanity of the bloodlust cleared, and he recognized her.

"Risa. Christ, get out of here!" Fear for her popped sweat out on his neck and back.

She undid her bra, ripped it off her arms and flung it to the floor.

Linc stared as her breasts bounced free, the sweet tits with dark nipples. He couldn't look away. Not until he saw her reach for her panties and slide them down her long legs, revealing her mound to him, with the tight little strip of dark hair running straight down between her toned thighs, shielding what he wanted most.

The memory of her taste tormented him. He'd had his mouth between her thighs and wanted that again. Needed it. Nothing tasted like Risa and her desire. Flames of lust licked at his cock.

When she kicked the panties away, he saw a flash of pink right at her center.

His mind stuttered, and a longing, deeper than lust, bigger than anything he'd ever experienced, wrenched through his entire being. The drive to claim her. All of her. Not just her body, but her very essence.

Risa strode toward him, awash in confidence and the magic she was using to help the bird hold him. Her scent, like a red-hot candy left to melt in the sun, flowed around him, staking a claim.

A second later, a shock of dark, angry need ripped through his veins and pulsed beneath his skin.

Take her down. Disable her magic.

He narrowed his eyes, ready to kick her in the solar plexus.

Her cool hand landed on his chest.

Clean threads of magic streamed into him, pushing through to clear his brain. In the moment of clarity, he understood the curse recognized her as a threat and battled hard to force him to kill her.

He didn't know if he could resist. "Get out," he begged her, his voice raspy. He didn't want to hurt her, couldn't bear it.

Determination shot her chin up and shoulders back. "Not until your curse is broken. You have to help me, Linc." She dragged her hand down his skin, between his ribs, over the ridges of his stomach to glide her fingers along his cock, from root to tip and back. The erotic sensation slammed his head back against the wall, pushing his erection deeper into her hand.

She closed her hand over him. Stroked down. Up. Rubbed her thumb over the head. "We can do this. The two of us together. I won't let you die."

Together. That single word reached into him, sparking a longing and hope as strong as the curse. In all the years he'd been trapped in a cage, no one had tried to help him. He'd been alone. She gave him the will to try to hold on to his humanity and work with her. "Together."

"Yes." She looked up at him with bewitching eyes. "But I need your help. I can't climb up you and hold my magic at the same time."

For the first time, he felt the bird on his back struggling. The creature burned in his skin as he tried to fully awaken and help Risa with her magic.

You could snap their hold. Take her, cut her...

No. Shit. He knew he was ninety percent into the murderous insanity of the curse, with only a single toe holding on to his sanity.

And his soul.

He had to do this. Otherwise Risa would never get out of this room alive. That alone kept him focused. "Hurry."

The feathers pulled back. Risa put both hands on his shoulders. "Lift me."

Need rocketed through him. He caught her by the waist, lifted and turned, positioning her back against the wall.

She spread her thighs, settling her long legs around him.

"Can't wait." He didn't want to take her this way, wanted to slow down and give her as much as she gave him. Show her some care, at least, in this hellish situation. He tried to breathe and regain a little control.

Then his cockhead touched her center, feeling the heat of her, the dampness. Not wet, but damp.

Paradise.

Need slammed his hips, and he plunged inside her channel. Hard. Deep. Tunneling through with nothing but the primitive drive to come. To release. Heart hammering brutally, his lungs burning, he buried his face into her neck. Groaned and pulled out.

Back in.

So deep. Feeling her slick walls accepting him.

In and out, racing higher.

Have to come! Goddammit. Why couldn't he come?

A flicker of her magic rippled through her walls, gloving his dick.

He pumped harder, chasing that, needing it, his balls starting to draw up.

Then it vanished, leaving him on the very edge of the desperate need to orgasm.

Sweat rolled down his back, and frustration had him snapping his hips, driving into her over and over. So close, but just out of his reach. The raging edge of release teased, then retreated.

Wrong! The word screamed through him. But what? Risa wasn't fighting him. She was moving, trying to match his rhythm. But it wasn't right. It was...

Forced.

Fuck.

Linc lifted his head and saw her tight face with only the barest trace of her witch shimmer. Just sparse little pops here and there. Her magic wasn't flowing any longer, but receding away.

And he was slamming her into the wall trying to chase it.

He slapped his hand against the painted bricks over her shoulder, struggling to get control of himself. He dragged in another ragged breath. Didn't help. He couldn't stop pumping into her.

"Get help. Hurry." It came out desperate.

Her fingers tightened on his shoulders. "What's wrong?"

"Can't come," he panted, the agony of need ripping through him. He was truly a feral animal now. Beyond help. "Scream. Tell them to kill me."

One of her hands caught his hair, jerking his head to her face. "Tell me how to make you come."

"Magic." He barely got the word out. "Need it."

Panic flared, tightening her thighs, rippling around his driving cock.

He couldn't bear it. He didn't want to be the beast that had lived in a cage, a creature so vile it destroyed women. "Risa, goddammit, scream! Make them stop me!"

"I can do it. Just need to summon more." She closed her eyes, her body relaxing into his arm wrapped around her. She arched back against the wall.

He drew his gaze down over the lines of her taut shoulders that contrasted with the enticing softness of her breasts. As he watched her, her nipples began to harden, growing tighter, darker.

He slid a finger over her damp skin to circle one mound.

He felt the answering touch of her magic, thin but there. A wave of heat shuddered through him.

Loud pounding and shouts sounded. A fraction of his brain grasped that the other hunters had heard him and were trying to get in. But all Linc could focus on was Risa. She'd stretched her arms up, her hands skimming the air in a graceful dance that flowed down her body and straight to his dick. A faint, translucent, silvery-blue shimmer flickered on her skin—tiny sparks of her magic. He wanted more, wanted to feel it wash over him, own him. Struggling to focus on her and what she needed, he skated his finger over the ridges of her belly to the very top of the neat, short strip of hair. She was so damned sexy. Linc surged inside her channel, feeling every sweet inch of her, every fold and...

There! Her magic. It began to swirl and pulse, teasing his cock. It gathered, growing stronger and stronger with every second. The bird flapped his wings while Linc's entire body sizzled with the amazing sensation of her power lighting him up. The scent of her desire, warm, wet and with that spicy edge, ripped away any control he had.

Groaning, he leaned down to take her mouth, tasting her intoxicating flavor. It wasn't just what he needed, it was so much more. He could feel her giving him a part of herself. It flowed, stroked and touched. With both hands, he cupped her tight ass, using his thumb to caress her skin as he thrust.

Fiery desire, more real and vivid than he'd ever experienced, slammed through him. Risa's body arched and opened, her magic swirling around them, encasing them in a bubble. Linc didn't hear anything but their harsh panting and the sexy sounds of their bodies gliding together.

He pulled her closer, kissed her deeper. Pleasure flooded him, hot magic and sweet surrender as the witch, this woman, owned him, and he couldn't hold off. *Wait, damn it, Risa's not there yet.* But his orgasm began at the top of his spine, raced down and exploded.

Ripping his mouth from her, he buried his face in her neck, inhaling her as he pushed farther into her sultry, swirling magic and let the pulsing hot gratification have him. Mark him. So intense he felt a profound change remaking him. Helpless beneath it, Linc held on to her, breathing her in as Risa became a part of his soul.

Finally, his heart stopped pounding, and he opened his eyes. The afterglow of bliss kept his brain idling in neutral. As he drew in a breath, it dawned on him—no bloodlust. No dark, sick hunger crouching in his chest, waiting to explode. Not even an echo of it remained.

The curse was gone. He was free.

His brain snapped into drive. Gently sliding out of Risa, he gathered her close and spun her to the middle of the room, so damned happy, so fucking amazed, he wanted to share it with her. They'd done it, he'd broken the curse. "Did you feel it? We did it!" She'd given him her body and magic in this shithole of a room.

Regret edged in. He'd never wanted it to be like this. "I'm taking you to our room, laying you on a soft bed, and I'm going to show you pleasure, sweetheart. Real—"

His words froze as the bird ripped across his back, clearly in anger or worry. He stopped. That didn't make sense. The bird should be happy. Dread built deep in his guts, and he looked down at Risa. Threading his hand into her heavy hair, the strands warm and soft, he tilted her head back.

Her eyes were closed, tension fanning out a spray of tiny lines at the outside edges.

"Risa?" Her scent was going too sweet with pain or fear. Worry crashed into the base of his skull. "What is it? What's wrong?"

She opened her eyes.

Blank. The rich blue that had been so dark it had been nearly violet had faded to dead gray.

Horror flooded him. "Risa!" he yelled, shaking her slightly, trying to jar her.

She went rigid, all her muscles locking in pain, and began to scream.

Soul screams. In a blinding instant, he recalled the beauty of her weaving her hands, her entire body going sinuous with the magic—Risa had thrown her shield around them to keep the guys out.

She'd saved Linc.

And in return, he may have broken her mind and destroyed her.

≋ 16 ≋

LINC SAT ON THE EDGE of the bed, his hand on Risa's face, drawing out as much of the violent pain as he could get from her trickle of weak magic. Fifteen hours and she'd only shown one or two glimmers of sanity. The rest of the time...

Fuck.

She lay still now, her body exhausted from the mental and physical battle. Twice he'd had to restrain her when she fought, screaming at terrors only she could see. Jesus, he'd rather fight an enraged pack of lions than watch her torment.

A hand came down on his shoulder. "I'm sorry, Linc. Her mind is too badly fractured, and without more of her magic, it just won't heal."

He looked up at Darcy MacAlister. She'd come with Axel, and both she and Carla had tried and tried to reach Risa. Their magic was so powerful, his entire suite had hummed with it.

Risa's magic had barely flickered. And yet, "I felt it, Darcy. Her magic is still alive."

Carla sat on the bed, facing him. She looked over at Risa curled on her side, nearly in a fetal position, and sadness filled her kind face. "Barely. Her magic is dying. Nothing we've done has been able to stop it."

"So, what then, we just stop trying? She saved me. I'd be dead or rogue if not for her." Helpless rage snapped and snarled deep where the feral animal inside him lived. The old marks on his back burned as the beast crouched, ready to strike out and kill. "She kept her end of the bargain, but I haven't." She'd given him freedom from the curse, but he hadn't found her baby.

God, he remembered the way she'd cast her shield around the two of them, her magic pulsing hot and cloaking them in an intimacy that Linc had never experienced. She'd freely given him the things she'd held back from other men.

Her desire and magic.

"I'm not giving up. I can feel enough magic to draw off some of her pain. I'm going to fight to bring Risa back, and I'm going to find her baby for her." He owed her that. But it was more than that, damn it. He liked her. Linc had women fawn over him, angle for his attention...all because he could give them great orgasms and spoil them. Hell, he'd enjoyed it. Every woman he'd made smile was a victory over the animal in him that had been forced to use and abuse other women.

But Risa? Her sheer bravery and iron will attracted him. She'd refused to take the easy path in life, fighting against her father, becoming a bodyguard for women running from abusers, and loving her child. She wasn't looking for him to coddle and spoil her. She wanted to gain her magic and take care of her child. That was hotter than anything he'd encountered.

"No one's giving up," Darcy said. "We just don't know what else to do right now."

Everyone was exhausted. They had injured witches in the infirmary. Axel, Sutton, Eli and Ram had gone back out, hunting for any sign of Archer and now Quinn Young. They were all frustrated and tired. Time was ticking down, and when Archer resurfaced, it was going to be bad. But all Linc could concentrate on right now was Risa.

Linc forced himself to calm and nodded. "Go get some rest."

Carla placed her hand over his. "Risa's one of us. We'll keep trying. She fought to save you, throwing her shield to keep Sutton and the guys out when you told her to scream for them. Sutton even tried to punch through the window, but her shield wouldn't budge."

Damn, his witch was fierce. Pride spread through him, followed by deep remorse. "I'd rather Axel had killed me than let her make this sacrifice." He meant it.

"It was her choice," Carla said softly. "I swear it, Linc."

"I know. She needs me to find her child. She'd risk anything for her." Risa had been used over and over, emotionally and sexually. He'd wanted to give her more than that, to take care with her. Show her that she was so much more than just a body to him.

So much more.

"You're the only one she's reacting to and who can calm her. The soul-mirror bond is there. It's fragile, but there. Find a way to reach her and strengthen it. Maybe more blood, or just skin-to-skin contact, letting her magic feel you." Carla shifted her gaze to the bed. "Give her a reason to come back."

Once they left, he turned to Risa. She was curled on her side, the knuckles of her fingers white with tension as she fought whatever torment played in her head. Her breathing was fast and choppy, the pulse at her throat rapid. She wasn't asleep, but trapped in the soul screams.

The reason to come back was easy—Kendall. But he

had to access Risa's magic to get through the cracks in her mind and reach her wherever she was. Taking off his shirt, he gently picked her up.

She startled, her body bowing, fists flailing.

"It's okay, love."

Her eyes opened, but they were clouded with murky gray.

"We're going outside." He tucked her against his chest. "No one's going to hurt you." He didn't want to think of the things she'd screamed out, things men had done to her, horrors she'd seen. Leaving the room, he headed past the kitchen and table to the balcony. Bright sunshine made him blink, the day's heat contrasting sharply with the chilled air conditioning of his suite.

Going to the padded chairs, he sat and pressed her against his chest. To his surprise, Risa relaxed more than she had in the past dozen hours. Maybe being outside helped, feeling the sunshine and air that were part of her magic. Stroking her hair, he said softly, "Kendall needs you, Risa."

She held her breath. He could almost feel her straining to hear.

"We can't find her without your magic. When I met you, you were in a cage fighting to live and find your baby. Keep fighting, Risa. I swear if you come back, we'll find Kendall together, and I'll get her for you." Even if it killed him. Linc didn't have immortality, not yet anyway.

He stroked his hand up and down her back. "I know you're scared right now." Hell, so was he. "But we can do this together." There was that word again.

The bird fluttered on his back, soft, cooing sounds echoing in his head.

Risa lifted her hand toward him.

The bird's cries ramped up, and it hit him what she was doing, reaching for the falcon. They were trying to connect. Holding her wrist, he pulled her arm around his back, laying her hand on the tattoo.

Instantly, the bird's cries gentled. In seconds, he felt a tiny flicker of her magic. "He's yours now," he told her as he kept stroking her. "He'll help us find Kendall, but you have to fight, Risa. Come back to us." Linc needed to give her a stronger reason. "Kendall will need her mom. There's no one else, Risa. You have to come back."

"Kendall."

He sucked in a breath. "Risa?" Her eyes were opened. That had to be good, right? He saw bits of blue floating around, like slivers of sanity. For seconds, she was there, struggling past the shattered part of her mind. Hope flared to life in him. "Hold on, sweetheart. Don't let go."

"He's singing. Feathers."

It was little more than a hoarse whisper. Could be random mutterings, except he heard the bird's calls in his head too. "He's calling you, trying to lead you back to us." Quickly he added, "For Kendall." Kendall was what got her attention in the chaos of her shattered psyche.

The dots of blue faded before his eyes, and she began to tremble. Panic stiffened her muscles.

And just like that she slipped away again, leaving him bereft and desperate. And so fucking helpless.

Ginny headed into the small staff kitchen of the infirmary to join Darcy and Carla. "How many injured are still here?" The other two women had been healing injured witches while Ginny did what little she could or stayed with Risa when Linc had to leave her.

Carla leaned back in her chair, rubbing her temples. "Two left. Both are healing and asleep."

"Any more coming in?"

Darcy looked up from her mug of tea. "No. Axel said the guys are calling it a night and on their way back."

Sinking onto a chair, she glanced at the clock. A few minutes before three a.m. "Linc's already back, I just left him and Risa." Linc had come into the suite, shirt torn, cuts healing on his arms from fighting rogues, weary frustration riding his face, then it all softened when he looked at Risa curled in the recliner. Even though she'd been in the soul screams for more than twenty-four hours and was unresponsive to Linc, he'd held her hand, brushed her hair back...

It had sparked a longing in Ginny's heart. She craved that touch from Ram, so much her skin hurt and her aura actually ached. She understood Ram feared hurting her with the electrical zaps he put out, yet emotionally it stung, leaving emptiness swirling inside her.

Shaking it off, she focused on Darcy and Carla. "I've got this. Go get some sleep." They'd both been using tremendous magic healing the witches and assisting the hunters.

The air in the room changed. Axel strode in, his bare chest marked with angry red-and-black streaks.

Darcy jumped up. "What happened?"

He went to her, wrapping his thick arms, which were marred with the same ugly marks, around her. "I'm fine."

"You're burned."

Anxiety rippled down Ginny's back as the marks began fading. Darcy was healing him. But what were they from?

"Sutton! You too." Carla went to the bald man as he strode in.

"Ram." Ginny shot up, worry churning her stomach as she recognized the marks. "Those are electrical burns."

Axel turned, his eyes shadowed, face tense. "We

JENNIFER LYON

drained most of it. He's okay." Sighing, he added, "For now. Go see him, Gin. Darcy and I will sleep here in the infirmary."

The need to get to Ram pushed at her spine, but Axel and Darcy were both tired too. "There's only twin beds and—"

His mouth twitched. "Darcy's a witch, she can magically stretch the bed to accommodate us." Shifting his gaze to the woman he held, he laid his palm on her face. "But it wouldn't matter as long as she sleeps with me."

The kitchen closed in, too thick with intimacy and the confidence of knowing whatever the future held, you faced it together. The need to find and help Ram took precedence over everything else. "Where is he?"

"Weight room in the gym. He's drained of most electrical energy, but the bloodlust is riding him hard."

He needed sex. All the unmated hunters used sex to ease the bloodlust. *No he needs Shayla, his soul-mirror witch.* Bitter-tasting jealousy spiked as she headed out into the crisp, desert-dry, early-morning air. She launched into a run, crossing the distance easily—being a halfling had a few perks. Going around to the entrance, she opened the door. Pounding music blasted her.

After jogging down the hallway, she stopped in the doorway of the weight room, which was filled with racked weights, benches, various pull-up bars, and Ram. He'd stripped down to loose shorts and shoes, and stood with his legs shoulder-width apart as he raised a fully loaded barbell from the top of his chest, straight up and back down. There had to be three hundred pounds of weight on the bar, yet he did it with extreme precision.

A sheen of sweat emphasized the sinewy muscles popping in his arms, shoulders and back.

Ram racked the bar with a clang and turned.

Her mouth dried. His once-regulation-cut blond hair had grown a few inches long and had a wildness that made her want to drag her fingers through it and keep going, over the stark planes of his face, the granite edge of his jaw, to trace all the lines of his powerful body. Dropping her gaze to the bronze thunderbird tattoo inked on his chest, she fought back tears. The creature had his wings up, with two streaks of lightning fanning out from his barely open eyes. That bird hated her.

The endless well of loneliness churned inside her. Each night, Ram let her press up against him to fall asleep, although he was careful not to touch her with his hands. Then she woke alone to find he'd moved to the floor, afraid he'd burn her while they slept. Would he turn away from her now? Going inside, she shut the door. "I'm not leaving. You need sex."

Ram stilled, only the barest movement in his chest indicating he continued to breathe. He took one step toward her. "Wrong."

The quiet challenge in his voice matched the pantherlike way he stalked her. Watched her. "I'm right."

"Willing to stake your..." he dragged his gaze down her tank top and shorts, "...safety on it?"

Was he trying to scare her? "You won't hurt me. I heal fast. I'm a halfling, not a fragile mortal." Her skin tingled at the memory of the way he'd used his sparking fingers to ramp up her desire. She'd loved the slight bite of pain mixing with pleasure. Her skin tightened, and every touch of his gaze sent tiny bolts of heat through her.

"I don't just *need sex*. You're more than sex. You're my angel. I've always had a control kink, but you bring out the primal beast in me."

"I do?" This wasn't about the electrical energy, it was about something deeper. More basic.

"Oh yeah. Right now, he's clawing at me, raging for me to take you. Not *just sex*. But take *you*. Pin you to the ground, under my control, and bury my cock in you so deep that you can't get away and vanish." His voice pitched down to gravel. "So every being in the whole damned universe knows you're mine."

Her pulse skittered, her nipples ached, and she squeezed her thighs together.

"Four nights since you got here..." he took another step until three feet remained between them, "...I've held back, kept in control so the electrical energy didn't hurt you. But that's drained down to a spark, and my control is fraying by the second. If you don't want the real me, then turn around and go out that door."

Her entire body hummed with sensual energy. Need. "Not leaving. I—"

Ram shot forward, scooped her up and dropped her down to the mat. Before she could gasp, he slammed his mouth over hers, kissing her possessively.

He tasted wild and untamed, like the jungle— where animals fought for dominance. Ginny wouldn't go down easily. No, she wanted him to fight to tame her. Adrenaline flooded her muscles. Hooking her leg around his, she flipped him to his back.

Ram reared up instantly, grabbing for her.

Excitement sent another wave of elation through her. She threw herself to the right, rolled and came up into a dead run. Without looking back, she laughed, knowing she'd caught him by surprise. The sound spilled from her heart as her aura flared out, her halfling power surging. This was the real her—half mortal, half angel and all woman. Leaping over a weight bench, she reveled in the sheer freedom of flying.

A force slammed from behind, and arms snapped

around her and rotated her. She landed with her back on Ram's chest. She tried to struggle, but Ram locked his thighs around her, pinning her to him. His chuckle brushed by her ear and slid to her belly. A throb bloomed between her thighs, making her wet and needy.

"Your aura's out, angel. You looked like a goddess leaping like that."

"Let go and I'll do it again. This time you won't catch me."

"Too late. I have you." He kissed that tender spot by her ear, and used one hand to push up her shirt and bra, exposing her breasts. Then he unbuttoned her shorts and shoved them down to her thighs, all the while holding her pinned.

"Ram." It slid out as a plea.

He shifted, rolling her to her knees. "Can't wait. Now."

"Yes!"

With an arm hooked around her waist, he helped her face the padded weight bench. "Hold on."

Ginny flattened her hands on the black padding. She moaned as Ram leaned over her back, lining up his cockhead to her entrance.

"Mine, Ginny." He thrust in, impaling her. His chest pressed her to the weight bench. One thick arm lay next to hers, and his other hand slid down her belly and circled her clit with a maddeningly light touch.

Tiny sparks teased but didn't hit the mark. He pumped in and out in smooth, easy strokes while holding her, surrounding her, controlling her.

Hot tension built with every thrust, higher and higher.

Not enough. He held her there on that edge, need coiling tighter, ache throbbing deep in her pelvis, just out of reach. "Ram."

He sucked in a breath, his cock swelling inside her. "Beg," he growled.

That threw her so close to the edge, she hurt and she loved this—the way they stripped each other down to their bare selves with no fear. No reserve. The need climbed into her throat and she implored, "Please, Ram. God, please. Only you can give me this."

"Fuck." His control broke, and he reared up and slammed into her, driving her higher, energy sizzling between them.

Then his fingers pinched her clit, sparks shooting into the nerve center.

Ginny cried out as her orgasm exploded, her body bowing beneath the wild pleasure. Ram was right there, coming hard as he panted against her ear.

Ram held Ginny in his bed, caressing her skin, her aura down to a soft glow in the dark room. It was edging toward sunrise, but he didn't want to lose a moment of this time with her by sleeping. "I don't know how long this drain will last."

His fingers sparked lightly as he cupped her breast, but he didn't mark her skin or hurt her.

God, he couldn't bear the thought of injuring her. He didn't care how strong she was or how fast she healed, he wanted to protect her, not cause her harm.

"You used Axel and Sutton to drain the electricity?" Ginny asked. "Both of them had burn marks."

"I was so jacked with the electrical power, my veins had a toxic glow. Once we got back to the academy, Axel insisted I try draining the electrical energy on him." He grinned. "I did it and shocked the fuck out of him. The jolts were harsher than he expected." Yeah, he and A went back a ways. Once, they'd been equally matched. Then Axel got wings and an edge on Ram. It was nice to even things up. "But it's not going to work for too long. Axel's strong and immortal, but soon it's going to be enough to disable him for a time, and we can't afford to have our hawk down. Same with Sutton too."

She trailed her fingers up his arms. "I talked to Risa about that before she got sick."

A stab of regret pierced him. He'd never forgive himself for letting Risa go in that room without Linc chained. If he had been restrained, maybe then Risa wouldn't have felt compelled to use her shield magic to keep them out. "Does she know something about the thunderbird?"

"No. But we discussed a lightning rod..."

Ram grew intrigued as he listened to the plan to create a shielded box to contain the electrical energy. Could it work? If it did, then he'd be able to hold Ginny and make love to her. A glimmer of hope flickered. This was what he wanted, to embrace his angel, care for her, and not see that look of desolation in her eyes when he was afraid to touch her and accidently shock her.

Stroking his hand, she finished with, "If Risa recovers and can do it, it'll work. Look at how you are now that you drained it off on Axel and Sutton. And if she can't, maybe Carla and Darcy can figure out a way." Turning to face him, she said, "Will you try it?"

He'd do anything for Ginny. "Yes. I'll get a rod and find an insulated box, and then we'll see what happens with Risa." He tucked her closer. "I know it hurts when I can't touch you. And when I leave the bed. I hate it too."

She pressed against him. "I'm scared to sleep without you. If you're holding me, I feel like my father can't take me. But when I'm alone..."

Ram couldn't bear thinking about it. Ginny being gone from him, completely out of his reach, would destroy him. But knowing what would happen to her when her angel sire stripped her of all her emotions, leaving her a shell, ripped a hole in his guts. "That's why I stay close. Even if I can't touch you and sleep on the floor, I'm here. I won't let him have you."

"All this is just a Band-Aid. You have to find out what happened with the thunderbird to fix this." She lifted her head. "Have you talked to Shayla any more about this mystery man she's looking for?"

"No."

Her entire body tensed, and her aura blinked out entirely. "She told you on the phone she needs more magic to unlock her mother's witch book. That comes from being near you."

The bird in his ink sent a crackle of hot energy down his arms, then it fizzled into limp sparks. The energy drain still held, but the internal pull woke up.

The need for Shayla.

Fuck. Ram loved Ginny with every breath he had, and she needed him to keep her in this realm and out of her father's cold clutches.

The bird wanted Shayla and was willing to hurt anyone, and kill him, to get her.

"I don't want Shayla, I want you."

"But you need her. And she needs you."

Her tortured whisper cut him worse than any knife. The truth often did.

≈ 17 ≈

THE SUDDEN PAIN RIPPED HER from sleep. It hurt. Like knives slicing her belly. Her baby—something was wrong.

Nausea roiled, and Risa stumbled out of bed, barely able to stand before she made it to the dresser in her huge room. The bathroom, she had to—

"Sick?"

That low voice wrenched through her. Clutching the top of the dresser, she lifted her gaze to her father. Vic Faden wore silk lounging pants, his thick chest covered in a light dusting of hair. His eyes were dark blue, just like Risa's. But while her hair was sweaty and lank from sleep and sickness, his had a perfect, careless wave. "I must have eaten something bad." Another biting pain stabbed her belly, doubling her over.

"No doubt from the powder I put in your tea tonight."

His icy words pierced her building agony. Unable to straighten, she craned her head up. "What?"

"To induce abortion."

He knew about the baby. Oh God, she was only four months along.

"I got it from a witch. I'm told you'll spend a day or two in misery, but won't die."

Her baby! She had to save her baby. She sucked in air and tried to force open her chakras. Was it too late, or could she shield the child? The pain ripped through her, but she got one chakra opened, then two. Magic trickled out in a thin, uncertain stream. Risa wove her hands, struggling to gather the strands and build a shield. Even just a bubble around her child.

Agony sliced hot and vicious down her center. Something wrenched in her belly. Her thin, fragile shield shattered like an eggshell. He was doing it, killing her baby.

Sudden adrenaline powered through her. Escape. Run. Her father stood in the doorway to the hall, so she spun, racing for the doors to her balcony. She made it past her bed and the pink-striped chair, reaching for the French door.

A hand caught her hair, whipping her around. He just stared at her. Once, she'd loved him, adored him. He was so handsome, and he always smelled good. He'd bought Risa her beloved pet miniature horse, Shelby.

And years later, he'd shot the animal right in front of her as punishment for warning one of his marks.

"You're a monster."

His lips moved into something cold as he slammed his fist into her stomach.

"Risa."

Terror gripped her throat. Her father was in her room again. She rolled away, flying off the bed, running. Where to? Wait, this didn't look like her room. The bed was too big, with a heavy dark-wood frame. Confusion and fear drove her to get away. She ran out of the bedroom into a sitting area and spotted a door.

She had to escape—

She slammed into a massive chest. Hands gripped her shoulders. Fisting her fingers, she punched and then yelped. Ugh, like hitting a damned Hummer.

A warm palm lodged beneath her chin and forced her gaze up.

Golden eyes stared back at her. "I'm not going to hurt you."

The liquid voice flowed over her terror and brushed her skin with feathery softness. The familiar sensation stirred memories, but they slid away as more pain pierced her skull and stole her breath. Screams bounced in her head, trying to drag her away. She didn't want to go and squeezed her eyes shut, clenching her fists.

Gentle fingers brushed across her forehead, down her jaw, skimming her throat. In the distance, she heard a bird singing. The rise and fall of that sound soothed and drew her.

Her magic bubbled low in her pelvis and up the center line of her belly, and the pain began to lessen. As the fierce stabbing softened and the bird's singing steadied her, flashes of clarity cut in.

She eyed the familiar man stroking her face. "Linc?"

His fingers kept brushing her skin, sending warm tingles of relief. "You know me?"

"I..." She frowned. "I think so. I mean..." Images flickered then winked out. What was wrong with her?

"It's okay, love. Don't try too hard."

Another memory opened. She and the man had been in this room and he'd kissed her. Her lips tingled just thinking about it. "You kissed me." A slow kiss that had built to something more, like he'd wanted to kiss her forever.

His mouth curved in a grin and melted more of her fear. "I did. But right now I want you to rest. Come back to bed."

Confusion sprayed a fine mist in her mind, dampening the sounds of the bird. "Why am I here?"

"So we can take care of you. Protect you."

There were others here? Old fear and panic edged along her nerves. "There's more men?" Why had she thought him different? How many men would she be forced to let use her before her father showed up and killed everyone?

His fingers tightened on her jaw for an instant. Then he took a deep breath, expanding his brawny chest. "No." Stepping back, he turned around. Gazing over his shoulder, he said, "Just me and the falcon."

Inked over the surface of his back was a stunning creature. The sight of the bird eased and comforted her with a deep familiarity and connection she didn't quite understand. She knew him, recognized him so deep in her bones, as if the bird were an essential part of her. Unable to stop, she drew her fingers over the big tat. There were odd ridges beneath the color that troubled her. They shouldn't be there, but she couldn't work out why. Instead, she laid her palm on the bird's chest. Warmth chased out the cold in her, slowing her breaths. A quiet broken only by the singing of the bird filled her mind, and against her palm she felt a fast beat.

A heartbeat. Every tap of that tiny yet powerful bird heart made the room more vivid, her thoughts clearer. A new sensation joined the heartbeat, the soft brushes of his wings fanning her magic.

Hot tears burned as reality snapped into focus. "How long have I been like this?" Her voice sounded as broken as she felt.

Linc hesitated, his shoulders bunching beneath her hand.

"Tell me. Please." She didn't know, couldn't track time. She'd surfaced a few times but couldn't hold on no matter how hard she'd tried.

"Two days. But you're improving, I swear it." He reached back and settled his large hand on her hip. "Each time you come back, you're staying longer."

Two days? No, don't cry. Don't. What would happen to her? Shivers wracked her body. Not knowing what else to do, she leaned against his thick, sturdy back, pressing into the softness of the bird. "What's going to happen to me? To Kendall?"

Linc spun so quickly, she barely registered it. His eyes burned into hers. "You're mine. You belong with me, and together we're going to find the baby. I have people out there looking, and I've gone out twice searching for her, but I can't leave you for long. You get agitated when I'm not here."

"So you stayed?" With her? While she was crazy?

"When I'm not here, Ginny stays with you. You're calmest with her." Linc held out his hand to her. "Let me take you to bed, and we'll talk there."

"Bed?" Linc had on gym shorts and nothing else. Part of her was drawn to him, craving the feel of his skin against hers. In her deepest terrors, she remembered that, him holding her and the bird singing. But another part of her was scared—if she slept, would she slide back into the soul screams and never return? "I don't want to sleep." Panic nipped at her chest.

His eyes searched hers. "Then let's go for a walk."

She glanced at the doors to the balcony, noting the darkness. "It's night. And what if I, you know, start screaming?" God she couldn't even trust herself. She'd been gone for two days. It felt like she was standing on a fragile layer of ice over black water. One more crack and she'd be thrust down into the depths forever.

"Then I'll shield you, making us both appear invisible. No one will see or hear, and I'll bring you back here."

She believed him and laid her hand in his. His

warm strength closed around her fingers. Despite her confusion and fear, the constant tug in her mind trying to suck her back into the soul screams, she felt safe. Protected.

She probably was insane, she thought as he grabbed a zip-up sweatshirt and wrapped it around her. He led her down to the first floor and out into the cool, dry night. Spheres of light spilled from fixtures on the buildings.

After a few minutes of walking, her muscles elongated, and the stiff achiness from two days of inactivity eased. Her thoughts centered on Kendall. "Linc. Is there any news about Kendall? Please." She squeezed his hands. "I have to know."

"Not yet. Phoenix and Key talked to all the employees at Lustrate Publicity."

She considered that. "The employees were willing to talk to some guy off the street?"

"Hunters have the ability to use memory shifting to help get people to cooperate. Anyway, it turns out things started going bad for the company about a year ago. After nearly three decades of wild success, clients started dropping them, a nasty lawsuit was filed, their insurance company cancelled them. I took a look at their financials."

She turned to eye him. "Are they a public company?"

"No. Sutton hacked in." He shrugged. "They were hemorrhaging money."

"What do you think that means?"

"Asmodeus. The timing fits. Twenty-nine years ago, Petra started the company, and it became an overnight success story that never hit a snag. Until a year before Archer's thirtieth birthday, when he had to choose either his human or demon side."

Risa listened, her mind still sluggish. "What if Archer didn't want to choose his demon side? He was a playboy, partying, throwing money around, screwing a multitude of women. He only fixated on Blythe in the last few months." Before that, he'd had zero interest in the kid. He had paid Blythe not to name him on the birth certificate or connect him to the baby. At that point, Blythe figured Kendall was better off.

"Exactly, and maybe he didn't want to give that up to become a demon and answer to Asmodeus."

"So where's his mother now? What happened to her?"

"Not a trace. They've run down every lead. She was last seen going home after work and then disappeared. Her car's in the garage, but there's no sign of her."

Risa couldn't understand it. "Maybe she's dead." So where was Kendall?

"Could be. Or Asmodeus used her as blackmail to force Archer into choosing his demon side. Since Petra's a demon witch, Asmodeus could pull her into the Underworld."

Oh. She stopped walking. That would explain Archer's sudden interest in Kendall, if Asmodeus had demanded he get the baby and spawn to release his mother. But it was all speculation. What really worried her was, "Is Kendall in the Underworld?"

"The witches say unlikely. The only reason Asmodeus could have pulled Petra in would be because she gave him her soul."

But Kendall wasn't a witch, she had demon blood. "What about Archer? If his mom was there, could he go back and forth between Earth and the Underworld?"

"That's the beauty of a hybrid, they belong in both worlds, so yeah, Asmodeus could have pulled his son to the Underworld and then had his demon witches call him back to the earth while a hybrid. But, once he wakes from his hibernation state, his human side will have died off. Then if you witches banish him, he won't be able to come back in his demon form. He'll have to be summoned into a host body, which won't be as strong and able to shoot hellfire, making him easy to banish again and again."

Worry buzzed in her ears, and the souls tugged at her.

"Risa? Kendall isn't in the Underworld, you felt her with your magic. Remember? You wouldn't be able to do that if she wasn't on the Earth realm. Besides, it makes more sense that Asmodeus sent Petra back to Earth to do his work, including raising Kendall to become another demon witch to serve him."

Cool relief calmed her frantic anxiety. She had felt Kendall, and it did make sense, although not for the reason Linc thought. Asmodeus would want Kendall raised on Earth to eventually choose her demon side and fight his battle.

"Risa, we're looking for the baby, I swear it."

"What if I don't get her back?" It just hurt. Blythe would hate her for eternity. And Risa deserved it.

"Don't give up." Linc started walking again, urging her along. "But right now, you need to heal, or you won't be any help to Kendall. Focus on getting strong enough to find her."

The truth of that washed over her. Letting the silence of the night settle around them, Linc's hand holding hers comforting and solid, she tried to think about something else. Much as she loved Kendall, worrying herself sicker than she was wouldn't bring the baby back.

He looked over at her. "I've increased the reward on her too. A hundred K. I won't give up until we have her with us."

Us. What was happening here? There wasn't any us, was there? Yet he'd been taking care of Risa and searching for Kendall. Her curiosity bubbled to the top. "Why are you doing this, Linc? Your curse is gone, right?"

"You remember that?"

She shivered again. "Right now I do. I remember how hard you fought not to hurt me. How good it felt. God I wish I could have held the screams off longer. Felt you come inside me and..." She trailed off, embarrassed. Ashamed. She was the one who'd broken apart, not him. Her emotions ping ponged. "Sorry, I'm rambling."

He stopped and pulled her around to face him in a circle of light outside the pool area. Steam rose from the water while Linc's eyes darkened from gold to bronze. He settled his other hand against her cheek. "You will feel that. As many times as you want. We're not over, love. You're mine. You gave yourself to me that night, trusted me with your body, magic and mind. We're not over."

The passion in his voice vibrated against her chakras. Whispers of longing threaded in her stomach. But even in her confused state, she knew Linc hadn't ever wanted a real relationship. "You can't mean that." Could he? "I'm having a sane moment now, but any second I'll be dragged back into that craziness. How can you want me?"

"Because you fight for what you believe in and the daughter you love." Shadows dimmed his eyes. "Because I know what it's like to be trapped in a cage, helpless. Used. Forced to do things..." he rubbed her arms through the sweatshirt, "...haunted by the ones I couldn't save, but I will save you."

Risa leaned closer to him, drawn to the man who was so strong, yet in this moment he was showing her a deep vulnerability. "Who couldn't you save?"

Linc shook his head. "Not tonight. You don't need that shit in your thoughts." He lowered his mouth to hers in a soft, quick kiss. "You're going to heal, and we'll get Kendall and figure out how to release the souls so you can live in peace."

Before she could process everything he'd said, he tugged her inside a gate. At the edge of the pool, the warm mist hovering over the water caressed her bare limbs. "Is it heated?"

"Yep."

It tempted her. She sat down on the edge and put her legs in. Warmth encased her feet and calves, wringing a sigh from her. Such a little thing, but it felt wonderful.

Linc dropped down next to her. She lifted her head, looking up at the velvety sky dotted with silvery-white stars. "It's so peaceful. I wish I could hold on to this."

He threaded their fingers together. "Hold on to me."

She stared down at their joined hands, his fingers long, thick and scarred. He might have a pretty face, but he had fighter hands. What was driving him? Memories percolated, one rising to the top. "One of the times I was awake, you made me macaroni and cheese."

He shrugged. "Not my preference, but you conjured the box, and I took the hint."

Startled, she said, "I did that?"

"Oh yeah. Shocked the hell out of me. I was combing out your hair, asking you if you were hungry, and the next thing I knew, I'm holding a box of macaroni and cheese." He leaned closer. "And damn near covered in your magic. Totally unfair, little witch."

Her eyes widened. "I didn't realize I'd done it."

"It was incredible. The feel of your magic is hot as hell, but more importantly, it was the first true sign that your power was rising. And your magic is what will heal your mind. At least as much as possible until you release the souls."

She was still trying to take it in. "So you made me the mac and cheese."

He lifted his nose. "Disgusting stuff, by the way. However, you ate almost the entire batch. And that time when the soul screams came, you fought, Risa. Begged me not to let them have you."

She remembered Linc pulling her against him, and telling her, *Listen for Falcon. He'll show you the way back to us.* The hairs on her arms lifted in an electric reaction. Linc and the falcon, they'd been her lifeline. Her only hope.

"You're remembering a lot more now. How's your head?"

It dawned on her then that she only felt a dull throb. "Doesn't really hurt." She tilted her head, considering that. "The pain began to fade when you were stroking my face in the room. How?"

"Soul mirrors. I can take your pain." He squeezed her hand. "At first I couldn't get much, but the more chakras you opened, the more pain I could draw off."

Recoiling, she tugged on her hand. "No. It's excruciating. How can you bear it?" Why would he?

"Doesn't bother me. I learned a long time ago to block out pain or most anything done to me." He clamped his mouth shut and breathed in.

Why? What had been done to him that he'd had the ability to resist pain? He'd said earlier, *Because I know what it's like to be trapped in a cage, helpless. Used. Forced to do things.* Forgetting about herself, Risa slipped her hand from his to stroke his back. The bird reached out to her, his feathers caressing her fingers. She searched for the ridges buried in the tattoo and found them.

A sick feeling welled in her stomach.

"This tat, it covers something, doesn't it? Some pain." Something they'd done to him. Hurt him with. Oh God, could she bear to know?

JENNIFER LYON

"Risa—"

"Tell me." Adrenaline burst into her veins, pumping anger. "Tell me what they did to you."

"It's a brand."

The horror sickened her.

"I wouldn't do something they wanted me to. I got dragged out of my cage, held down and branded with the word feral." His pupils swelled, the lines in his face shifting from handsome to lethal. "And I still wouldn't do it."

Sweet Ancestors, they'd been monsters. He'd been just a kid. She swallowed the vile rage choking her. "Do what?"

"Rape a young woman they put in my cage."

A clang rang in her head. Not soul screams, but shocked outrage. "Why would they want that?"

His eyes iced. "They wanted me to be exactly what they branded me with—feral. They treated me like a fighting dog, and they worked to make me mean enough to never lose. But they couldn't break me with pain or any humiliation."

While she'd caved under pain, dropping her shield, allowing her father to kill his marks. Some of them had just been in the wrong place at the wrong time, not evil. But if a person paid her dad enough, he'd kill whoever they wanted him to. He didn't care if it was a young woman, a man with a family—nothing mattered. But Linc cared. Oh, he'd killed—she'd seen him do it in that cage. Then he'd been gentle with her. "You're so much stronger than me."

"Wrong, baby. They just hadn't found my weakness yet." His back knotted beneath her hand. "Not until they chained that girl to the wall and held up the brand, ready to press it to her back. I can still hear her screams of terror." He turned away from Risa. "I did what they wanted. Anything to spare her the agony. I became exactly what they branded me."

246

No! Risa couldn't even imagine being put in that position. "You didn't have a choice." It came out in a painful whisper. He was as much a victim as that poor girl.

"I tried not to hurt them, to make it as easy as I could. Most even figured out I was the safer option and clung to me. I wanted to care for them and keep them safe, but the captors always killed them at some point. It would've been more humane if I'd killed them the first second they were put in my cage." His jaw was rigid, tone vibrating with anger. "When I got out, I killed every last one of those bastards."

His regret and guilt were so thick it made her chakras ache then pop open, spilling out magic. She didn't think, but went with her instinct and laid her hand on his arm. "How did you find your way from that, to the man you are now?"

"Hilary pushed me to learn, and Baron taught me street smarts, and I used both to acquire money and polish. I built a house, hoping that would make me feel more settled. In control."

Risa could only imagine what a home represented to Linc—not just a place to live, but control over his world. His house had been open and beautiful, not an ugly confining cage. And yet, she sensed that it didn't give him what he'd needed. "But the house didn't help?"

He hesitated, eying her for several beats, then said, "Nothing changed the reality that beneath all the clothes, manners, wealth and home lived a violent, feral man saddled with a curse for witch blood. The need to fight was always there, driving me to the underground cage fight. I hated it, detested that I couldn't shake what my captors had made me into."

Her heart ached for him. "So you left Vegas?" Still trying to escape the cage, even though he'd been free for years.

He nodded. "I found the Wing Slayer Hunters run by Axel and other men just like me. Fighting to be better than we were. There's an induction ceremony that the hunters do. First, I chose my tattoo, a falcon, and had the outline done. After that, at some point, there was a test."

"What kind of test?"

"To show commitment to our god. It's the one thing Wing Slayer needs to invoke his god power—real belief. Anyway, it's different for every hunter."

She debated asking him what his test was, but deep down, she had the sense that it was between him and Wing Slayer. Instead, Risa said, "How do you know you passed?"

"Axel knew. So we held this ceremony with just the Wing Slayer Hunters, and once I gave my vow, there was this hush of power on the air, then it vanished. After that, my tattoo had been completed."

"He accepted you." She whispered it, understanding that it meant so much to him.

Linc nodded. "For the first time, I belonged somewhere."

With her magic flowing into him, his sincerity streamed back. Despite her enviousness of his acceptance, she welled with joy for him. "I'm glad you found them. That you have a place. A purpose."

Linc seemed to shake off his thoughts as amber lights flared in his eyes. He latched his gaze on to hers. "What are you doing?"

"Magic. You were so tense talking about your past. I want to help. Comfort."

"Risa." His low voice shivered in her chest.

"What?"

"I'm not feeling comforted."

Oh. "You're not?" She'd only done this with Kendall and the witches she'd helped heal in the infirmary.

"Hell no. I was half hard just sitting here with you,

but this?" His voice dropped to a growl, and he leaned into her, wrapping a hand around her head. "Baby, this is desire. And it's making me burn to kiss you."

He was so close she could see the flecks in his eyes, feel his breath on her face. She forgot about everything but Linc and the way he made her feel centered and desirable. Not crazy, weak and broken. She didn't know how long she had before she'd be dragged away from him again.

But she wanted this. "Kiss me."

For a second, he stayed perfectly still.

Would he retreat? Second thoughts? He'd said earlier they weren't over.

He unlocked his muscles and swept her up, her legs splashing in the pool water as he settled her on his thighs. Curving his hand around her jaw, he angled her head up and pressed his mouth to hers.

Her magic surged, rising and swirling.

Linc groaned against her lips, his tongue sliding in to stroke hers. His other hand wrapped around her hip, holding her as he ate at her mouth, dipping deep inside, then nibbling at her lips. He trailed wet licks and kisses down her throat.

Her magic chased every touch. Chills and heat collided, making her nipples tight and hard. She dropped her head back, caught up in kisses so potent she could only feel. "Linc."

He lifted his head, looming over her. His nostrils flared, and in his eyes, she could see spread wings. Feel the connection between them, bigger than sex. Stronger. Deeper. "I see the bird."

"He feels you. We both do." He swallowed, his Adam's apple sliding down the long column of his throat. "God I want you."

Those words sank deep into her, wrapping around all her scared and lonely places, making her feel safe and sexy. Linc had seen her at her worst and still wanted her. Not for her beauty. Not to break his curse.

He just wanted her.

Could this be real?

It took everything he had to pull back from the woman in his arms. Linc meant it, he wanted her. However... "The next time we make love, it's going to be when you're ready."

"I think I'm ready now." She shifted on his thighs, rubbing over his cock. "I'm swollen, wet."

He hissed, her sweet ass torturing him and the image of her wet and swollen burned into his head. Didn't matter. Not happening. It was his job to protect and care for her. "You're healing. We're releasing more and more of your magic. I can feel it swelling. But we're not pushing you into another bout of soul screams." At her look of disappointment and uncertainty, he rested his forehead against hers. "Soon, very soon." Because Risa had become vital to him.

"As much pleasure as you can handle, love. I swear it." He wanted to give her that. She'd been cold and numb, unable to trust the desire that was part of her magic. Except with him. That hardened his cock even more. "I want to watch you come, see you let go for me." He kissed her, then shifted, rising to his feet and setting her on hers. "But right now, let's go raid the kitchen and feed you." He held out his hand.

Putting her hand in his, she tilted her head up. The moon cascaded its light over her skin, which was tinged with the lightest blue witch shimmer. He caught his breath and barely stopped himself from blurting out how beautiful she was to him. Risa viewed her beauty as something that had lured people to their murders, while Linc saw the strong lines of her face, vulnerable eyes and chopped-up hair as a reflection of a woman so strong and determined, she could carry and safeguard the souls of the dead.

Swallowing against a knot of emotion, he asked, "Hungry?"

"Not really."

Yeah, as they walked, he felt her tension building. "Thinking about Kendall?"

"Always." She raised her shoulders and added, "I'm not giving up. I'll get strong enough to find her. I'll eat something."

There she was, his warrior witch. The same one who stood up through the sunroof in the moving car and shot a rogue. She wouldn't ever give up. Fighting another wave of emotion, he said, "What would you like?" Trying to lighten things up, he added, "Don't say macaroni and cheese."

"It's too early for pasta." She gave him a guileless look. "Do you have Cap'n Crunch cereal?"

Okay, now she was playing with him. "Nice try, sweetheart, but there's no way you'd actually eat that shit. No one over the age of seven eats that." He firmed up his tone. "How about an omelet?"

"I'm not in the mood for eggs and all that cholesterol. Do you have Froot Loops? There's fruit in the name, so obviously they're good for you."

Hiding his grin at her attempt to tease him, he said, "Not happening. French toast?"

Reaching the front door, she turned, raising her eyebrows in mock disgust. "Witches aren't the same as you hunters. We have special dietary requirements."

Linc leaned his hand on the door over her head. "Is that right?" Risa was stalling, probably not ready to go back inside. Shadows of worry for her daughter lurked in her eyes.

"Absolutely. You need to eat all that protein and

whatever to maintain all your massive strength and super hotness you got going on."

A slow smile curved his mouth. She thought him hot? Yeah, he liked that. "With you so far. So what do witches eat then?"

"Lucky Charms."

He was so going to regret this, but even with the strain in her gaze, she charmed him. "Why?"

A grin transformed her face. "Because they're magically delicious."

He leaned his forehead against hers. "Baby you don't need cereal to make you magical or delicious." Nope that was all Risa, and damned if he wasn't falling under her spell.

≈ *18* ≋

LINC STOOD IN BARON'S CONFERENCE room, drinking the swill that vaguely resembled coffee. Baron and Vice were huddled at the front, while Ram and Eli were at the table in the back, rooting through a pastry box. Sutton had stayed at the academy to guard the girls.

Linc's thoughts drifted to Risa. Once he'd gotten her back in bed, she'd dropped off into a deep, healing sleep in his arms. Her trust in him humbled him, while her strength and will to fight ramped up his admiration and respect.

Admit it, you're falling hard for Risa. He'd never imagined he'd find a woman he'd want for a real, long-term mate. Oh, he'd desperately wanted to find his soul mirror and end the curse, but he'd assumed they'd come to some kind of deal. Maybe a sweet witch who just wanted her high magic and possibly someone to help pay her bills. He'd have done that, and enjoyed giving her something that made her happy. At least that's how he'd envisioned a soul mirror would happen for him.

But Risa? Oh, she had a sweet side, but she also had a fierce loyalty and loved her daughter, so much it'd melted Linc's walls. He'd even told her about his brand. The witch was getting to him.

He didn't want to just fix her world. He wanted to share her world, along with Kendall. His feelings for Risa scared the shit out of him. But he couldn't stop it. The pull of Risa was stronger than even the bloodlust had been.

When Linc had woken her this morning to tell her he had to go to this meeting, she'd been so warm and sweet and fully there with him that he couldn't resist kissing her. And then he'd wanted more. Wanted to make slow love to her, until she came undone for him.

Worry edged into the memory. Without him there, was Risa still doing okay? Holding on to reality? Or were the screams trying to pull her back?

A spark stung his forearm, yanking him from his thoughts. Snapping his head around, he cocked an eyebrow at the man who'd moved up next to him.

Ram shrugged and bit into a donut. Which made him think of Risa with her atrocious taste in food, and he smiled.

The door opened, and Axel strode in. "I got confirmation Quinn Young left Vegas and is back in Glassbreakers. One of my hunters there, Phoenix Torq, ran across him in a fight early this morning."

Vice crossed his arms. "I told you I got that from two rogues I killed. Young was just here to check up on them while Archer's in hibernation or regeneration or whatever he's doing."

"And I verified," Axel said.

"Don't trust my hunters, Locke?" Baron challenged.

Linc saw the possibility of this going bad in a heartbeat and opened his mouth.

Axel cut him off. "I don't trust Quinn Young." He stared down Baron, Vice and the other hunters. "Up till now, he's been the demon Asmodeus's pet here on Earth. Now the demon just sprang a son on all of us. I wouldn't be surprised if Young told the rogues he was leaving when he was hunting Archer to kill him and keep his number-two spot. This isn't about credit and trust. It's about making sure we know who our enemy is and where they are."

No one said a word. The tension was so high Linc slid his hand to the hilt of his knife.

Baron nodded in acceptance. "Our intel is that Quinn Young delivered a group of witches as some kind of token to the spawn. Checked things out, then left."

"Not before trying to kill my hunters in the fight club." Axel eyes went to Linc. "Young always has motives. He knew my hunters were here and tried to get the drop on them. The rogues are organized and share information."

"We chased him off," Vice announced. "Our crew came in, and Young bolted."

Axel faced the second-in-command. "I appreciate that you had my hunter's backs. We'll do the same for you."

That sucked some of the tension out of the room.

Baron said, "So our enemy here in Vegas is Archer. If he's still here."

"He's close by his spawning sight, probably within a fifty-mile radius," Axel assured him. "He needs magic through the ley lines to finish his transition."

Vice paced the front of the room. "Yeah, we could get the rogues we caught to talk about Young, but not the spawn. No amount of torture made any difference. If the rogues tried to say anything about the hybrid, they went into convulsions and died. They couldn't even write it down or point on a map."

"Demon magic." Axel's frustration showed in the tense lines of his shoulders. "It's blocking the witches from finding him too."

"Can't they remove it?" Baron asked. "Say we

capture a rogue, can a witch remove the demon magic stopping him from telling us?"

Axel shook his head. "Too dangerous. Demons can magically latch on to a witch's power that way. The witches are trying to use their third eye and get above the block to find him, or go to the astral plane and track him. So far, though, nothing has worked."

Vice eyed Axel. "What about Wing Slayer? You're supposed to be so close to him."

"He can't see Archer either. Asmodeus and Wing Slayer go back centuries. They both know each other's tricks and magic."

"Hell." Baron rubbed the bridge of his nose. "What now?"

Ram walked to the laptop and brought up his PowerPoint on the big screen. "We keep working the grid, going farther and farther out. We've cleared the Strip and tunnels beneath."

Baron nodded. "A few of our men are going to do surveillance and follow any rogues who snatch witches to see if they take them to Archer."

Eli twitched. "Will we let them deliver the witch?"

Axel turned. "No. Any point the witch is in danger, we move in and save her. Wing Slayer is adamant about saving earth witches first. Always."

One of the other hunters said, "Sacrificing one witch to find the demon spawn—"

"Is unacceptable," Baron snarled, moving toward his man who had spoken up. "Clear?"

The blond man paled but held his ground. "Got it."

Baron looked around the room. "Any witch out there could be *your* soul mirror. Any one. We save them all if we can."

Ram and Vice gave out assignments, while Baron came up to Linc. "Interesting that you found your soul mirror here in Vegas. Not in California."

"Think so?"

"I think a lot of things, Dillinger. Including that I made you and you bailed."

"I didn't bail. I've come any time you called for backup." That was true. Linc would die for Baron, but he wouldn't be a part of strip clubs and prostitution.

"You think you weren't paying for sex when you gave women gifts or vacations? Flying them to France for dinner and shopping?"

Linc didn't flinch or show a flicker of emotion. He was too well trained.

"I'm more honest. And I protect my girls. Once they want out, they can work in our other businesses. We still protect them."

That much was true. Lay an unwanted hand on one of Baron's girls and the idiot paid in blood. But that changed nothing for Linc. "First, I'm mated, and I have what I want waiting for me in my bed." His days of searching for relief were over. Instead of that magically fueled drive for release, he had clean and very real desire.

Baron nodded in acknowledgment.

"Second, I'm not profiting off women as a commodity."

"Son, I've been to Axel's club in Glassbreakers. The whole purpose of starting that nightclub was for sex."

"He's not wrong," Axel said from behind Baron. "But I didn't pay the women or allow prostitution. That kind of shit turns ugly too fast. Our job is to protect women. Not turn them into a merchandise to be sold." Axel paused then added, "And I don't like my hunter being poached."

Baron turned to face Axel. "He was my hunter first. And Vegas is his town. The stubborn idiot just won't admit it." The man walked away.

Linc watched Baron, disloyalty tearing at him. Baron had shown him how to deal with his witch hunter and feral side. And now that Linc was here fighting for Vegas, he had to admit to a certain possessiveness over the town. But Axel, Ram and all the guys, they'd shown him how to be a Wing Slayer Hunter and find his soul mirror.

Axel laid a hand on his shoulder. "As hunters, our first priority is to fight this spawn. And as individuals, our first priority is our mate. Yours is Risa."

Risa. She tugged at the deepest part of him, as if she were his true home. Not Vegas or California, or Axel's group vs. Baron's crew. That clarified things for him. "In the end, it's going to come down to what Risa and her baby want and need."

"Whatever you choose, we're your friends and will always have your back. Always."

Risa couldn't hide forever. For the last thirty hours, she'd stayed in reality, and the souls remained quiet. Linc had taken her out on more walks, and they'd eaten together and swam. He'd even jogged with her.

But they hadn't run into anyone when they were out of the room. Did they all view her as the crazy witch? Or had Linc asked them to give her a little time to recover?

Didn't matter, she had to find Kendall, and Linc kept resisting. He didn't think she was strong enough yet to use that much magic.

But what about Kendall? She'd been missing for just over a week. Risa'd tried on her own to find her, but couldn't do it. Since Linc had left to meet with other hunters and search for Kendall, Risa decided to ask Carla for help. The woman had tried once before, so hopefully she'd be willing again.

Her stomach clenched as she headed down in the elevator. What did the others think of her? They'd seen her screaming in the room. Would they want to avoid her? The elevator doors opened to the first floor.

Guess she'd find out. Walking out in the living space, she glanced around and heard voices.

"I didn't okay that. Phoenix, what the fuck were you thinking?" The voice boomed through the room, throbbing real anger.

Risa shivered at the vaguely familiar tenor. Where had she heard it?

"That it's been a goddamned week and we haven't located the missing baby. It's pissing me off. Then I started wondering, what if Quinn Young went to Vegas for more than delivering witches to the freakazoid spawn?"

She followed the voices and sprinted to the computer room. Honing in on one of the big monitors mounted on the wall, she eyed the man wearing leathers and a mutinous expression. Phoenix, the hunter mated with Ailish the blind witch. Risa blurted out, "You're talking about Kendall? Did you find her?"

The two couples in the room spun around. Sutton was at multiple keyboards. Carla and another woman sat on stools, and behind the dark-haired woman stood a huge man with raven-black hair, piercing green eyes and crackling with authority. He wore a T-shirt and jeans the way other men wore a power suit.

Now Risa placed that commanding voice—Axel, leader of the Wing Slayer Hunters. Carla had told Risa he was coming the night she'd had sex with Linc to save him. The other witch would be Darcy, his mate.

"No."

She jerked her gaze back to Phoenix on the screen.

"Key and I got into the rogue compound. Turned into a bloody battle, but the kid's not there."

She closed her eyes, defeat sagging her.

"I'm not giving up. If that kid is anywhere in L.A., we'll find her."

Pulling herself together, she said, "Any other leads?"

"Nothing. But I have people watching the employees of her company to see if one of them leads us to her, and we're searching for any demon witch activity in the area. If Petra's here, she can't hide forever with a baby."

She held on to hope. "Thanks."

"What about you? How are you holding up, Risa? Linc says you're a fighter."

The kindness in the rough-looking man's dark eyes surprised and touched her. But how did she answer him? Several of them had seen her in the soul screams. Yet Linc had called her a fighter, and that made her feel braver. "I'm okay. I'll be fine once I have Kendall."

"Then let's get to work and find your daughter. Later."

The screen went black.

Carla sprang up. "Risa, you're looking better."

She half laughed from nerves. "Yeah, I bet." She didn't want to know how she'd looked while trapped in soul screams.

"Nice to see you, Risa. I'm Darcy. Carla and I tried to help you, but your magic wouldn't respond to us."

Risa winced, unable to help herself. Humiliation that this powerful woman who was mated to the leader of the Wing Slayer Hunters had seen her like that burned her face. "Thanks for trying."

"Frankly, I'm amazed you're sane at all. You had so many cracks in your mind it was like a shattered mirror."

"Darcy," Carla groaned. "A little tact is called for here."

Risa blinked, then laughed. She liked the woman's bluntness, it made her feel less fragile and nervous. "It felt worse than it looked."

The witch touched her shoulder. "It was hideous to see, Risa. And frustrating that I couldn't help you. I could feel you suffering, and I saw enough flashes of what you were enduring to know I would have crawled into one of those cracks and never returned."

"The hell you would," Axel said, his voice low and possessive as he moved up behind Darcy. "I'd find your ass and pull you back." Axel reached past Darcy and held out his hand to Risa. "Nice to meet you in person. I'm Axel Locke."

Manners trained into her from birth had her quickly shaking his enormous hand then releasing it. But manners only went so far when she recalled Carla had told her why Axel had come. "Would you really have killed Linc?"

"Yes."

Silence rose in the room.

Sutton joined them. "Risa, it's a pact we all took before we were mated. Dead is better than a soulless rogue." He glanced at Axel then back at her. "I was blooded and nearly lost my soul. Axel would have killed me if Carla hadn't been able to save me. It's what Linc would have wanted too."

This group had a deep bond, one that was more than friendship or a cause. She was the outsider.

"He would have," Axel agreed. "But I'm damned glad I didn't have to. Thank you, Risa."

She flushed. This wasn't at all what she'd been dreading when coming down and mixing with everyone. "I'm glad I could help." She turned to Carla. "Will you help me with my magic? I know it's stronger. I can feel it in my chakras, but I can't really control it."

Carla hesitated. "Maybe we should wait. Linc needs to be here. His falcon will help you with control."

Frustration rattled her nerves. She wanted to find the baby soon, both for Kendall's sake and to stop lying. "He's being too protective and refuses to help me yet."

Darcy snorted. "They're all like that." Grabbing

Risa's hand, she tugged her. "Come on, I'll help you. We'll go outside."

"Darcy." Carla trotted beside them. "This might not be a good idea. Risa's still healing."

Out in the warm sunshine, Darcy turned to them. "We need Risa, Carla. We don't have time to be cautious. Archer is hibernating, recovering from his spawn, and once he wakens, we're going to need all the help we can get. And Risa has some kickass shield magic that held off Archer's hellfire arrows. We need her, and we don't have the luxury of time."

"True," Carla relented. "But no shield magic today. That triggers the soul screams."

Risa held up her hand. "Believe me, I don't want to trigger that. Darcy's right, I'm going to have to attempt my shield magic at some point to see what the souls do." She repressed a shudder. "But now, I just want to test how many chakras I can open and see if I can reach Kendall. You said you might be able to see her with your third eye through my connection to her, right?"

Carla's eyes searched her face. "Possibly. Let's go to the field. Being in the open with the elements should help." As they walked, Carla asked, "How did you learn you were a shield witch? Was your mom one? It's normally impossible to control without your high magic."

At least this she could answer honestly. "My mom and her family were music witches. They would play and weave their magic into the notes, invoking emotions and spreading comfort or calm." She'd heard their recordings, and even those evoked a deep response in her. "Most of her family are dead now. Their music attracted rogue's attention. The few in hiding won't talk to me."

"Why?"

"Because my mom ran away, left them and her

career, to be with my father. They tried to tell her he was evil, but my mom fell for his charm and wealth. He isolated her."

Carla sighed. "It's the way of any brainwashing, take the victim from their support system and immerse them in reconditioning."

Risa turned and said, "You know a lot about brainwashing?"

"I specialized in it for years as a psychologist. It's not as hard to break down a psyche and get control as people want to believe."

Impressive. Carla had struck her as intelligent, but this amazed her. Old feelings bubbled and spilled out. "When it was me and my mom, she was kind and loving. And brilliant when she played the piano. I loved her. Then after she died, I found out she helped my father kill people. I don't know how far she went—maybe she even had sex with the marks to distract them. Yet she insisted my father loved her, that they were this great love story." All her feelings about her mom poured out of her in a huge wave.

Carla nodded. "He broke her, Risa. Took her from her family and her audiences that fed her music. I'm not excusing your mother, believe me. She made bad choices, which led to worse choices. But at the same time, it's important to understand it's very likely your father controlled her." She brushed Risa's arm. "And it's okay to love the woman you remember as your mom while hating the choices she made with your father."

Something old and tight unlocked in her chest as Carla described exactly how she felt. She did love her mom. "You're good at this."

Carla smiled. "Do you have any ability as a music witch?"

"Marginal." Although more since she had met Linc. "My mom was baffled by that. We both assumed I was weak as a witch."

"When did you realize you could weave a shield?" Darcy asked.

"Shelby, my miniature horse. He was barely thirty inches tall and the love of my life." She smiled at the memory of her sweet, stubborn horse. "I was grooming him in the barn, and my mom came out there to find me when she accidently knocked a pitchfork off a hook. It fell straight toward Shelby. I panicked, my magic surged out, and I threw up my hands. The pitchfork stopped mid-fall. I felt the impact rattle through me like a tuning fork. Freaked out, I grabbed Shelby and moved. Then the pitchfork hit the ground. My mom was stunned. She said she could see my shield."

"How old were you?"

"Thirteen. About a year before my mom was killed."

Carla nodded. "Most of us come into our magic around puberty. Fear and panic probably released the hormone surge you needed to make that happen."

They passed by the pool area. A glance over at the water made her think of talking out there with Linc, his kiss...*Focus*. "Probably," she agreed. "But it was a weak shield, barely holding up a pitchfork for maybe thirty seconds. Looking back, I know it wasn't a true and strong shield, more like a couple threads of yarn. It took years to learn to grab the threads of magic and weave them together into a shield, throw it and hit the target. Anyway, my mother recognized it as shield magic and pushed me to learn. We'd practice together when my father wasn't around."

"Interesting," Carla said. "She hid your power from your father?"

Risa nodded. "She kept telling him I was weak..." And for the first time, she understood. "She was protecting me."

"I can't say for sure. I didn't meet her. But I'd guess

the mom in her was, yes. She knew what your father was and what she'd become, even if she couldn't admit it."

Darcy stopped in the middle of the athletic field. "When did the soul screams start?"

Risa thought back. "At first it was a headache and ringing in my ears. But by about the fifth soul I failed to save, it pitched up to screams. I could hold them off for a couple hours, but once I relaxed at all, they'd attack, and it'd be like a migraine for an hour or so. It progressively grew worse over time."

Darcy pursed her lips then said, "Mating makes your magic stronger and more controlled, so in theory, you should be able to maintain your hold on your magic, which would keep the souls from taking over. But the pressure on your mind is intense. You need to access your high magic to figure out how to release the souls."

Risa looked down at the grass. "Will they know where to go?" And what about Nola? Risa hadn't seen her since the night she'd mated with Linc.

Carla glanced around, then said, "Let's sit here in a circle."

Tapping down her impatience for an answer, Risa sat on the dry grass and crossed her legs, with Darcy on her left and Carla on her right.

Carla squinted into the sun. "Now that you have a familiar, if you cast a shield and someone dies, your bird will keep any other souls from lodging in your magic. But for the ones already trapped in your magic, you need to ask the Ancestors how to do the spell to release them to their afterlife. That will require your fifth and sixth chakras."

Risa nodded.

"If you haven't already," Darcy added, "you should start a witch book to store your magic and knowledge in."

"I had one. It was in my luggage in my car that burned."

Darcy slipped off a silver ring from her thumb. "Here you go. Size it with your magic and you have a witch book."

Risa stared at the bold yet elegant ring made from polished silver that wrapped around the thumb, two sides passing each other and arcing away. She hadn't worn jewelry or anything pretty in years. She hated even looking at herself in a mirror. What others saw as beauty, she saw as something ugly. Hideous. But she wasn't that girl anymore, was she?

Risa took the cool ring and slid it on. "Thank you. I'll return it when I get something else to hold my magic."

"I'd like you to keep it, Risa. You'll know you have friends, and the ring will help connect us if we have to circle our magic when we're not together. It's a symbol of friendship."

Her throat clogged. "I'd like that."

"Good. Let's work on transferring what you know about your magic into your ring. You'll need to open your fifth chakra—communication with other realms—to do that."

Excited and hopeful, she concentrated.

"Wait," Carla said. "You use your hands for shield magic, right?"

Risa nodded.

Carla took her right hand. "We'll hold your hands. It will help us circle magic together and stop you from using shield magic." Once situated, Carla said, "Start opening your chakras."

The hot sun poured over her, a light dry wind blew and the ground beneath her vibrated with life. Her first four chakras opened in seconds, spilling out power. Heat spread, whispering sensations filling her belly, making her nipples pebble. Too weird, especially without Linc here. Her magic slowed, beginning to retract.

"It's normal," Darcy said softly. "It's in all our magic. Accept it."

Risa took a breath. How did the other witch know? "Really?" All witches felt this?

"Yes," Carla assured her. "All of us know that part of our magic belongs to our soul mirrors. Believe me, Axel and Sutton are feeling it right now. They won't interrupt us, but they feel it."

"Oh yeah." Darcy laughed. "Axel will make me pay for torturing him."

A giggle bubbled up in Risa's chest. "It tortures them?"

"Instant boner if they're close enough." Darcy flashed a wicked grin. "Try it sometime."

Oh she would. Risa loved feeling like a part of their world. Doing magic with the other witches, talking about sex, chuckling a bit about their mates. She had the sensation of belonging, of being home. Wanting to make the girls proud of her, she pushed her magic, and it rose through her heart chakra, then down to her pelvis in a continuous stream. Pressure began to build in her throat, her magic slowed, and strands leaped out of the stream. Seconds later, Carla and Darcy's magic joined hers.

"Don't worry about the stray magic right now."

Darcy squeezed her hand. "Normally your familiar would help you with that. Just concentrate on opening your throat chakra."

Risa closed her eyes, picturing the stream of power growing and thickening, pushing it harder and harder.

Pop.

Her fifth chakra opened, and more magic poured out.

"Perfect." Carla's voice was nearly hypnotic. "Now direct your power into the ring."

Shifting the magic stream was like trying to turn back a tidal wave. But she focused and mentally drew the magic down her right hand to the ring, willing it to saturate every atom.

Her skin tightened, and heat spread. The souls sat quiet and undisturbed like stones at the bottom of a riverbed. But she had a weird vibration at her throat. "I feel something."

"Your communication chakra. It's sending info to your witch book. Everything your magic knows from experience is being stored in there."

The vibration stopped. "I think it's done."

"Doing okay?" Carla asked.

Power zinged along her veins, her awareness sharp and vivid. "Yes. I want to see if I can find Kendall. Or at least connect to her."

"Concentrate on her."

She filled her mind with the baby. Kendall's round face, her grin and laughter. A vibration sparked in her throat. Her pulse shot up. It was working. She might really—

Her magic slammed into a wall that reeked with sulfur.

"Demon magic." Carla squeezed Risa's hand hard. "Pull back. Now."

Her magic scattered at the impact, and she couldn't catch it all. Panic spiked. Oh God. What should she do? Her magic spun too fast, and she couldn't get control.

Huge wings swooped in between her and the demon magic wall, and a screech rang out. *Falcon.* Every cell in her recognized the bird and honed in on him. The creature's wings flapped in long, smooth strokes, corralling her magic and pushing it into a stream and back to her chakras.

Away from the threat.

The sensation of the bird moving through her,

weaving in and out of her magic, was like discovering a missing piece of herself. She called her power back, and the falcon easily chased down the stray threads. Deep joy filled her heart, even as the threat of demon magic lurked in the back of her mind.

Finally the bird slowed and relaxed, indicating that the threat was over. Opening her eyes, she took in Carla and Darcy. "That was a rush."

"Sugar, you have no idea," came the deep, golden voice behind her.

≋ 19 ≋

IT TOOK EVERYTHING LINC HAD to resist tugging Risa
up into his arms and kissing her. Tasting her. His
entire body buzzed with the sheer power of her vibrant
magic winging through him. Heat coiled low in his
stomach, his cock thick and hard, aching.

He'd returned to the academy after more searching
for Archer, chasing down leads on Kendall and a few
other things. As soon as he'd gotten out of the car, he'd
been slammed with Risa's magic. Not bloodlust.
Instead it'd been the incredible magnitude of her
power that had sent him into a run, pulled both by
attraction and concern. What he'd found had ripped
the air from his lungs. The three witches holding
hands, sun gleaming off their witch shimmers. Carla
and Darcy were pretty girls, but his witch?

Stunning. Just days ago, she'd been trapped in the
cracks of her mind, and now? She radiated strength,
magic and pride in what she had done.

Until he'd heard two words—*demon magic*.

She rose and whirled to face him. "You're back."

He nearly laughed at her half-defiant, half-busted
look. Where did she think the falcon had come from?
He knew she'd felt the bird—the connection between

them at that second had been intense and vivid. Linc couldn't see what the bird did, but he'd sensed danger like a physical threat, and he'd smelled sulfur. Now that the bird had chased off the threat to their witch, the creature made ridiculous, happy noises.

Taking a step closer, he locked gazes with his witch. "Just in time, it would seem."

She glanced back over her shoulder.

Linc resisted the urge to grin. Risa fit right in, clearly having bonded with Carla and Darcy, now looking to her girls for support. "They aren't going to save you."

She turned back around, her eyes taking on fire. "I don't need them to deal with you, birdman."

He jerked up an eyebrow. That was new.

Risa hurried on with, "So here's the deal. I need my magic. And I need you to help me. But if you won't, or you just don't believe I'm strong enough—"

He moved so fast, he had his hands around her arms and her chest pressed to his before she could react. "You almost drove me to my knees with your power. I'm not worried about your strength, toughness or bravery. You don't know the meaning of giving up. And for your daughter? You'll risk anything, including your sanity." He drew one hand up her arm, gliding over her shoulder until he got to the delicate skin of her throat. The residual magic from her fifth chakra tingled up his arm and straight down to his cock.

A shudder ran through him. His mouth watered, but he needed to stay focused.

Risa stilled, wonder sliding into her expression, softening the distrust and frustration into something so beautiful it captivated him. "You think I'm brave?"

"You talked your way into a locked room where I had been losing the battle to hold on to any shred of my humanity. Then you cast your shield, knowing you'd pay a heavy price. Your bravery isn't in question."

She opened her mouth but said nothing.

"I didn't stop you, Risa. When we were in that room together, I was *inside you* and didn't stop you, didn't protect you. I used you, drank in your magic, and was so goddamned lost in you that I didn't protect you. That's what scares me." Linc hadn't forgotten the other two witches, he just didn't care. Let them hear. What mattered was he and Risa came to an understanding.

"Linc." She wrapped her hand around his resting against her throat. "I didn't even know you were here, yet your falcon linked with my magic and pulled me back from the block around Kendall. I didn't fight him, even though Kendall was behind the danger that he pushed me away from. I won't do her any good if I'm dead, incapacitated from demon magic, or let them track us." A heavy frown settled between her brows. "Oh God, that's how Archer found your house. I was trying to reach Kendall and hit the demon block—"

"Stop. You were trying to find your baby." Linc didn't like the dawning horror on her face. "You couldn't have known what would happen, and neither did I."

Some of the tension eased in her. "But that's why you were being so cautious about helping me do high magic."

He pulled her tighter against him. "That's half the reason. The other half is that I didn't know if our bond was strong enough yet for me and the falcon to protect you." Linc looked down at her, seeing a woman who'd been used and hurt but who'd trusted him to touch her magic. A growl worked up his throat, and he shifted, lifting Risa in his arms.

"Linc! What are you doing?"

He glanced down. "Claiming you. Our bond is strong

enough, and I'm done being careful." He couldn't wait, couldn't hold back, and launched into a run.

Laughter followed them. "Been there!" Darcy called out.

"Done that!" Carla followed.

Linc raced by the pool and student dorms, enjoying the freedom of running flat out with Risa in his arms. The wings tattooed on his back itched, as if trying to push out.

Damn he'd love to fly one day.

But now he had other plans. Shifting his path, he headed for the garage.

"Where are we going?"

"To a place where it'll just be the two of us. I was coming to pick you up when you blindsided me with your witchcraft. We'll work on your magic to find Kendall." He looked down into her flushed face. "After I keep my promise to you."

"What promise?"

The first time he'd taken her in a concrete room with a window that gave the others full view. That bugged the shit out of him. Tortured him. Risa had been used in ways he didn't even want to know about. There'd been no one there to protect and care for her. But now she had him.

"All the pleasure you can handle when we make love. We'll experience it together."

"Can I drive?" Risa watched the way Linc, wearing dark slacks and a crisp white shirt with the sleeves rolled up to reveal a hundred K watch on his thick wrist, shifted through the gears of the gray-striped, ceramic-blue Viper. The car's engine rumbled with the same restrained power that lived in Linc. She'd love to get her hands on it.

"I'll buy you your own car. Anything you want."

Amusement tugged at her mouth. "You'd buy me a car to keep me from driving yours?"

"Well, I don't want to be an ass about it."

Oh my God, he was serious. She couldn't resist and asked, "Can I eat Twinkies in this car?"

His jaw clenched. "No."

"Sno Balls?"

The tendons in his neck stood out. "Not happening."

She had to bite the inside of her cheek to keep from laughing. "Ding Dongs?"

Linc snapped his head around, lowered his chin and glared at her over the top of his shades. "You wouldn't dare."

Don't do it. Don't. Yet her magic swelled in her chakras, then burst out. A twin package of Twinkies appeared in her hand.

Comical shock stamped onto his face, and he nearly missed a corner.

Risa doubled over laughing, her body shaking with the force of it.

Linc swung the car around another corner, then refocused on her. "Having fun?"

Wiping tears, she lifted her head. "Yes. And it feels so damn good."

His face softened. "Yeah?"

"Yeah. I can tease you, defy you, and you won't hurt me." It came out before she thought about it, but it was the truth. She held up her Twinkies. "Besides, you bought me a box of these, Sno Balls and Ding Dongs." She'd been so touched when he showed her the cupboard in the small kitchen with all the treats. He'd done that for her while she'd been in the soul screams. She grasped the package, wanting to tear into it and bite into her Twinkie.

"You don't want to defy me on this."

His low voice got her attention. "No?"

"You open those and I swear to Wing Slayer I won't let you come. I'll kiss you, touch you until you moan, but I stop right there when you're begging me. Still want to open that package?"

"That's... You'd really do that?"

"Want to test me?"

She looked sadly at her Twinkies, then waved her hand, sending them back to the box in their suite.

His laugh rang out in the car. "You're pouting."

"I like Twinkies."

He reached over, his large hand folding around her thigh. "I'll make it up to you. We're almost there."

Excitement bubbled in her veins. The worry for Kendall was always there, but now she had real hope, and with Linc's help she'd find the baby with her magic. To distract herself, she said, "This car wasn't in the garage the night we arrived." She sniffed, the new-car smell tipping her off. "It's new."

"Yep. My other Viper was destroyed the night Archer spawned. This one came in as a special order for another client."

"And the dealership sold it to you?"

"I own the dealership."

Interesting. Every tiny thing he told her increased her curiosity, her desire to really know Linc. "What does this car mean to you? You took the time to go get it while dealing with all the other shit going on. I know you have other vehicles. Why, Linc?"

Linc guided the car into a gated parking garage. Once parked, he turned to look at her. "You really want to know?"

"Yes."

"When I was caged, one of my handlers had a Viper. He'd showed me pictures of it, telling me how many fights I'd had to win to get him that car. Taunted me with it. The day he bought it, all of them talked about it. I could smell the leather on them..." His hand caressed the seat, his eyes distant.

"Linc?"

"It was the smell of freedom to me. Power. Controlling my own destiny. After I escaped and could afford it, I bought a Viper. I have a lot of cars, but the Viper, when I see it or drive it, it feels like I made it out of that cage."

She put her hand over his on the seat. "That's why you don't want anyone else driving it?" Linc's entire life and future had been ripped from his control the night he'd been taken from his bed. Not waiting for his response, she answered her own question. "You don't want to give anyone else the keys to your freedom."

Their eyes connected, and tension thickened the air like a summer storm. She held her breath, waiting for...something.

Linc twisted away, breaking the moment to shove open the door.

Startled by the abrupt change, she turned to get out.

Linc shot around the car and opened her door before she could reach the handle. Taking her hand, he eased her out, shut the door and led her to an elevator.

"What's this place?" It didn't have any signage on the outside. "Condos?" she guessed, since it was a high-rise building.

"L.C. Family Recovery Center." As the elevator doors slid closed, Linc hit a button and added, "It's not open yet, and the building is damned secure. Unless Archer wakes and destroys it with hellfire, no one uninvited is getting in here."

"Part of the L.C. Group that Hilary mentioned?"

He leaned back against the side of the elevator, one perfectly draped pants leg over the other, and inclined his head.

"Recovery center for drugs?"

"And other issues, yes." Once the doors opened, Linc led her out. Two steps later, she stopped, tugging on his hand as she took in the huge room. It was a kid's paradise. A rock climbing wall, playground equipment, a sectioned-off room with trampolines, even a snack bar.

"What's this?"

"Child care. Children will live here with their parent or parents. Our goal is to help families that want to stay together. You can look later. We're going to the roof."

As she followed him up the stairs, the scope of what he and Hilary were doing sank in. They weren't just building a school for lost kids, but also a center for fractured families. He led her to a hallway and up a flight of stairs. Linc opened the door, stepped out and held it for her.

Risa walked out into an oasis in the desert. On one end of the roof bloomed a full garden of desert plants mixed with greenery. The other side had a built-in kitchen, couple big BBQs and in the center was a massive fire pit surrounded by wide lounge chairs covered in thick cushions and sitting areas. Looking up, she saw retractable canopies. Linc flipped a switch and misters sprang to life, cooling the hot air.

"This is amazing." The entire roof had metal-and-glass fencing that came up to her chest. She walked over, placing her hands on the glass. She could see the casinos in the distance.

"Shatter and bulletproof. Completely safe." Linc covered her hands with his and pressed his body against her back and ass. "And treated so no one can see in." Leaning down, he kissed the side of her neck. "You're the only woman I've brought here, Risa. And the only woman I want to make love to."

She closed her eyes, sexy chills skittering down to

her nipples. Magic rippled in her belly, and longing built in her throat. She turned, forgetting the world beyond the glass.

This was their time. He'd brought her to this place that held some meaning for him. Shared a part of himself with her. And he'd seen all her darkest parts.

Except one—the lie that would tear them apart.

But for this moment he was hers. Rising on her toes, she kissed him.

He wrapped his arms around her, lifting her off her feet and ravaging her mouth. One hand covered her ass, kneading as he pulled her tight to his thick erection. He walked, every rolling stride pushing his cock through their clothes against her center.

Each beat of her heart ramped up her need. Magic rushed and bubbled, heightening her senses. When he broke the kiss to lay her on the thick cushion of the wide lounge chair, she clung to him, craving the feel of him surrounding her. A harsh, deep ache grew below her belly button. In bold desperation, she focused her magic, taking their clothes and tossing them to a nearby chair.

"That's hot," he growled in approval. Linc kneeled at the side of the spacious chair, the sun catching the highlights in his brown hair and gleaming off the fine sheen of moisture from the misters that was beading on his broad shoulders. He slid his fingers down her throat and chest to cup her breast, thumbing a nipple. "I want to explore you, give you pleasure you've never imagined."

Fire streaked from his touch, making her writhe. She shook her head, a near-frantic sensation riding her. "I need you inside me. I have to feel that again." Thick want tightened her throat. "I hurt for it." Linc's belief in her had freed her ability to feel desire, to embrace it as normal and healthy.

"Hurt where?"

Taking his hand, she led him to the spot right over her mound between her hipbones. "Here." Her magic surged up to touch his hand and spread more agonizing want. The heat of his touch branded her skin.

Trailing his fingers down, he brushed her thighs.

Magic chased his touch, making her clench.

"Are you wet, Risa? I want you soaked, so slick that I glide into you, filling up the emptiness." His voice dropped to a sexy growl. "Show me."

She opened her thighs, spreading them far enough to feel the gentle mist and Linc's heated gaze. He dragged his fingers along her cleft, then parted her. "Oh God, wet. So wet." He sank his fingers into her depths, while his thumb circled her clit. A deep moan rumbled out of her, and Linc moved with blinding speed.

He took his fingers out, and just when she missed the feel of him stroking her, his massive body covered hers. The weight and heat of him pressed her into the chair, his legs pushing her wide, and his cockhead, thick and hot, seated against her entrance.

His face flushed, eyes burned. "Put your hands on my shoulders. You need your hands for shield magic, and I'm not taking any chances. Keep your hands anchored there." Leaning nose to nose, he said, "You're mine now. I'm not letting you slip away from me. You're going to feel what we do, every slide of my cock." Each word bled possession. Raw need. "Hang on to me."

As soon as her palms hit his shoulders, he pushed in, tunneling fast, hard and deep, filling the emptiness inside her. She arched beneath the sensual assault, her vaginal walls fluttering with pleasure and magic. Desire rose and twisted, until she had to move. Wrapping her thighs around him, she held on. With her eyes closed, she rode the wild sensation as he pumped his cock into her, hitting nerves that made her gasp and writhe.

"Look at me. I need to see your eyes."

Following the growled command took everything she had, but she forced her lids up.

Linc's jaw was rigid, tendons bulging his neck and arms, nostrils flaring. "There's my girl, my Risa. So fucking beautiful." He kissed her hard, stealing her breath as he thrust deeper, driving her higher. Her womb tightened mercilessly, and her muscles locked as she arched up, reaching for that pinnacle.

She yanked her mouth free, gulping air, clawing at his shoulders. "Too much."

He pulled back and locked gazes with her. "It's never too much. Surrender, sweet witch. Let the pleasure have you."

Linc shifted his hips, and her body lit up, ripples of fiery waves rolling and spasming, so exquisite she was helpless beneath the onslaught.

And through it all, Linc held her gaze.

The dazzling blue of her eyes warmed to fire as she showed him her pleasure. All of Risa was there, completely with him. Her channel rippled around his cock from her orgasm, her magic swarming him, making his heart pound.

His balls drew up. He tried to hold back, determined to give her more. To watch her again, experiencing the pure trust in her as she came apart. Letting her tumble into that exquisite place while he and the bird stood guard, keeping her safe.

Priceless.

Risa drew her hands down his shoulders and stroked the ink, her fingers tracing not the bird but the brand. "Don't hold back. I want all of you right down to the feral side you keep leashed."

She saw him. Knew. Cared about him anyway. Her

words and touch snapped his control. An inferno ignited and spread, bowing his back until he rose stiff-armed over her, pumping fiercely into this woman. Her glove-tight sheathe rippled and milked him as she met every thrust.

Linc looked down at Risa, swimming in her magic, surrendering everything to him. He felt her tightening, her legs trembling around him, panting as her fingers dug into his back. He didn't feel the brand, only her touch.

He fucked her harder, digging his toes into the cushion, snapping his hips in a feral need to claim her, mark her as she'd marked him. "Risa." He slid his hand beneath her ass, raising her hips to take him, making her completely open and vulnerable to him. "Now. With me. Let go and come." In this moment, Linc wanted to be the center of her world and to shatter with her into total bliss.

She cried out and lost control, her head thrown back, neck exposed and her magic slamming him. His orgasm ripped down his spine and exploded. He powered into her, jetting hot seed and giving her everything he had. Finally he buried his face in her neck, inhaling the scent of his soul mirror.

She smelled like home.

Risa shivered as she stood at the treated glass wall, looking out as darkness fell over the city. She'd pulled on her panties and T-shirt, but the scarcity of blazing neon lights that normally lit up the Vegas night had drawn her before she finished dressing.

"Hey, sorry." Linc's heat spread behind her. "I had to take the call from Carla."

She flattened her hand on the glass. "Everything okay?"

"At the moment, yes."

Out in the distance the high-rise casinos that dominated the landscape should be lit up, but many of them remained dark like gaping holes, either burned down or the power still out. Even the energy in Vegas was different. Just like Risa was different from the woman she'd been a week ago when she, Blythe and Kendall had arrived.

"Is something wrong?"

Yes. She was falling for this man, but it didn't matter. "No. I was just thinking how you gave me a beautiful memory by bringing me here, making love to me." She craned her head to look at him and smiled. "Thank you."

His eyes darkened, the gold taking on veins of bronze. He wrapped an arm around her waist, tugging her back against him. "It's more than that. I can feel your turmoil and sadness."

God. Turning her gaze from his, she stared out into the night. "It's just more than I expected."

The sounds of traffic drifted up, and Linc's scent swirled around her. "The sex? Or us?"

Did it matter if she told the truth? "Both. You're a just man when you have every right to be bitter. You care about kids and those who can't fight for themselves, like Kendall. You built a school, this family recovery center. You're kind of a modern day Robin Hood, using your money won by gambling with the rich to give back to the poor. And you believe in me even though you've seen me broken by soul screams." He'd taken care of her then, holding and comforting her, coaxing her back to reality. "I've never met anyone like you."

"Risa." He stroked her hand and paused. After a couple seconds, he added, "I've dated a lot of women."

Her stomach twisted in awful humiliation. Of course he had, she'd heard the tales. And she was acting like a teenager with her first lover. "You're right. My experience is limited. This is probably just—"

Linc caught her chin, tilting it up for his gaze to blaze down into hers. "But I've never felt like I do with you. You're more amazing than anyone I've met. I've told you things, trusted you with the parts of me I've told no one else, not even Hilary. You touched my brand, felt that there when no one else cared."

Her eyes filled with tears. "I care. You're not feral, Linc. You're a man who does the right thing, makes the hard choices. That brand...you let them brand you rather than hurt a woman. Don't you see?" God, she was crying. But her heart hurt for him. "That's your mark of honor. Not shame." Risa knew what he'd been forced to do, but his care with her when her mind shattered told her that he'd been just as kind to those poor girls.

"You scare me, little witch. You have far more of me than I've shared with anyone else. Ever." He kissed the top of her head tenderly.

Dear Ancestors, he trusted her with too much. Something rare and special was growing between them. She touched the glass again, wishing she had a way out of the lie. Regret pushed into her chest. She was going to destroy their relationship when the truth came out. Could she tell him? God, she wanted to, but fear kept her silent. Kendall was one-quarter demon, the daughter and granddaughter of the hunters and witches most hated enemies.

He'd never forgive that lie.

But what could she do? She couldn't risk them not helping her find and rescue Kendall.

Linc's hand settled over hers against the glass. "I feel your magic in this ring." He fingered the silver wrapped around her thumb.

"It's my witch book. Darcy gave the ring to me." She closed her eyes, drinking in the feel of Linc pressed up to her back and the memory of doing magic with Darcy and Carla. "It was so amazing to circle magic with them. They helped me until we hit the block."

"You have friends now."

See that? Linc got it, understood how much it meant to her, which made her care even more for him. Trying to remind herself of her priority, she kept her gaze over the city and said softly, "Kendall's out there somewhere."

"I'll help you, sweetheart. That call I just took from Carla? She told me to try to get you to open your sixth chakra."

"My third eye?"

He nodded. "She's surmising that your third eye can get above the block on Kendall to see her location. That means we push your magic past your communication chakra." He lifted his hand to her throat. "It's a lot of magic. You have to trust me to help you. Do you think the souls are up to it?"

"They didn't react to the magic I did today. Not even when I moved what I know into my witch book, which included my shield magic. Before, that would have stirred up the souls." She closed her eyes, feeling the weight of them in her magic. "I think they're used to the falcon now. He was there a lot when I was in the soul screams, or at least I could hear him."

"He was there singing to you."

"How did he know to do that?"

"Because you told us. Your mom and you, you had music together. That was your good memory, your bond. He knew you'd follow his music, even if you couldn't hear anything else."

Her heart hit the top of the highest cliff and tumbled right over, giving her that bottoming-out sensation. *This is what it feels like to fall in love.* "You have too much of me too."

He kissed her hair. "Open your chakras and gather your magic." His voice flowed whisper soft against her ear as he lifted the hem of her shirt.

Her chakras popped open with a hiss, magic pouring out as she let him slide off her shirt. He'd told her no one could see, and she believed him. She relaxed as he trailed his fingers up the center line of her belly, between her breasts to her throat.

Then down.

Tingles broke out on her skin. Her powers began to spin, chasing his touch. A flush rose, and she moaned as her magic swelled. Desire rushed up, her nipples hardening and folds softening. "Linc."

"I feel it. Jesus, I feel it right to my cock." He pressed his erection constricted in his pants against her lower back. He hadn't bothered putting on a shirt. "Keep going, Risa. Feel it."

His caress slid down into her panties.

More magic burst out, causing her to gasp as he penetrated her with two fingers, brushing hot spots deep inside her. "You're so wet. Slick."

"That's from you too." She wasn't even thinking now, just feeling the magic rushing, his fingers pumping.

His dark laugh spilled over her. "That makes it hotter." He gathered her slickness and rubbed it on her clit.

Power pushed at her throat. She stiffened, trying to breathe past the pressure.

Linc wrapped his other hand around her neck, skating his fingers up and down as he continued the sexy invasion between her legs, gliding in and out in a maddening rhythm. Every touch made her hotter, needier. She arched into his thrusting hand, riding it out, secure that Linc only gave her pleasure.

Her fifth chakra opened with a vibration. Sudden, sharp awareness hissed through her. The bird's wings pumped powerfully, corralling her magic while emitting musical chirps, whistles and trills. They were beautifully familiar to her, the same calls he'd used to lead her out of the soul screams. Why was Falcon doing it now? Understanding dawned. The bird's music had calmed the souls while leading her out of the cracks in her mind.

Singing. He's singing to the souls.

Linc jerked behind her, his fingers stilling.

Panic edged in. "What?"

Shh, it's okay, love. You just surprised me. You projected your thoughts to me like I am to you.

I did? She'd never felt this close to anyone. It thrilled and terrified her.

Soul-mirror connection. The mind link forms over time. You told me the bird is singing to the souls, keeping them calm.

The heat and safety of Linc surrounded her from the outside and caressed her internally. It was so powerfully amazing it caused her magic to surge again, pushing higher, making Linc's touch more vivid.

You're so beautiful to me like this. Real and trusting. Let the magic have you, Risa. I'll hold you, I won't let go.

Linc's mind connected with hers. That intimacy shuddered through her, creating a roar of magic and desire. Her entire lower body clenched around his fingers. His thumb pressed against her clit as pressure built in her forehead. The roof and night slid away, until all her awareness centered on Linc and her magic swelling and pushing and...

Her climax hit, stealing her breath, hot pleasure pulsing wildly. It didn't ebb and soften, but grew until it *unanchored* her. Pulling her away.

Terror slammed into her.

Don't fight it, sweetheart. I have you, I swear. Trust me and your magic.

Risa hovered, aware of a dime-sized pain in her forehead, yet her mind clutched the very last tether holding her—fear. The bird worked at a furious pace, pushing her magic into a stream so strong, it glowed like blue fire. He only waited for her.

Just like when she'd been so scared, locked in the cracks in her mind, she reached for the bird. The second feathers touched her hand, he pulled her free of her body.

Her third eye snapped open. Everything passed in a blur, then slowed.

Kendall! Oh my Ancestors. The child sat in a crib, her eyes drenched in tears, surrounded by an oily gray shroud.

Kendall looked up, a sob wrenching her whole body as her gaze focused. A trembling smile lit up her face, and Kendall held up her fat arms.

To her. Somehow the baby saw her. Unable to bear it, Risa shot forward, desperate to get to the child.

The bird screeched, streaking in to push her back and up. For a second, magnificent wings filled her third eye.

Risa. Come back, now.

Linc's gentle, coaxing voice created a pull in her magic to go to him. No. She couldn't leave Kendall. She had to at least figure out where the baby was. But despite herself, she retreated, Kendall growing smaller until it appeared Risa was looking down on a dollhouse with no roof, just a maze of walls. Frantically she scanned the rooms but couldn't find anything to identify it. She spotted a woman and two men around a card table.

The woman frowned, turning her head so that Risa got a good look at her. Shoulder-length dark blonde hair, light eyes...Petra! She'd found Archer's mother with Kendall, but where were they?

Pulling farther away, she saw the outside of the

main two-story building and outbuildings. Was that kennels? All shabby and in need to paint. Where was this? Finally a fading sign leaned up against an abandoned car came into view. She concentrated with everything she had to make out the words.

Izzy's Kennel Club.

She barely read that when dizziness spun her away and she plummeted into a freefall.

⤜ 20 ⤛

DREAD HIT HIM THE SECOND Risa's magic dropped off, and she collapsed in his arms. Oh fuck, not the soul screams. He lifted her and sank down on the lounge.

"Risa." He pushed her hair back. "Open your eyes."

Nothing. She just lay there, limp.

He'd screwed up again, so caught up in her, in the untamed beauty of Risa in her magic, the feel of the bird moving with her, the heat...

Wait, the bird was quiet on his back. Not agitated.

Risa. He tried their brand-new mental link as he stroked her face.

Her eyelids lifted.

Linc braced himself, and the dread reappeared to fist in his belly until she fully opened her eyes. Dark blue with no gray. Blowing out a breath, he relaxed. "You okay?"

"Hard landing back into my body." She shook her head as if clearing any residual fog, then sat up abruptly. "I saw her, oh God, Linc, I saw her." Shooting off his lap, she grabbed her pants and dragged them on. "Kendall's at a house with a woman and two men. It's Petra, Archer's mother. She has Kendall. Where's my shirt?"

289

"Whoa." He caught her arms, needing her to stop and explain more. "Did you see any markings that will give us a location?"

"Yes." She took a breath, obviously trying to calm down. "I saw a sign. *Izzy's Kennel Club.* We have to find it."

All his muscles locked. He couldn't have heard that right. Memories spun while the brand on his back burned as if the red-hot metal were being held against his skin right now.

"Linc? Did you hear me? We have to go get her!"

Right. He pulled himself together. "Izzy's Kennel Club? You're sure? That place has been abandoned for nearly a dozen years." As soon as the words were out, he realized how fucking perfect it was, a great place to hide. After all, who wanted a property where there'd been a mass murder? Linc had killed a half-dozen men the night he escaped, and rumors had spread like wildfire after that.

"I saw the sign leaning up against an old rusted car. Do you know—?"

The building jolted sharply, then settled. In the distance, car alarms blared.

"Earthquake." That jarred him out of his memories. He grabbed her hand and yanked her to the door. "Let's go."

Risa stumbled. "Wait, I'm dizzy."

The building swayed again, triggering a deep need to get her out of the structure that could collapse. Too many years in a cage made him hyperaware of how easy it was to get trapped.

"No time." Linc scooped her up and wrenched open the door. The stairs split into two sections. He leapt down one, then the next and kept going down each floor until he got to the garage level. Quickly scanning the empty structure, he raced to the car, a bad feeling riding his spine. Natural earthquake, or Archer rising?

After dropping Risa to her feet, he opened the door. "In."

She complied, and he shot around the car, jumped in and started it just as another jolt hit.

"Crap. I feel it in my magic."

Peeling out of the garage into the dark night, he asked, "What does that mean?"

"It feels like the night Archer spawned."

Fuck, fuck, fuck. The bastard had to wake some time, so why not now when Linc had Risa out in the open? He spun the wheel, taking a corner. His phone rang, and he answered it through the car's Bluetooth. "Dillinger."

"Rogues are attacking," Axel said. "We have all the women in the multipurpose room in the center of the school."

"Anyone hurt?"

"Nothing significant, but Darcy and Carla feel demon magic in the ley lines."

"So do I," Risa spit out. "It's Archer. He's waking." She grabbed Linc's arm. "Kendall! We have to get her."

Goddammit. What should he do? Go help his friends or rescue his mate's baby?

"You know where she is?" Axel's voice cut in.

"I saw her with my third eye," Risa confirmed. "Petra's there too."

"Where?"

Linc jumped in. "Izzy's Kennel Club. It used to be an underground dog-fighting place. They had gambling, prostitution and other illegal activities." Like deathmatches with Linc as their star attraction. "It's been abandoned for years. I can make it there in fifteen minutes. But I have Risa with me, and it's too dangerous."

The car shook as another earthquake jolted. More car alarms went off, people ran out to the streets, and two cars collided. All hell was breaking loose.

"No time!" Risa's fingers dug into his biceps. "You swore, Linc!"

He spun the wheel, turning the car to head the other way. "Axel, get the women to Baron's gun range. He has a bunker belowground on the site. Put the girls there. Risa only saw two men and a woman. I should be able to get the baby." Two rogues and a woman—even a demon witch—he could handle.

"Archer might be hibernating there. You can't take Risa into that possible danger."

"I'll be able to tell," Risa blurted out.

"What?" Linc glanced over at her white face and clenched hands.

"I was right there outside the Mystique Hotel when he spawned. I feel his power now. If it increases as we approach the kennel club, then we'll know we're getting closer to the source."

That made sense, but his muscles locked up at the idea of putting her in any more danger.

"Go and report back," Axel said. "Don't get too close, just enough to know if Archer's there, then we'll figure it out. Right now... Fuck."

"What?" How much worse could this night get?

"More rogues attacking."

"Do you need me?"

"No," Axel ordered. "Get the kid first. But we're not leaving. Moving the women in a vehicle makes them too vulnerable. You find out if Archer's at the kennel club. Update me." The line cut.

Ignoring the deep urge to go protect his friends, he gunned the engine, breaking speed limits and pushing the car to the max. He swung around a motorcycle. "I need the truth, Risa. Will you really be able to feel Archer if he's there?"

"Yes. It's a heaviness now, but I'm still in control. What I remember was that the closer he got to me, the stronger an oily, smoke sensation coated my mouth. If he's close, I'll know."

"You didn't realize he was at the house when he attacked with the hellfire." Was he doing the right thing? But damn it, he'd sworn to get her baby for her. Axel and the others could handle rogues.

Risa sighed. "My magic was numb then."

That was a punch to his ego. Linc hadn't forgotten trying to kiss and arouse her, and she'd gone cold on him, her magic protecting her. He understood it, but it still rankled. "Yeah, well, your magic loves me now."

She snorted. "Your bird sings to me."

Despite the hellishness, he turned to face her. Dark choppy black hair falling around the bare shoulders of her tank, her usual camo pants, clunky boots. *Hottest woman I've ever seen.*

Risa met his gaze, her eyes softening. "I heard that."

"Good." He wanted her to know.

She shifted to look at the road. "Linc!"

Jerking around as another earthquake rumbled, he spotted a fissure splitting open in the road, the sides caving in. Reacting, he cranked the wheel, just missing it, and careened up the sidewalk toward a trailer park.

The bumper scraped and moaned as the low-slung sports car struggled to jump the curb. Tires better not blow. Finally, the car straightened, and he guided it around the sinkhole back onto the street.

"Second Viper destroyed in a fucking week," he growled.

"Maybe you should get a Hummer. They eat curbs for breakfast instead of crying and whining like a little bitch."

Linc laughed, some of the tension easing in him for a second. "I'll get you a Hummer." Pink, just to piss her off. Sobering, he said, "We're almost to the place. That sinkhole might indicate Archer's close by.

Are you feeling anything more? Tasting anything?"

"Same pressure in my chakras, nothing else." She twisted in her seat, nerves and worry making it impossible to sit still.

He turned into a storage yard. Rows of lights showed the locked units. Linc pointed to a dirt road. "The kennel club is down there a half mile."

Risa unsnapped her seat belt.

He reached past her into the locked glove compartment, pulled out a gun and handed it to her. "If anything happens to me, use this gun, hightail your ass back to this car and get the hell out of here. Call any of the guys, or Baron. They'll protect you."

"I can't leave without Kendall."

"You will if you have to. If I'm down and you die tonight, then that baby has no one. Live to help her later. Got me?"

Risa nodded.

Linc rolled up his pants legs, then reached under the seat, grabbed his holsters and strapped his throwing knives to his calves. "Open your magic. What can you feel?"

Her magic rolled over him, buzzing through his veins. The bird spread on his back.

"Kendall and demon magic. But it's not Archer."

He nodded. "I smell copper and sulfur, but not as strong as the night Archer spawned. Pretty sure the sulfur is Petra the demon witch, not the spawn. Even if he was hibernating, he'd be giving off scent."

"He's waking though. Soon." She shifted in her seat. "I need to get Kendall before he fully wakens."

Her agitation rode her magic, pricking his skin as he unbuttoned his shirt and slid it off.

"What are you doing?"

"It's white—it'll stand out like a beacon in the night. Especially with the nearly full moon." He tossed the shirt, clearly sliding into hunt-and-kill mode. He grabbed his phone and sent off a quick text update to Axel, Sutton, Ram and Eli.

Done with that, he looked at Risa. "Let's get your baby."

Risa's heart pounded as she watched Linc peel off his civility and James Bond charm. Wearing rolled-up black pants, his bronzed skin and a wicked knife expertly fisted in one hand, the others gleaming against his powerful calves as he moved with incredible stealth, he looked rough and feral.

Kendall's nearness sparked a huge, empty ache inside Risa. The baby may not be her biological child, but Risa loved her desperately. Should she have told Linc the truth?

Don't think about it now.

Linc stopped, catching her hand. "I'm going to shield us so we appear invisible."

Both their hands vanished. A quick glance at their bodies proved his claim. She couldn't see either of them. "Wow."

"I can't hold it if I engage in a fight. Quiet now, rogues might be shielding too."

She squeezed his hand to let him know she understood and followed him as they stayed off the road, stepping around weeds and rocks. They passed the old stripped-to-a-shell car with the sign she'd seen with her third eye. Her shoe snagged on something, causing her to stumble. Regaining her balance, she made out the shape of an old mattress.

Linc abruptly stopped. "Don't move." It came out a bare whisper.

She strained, trying to hear or see what he did. In the moonlight, she could see the house about half a block's length away. To the left should be the building with kennels, but it was hard to see now. Straight ahead, something flashed, followed by a *boom*.

Linc shoved her to the ground, materialized and threw the knife in his hand.

A grunt and scream sounded.

Risa jerked her head up in time to see a man materialize twenty feet away, dropping the gun in his hand to clutch the knife buried in his chest. His knees gave out, and he hit the dirt.

A second man materialized next to him and fired his gun.

Linc dove, rolled, yanked thin wicked blades from his calf holster, shot up to his feet and rocketed the two knives.

All before Risa could get the safety off her gun.

The second gunman bellowed and thumped to the dirt.

Her stomach clenched at the sight of the blades lodged in his throat and chest. That was all she saw before Linc bent over the men and retrieved his knives.

Gaining her feet, she raced to him. "Are they—?"

"Dead. Two rogues. Let's go." He shoved the two guns into his waistband, grabbed her hand and tugged her into a run. "Stay low." They passed two rows of kennels with an attached building.

Linc's hand on hers spasmed.

An image flickered in her mind. A big but young man shackled on his knees...a red-hot brand pressed to his back. "Oh God." She tripped, her entire head blazing with sudden pain and horror. Going to her knees, she yanked her hand free. "It was here. You were kept here." She stared at the rows of kennels. Linc had said he was trained like a dog, and he'd meant it. Sickness and aching fury roiled in her.

Linc dropped down, one hand on her face. "Look at me."

"I saw it. You showed me. I saw them branding you."

"Fuck. My fault. The memory hit, and I must have projected it." His face hardened. "Push it out, Risa. Do you want to get your daughter? Or do you want to sit here and cry over something that happened over a decade ago?"

Shadows of the past haunted his eyes, yet he hadn't let it stop him from helping her rescue Kendall. There was no time for her to melt down. She nodded, put a hand on his shoulder and jumped to her feet. "I'm—"

The ground pitched, rumbling and rocking as another quake shuddered the earth.

Her chakras cramped, stealing her breath. It took an effort to fight it. "He's waking more, almost fully awake. I can feel it. He's sucking magic through the ley lines away from here. Like a supersized Hoover." The shaking stopped. "Hurry!"

He took off, and she stayed with him despite the constant tug on her magic. The house loomed up, two stories of brown paint faded to dried, cracked mud and blacked-out windows.

"You sure she's in there?" Linc asked.

"Yes." The need to get to Kendall propelled her forward. Sudden gray and black fog billowed up from the ground in a circle around the house. Her magic cringed, and sulfur burned her nose. "Demon magic." Risa skidded to a stop. "That's the black that's been around Kendall. But it's not around her, it's around the house."

"Has to be Petra's magic."

"How do we get through?"

Linc touched the edge of the fog and jerked his hand back. "Huh." The skin turned black at his fingertips and hung off in strips. Blood welled. "Demonic acid."

That had to hurt, but he just shook his hand.

Looking around, he found two empty beer cans. After grabbing them, he threw one into the fog.

It melted and twisted hideously.

Risa backed up a step.

Linc threw the other one over the fog.

It landed perfectly intact on the other side. Linc tugged her back a few yards and crouched. "On my back. Hold on, and don't fall."

Risa jammed the gun in her pants and climbed on. "You sure? It's rising fast, up to your knees now."

"No problem. Hold on." He launched into a run.

She locked her arms around his neck, instinctively burying her face in his shoulder as he leapt up. And up. For a second, they were flying. Would the fog surge up and surround them?

He landed, bending his knees to let her slide off.

She turned. "It's coming this way!" The fog had stopped rising and now oozed toward them rapidly. Instinctive fear gripped her, and she ran for the door.

Linc blew past her, slamming into the door, shoving it open, dropping to a crouch with his gun out and sweeping the interior. Lights spilled over a bare room holding a card table littered with dirty paper goods, laptops, and a huge trash can brimming with fast food containers and beer cans. The place reeked.

Risa spun around to see the encroaching fog. Too close, moving too fast. Fear slammed her heart against her ribs, and she banged the door closed, hoping to slow the vapor down. That shit would skin them alive. No time to think about it. She spotted Linc checking a closet and doorways, and caught sight of a staircase across the room.

A low hiss spun her, and she stared in horror. Fog leaked through the cracks of the door, then the solid wood began to bulge inward. "Linc!"

He ran out from another room by the staircase. "Shit. Upstairs!"

Risa tore across the room. Halfway to the stairs, the door exploded open. Linc got there first, yanked her off her feet into his arms and ran up. His heart slammed against her chest. Tilting her head around his shoulder, she saw the fog billowing wildly, filling the room below and getting closer.

Broken, exhausted sobbing reached them. "Kendall!" The walls and doors blurred as Linc ran, rounding through an opened door. He dumped her on her feet.

Risa stumbled into the bedroom and focused on the crib. Her knees almost buckled when she saw the little girl. Kendall's blonde hair was matted, her face drenched in tears, and she rocked in distress. She wore a dirty T-shirt and diaper. "Kendall." It came out a thick whisper. Risa reached into the crib. She couldn't quite believe it. Had she really found Kendall? Was the baby real or a figment of her desperate imagination?

The baby lifted her head, her eyes fixing on Risa. For a second the rocking stopped, then she let out a wail, holding out her arms. The look on the baby's face ripped out Risa's heart—pure fear that Risa would leave her.

Never! Hot emotion squeezed her chest, too much to process. She scooped her up and hugged her tight. Her nose clogged as those fat little arms wrapped around her neck.

"I have you, baby. I won't leave you ever again." *See, Blythe? I'm keeping my promise.* More emotion stole her breath as she thought of her friend who'd loved her child so much.

Kendall grabbed fistfuls of Risa's hair, as if afraid to let go.

"Fog's in the hallway."

Linc's sharp voice cut into the moment, jerking her back to their imminent danger. Where was Petra? She had to be here.

He shut the door and ran to the window. After wrenching it open, he slid through. "Come here."

Risa leaned her head out the waist-high window to hand him Kendall. The baby whimpered, burying her face into Risa's neck.

The door creaked and groaned.

Linc shoved his gun into his waistband. "Hold her tight." Gripping Risa's arms, he hauled her out the window and steadied her on her feet. "Careful." He closed the window just as the door burst open inside the room.

With the light spilling out the window, she studied the ten-foot length of sloped roof that ran the width of the house and wrapped around the corner. "What now?" Taking a couple steps, she eyed the solid six feet of fog rising from the ground to surround the house.

Striding to her with sure footing, he said, "We'll have to jump."

He'd jumped from his second-story window holding her before. But now she had Kendall, the baby clinging to her desperately. "But—"

A shot exploded.

"Fuck." Linc stumbled, caught himself and pivoted around, a gun in his hand as he fired back toward another window.

Kendall screamed, her body spasming in fear. Struggling to keep her balance, Risa looked up. Linc's huge body blocked her and Kendall. He had his knees bent, arms up aiming the weapon. A line of blood dripped from his right biceps. *Shot! He'd been shot.*

Refusing to panic, she shifted Kendall to one arm, pulled out her gun and leaned around to see a dark shape with shoulder-length hair leaning out an opened window. The acid fog split around her and raced toward them.

Petra. She's controlling the fog. She barely thought it before Linc fired his gun.

The shot threw the witch back from the window, but the fog kept coming.

Linc turned, reaching for her, blood pouring from his arm wound. *Do something! Help him.* That thought snapped her into action, and she concentrated on opening her chakras.

The house shuddered, followed by a rocking jolt.

Pressure cramped down on her chakras, wringing a gasp from her. Dropping the gun, she struggled to hold the baby. The earthquake pitched the house, and Risa lurched toward the end of the roof.

No! She couldn't stop. Couldn't use her arms to catch her balance with Kendall in them. Her thighs burned as she fought to gain purchase. *Don't drop the baby!* Two feet from the drop off, the house settled, and Risa caught her balance.

Gushing out a breath, she shifted Kendall, when the house rocked again. Her foot hit the edge. Desperate, she reached out one arm to Linc.

Linc lunged to Risa, snapped out his hand and closed his fingers around her arm. Thank fuck.

Another jolt hit, wrenching the entire house.

Risa tumbled out of his grip.

Everything slowed down into utter horror. Linc saw her wide eyes, the shrieking baby clamped against her chest, then her arm sliding from his blood-coated hand.

She tumbled over the side of the house.

Every instinct in him lit up. *Catch them. Jump with enough force to get past the acid-fog line.* Running, he dove into off the roof toward his witch. The bird screeched and spread his wings in the tat.

He had to succeed. He stretched, pushed, willed himself to defy gravity and arrow through the air. His gaze focused on Risa. She'd twisted midair so her back would hit the acid fog sizzling below her.

Oh fuck no.

Heat flashed from his shoulder blades outward, then sudden weight whooshed out of his back. His muscles twisted and torqued as they fought to adjust to wings and flying, but all he focused on was reaching Risa.

He shot forward and scooped his arms beneath her.

His stomach skimmed the acid, but it didn't matter. He'd caught them. The pain searing his skin didn't compare to the relief ballooning through his entire being as the wings that had burst from his back took them up. And up. Sweat coated him as he powered through the air.

"You have wings." Risa shuddered in his arms, the baby pressed to his chest.

"You have your child." He'd never seen anything more beautiful than this dirty baby cradled in his witch's arms.

"Did you know your wings would come out when you leapt off that roof?"

Everything on the ground was going to hell, but up here they were shrouded in the sable night dotted with crystalline stars. "No. I only knew one thing."

A flush warmed her face, and her eyes reflected the starlight. The pulse at her throat fluttered. "What?"

He wrapped his arms tighter around her, ignoring the pain of his gunshot and the acid burns. He'd never known what this felt like, holding a woman and baby, and it tripped a well of want he hadn't acknowledged since he was thirteen years old.

To love and be loved in return.

That thought scared the shit out of him. Even his wings trembled as if they'd hit a pocket of turbulence. Love. That was too risky. Gave the other person too much power. As a boy, he'd loved his mom.

He'd paid for that love and trust with six years in a cage and a brand on his back.

But Risa wasn't his mother. She was a woman who would go to any length to save her child. He told her the truth.

"I love you."

≫ *21* ≪

RISA HAD HEARD STORIES THAT hunters got their wings to protect their witches. After falling off the building, she'd twisted around and saw him leap, his eyes fierce, jaw clenched, entire body undulant with muscles. His wings had whooshed out, easily spreading six feet on either side of him. The feathers were intricately formed, the wings striped with shades of brown, bronze, gray and white.

Then he'd caught her and Kendall.

Caught them.

No one had ever caught her. But Linc had cared enough to leap off a building and do it. He treated her the way Axel and Sutton treated their mates—cherished, protected and respected.

Sure, that was amazing, but what really rocked her more than any earthquake? Those three words: *I love you.*

Emotional shudders wrenched her heart. "I want to stay up here forever." She didn't want to face the ground and reality. For just a few more minutes, she wanted to be free like this, able to have the two things she wanted—Kendall and Linc. Wanted to live in the fantasy that together they'd take care of

Kendall, love her, never use her for their own benefit.

"If we could fly anywhere," Linc asked softly, breaking into her thoughts, "where would you want to go?"

"Close by? Our rooftop. Put Kendall to sleep in a crib under the stars, but close to us so she knows she's safe and cared for. I don't want her to ever be that scared and lonely again." Once Linc had caught them, Kendall's shrieks had calmed. Now she watched the wings, her gray-blue eyes wide and her tears drying.

Linc's arms tightened around her. "And us? Where would we sleep?"

She smiled. "Who said anything about sleeping?" She pictured him on that rooftop, naked in the moonlight, all hers to touch and explore. The first thing she'd do, though, would be to circle behind him and ask the bird if he and the ink could move aside so she could see the brand. Touch and kiss each line of pain and shame he'd endured...

"Risa," he choked the word out, thick and needy. "You're showing me."

"Because I want you to know." He'd shared a piece of himself with her as they'd run toward the house. Trusted her with that single, horrible memory of being branded.

"Know what?"

Up here in the sky they were unbound by fears and the threat of bad things. Up here it was possible to have it all, and she gave him her heart in words. "That I love you. All of you, even the scars."

His eyes burned into hers, his arms tightened, and Linc leaned down, smiling first at the baby, then kissing Risa. His mouth touched hers with a tenderness more powerful than magic or weapons.

Breaking the kiss, he said, "Once we defeat the spawn, we'll go somewhere, just the three of us. Kendall and I will get to know each other, and when she sleeps, I'll teach you to play poker." His grin turned wicked. "Strip poker. And, baby, I don't lose."

Everything in her wanted that—not the trip, but the family. To have both—this baby she'd sworn to care for, and the man who had won her heart. She'd never know if she could have it all if she didn't take a chance and tell him the truth.

Could he accept a child that was one-quarter demon? Fear and hope tangled into a thick knot at the base of her throat. She hoped to God he didn't make her choose between him and Kendall. "Linc, I have to tell you something."

Tension rode into his body, and his head lifted as he scanned the night. "Tell me when we're safely on the ground. We're near the academy. I have to make sure it's safe, then figure out how to land. I see cars in the parking lot. Something's going on."

Since Risa faced upward in his arms, she couldn't see, nor did she have Linc's super-sharp hunter vision. But his sudden tension told her he had concerns. "What? Rogues?" She focused on her magic. "I don't feel Archer." She still felt the heaviness of his power suck, but it hadn't increased.

"Doubt it. I just saw Ginny helping a bloody woman, probably a witch, out of a car. The guys wouldn't let her out in the open if rogues were still around." He kept scanning. "We're going to the field."

"So, um, you don't know how to land?"

He glanced down, amusement quirking up one side of his mouth. "Baby, I didn't even know I could fly. I'm going by pure instinct here, plus from having watched the other mated hunters do it. Landing's going to be tricky."

Risa tucked Kendall in tighter, readying to protect her as Linc banked around the athletic field.

"We have an audience."

"Who?" She craned her head around.

"Axel." Linc flew low over the ground, getting a feel for it. Then he slowed and shifted until they were vertical, and landed on his feet.

"Huh. Not bad," Risa said as he set her down.

Axel strode up.

Kendall cringed back into Risa's shoulder, a whimper escaping her.

Before Risa could do anything, Linc's wings folded around her and the baby, pulling them against Linc's chest.

Axel stopped, his green eyes taking in the action, then he sighed. "Risa, tell the bird I won't hurt you or your baby."

"The bird? But isn't Linc controlling the wings?"

"The bird did it," Linc said. "I can feel his protectiveness."

Was it wrong to freaking love that? A creature that wanted to protect her and Kendall? She stroked the feathers, which were soft and strong. "Falcon, Axel won't hurt us."

The feathers wrapped around her fingers.

"Good," Axel said. "Now ask him to go back into the ink. Tell him you're safe."

Risa should have felt stupid, except...the wings were real. And for her. "You and Linc saved us tonight, Falcon. Thank you." She had to tell the bird that she was grateful to him for helping her find and save Kendall. If Linc rejected her, the wings would die. "You can go back into the ink now."

The wing slid up to glide along her face, then vanished.

Kendall craned her head around, her bottom lip jutting out, reaching for the vanished wing.

"It's okay, Kendall," Risa soothed the baby. "He'll come back."

"Let's get inside where it's safer," Axel said. "We've

moved the women to the infirmary to take care of the injured."

The two men positioned Risa between them as they walked. After shifting Kendall, she opened her magic and settled a hand on Linc's right arm to heal the bullet wound.

"What happened with the rogues?" Linc asked. "Anyone hurt?"

"None of ours. The fuc—" Axel cut himself off, eyed Kendall and went on, "—cowards cut and run after we killed a few. But rogues attacked Baron's tower too. That battle got ugly. He lost four men, and there's a few more here Darcy and Carla are healing. But we can't keep them in the infirmary since we also have unmated witches healing there—bloodlust. We're putting them with Ram and Eli over in the student dorms."

"Complicated," Linc said.

"We also got calls from witches who were kidnapped and dumped."

"Dumped?" Linc snarled as he opened the door to the infirmary. "They must have been alive if they called. Rogues don't leave them alive."

Risa carried Kendall inside.

"Exactly." Axel followed them. "This whole night has been a setup to keep us busy. Darcy and Carla are running ragged, working to heal the injured, and assisting us while trying to track the pull on their magic to find the spawn. Which is getting worse every hour. And there're rogue attacks in Glassbreakers keeping Phoenix and Key occupied."

Linc made a frustrated noise. "So they can't leave to come help here. Rogues are really organizing to support the spawn."

Kendall shoved her tiny fist in her mouth, frowned and cried. Risa patted her back and said, "She's hungry."

"There's a room in the back set up for her. Crib, supplies, whatever shit... Sorry." Axel grimaced. "Go get her settled. You need to stay in here. If you get her situated, can you help the others?"

"Yes." She could put Kendall in a carrier and work. Glancing at Linc, she said, "I really need to talk to you."

Ram yanked open the door. "More trouble. Rogues set a mobile home park on fire. Residents trapped."

Axel turned to Linc. "Let's go, Dillinger."

Linc rubbed her arm. "Stay inside here, Risa. We'll talk when I get back." He kissed her and raced out with Axel.

Risa watched from the doorway, amazed as his new wings sprang out on his back, and he lifted into the air. Magnificent and powerful.

A scream from the back jerked her around, and tucking Kendall against her, she ran to help.

Hours later, Linc circled the academy, ignoring his torn, bloodied hands. That would heal, but the memory of the screams, of the people he and Axel couldn't get to, burned in his guts.

God he hated rogues and demons. But at least the earthquakes had stopped and—

Sparks shot up from the field. "What the hell?" Flying lower, he spotted Ram standing still, arms crossed, feet spread and shooting enough sparks to light up the city. What was he glaring at?

Linc's stomach dropped when his gaze landed on Risa and Ginny, five feet away, glaring back at Ram. They were out in the open, damn it. And where was Kendall?

He and Axel banked around the field and landed. Axel's feet barely hit the ground when he barreled straight to the group. "What now?"

Linc moved up behind Risa. "Do you know how dangerous this is?"

She turned, hot determination glinting in her eyes. "We're trying to help Ram."

"Not in the middle of a shitstorm." Ram's coldly angry voice cut through the night. "Archer could rise any moment, and you two trotted out here like you're going to a garden party." He glared down at his hands then back at them. "And I couldn't stop you without burning you."

"Which we're trying to help you with," Ginny pointed out. "You promised you'd try."

Axel rubbed his forehead. "Try what?"

Risa jumped in. "Lightning rod set into a box that I seal up with my shield magic. Ram will hold the pole, draining his electrical energy into a sealed box, which will contain it so it doesn't get into the ley lines."

Linc stiffened. "It's risky for you to use your shield magic."

"It's a small amount to do this. If you help me, it'll be better. The bird can keep the souls quiet."

"Axel," Ginny to turned to face him. "It worked when you and Sutton drained Ram's electricity. This is a more efficient way. Carla agrees."

Axel closed his eyes, going quiet. Then he opened them. "So does Darcy. Are you sure you want to risk it, Risa?"

Linc held his breath. Part of him wanted to say no to protect her. But today she'd been magnificent in her power when she'd opened her third eye. He'd felt the magnitude of it whipping through him, and the bird had helped her keep control of it. What's more, his wings had come out for her.

He and this witch had a bond, and he had to start trusting her to know her real limits. He projected the thought to her: *Up to you, Risa. I'll help you as long as you think you're safe doing it.*

Risa craned her head around, a smile lighting up her face and melting the utter exhaustion from his bones. "You mean that?"

Touching her face, just needing that contact, he answered, "Yes. One question though. Where's Kendall?"

Her smile gentled to the one that was exclusively for her baby. "Asleep. Hilary was exhausted, so she's sleeping in the room with her. I've checked them both, and I can hear Kendall if she wakes."

Like the mental link we have?

Actually..." she reached into her pocket and pulled out a disc, "...a baby monitor."

He laughed. After all the misery he'd seen at the trailer park, it felt good. Cleansing. "That works too."

Risa's gaze clung to his for one more second before she faced Axel. "I can do it." Then she looked at Ram. "And I want to."

Ram nodded. "Let's do this fast."

They all headed to the side of the field near the fence line, where a metal pole set into a box roughly the size of a small fireproof safe rested next to a deep hole. Linc eyed Risa.

"Wasn't me."

"It was us." Ram had his chest pressed to Ginny's back but didn't touch her with his hands. "But we weren't going to push Risa. That was our agreement."

Ginny looked up at him. "You set a bed on fire tonight helping Darcy move an injured rogue. We don't have time to wait."

The reality of Ram's situation hit Linc. If electricity built up enough, he'd combust into flames and die. He asked Risa, "What do we do?"

She went to the pole and crouched down.

Her magic surged over him, silky warm and tasting of cinnamon. Instinctively he crouched behind her, laying his palms on her shoulders.

He was mesmerized by the way she used her hands to weave intricate patterns, moving up and down, then back and forth fluidly. Every dip of her finger and rotation of her wrist had a purpose. It was like watching her play the piano—she captured her magic the same way she captured notes.

Gossamer threads shimmered around her fingers, growing bigger as she added to the shield. Curious, he glanced at the others. "Can you guys see that?"

"See what?" Axel asked.

"The translucent threads weaving together in the air." He couldn't stop staring even as the bird's wings stretched wide. He realized the creature had gone back into his tattoo.

"No."

Huh. So only he could see her magic? He wanted to ask her if she was showing him mentally, but stayed quiet and let her work.

Risa took a breath, gathered a wave of power and magically *pushed*. It was the only word he could think of to describe the sensation. The shield shot forward and snapped around the box.

"Done."

Her magic closed, and Linc caught her beneath her arms to help her rise, pulling her against him.

"I'll bury it." Axel set the pole in the hole, grabbed the shovel and started scooping.

Linc wrapped his hand around Risa's throat to tilt her chin up, relieved to see her eyes were clear and blue, but her jaw was tense. "How do you feel?"

She opened her mouth, then closed it.

Alarm flared along his nerves. "What?" Not the soul screams, he could see her eyes were fine.

"That oily sensation." She jerked back, whirling around, her gaze frantic. "He's here. Oh God, Kendall!"

"Who?" But he knew, and whipped out his knife while hooking his free hand around Risa's arm.

"Archer! He's coming for Kendall."

No time to dick around, and yet something kicked in his brain. Twice after they'd rescued Kendall, Risa had said she had something to tell him. "Why does he want Kendall so much?"

Risa stopped tugging and stilled. "Because she's his daughter."

What the fuck?

"You brought a demon baby here?" Axel roared at her, his voice throbbing with anger.

It took everything she had not to cringe. No matter what he did to her, she had to stay ready to shield. "She's only a quarter demon. Three quarters human. Mortal."

"Not witch?" Linc's hand bit into her arm until the bone hurt. "Not your kid at all?"

The oily taste grew. She shook her head, straining to make them understand. "We have to get Kendall and run."

"Keep her away from my mate. From all of us." Axel turned and launched into a run toward the infirmary.

Desperate, she cried out, "Kendall's just a baby!" Ripping her arm from Linc, she raced after the man. She had to get—

Fire lanced the sky, streaking down almost as fast as a bullet.

"Axel!" Ram bellowed, his knife out, sprinting. "Arrow headed for you!"

Risa tracked the fire-blazing arrow chasing Axel. No! Oh God. If it hit, he'd burn in hellfire. *Shield. Do it.*

The arrow's too damned fast.

Wait, she already had a shield. Not big enough to

cover Axel, but she had another idea. Stopping, she forced open her chakras. The ley lines tried to pull, but she fought it, using everything she had to concentrate on the shield she'd made for Ram's lightning box. *There.* Magically grabbing it, she wrenched it free of the box and threw it, aiming for the arrow.

For a second, she couldn't tell if the shield would hit the arrow in time. Axel leapt into the air to evade it.

The arrow chased him, and her shield chased the arrow.

Risa focused, pushing her shield harder, willing it to catch the damned arrow.

But the fire-laced shaft gained on Axel. Six feet away from him.

Five.

Four.

Her shield caught the arrow and snapped around it. Heat flashed over her body, pain lancing every cell as the demon magic fought her shield. She wove in more magic, grabbing every strand. Desperation clamped down on her shoulder and neck muscles. Her arms ached with the effort of holding it.

The flames sputtered and died.

"Another one!" Ram called out. "Fuck! Heading for Ginny. Run!"

Ancestors, help me. Give me the magic. Her power streamed up wildly, then raced down in an undisciplined torrent. She needed the bird, but the connection between them had shut down. A small part of her mind knew Linc had mentally shoved her away. But she didn't dare let herself feel the rejection and loss right now. *Keep going.* Tugging every thread she could snag, she wove fast. Furious adrenaline burned in her veins.

The souls shifted, agitated without the bird there to calm them.

"Where is it?" She screamed the question, unable to look away from her shield.

"Twenty feet," Ram shouted.

Linc blew past her, his wings flashing out. He grabbed Ginny, leaping into the air.

The arrow chased him. *No!* She wove faster.

The flaming shaft just missed as Linc banked and came toward Risa.

The hellfire arrow spun as if searching for its target. Then stopped, locking in, and shot forward.

Now! Risa flung the shield as Linc and Ginny flew past her.

Her shield caught the arrow.

The impact pitched Risa five feet back and dropped her to the ground. Rolling, she jumped up, weaving and pushing to fight the demon magic.

A vessel popped in her nose. Blood poured out. Her ears rang. Her legs gave, and she sank to her knees but kept her hands up.

"Help her!" Ginny cried.

Linc's hand settled on her shoulder. The bird screeched into her head, gathering and feeding magic.

The hellfire spewing from the arrow spurted out.

A bellow of rage sounded as a shadow streaked across the sky. Leathery wings flapped as Archer appeared overhead, pulling another arrow from the quiver on his back, nocked it and fired. Flames lit the path.

Axel screamed into the air, evading the arrow as it chased him.

Risa worked feverishly, refusing to give up. Her thumb ring heated, and more magic joined hers, Darcy and Carla circling magic with her. Thank Ancestors. Grabbing the boost of thick, powerful threads, she wove it as Axel danced and darted, the arrow twisting and turning to follow.

Another winged man shot into the fray.

"Sutton," Linc muttered.

Risa threw the shield, catching the arrow. Archer readied to shoot another when both winged hunters attacked him.

She couldn't see the battle as she fought the arrow with her magic, until the flames died. Nausea roiled, and her head pounded. She looked up.

The three of them tumbled and fought in the air, blood flying, weapons flashing. Then all three slammed to the ground.

Archer shot to his feet, grabbing another arrow and nocking it.

Only a dozen feet away, he aimed right at her.

She got her first full look at him. Archer's face had thinned and stretched, his hair wild, his skin the color of yellow fire, leathery wings billowing out. "You'll burn now, witch."

She'd failed and—

Her thought cut off when Ram slammed into the spawn and stabbed his knife into the demon's chest.

Time stopped as Ram's hand sizzled, and the knife glowed white hot. Thin zaps of jagged lightning streaked all over Archer's exposed skin.

Hope flared weakly in her head. Could Ram kill the spawn?

The demon thing roared, flung Ram away, shot straight up into the air and fitted another arrow. He shot it at Risa.

Empty, bleeding and so weary it hurt, her brain screamed, *Linc! He's right behind you. Shield him. Save him.* She tried, but all she could get were limp threads.

Linc locked his arms around her waist and leapt skyward. The arrow passed beneath them.

They landed close to where Archer's arrow stuck up out of the grass, unlit. It had never caught fire.

The earth trembled and suddenly sucked the arrow down and gone. Vanished.

Axel alighted next to her. Ram walked over with Ginny.

"Where's Archer?" Linc snapped out the words from behind her.

Risa focused on the blood dripping on her shoes and the grass. Gushed really. Not good. Would she be able to throw another shield? Where was Archer?

Sutton touched down by them. "Gone. Flew off when his arrow didn't light."

"Ram's jolt stunned him, shorted out his arrows," Axel said.

"The hellfire comes from the Underworld." Risa barely heard her own voice over the writhing screams building in her head. Everything moved in slow motion, receding back. For some reason, it seemed really important they know this, and she struggled to explain. "He was pulling it through the ley lines, and my shield smothered..." Words failed her as grayness swirled in her mind.

"Risa. Look at me," Linc demanded.

"She's lost a hell of a lot of blood," another voice said.

And then all the talking stopped. Only screams remained.

➤ *22* ⬅

RISA CLUNG TO A TREE branch and looked down at the souls snapping and snarling like rabid dogs, leaping up trying to grab her and drag her down.

She didn't want to go. Clinging to that one branch jutting out over the souls, she dragged her legs up, huddling into a ball. Their hatred spewed with the power of a geyser, soaking her in their need to make her suffer as they had.

Among all the souls, she searched for one.

Nola. Risa hadn't seen her since she'd bonded with Linc and her mind had shattered. She missed her so much. Nola was the only one who'd ever truly loved her. Wanted to be with her.

Did the baby hate her too?

All the souls leapt, springing up, crazed, bloody hands, rotting teeth...

A shadow soared over her, trilling a low melody that caused a hush. Falcon. His wings were spread against the bright blue sky, the baring of his colors showing his magnificence. Banking with the effortlessness that only birds exhibit, he glided down, his song spreading a mellow, warm blanket.

The souls settled back, sinking into the threads of Risa's magic, as the bird sang them into the place between life and death, between wakefulness and sleep. The tranquil place.

The geyser of hatred petered out.

Falcon hovered between the souls and her, and sang, the rise and fall of his melody beseeching her to let go of the tree and trust him.

Part of her wanted to stay right there, clinging to the branch. But there was another child waiting for her. So she let go.

The brutal lights pierced her eyes, and Risa squeezed her lids shut. Her magic flowed, creating a warm tingle in her nose. That had to be healing magic. So she'd been injured? No, wait, the memory swam for a second, then burst up.

Her shield magic. There'd been so much power she couldn't control it, and something had torn.

Archer. Oh God, the demon spawn had come for his daughter. "Kendall!" She jackknifed up, pain stabbing her head, the room spinning.

"Easy." Linc's hands settled on her shoulders. "The baby is sleeping. Fine."

Blinking helped her bring the room into focus. She sat on a thickly padded table in one of the treatment rooms. Carla and Darcy were on one side, their glowering mates behind them.

Linc was on the other.

How long had she been out?

"You burst several veins, getting a little close to your brain." Carla's eyes went to Linc. "You were using too much power without your familiar."

She cast around, trying to remember. "Everyone's okay?"

Darcy nodded. "Ram has electrical burns and a bruised sternum, but we healed that."

Sutton added, "Everything is quiet now. Our guess is Archer went back to his lair, wherever that is."

"He'll come again for his daughter," Axel said.

Like a coward, Risa dropped her gaze to her hands. "I'm sorry. You have no idea how sorry I am. I didn't know what else to do."

"Why, Risa?"

Linc's two words held a dictionary worth of meaning. She still couldn't look at him. Or any of them. "Blythe is—was—Kendall's mom, and Archer her father. Archer wanted nothing to do with Kendall and paid Blythe to keep him off any public records. Then four months ago, out of nowhere, Archer showed up and tried to physically take the baby from Blythe. He really scared her, so she came to me in Phoenix."

"Four months ago. That's when his mother vanished," Sutton said.

Risa nodded. "He came around a couple times trying to sweet-talk Blythe into going back to Vegas with him. But she wasn't biting. It escalated into violence, but when we tried to file a police report, the report would vanish and the cops had no memory of it. I knew it was magic, but not what kind."

"Asmodeus could easily have gotten one of his demon witches to do that," Darcy pointed out. "That's assuming Archer's mother wasn't around to do it at the time."

"Someone helped him. Another time, I took Blythe and Kendall to Utah, being very careful not to leave a trail, but Archer found us there too. Nothing stopped him." They'd been so desperate, his fixation on Kendall growing more and more evident. "He let his hair grow, stopped shaving, showed up in ragged clothes. All he cared about was getting Kendall." Blythe had been so scared, truly afraid for Kendall.

Archer went from arrogant, well-dressed, spoiled playboy, to obsessively dangerous.

"So why were you here in Vegas?"

She flinched at the ice in Linc's voice. But they deserved an answer. "Archer and two thugs with guns broke in and tried to get Kendall. They intended to kill Blythe too. I used my shield magic to get us out. The last thing Archer screamed at us was *Once I spawn, you won't be able to run fast or far enough.* I didn't know what that meant, but it scared the hell out of me. By then I knew he wasn't mortal, but I didn't know what he was. I had to get us away from him." She squeezed her eyes shut. "And even then, I'd never imagined what would happen. That he'd become a demon and burn Blythe to death." Tears stung her eyelids. Sick grief churned.

"So you came here where you knew Archer lived?"

The jagged doubt in Linc's voice cut, but Risa had no damned right to hurt. None. She'd lied to him, to all of them, and they'd been good to her and Kendall. Swallowing the pain, she stared at the floor. "I grew up here and knew someone who could get us out of the country undetected on a private plane. He booked us at the hotel under assumed names. I trusted him. He was the one who helped keep me hidden after I turned my father in."

"Did he set you up?"

"I don't think so," she said. "He was one of the victims that night. I think Archer tracked us and spawned there to get Kendall." Too many memories spun in her head. "We were running, I'd taken Kendall, and Blythe was right behind me. He shot her with the hellfire arrow. The last thing she screamed to me was to take Kendall, that I'd sworn to protect her." She shuddered, unable to contain the raging anger, fear and sadness at knowing that she'd never see her best friend again. Never hear her laugh, share

Twinkies and ice cream, talk about anything and everything.

"And so you lied to us," Linc stated flatly.

Her throat ached, and finally she turned to his harsh and unforgiving face. "Would you have saved her if I told you she was the daughter of Archer? The granddaughter of Asmodeus, the demon you're all sworn to fight?" Terrible loneliness welled in her. "Or would you have left her there in that horrible place?"

"We'll never know now. You didn't trust me to find out." Linc circled the table and paused by Axel to say, "I'll take the next watch." He vanished out the door without a backward glance.

Risa's eyes burned, and her nose clogged. He'd walked out. Left. She closed her eyes, trying to breathe past the savage pain.

"You need to sleep," Carla said.

She slid off the table, fighting more dizziness. Blood loss, she supposed. "I can take Kendall and go to another building."

Axel wrapped his hand around her arm, leading her out of the room, down the hall toward the back where the staff rooms were. He stopped. "You'll sleep here where we can protect you."

He'd let her stay? Protect her? "Why?"

"Because like it or not, we need you to defeat Archer. Your shield magic saved us tonight."

Right. Yeah, they needed her magic, not her. She nodded and went into the small room that normally held two twin beds in the dorm-room style. The bare-bones rooms were meant for staff who needed to rest, not live in. One of the beds had been removed and a crib placed there. Risa dragged herself to the crib.

Kendall slept on her back, arms flung wide, legs relaxed. Once she'd been bathed, dressed and fed, the baby'd conked out. Risa didn't know what the last week had been like for the child, but Kendall seemed to know she was safe now and rested in the deep way of innocent children.

It wasn't the baby's fault that her father was a hybrid who chose to spawn his demon side. It was bad enough she'd lost her mom who had loved her with such fierceness. If they all survived this, Risa was going to tell Kendall every day how much her mom had adored her. And that Blythe's last wish, last words, were about the daughter she'd loved so much.

She crawled into the small bed, and the memory, the one she'd been trying to avoid, swallowed her up.

The second Linc had yanked the bird and himself from her. Like ripping her soul in half, taking away the love she hadn't deserved.

Hot tears seared her eyes. He had loved her for a few moments.

Then she'd destroyed it with her lie.

Her throat ached. Eyes bled tears. Chest burned. Her sobs wrenched her whole body until her back hurt, but none of it came close to the anguish in her heart.

Linc nodded to Sutton as the man relieved him from watch duty. He needed a couple hours' sleep and headed down the hall to find an empty room.

Not the one Risa was in, or he'd lose control of the anger and betrayal festering inside of him.

Because I want you to know.

Know what?

That I love you. All of you, even the scars.

Did she? Did people who loved someone lie to them? Distrust them with something so important?

He'd trusted her with his worst moments, including mentally showing her a picture of the moment he'd been branded. It hadn't been his intention, but he'd trusted her deeply enough to do it unconsciously.

And she'd lied to him, unable to trust him. It hurt as badly as the night he'd been dragged out of his bed, sold by his own mother.

Laughter filtered from the kitchen, stalling out his thoughts. "Perhaps you're not ready to feed yourself?"

Risa. God, his entire body heated at the sound of her amused voice. *Shit. Keep going. You're not in a good frame of mind to deal with her.*

And yet he turned, stopping in the doorway. The small fridge stood on the left, with an L-shaped counter next to it. Directly across from the door was a table, pushed up against the wall. The baby wiggled in a car-seat-type device, kicking her feet while Risa tried to wipe her hand, which was covered in some sort of oatmeal-colored goo. The same stuff covered the kid's mouth, chin and cheeks. Yet the baby grinned proudly.

"Spoons work better than hands with cereal, K-doll." Risa leaned down, kissing the baby's soft hair. Then she picked up a spoon with a puddle of cereal and held it up. "More?"

Kendall kicked her sleeper-covered legs again, bouncing in the chair and opening her mouth baby-bird style.

Risa kept feeding her, chatting away. She had her hair scraped back in a ponytail, wore a tank top, dark-colored yoga pants and was barefoot. She laughed as Kendall happily smacked her gums around another bite of food.

His anger still ached like a living thing, but she hadn't lied about loving Kendall, a child that wasn't her biological kid. Even the bird sighed at the sight the two of them made.

Risa did another pass with the washcloth over the kid's face.

The baby gave her a frown, batting at the rag with her small hand and babbling sounds that made zero sense.

"You're all clean now, quit your scolding." After setting the rag aside, Risa scooped the baby up and reached for a bottle. She turned to sit and froze, her gaze widening. Her happiness drained to something heart-wrenching. "Linc."

His chest kicked, and the bird stretched in the tat, as desperate to touch her as he was, pissing him off. He didn't want to feel this yearning for her.

"Sit." He went in, filled a kettle with water and put it on the stove. "You're up early."

"Kendall woke up hungry."

Damn it, her voice pulled hard at him. Turning, he leaned against the counter, keeping a dozen feet between them. Her eyes were bruised, tired. "Did you sleep at all?"

"Some. Did you?"

"Watch duty." The gulf between them widened with every word. "How's your head?" Guilt swam beneath the surface of his emotions. He could have helped her with the pain. "Any more soul screams?"

Risa looked down at the child, a tender smile softening her mouth and making her eyes glimmer with real and guileless love. Her expression roused dusty memories that had been shoved into dark corners of his mind. Flashes of his mom when she'd been sober and smiling at him with love. Linc thought those memories had died.

Oh, she'd loved him once. Intellectually he understood addiction had destroyed her, and she hadn't had a true grasp of what she'd sold him into that night to pay off her drug debt. But he'd lived it each day. At first, in those early nights, he'd cried for his mom, sure she'd come. He'd believed she'd sober up and realize what she'd done.

No one came. Ever. One day he'd realized no one would ever come and his tears meant nothing.

Now he looked at Risa, gazing at her child with a

tenderness that ripped a scab off his old wounds. How fucking pathetic did that make him? He had a Feral brand. He really needed to toughen the hell up.

"No soul screams. You let the bird help me, and the souls calmed."

Her comment jerked his gaze to hers. "Let?" There it was, anger blasting his veins and stripping him down to a pure, hurting animal. "What did you think would happen? You piss me off, so I leave you to suffer? That I would abandon you in the time you needed me?"

The baby stopped sucking on the bottle, her eyes widening.

Excellent. He'd scared the kid. The one person in this room who deserved to feel safe and he'd scared her. Going to the stove, he shut it off. "Forget it." He kept his voice soft.

"I should have told you. I wanted to tell you."

He stared down at the blue teakettle. A tiny stream of steam escaped the pour spout through the hole in the stopper. It was exactly how he felt right this second, boiling with only that miniscule pinprick for the pain to escape. "I would not hurt a child, Risa."

He heard the chair move. Cloth rustled as she adjusted the baby. Heard the milk or formula or whatever she had in that bottle slosh. "I had no right to ask you if you would have rescued Kendall if you'd known who her father was. You would have. I just didn't give you the chance." Her voice moved a few steps away. "Or us."

The lid blew off his steaming emotions, and he shot across the room, blocking her from the exit.

She stopped, tilting her head back, the baby on her hip.

This close, he got the full impact of her red-rimmed eyes in swollen lids. Faint purplish smudges half-mooned below. "You didn't sleep." No, she'd cried. Alone.

Her breath hitched.

Unbearable. He used to look beyond the bars of his cage. Freedom had been there just on the other side. He could stick his hand through the bar but never quite touch freedom.

That was how he felt right now. She was right there. He could touch her, but he couldn't recapture the moment when he'd thought she really knew and loved him.

The air between them thickened. Half of him wanted to pull her into his arms, and the other half snarled in pain. "Was any of it real? Telling me you loved me?" He took a breath, forcing his voice to stay level for Kendall's sake. "Was any of it real?"

She didn't answer for several heartbeats. The baby developed a serious interest in his arm stretched across the door, while he stayed trapped in Risa's eyes.

She swallowed. "So real I go to bed each night with the taste of your kiss and wake to it in the morning. When other men touched me, I felt nothing. But when you touched me, I felt everything. You're the most real thing I know."

Her words shredded him syllable by syllable, cell by cell. "I want to believe you."

She nodded in the jerky bobble-head fashion. "But you can't. Will you ever believe me? Trust me again?"

Linc drowned in the hope warring with hurt in her eyes. "I don't know." Carefully removing his arm from the baby's hold, Linc walked away.

"Risa?"

She looked up from changing Kendall as Carla walked into the small room. "Hi." Taking the baby's arms, Risa tugged her up to a sitting position on the bed and handed her a cloth doll.

The other woman sat on the bed, smiling at Kendall.

Dropping the doll, Kendall reached up both arms to Carla.

Laughing, Carla lifted her. Kendall latched on to the silver eagle cuff around Carla's upper arm. "Ah, that was your real target all along." She looked at Risa. "I've been had."

Risa didn't know what to say, how to act. Nerves and endless regrets cramped her stomach. Did Carla hate her? What did she want? "She likes shiny things."

Carla slipped off the cuff, settled Kendall in her lap and let the baby have it.

Kendall immediately stuck it in her mouth. Worried that she'd ruin it or something, Risa asked, "Isn't that your witch book?"

"It is. Originally it was an infinity sign, but Wing Slayer remade it into eagle wings. Magic keeps it clean. It won't make her sick."

"Oh. That hadn't even occurred to me. But that piece must be valuable. I don't want her to damage it."

Carla laughed. "Wing Slayer's power can stand up to a baby, trust me."

Confused, Risa glanced around, and unable to help it, blurted out, "I am sorry for everything. I know you all must hate me for lying."

Carla put a hand on Risa's arm. "I hate that you and Linc are hurting. But the lie I can understand. You were scared and didn't know us enough to trust us. I didn't believe Sutton loved me at first either. I was sure that he loved my twin sister."

Surprised, she said, "You have a twin?"

"I did," she answered. "Keri. She died in a rogue attack, her soul trapped in a knife. It's complicated, but I was able to keep her soul alive."

Risa leaned forward. "Like the souls trapped in my magic?"

She nodded, her blonde hair swinging, catching Kendall's attention. "Yes. I believed that when Sutton touched my blood, it wasn't me he felt as his soul mirror, but Keri's through our twin bond."

"Was he?"

"It's a long story, but the end is this—his love was real even though I doubted it." Squeezing Risa's arm, she added, "You were afraid to trust that Linc's love was real. That he would fight for what you loved."

She understood. The bottom dropped out of her stomach. "He doesn't know if he can trust me again." Tears filled her eyes, and she swiped at the moisture. "I managed not to cry in front of him this morning."

"Girlfriends..." Carla captured Kendall's arm as the baby tried to shove a length of hair in her mouth, "...are much better for crying with. Guys either try to fix it or cure it with sex."

Laughter mixed with her tears, causing her to snort, then she laughed harder.

Kendall looked up.

Risa got a hold of herself before she scared the baby. Kendall went back to playing with the arm cuff.

"I feel your magic all over her, like a security blanket." Lifting her eyes, Carla said, "Shield magic."

"I wove security and love into it and settled it around her in the middle of the night. She woke scared, clinging to me, and it just..." No more crying. But she worried about any lasting effects Kendall would suffer from her ordeal.

"So you risked shield magic after nearly bleeding out in the fight with Archer."

"It wasn't a lot. I'm not shielding against physical danger, just wrapping her in the security of what I feel for her. Her mom's soul is in my magic. Maybe she can feel that too."

Carla smiled. "She'll be okay, Risa. And we'll all give her lots of love while she's here with us."

Her stomach clenched with the sick reality that she'd gotten Kendall back, but she was losing Linc.

Carla stood up. "Come on."

"Where?" Risa asked, following the other witch.

"Time to get to work. The guys are strategizing and training. But they aren't going to be able to kill Archer. He's immortal and like nothing we've seen before."

"I agree. Ram stabbed him right in his heart. Archer lit up a like a Christmas tree, but he didn't die. He threw Ram back as if he'd been no bigger than Kendall."

"Exactly." They exited the hallway into the reception area.

Darcy, Ginny and Hilary all converged on them, wanting to see Kendall.

The baby was shy for about four seconds, until Hilary dangled some keys in front of her. Kendall dropped Carla's cuff. Ginny caught it without really looking. Kendall happily went to Hilary to get the keys.

"Traitor." Carla laughed, slipping the beautiful cuff back on her arm.

Risa touched the ring around her thumb, but her thoughts went back to Archer. "How do we get rid of the spawn if we can't kill him?"

Darcy answered, "We have to find and then banish him. That will keep him from returning, at least in his current demon form. But we'll need to hold him to do the banishing spell. Think your shield could do that?"

Could she? "It'll be hard. Just holding his arrows was a battle." Everyone turned to look at her. "But I'll try."

"You won't have to hold him for long," Carla assured her. "We believe Ram's electrical charge shorted out Archer's hellfire. If Ram can do that again, maybe by discharging his electrical energy into his knife and throwing it into Archer, then you cast your shield, at that point Darcy and I could banish him."

"Oh." The possibilities opened in her mind. "Can Ram get close enough?"

"Even if he can't, Axel or Sutton probably can," Darcy said.

Ginny frowned. "But can they touch the knife if Ram discharges into it? Will their touch drain it? Or the burning slow them?"

Risa considered that. "I bet I could shield the base of the knife. Does anyone have a knife? Let me see what I can do."

Linc flew maneuvers again and again, landing and taking off while Baron and a few of his hunters training with them threw knives for Linc to dodge. Eli added his whip to the fun when Linc got close enough to the ground.

Axel attacked from the air.

Linc was getting damned good at flying maneuvers, which could save him from Archer's arrows. But it did nothing to soften his inner turmoil. How could he trust Risa now?

The lash caught his thigh. Fuck, that stung. He shot up, wings pumping, then dodged a knife coming at his face, while Axel arrowed toward him from his left. Linc banked out of the pathway, barely avoided another knife and decided to land.

Drenched in sweat, bleeding from his mistakes, he touched down when he heard the whistle of the whip.

He spun, caught Eli's lash, jerked the hunter forward and rammed his fist into the man's jaw.

Eli absorbed the punch and whirled into a roundhouse kick.

Linc jumped back, grabbed Eli's foot, dumped him on his ass and dropped all his weight, intending to drive his elbow into the hunter's ribs.

Eli rolled.

Linc halted, pushed up to a crouch and eyed Eli. "Any reason you're riding my ass, Stone?"

The other hunter circled him. "Ginny could have been killed. If that arrow had hit her, she'd be taken. Gone."

Taken where? But knowing better than to ask, he said, "Archer could have killed all of us."

"Death won't treat all of us the same, Dillinger. What awaits Ginny..."

"Don't," Ram snarled.

Eli lifted his hand.

The whip rose off the ground where he'd dropped it, flinging though the air and hitting his palm.

What the fuck? Linc blinked. Had he really just seen that? He'd fought by Eli's side over and over, and not once had Eli's whip flown to his hand like magic. "Witch hunters can't do that." Eli was a hunter. He had the tat. Wing Slayer had filled it in. What was going on?

"Well I can. This whip?" Eli held it up. "It's one of those unwanted gifts that you can't return. I can't lose it or destroy it. I've tried, but it always comes back. At first I refused to use it, but it started attaching itself to me."

"What are you?" Baron asked. All twenty men training on the grounds had quit training to watch.

"I was born a witch hunter, but I was hijacked." Eli turned to Linc. "Now you're harboring Archer's baby. He's coming back for that kid. And he'll kill us all to get her. But Ginny and I won't die." He stalked off.

"What will happen to you?" Baron called.

Eli stopped, his shoulders bunching, the whip latched to his side, twitching. "Another unwanted gift." Then he was gone.

"What the fuck?" He turned to Ram.

Sparks flew from his hands. "I don't know, but my guess is that his fate is tied to Ginny's."

He remembered what Eli had told him. *Ginny's father destroyed my connection with my soul mirror. For that alone, I'd kill him if I could. Savi's alone out there. I was her lifeline and... Fuck.*

"But he has his tat. Wing Slayer accepted him."

Axel stared after Eli. "Apparently, some powerful being poached. It should be impossible, but the curse weakened our god's bond with us for decades."

"So who's this mystery being?" Linc couldn't figure it out. "Ginny's father isn't Asmodeus, right?" Was she another hybrid? It would explain her secrecy.

"No." Ram's tone was sharp and icy. "Let's focus on the problem at hand. Like the fact that we have a pissed-off demon spawn coming to get his kid."

"Over my dead body." Linc meant it. Especially after seeing Risa with Kendall this morning. The baby deserved a chance to grow up loved and safe. After seeing Eli's reaction, he began to get an idea of how afraid Risa had been that Linc would reject the kid based on her demon blood.

The others wandered off to resume training. Linc went to snag a bottle of water.

Axel grabbed another one.

"I mean it, A. I will protect Risa and the baby." No matter what happened between him and Risa, they had his protection.

"I remember when all witches hated us. Feared us," Axel said. "We were cursed with the drive to kill them and harvest the power in their blood. Most of them believed that we had all become evil."

He lowered the water bottle, looking at his leader.

"Kendall will have to choose for herself, just like we all do," Axel twisted off the lid and drank some water.

"But she'll have a better chance if she's with you and Risa."

"You were pretty pissed at Risa last night. Told me to keep her away from Darcy."

Axel shrugged. "It's possible I'm a tad protective of my mate and overreacted."

If by tad protective Axel meant insanely possessive, then yeah, he'd agree. Linc opened his mouth to answer when a wave of magic lit up his insides, sucking out his breath and making his wings twitch.

Axel laughed. "The witches are together, doing magic. No doubt planning how to take down the spawn."

His blood heated in reaction to the feel of her magic, and damn, he did not need a boner right now. Trying to distract himself, he asked, "Did you ever have doubts about Darcy?"

All the humor left the other man's face. "My doubts almost got her killed. I know you're pissed, but I saw your witch in action last night. She's fierce, courageous and willing to sacrifice her own happiness for the child of a friend. That's some deep loyalty. You might want to ask yourself, have you been completely honest with her?"

Linc started to answer, when he thought of something he hadn't told Risa. Shit, Axel had a—

Phones started going off. Linc yanked out his to see an alert from missing witches.

His stomach burned in fury. He had to stop Archer and the rogues. Before that fucking demon destroyed Vegas.

Or even worse—killed Risa and snatched Kendall. Rage clanged in his head, and his chest constricted. He wouldn't let that happen and took off at a run.

≫ 23 ≪

HOT WATER POUNDED ON LINC, draining off the blood and growing worry. They'd only managed to rescue a few witches and found more dead and dumped.

It was barely ten p.m., but he was going to grab an hour or two of sleep. They were rotating watches, searching for the spawn and rogues, and rescuing any witches they could find.

After turning off the shower, he toweled dry, yanked on some shorts and headed down the hall. Quietly he opened the door and slipped in. Crossing to the crib, he looked inside, able to see perfectly well in the dark. Baby Kendall lay on her back, arms and legs flung out, face relaxed and mouth open. His chest twinged at the sight of her safe and content. He could smell a gentle layer of Risa's magic around her.

"Linc?"

He turned toward the bed. Risa rose on an arm, blinking away sleep. He regretted waking her. She, Carla and Ginny had worked for hours, healing the witches he and the others had rescued. "Yeah, it's me."

"What's wrong?"

"I want to sleep with you." Yet he didn't walk to her, suddenly unsure of his welcome.

Her magic flared out, and the twin bed stretched into a double. "It's the best I can do in this tight space." Pulling back the covers, she said, "Come sleep."

His mouth dried. Long and lean, wearing only a tank and panties, her hair falling around her shoulders, she took his breath away. The sight of her created a need so deep it truly scared him. Going to her, he set his phone on the night table, got in and pulled her against him. Her scent chased out the smell of pain and death, easing his muscles.

As Risa stroked his back, her magic rolled over him, gently probing, then tingling when it found injuries. "You're healing me."

She tilted her head up, eyes so vulnerable. "I want to."

Desire rode in on her magic, swirling through him and thickening his cock. Wrapping his hand around her hair in some primal need to capture her, he told her the truth. "I missed you."

"Really?"

He was very aware of the baby in the crib, could hear her soft breaths, so he didn't kiss Risa, or the sweet desire simmering between them would ignite. It was enough to hold and touch her right now. "Yes."

She sighed. "I know it's going to take time for you to forgive me and trust me, but I'll be here if you want to."

He opened his mouth.

"Wait. Please. I can only say this once."

"Okay."

"If you don't want me..." she pressed her hand to his chest, "...I'll go away. Me and Kendall. I mean once this is over, because we have no chance on our own right now, and I'm not risking her life out of pride or a broken heart. That baby—she's good, Linc. I don't care what her bloodline is, she's a sweet, funny girl. And

I'm going to give her the chance to make her own choice in life. Just like you chose. They tried to brand you as feral. And you refused to be that. So..." She closed her eyes. "Sorry, I got off track. I won't try to hold on to you if you walk away." Her fingers tightened against his chest, anxiety bleeding off her.

"I'm not walking away, and neither are you. No woman who fights this hard for her friend's child walks away." He loved her more for that, but he'd just had to get past his initial hurt.

"But I lied."

He nodded. "So did I. There's something I haven't told you. At first, I didn't think you needed to know, that it'd only complicate things between us. But then...I didn't want to tell you and have you resent me for it."

"What?"

"Your father." Linc hated the wash of fear and uncertainty backing up his throat. One thing he knew for sure, no matter how much you hated your parent, you also still loved them. "I killed him."

She didn't move.

"Risa?" He stroked her hair. "I didn't know you then. I saw his picture in the media after his arrest and recognized him as the one man I'd never found. I waited, then once I decided he'd been in prison long enough to know what being in a cage is like, I got in."

"How?"

Dread tightened his stomach. "Did I get in? Or kill him?"

"Get in."

"Invisibility. But I'd studied the security too. Anyway, I cornered him in a spot with no camera angle, and killed him. In cold blood." Linc made himself tell her without softening it. Would she consider him an assassin like her father?

She nodded and laid her head on his arm. "I

suspected it was you. After you told me about what happened to you, my father's part in it, and that you'd killed them all."

"Why didn't you ask me?"

She shrugged, looking lost for a moment. "I didn't really want to know." Raising her gaze, she added, "I hated him. So much. But I never had the courage to kill him, not even after..." She closed her eyes.

Oh hell. "Another secret?"

"Not like Kendall." She rubbed her thumb back and forth on his chest. "I've never told anyone though."

It was late. They were both tired. "Do you want to tell me?" He could feel it bunching up inside her, worse than physical pain.

"One of the souls trapped in my magic..."

Linc stayed quiet and didn't rush her. Talking like this in the hush of the night, lying together with her legs tucked between his, Kendall nearby, safely sleeping—they were in their own special world. They could tell each other anything here.

Risa swallowed and said, "...is my daughter, Nola. She was never born. I was only four months pregnant with her when she died."

Given that her father used her to lure his victims, he ventured a guess. "Your father found out and did something?" He kept his voice level even as his anger brewed.

She nodded. "I was seventeen. He figured out I was pregnant and put an abortion potion in my tea. I didn't know until I woke in the middle of the night in pain. I tried to save her by shielding her."

She'd been so young and alone. No mother, no one who loved her to help her. Linc hated that he hadn't been there to protect her. "Who was the father of your baby?"

"One of the men my father forced me to be with then killed. I guess I was thinking maybe if I got pregnant, my father would have to stop using me. It was stupid, I know that now." She closed her eyes. "The baby wasn't full term or anything, but I still loved her. And I failed her."

God, he hated her father and was damn glad he'd killed the man. For the things he'd forced his daughter to do, and for hurting her, he'd deserved to die. Linc settled his forehead against Risa's. "Your loss made you more determined not to fail Kendall." Oh, he understood that.

"Not just Kendall, but Blythe. I want her to know I'll love Kendall, but I'll tell her about her mother too. Blythe was a great mom. Her last thoughts and words were for her baby. I'm going to honor that."

That hit him square in his heart. He'd been pissed and betrayed at her for lying to him, when all along she'd been keeping her vow to a dying woman. But now that he held Risa, fierce possessiveness and the desire to be the man she deserved solidified in his bones. But deep in his chest, a cold foreboding pricked his contentment.

He couldn't lose her. She trusted him fully, enough to tell him about Nola, even after he'd admitted to killing her father. She was his everything.

Yet the dread sat there like a ticking time bomb. Archer was coming.

Mama. I can't see you. You said you'd never leave me. Why can't I see you?

"Risa, wake up."

Jerking out of the dream, she opened her eyes.

"You're crying, love." Braced on his elbow, Linc brushed his thumb over her cheek.

She drew in a ragged breath. "Just a dream." But the sadness, the feeling that she'd betrayed Nola, left her aching. More tears welled in her eyes. "Damn it," she whispered, trying to turn her face away.

"Don't." His voice roughened. "Whatever this is, don't hide from me. Don't pull back out of my reach. It feels like cage bars between us and makes me feel fucking helpless. I can see you hurting but can't reach you."

Her chest hollowed. "Like when my mind shattered."

"Precisely. You'd surface then slip away and I couldn't catch you."

Like he had when he'd caught her and Kendall before they fell into the acid fog. He'd leapt off that roof without any hesitation, determined to save her and the baby.

He'd even sprouted wings.

All he asked now was that she turn to him, not away. "I dreamed about Nola. She was calling for me, asking why she couldn't see me."

"The baby you lost? You knew she was a girl or just chose to think of her as one?"

"I shielded her in my womb, and I could feel the seed of her magic there." She hesitated, but he'd been so honest with her, telling her he needed her to share with him, not hide. "After she died, I used to see her, talk to her. At first, she was just a little starburst, but I knew it was her. Then she started taking shape and we talked." God it sounded insane. "I know it was crazy. I was only four months along in the pregnancy when she died. But once I turned in my dad to the cops and went into hiding, she was all I had."

"Did you see her in your dream now?"

"No. I haven't seen her since my mind shattered. It's like I lost her again. After I promised her I'd never send her away." It was all spilling out of her, the way Nola had developed eyelashes and eyebrows and acquired the ability to talk. Risa ran out of words.

Linc slid his arm beneath her, rolled to his back and pulled her on top of him. His erection pressed against her thighs.

Ignore it. I'm always aroused around you, but our girl is sleeping just a few feet away.

His words feathered in her mind, creating a flood of internal warmth. Desire, yes, but there was more. This was what love felt like. *Our girl?*

I'm claiming her, love. She belongs to you, and you belong to me. See how it works? He moved his hand beneath her shirt and spread it over her back.

Who do you belong to?

You. And in time when Kendall accepts me, her as well. You're my girls.

She laid her head on him, listening to his heartbeat.

After a few minutes, he asked, "Do you think you saw and talked to Nola's soul?"

"I wanted to believe it and yet knew it was unlikely intellectually. I never saw any of the other souls when they were quiet."

He rubbed gentle circles on her back. "You needed her to be real, needed to feel loved and wanted. And you loved her, or at least how you imagined it would be to have your own child."

His words resonated deeply, striking a chord of truth so authentic, she raised her head. In the darkness, his eyes had a slight glow to them. "She told me she never wanted to leave me." Her eyes burned with more tears, but this time Risa let them fall. "Oh God, Linc, I was projecting my need for her. Not letting go." She couldn't go on. Her little baby had died at four months' gestation, and her soul was trapped in Risa's magic with the others. But Risa hadn't actually seen her, that part was a fantasy, because she couldn't accept the loss and had been desperate for someone to love her. And yet, Linc made her feel safe in facing the truth. Not judged, just sheltered and held.

"Because you loved and needed her. But now, when the time comes to release the souls, you'll be able to let her go. It's still going to hurt, Risa. Your baby was very real to you, but I'll be here to catch you. Me and Kendall."

"Why do you understand?" Most people would be freaked out.

"I used to see my mom. Sometimes, after a brutal day of training, when I couldn't even move, I'd lay in a heap of misery in my cage and she'd sit with me, telling me she'd find a way to get me out, that she loved me. Comforting me."

Her heart broke. More tears filled her eyes, this time for the thirteen-year-old scared and hurt boy who just wanted his mom. "She wasn't there."

His jaw clenched, then released. "No. But for a while I believed she was."

Unable to bear it, her chakras opened, pouring out magic. It wrapped around them like a blanket.

I love when you do that, but damn, woman, it makes me hard as stone.

She shivered, his cock branding her belly. *We could sneak into the bathroom...*

Her magic surged, springing wildly, straight up through her chakras and centering at her forehead. The pressure was so intense, her vision blurred and dizziness spun her away.

Linc! My third eye.

I've got you. I won't let you go.

His confident voice in her head calmed her enough for her third eye to snap open. Risa struggled to bring what she was seeing into focus. Soaring overhead, she took in the sight of an architectural marvel lit up against the night sky.

Hoover Dam.

She could see the dam wall, the intake towers on the Lake Mead side, the Spillway House, and on the other side, the bypass bridge. What did it all mean? Hoover Dam had been closed to the public since Archer spawned. The authorities believed the city was under a terrorist attack and had locked down the dam as a precaution.

Still moving, she headed closer to the Nevada side of the dam, honing in on the Winged Figures of the Republic, which was two mythical beings figures sitting on a block with their wings reaching thirty feet into the air. Between them rose a hundred-and-forty-two-foot-high flag poll. The figures rested on a massive black base that sat on a terrazzo floor inlaid with a star chart. Rumors had swirled since the monument was built that the celestial chart held a secret invitation to other realms. All the lights on the intake towers and along the dam flickered, the earth trembled, and the lake water boiled. Flames shot up out of the two winged statues. With another horrific rumble, the front side of the black base of the statue blew off, revealing a supine man with wings curled around him as streaks of fire raced over his skin.

His eyes opened, and he rose. *Archer.* That's where he'd been hibernating! But since Archer already had risen and attacked them, that meant she was viewing the past with her third eye. Probably yesterday when Archer rose.

She floated over to the Colorado River side, catching sight of the power plant below the spillover, then stopped. In a weird fast forward the sun rose, then set again. She guessed it meant a day had passed in her third eye, bringing her to the present. She continued to watch as a large man with wings flew into her vision and landed on the roof of the power plant at the base of the spillover wall.

Archer.

Lit up by the moon, he spread his leathery wings

wide, his quiver of arrows on display in the center of his back, his arms in the air with his bow in one hand. The entire ground shook, and the water in Lake Mead and the Colorado River boiled, turning red and blue beneath the lights and moon.

Lake Mead began to drain as if a massive plug had been pulled. With her third eye, she could see it filling the powerful ley lines below, rushing along the magical grid to shoot up through the power plant as pure energy.

Right into Archer.

Flames burst out from the spawn's skin and climbed to unimaginable heights.

Oh Sweet Ancestors. He was absorbing all the power in the dam and the ley lines.

Archer turned and looked right into her eyes. "I'll kill you and take my kid." He leapt into the sky, his massive leathery wings flapping.

Risa's third eye closed, and she dropped back into her body. She jumped off the bed and nearly fell from a wave of dizziness.

Linc leapt up and caught her. "Risa, tell me."

"Archer! He's coming!"

"Anything?" Linc asked into his Bluetooth. He, Axel and Sutton were flying around the school perimeter, looking for any sign of Archer in the sky or rogues skulking around.

"No sign of Archer," Axel answered. "No idea if he can shield and appear invisible."

Shit, Linc hadn't thought of that.

"Several empty vehicles a few blocks away," Sutton said. "Engines are warm."

"I smell rogues," Ram replied from his position on the ground. "Not strong, so they're staying back."

"Invisible," Linc growled as frustration rode his spine. They couldn't do anything but wait. "Fucker was hibernating at Hoover Dam the whole time." If they'd known, they could have killed him before he'd locked in to his immortality.

Now the witches had to banish him. Everything in Linc screamed to keep Archer away from Risa. But they needed her shield to hold the spawn long enough for Darcy and Carla to do the banishing spell.

"We need more men," Ram said. "Phoenix and Key are dealing with multiple rogue attacks in Glassbreakers. They can't leave."

Linc flew around the back of the gym to the running track. He could see in the dark but spotted nothing unusual. Dipping low, he caught the faint scent of copper. Rogues, but where? Were they hiding behind a cloak of invisibility, or had they been scouting and left? To answer Ram, he said, "I called Baron. He and his crew are coming."

Linc, see anything? Risa's worried voice flowed in his mind.

Not yet. See anything else with your third eye?

Nothing more. But I can feel him closer. Too close. I need to come out there so I can be ready.

No! He roared that. He didn't want her—

A flaming arrow arched into the school, heading for Axel by the pool. *Shit! He's here!* Linc pumped his wings. "Axel! Arrow on your six!"

The man flipped in a series of aerial cartwheels, came out of the turns, and swooped below the arrow.

Linc caught up to him just as another arrow blasted through the sky, right at him. He shot straight up, banking left toward the front of the school, when he saw Archer land on the roof of the student dorm and fire another arrow.

Linc tried to evade, but it was too fast. Clearly the

man's power had increased. Magic flooded Linc's body and cinnamon filled his mouth just as the arrow slammed into his left wing.

For one second, the shaft hung there with the tip piercing the feathers, flames spitting sparks. Damn that burned. Before he could grab the shaft, the fire sputtered, died, and the arrow dropped.

What the fuck?

Shield magic, Risa said in his head. *It's in your wings, and I'm feeding it.*

Oh yeah, that half-breed demon was his now. Linc spun, leapt in front of Axel and snapped out his wing to block the arrow chasing him.

The arrow hit, sputtered and fell.

"He's on the dorm roof," Linc said into his Bluetooth, making sure all the hunters knew as Archer fired more arrows.

Linc zigged and zagged, blocking them with his shield-enhanced wings.

"Rogues," Sutton yelled, diving down and slamming into two men sneaking up on Ram.

The growl of motorcycles filled the night as more than a dozen choppers exploded into the school. Baron's armed men riding the bikes mowed down rogues.

Archer leapt off the roof into the air, firing arrows. Linc pumped his wings, desperately trying to catch them. He got one, but another slipped by, hitting the gym. Flames shot up, lighting the building on fire. Another arrow struck a rider wearing a Baron's M.C. vest, chasing a rogue.

The motorcycle gas tank exploded in flames. A horrific scream rent the air.

Linc kept going, trying to catch as many arrows as possible.

"We have to get him on the ground," Sutton said through the Bluetooth earpiece. "I have Ram's knife filled with electricity."

Linc recalled the witches' plan to stun Archer with Ram's electricity. Would it still work now that Archer had sucked up a lake's worth of energy?

"Distract him, Linc," Axel ordered. "The witches are ready."

Fuck. He didn't want Risa out here, but they had to end this tonight. The only way she and Kendall would be safe was to kick Archer back to the Underworld. With his wings as shields, Linc could protect her.

Decision made, Linc flew as close to Archer as he dared. "That all you got, fire boy?"

The creature's eyes glowed crimson. He nocked an arrow and—

Axel and Sutton slammed into him from behind. Lightning flashed, flames shot up. And all three crashed to the ground on the athletic field.

In the tumble, the electrically charged knife jetted out of Sutton's grasp. Linc dove to catch it, but it embedded in a rogue. The man screamed as the electrical energy cooked his organs in a hideous death.

Oh shit. Now they had no way to short out Archer's hellfire. Risa would be trying to hold this supersized hellfire-shooting spawn at full power with just her shield magic.

Worry twisted his guts. Could she do it?

Risa climbed on the back of Baron's Harley and gripped his sides. Once ready, she yelled, "Go!"

The man gunned his motorcycle, roaring across the school grounds around death and fires. So much blood.

Don't think about it. Opening her magic, she let go of Baron and wove her shield, working every strand, making the strongest shield possible. She pushed more magic. She had one chance to get this right.

"There they are!" Baron shouted.

The three men battled on the ground. Axel's wing was on fire, and Sutton had blackened strips of skin peeling off his chest. Archer shoved them both off him and jumped to his feet, nocking an arrow, aiming at Risa.

A whip snapped around Archer's arm. Eli maneuvered the lash, keeping a hold on the spawn. "Do it."

Baron skidded the motorcycle to a halt less than ten feet from where Archer was restrained. Risa hung on with her thighs and prayed she could do this. *Please, Ancestors, help me.* If she failed... No. She couldn't. Determined, she threw her shield.

It snapped around Archer and his arrows.

Pain. It blasted her nerve endings like she was being electrocuted. *Hold it, don't let go.* Archer fought her magic, sending bolt after bolt into her shield. Her world narrowed down to just this, accepting the fiery jolts, keeping her chakras open while weaving more magic.

Burning seared into her chakras, making them cringe. Her magic stuttered. Screams echoed in her head, rising in pitch, dragging at her mind. No! This couldn't happen. If Archer got loose, he'd kill them all and take Kendall.

Risa, I've got you. Let me have the pain, baby. Linc's voice penetrated the screams. *Come on, love. Keep your magic going.*

The bird flew in, his wings working as he herded her magic into a stronger, more disciplined stream. Relief from the hurting spread too. Opening her eyes, she realized Linc had pulled her off the bike and was holding her in front of him, facing Archer.

"More blood," Sutton said.

Linc sliced his hand, laying it on her stomach where he'd shoved up her shirt. "Keep going, Risa. I won't let go, sweetheart."

Dimly, she understood he'd been giving her blood to help her. His strength poured into her, while he siphoned off her pain. The ring on her right thumb glowed as the witches fed her additional power. They were doing it! She skimmed her hands through the air, pulling more threads of magic into the shield.

Darcy's and Carla's voices rose in a chant. "Pure in whiteness, born of earth, feared by darkness, embraced by light..."

Archer struggled, his power a dark, living entity, firing bolt after bolt of pain into her, but Linc funneled it off. Sweat poured down her back, and her knees weakened.

Linc's arm tightened around her waist. "Got you."

The bird worked in her magic, corralling the power into strong streams and guarding from threats.

"...Salt open the door, to the demon's demise!" The witches finished the spell.

Pull back. She had only a second or two to drop her shield before Carla and Darcy threw the consecrated salt that would fully banish a demon. Lowering her hands, Risa waited for the relief in her magic. She'd done it, held the spawn long enough to complete the spell. Wait. What?

The shield didn't release. Instead it stayed solid and connected to her chakras.

The bird stopped, wings going still. In her mind's eye he turned to her, his yellow-ringed eyes wide as he screeched a warning.

"Risa? What's wrong?" Linc demanded.

The bird screeched again as something oily streaked into her magic.

"Pull back!" Linc yanked her against him in an unyielding grip.

Panic ripped into her as she tried to retreat, but nothing happened, her shield didn't budge. What was going on? She opened her mouth to scream, *Stop!*

Too late. Carla and Darcy threw salt on Archer and Risa's shield.

"No!" Linc shouted, jerking her off her feet. "Something's wrong!"

Oh Ancestors! Archer had locked on to her shield. She'd be dragged with him. But there was no help.

The unholy pull started at her feet and shot up her being. Oh God, Risa couldn't save herself. But Linc held on to her, so she only had one choice.

Save him.

She gathered what magic she could and shoved Linc and the bird away.

Sulfur billowed up from the bowels of the earth and yanked her into the Underworld.

≥ 24 ≤

THE BIRD SCREECHED IN AGONY as Linc was thrown back ten feet, landing on his ass. Rolling, he leapt up and lunged, stretching in desperation to grab hold of Risa.

A sharp burn ripped across the inside of his chest. The bird screeched again, both of them experiencing a sudden loss as Risa's magic vanished.

"Risa!" The scream blasted from his soul. He couldn't let her go.

His hand brushed the edge of her arm. Almost...

I love you.

Her words filled his head just as she was yanked away. Gone.

There was something warm in his hand. He looked down.

The ring Darcy had given Risa. The one she was so proud of. The loss of her was unbearable, leaving a ragged hollowness in him. Shoving the ring on his little finger, he dropped to his knees, frantically digging at the ground where she'd been, as if he could tunnel his way to her. Red rage and pain consumed him. "No!" He plowed relentlessly into the dirt, the bones in his fingers snapping as he struggled to reach her.

"Linc, stop." Axel crouched in front of him, his hands clamping around Linc's wrists. "She's not there."

He looked up to the man. "Archer took her. He locked on the shield magic and took her. I tried to pull her back, but she threw me off." The horror flooded him.

He'd failed her.

Now Risa was alone in the Underworld. The last thing she'd said to him lingered in his mind. *I love you.*

He stared at that silver ring on his swelling finger, the awful pain in his chest slashing and tearing at him.

"Linc." Hands on his shoulder shook him.

He forced his head up and returned his gaze to Axel. "I have to get her back. She's mine. I don't care what it costs. I'll do anything." Without the bird to help her, oh God, the soul screams would attack. They'd rip her mind to shreds. "I have to save her."

"The only one who can help is Wing Slayer."

Their god? He could help? Linc would do anything to get to Risa and save her. "Where is he?"

Axel said, "You have to get away from the salt and the banishing spell."

"What?"

"Wing Slayer's half demon. The consecrated salt Carla and Darcy used is a problem for him. He's waiting for you on the roof of the staff residence." Axel pointed to the five-story building.

Rising, Linc turned to a huge figure backlit by the sun looming on the building. Around Linc were dead and wounded men from Baron's crew, burned-out bikes and scorched ground. The second building of classrooms had burned, as had the gym. But now all the flames were out, no longer able to burn once Archer had been banished.

"Here, let me see your hands," Carla said.

He shook his head. He didn't care about the broken bones, and he didn't want anyone touching Risa's ring. He launched into a run, hoping his wings would carry him. *Come on, Falcon. Wing Slayer is our only chance.*

The bird shook out of his cry and spread his wings, catching the air currents to take them up.

Landing on the roof, he focused on the huge being hovering close to the building's edge. After dropping to his knees, Linc removed his knife, cut his hand and laid the blade down in the offer of blood and service to his god. "Wing Slayer." As his blood dripped onto the roof, he implored him, "Help me save Risa. I'm begging for her life." How many lives had Linc begged for? Memories spun and replayed sickening details of those poor girls he couldn't save—who were always dragged from his cage and killed. He wasn't worthy of his god or his witch. He knew it. "I'll go in her place." It was all he had to offer.

"Asmodeus doesn't want you, hunter. He wants his granddaughter, Kendall."

Linc snapped his head up, but his words froze for a second, too struck by the terrible beauty of Wing Slayer. The god easily topped seven feet, and his wings glowed gold with red streaks. His enormous arms were wrapped in bands branded with wings, and he wore a bronzed cloth draped around his hips and over one of his shoulders. Linc raised his eyes higher.

The god's harsh face had something fierce and fucking scary bulging in his forehead. Horns?

"You don't want to see my horns, hunter." The voice boomed out as if projected from a thousand surround-sound speakers.

Right. Focus. "I just want to save Risa."

"He's willing to trade. He'll give you back Risa, an earth witch, for the baby with demon blood."

That easy? Just trade and get—

What was he thinking? God, he wasn't that much of a monster. If he handed Kendall over to Asmodeus, he'd be his mother. He stared at his knife lying there between him and Wing Slayer. What the hell should he do? He couldn't leave Risa in the Underworld either.

An impossible choice. He loved Risa, God he loved her. But Kendall was a baby. "I can't. I'll fight or do anything, but I won't sacrifice a baby." And if the god wouldn't help him, Linc would find another way to get to the Underworld.

"Pick up your knife, hunter."

His broken fingers hurt like a bitch, the smallest one swelling around Risa's ring. He reached for his knife, ready to beg.

The silver lit up, and the golden light raced around his hand.

Frowning, Linc watched both his hands heal in seconds from god magic. Warmth bloomed against his palm. Lifting the knife, he turned his hand over and opened his healed fingers. Impressed on the hilt of his blade were wings. Wing Slayer had marked his knife.

He looked up. "I don't understand."

"If you'd been willing to hand over that baby without a fight, you'd have seen my horns."

Elemental fear slid down his back. That would have been bad in a way Linc couldn't comprehend and didn't want to. "So what now? How do I get Risa?"

"You're going to have to fight. There's no other way to get her out from Asmodeus's clutches alive. Once Risa dies, her soul will still go to Summerland, but Asmodeus plans to keep her alive and torture her until we give him his granddaughter."

Memories of his own torture burned in Linc. His muscles twitched, the need to get to Risa zapping his nerve endings. "I'll do it. Tell me what it is. We have to hurry." He couldn't kneel there doing nothing while she suffered.

"Be sure, hunter. Right now you have Kendall, but if you do this, you could lose her and you'll die."

He narrowed his gaze, impatience fueling his anger. "You said we aren't handing over Kendall."

"Without a fight. I had to make sure you wouldn't sacrifice her. You tore yourself away from Risa when you found out she was rescuing a baby with demon blood, leaving your witch unprotected."

Shame pressed in. "I fucked up." He had done it, so damned scared of being betrayed as he had been by his mother, he'd pulled back. "I have no excuse. But I'll never do that again." Swallowing down the internal rage and desperation to save Risa, he fought for the patience to find out what to do. "Please, what's the plan?"

"A cage-fight deathmatch between you and Archer. The winner gets both Risa and Kendall."

Shock blanked his mind for a second. A cage fight? In the Underworld? Was that a thing there? Regaining his wits, Linc said, "Why would Asmodeus agree to a cage fight and risk it all when he can just keep sending his demon witches, rogues and any other spawns he has out there after Kendall?"

"He didn't have a choice. I issued a *Provocatio* challenging his son to fight my hunter to the death. If he refused, I could claim my boon, which would be Risa."

What? "How did that work? And when did you have time? It's only been minutes since Risa vanished."

"Time moves differently in the Underworld. Now are you interested in demon rules and politics or getting your mate back?"

Easy answer. "Risa. I'll do anything." Rage pulsed beneath Linc's skin. He wanted to kill Archer. That slimy prick had taken his... "Wait." A new concern struck him. "The witches said we can't kill Archer."

He glanced at the knife in Linc's hand. "I gave you the power to kill him in the Underworld with that blade. The knife is your weapon against Archer's hellfire arrows."

"In a cage?" That was suicide if Linc couldn't maneuver. Unless... "I'll have Risa's shield in my wings, right?"

"That's another reason Asmodeus accepted the *Provocatio*. Risa can't reach her magic right now."

"Because she's in the Underworld?" How the fuck was he going to win?

Wing Slayer waved his hand. "See for yourself."

Screams pierced his brain, and he was dragged through one murder after another, experiencing the terror and pain as soul screams ripped apart his skull.

Then it vanished, leaving him sweat-drenched and nauseated. "Do something!" Frantic worry clawed at him. "She can't endure it, she needs the bird." Linc fisted the knife, desperate to save her. "I can't reach her, she shoved me away." Out of love for him and Kendall. Did she know he loved her enough to come for her? Or did Risa think she was alone in torment?

Wing Slayer said, "You'll have only a few minutes with her while I secure the baby. Are you willing?" The god held out his hand.

He'd hesitated once when Risa needed him. Never again. "Yes." He set his hand in Wing Slayer's, and the world split apart as he was cast to another realm.

The Underworld.

Risa cringed as a scream dug into her mind, dragging her through another murder. Sweat soaked her skin, and she shivered with icy dread and constant bolts of pain. Exhaustion made her want to give in.

Let her mind shatter.

No! Eyes squeezed shut, she tried to push out of the pit of agony. Bloody, rotting hands reached for her with hatred boiling in eyeless sockets. She couldn't get free. The hands tore at her legs as the screams battered her mind.

Soft singing caught her attention. Risa fought, trying to surface out of the screams holding her trapped. There, she heard the melodious sound again, so beautiful it redoubled her hope and will to survive. *Falcon.* He came for her, which meant Linc was there too.

What if it wasn't real? Just more torment in her mind?

The singing increased in magnitude, the power of the trills and calls urging the souls to relax.

Come on, sweetheart. Come back to me.

Linc. Her magic opened, flowing out and spreading tranquility. The souls settled back into the quiet place, surrounded by a shield of serenity.

"I'm here, Risa. Look at me, love."

The sensation of his arms around her solidified. Slowly she opened her eyes. It all rushed back to her. "Linc, how did you get here? Where's Kendall?" She tried to move.

He locked his arms around her. "Rest a couple more minutes. Your magic is still working to heal you. And Kendall's fine, safe. I swear."

That helped her relax. She looked around the eight-by-eight cell, which was made up of black concrete of some kind and had a door with bars as thick as Linc's arms. Hooks hung from the ceiling, and black spikes protruded from one wall and part of the floor. She tried not to think about what those spikes were for.

"Where are we?" She'd been shoved in here and left alone to endure the soul screams. At least they hadn't thrown her on the spikes.

"Some kind of demon coliseum. This is a holding cell."

Chills raced down her spine. What did that mean? "You didn't answer my question. How did you get here?" Hope welled in her, but it couldn't be that easy for them to get out and return to Earth. She eyed the door. It was shut. Locked. He was locked in here with her.

"Wing Slayer." He explained his meeting with the god.

Amazed, she took it all in. "What's a *Provocatio*?"

"Not exactly sure, some kind of challenge that Asmodeus couldn't refuse, or he would've had to relinquish you to Wing Slayer as a penalty."

Emotion welled up, knotting in her throat while her heart ached with the magnitude of Linc's love. He'd done so much for her, pulling her back from the soul screams, helping her find and save Kendall, and once he discovered Risa had lied about the baby, he protected them anyway. And tonight...he'd come to hell to save her.

Risa cupped the side of his face. "You found a way to get here. I hoped, but I didn't know if it was possible."

His eyes burned a dark gold. "You knew I'd try? Even after I nearly severed our bond the night Archer woke and attacked?"

The memory hurt worse than the screams, that wrenching rejection just minutes after telling her he loved her. Taking away the most beautiful part of her...their bond and the bird that linked them. As she'd told him before, once she felt nothing with other men, but with Linc, she felt everything. Every emotion was bigger, sharper, more beautiful or devastating and he was worth all of it. "Yes. We're not perfect, but you're not your mother. You regretted that moment and fixed it, helping me come out of the soul screams afterward."

He brushed her hair back. "You were hemorrhaging blood and nearly died that night. Scared the fuck out of me. I knew in that second I still loved you."

"But I'd broken your trust by lying to you."

"I understand why—"

She slid her fingers over his mouth, cutting him off. "I learned the price of not trusting you, of not believing in you, and I'll never doubt you again. So yes, I knew you'd try to get to me, and save me if you could. All I had to do was hold on to a thread of sanity."

"God, I love you." He shook his head. "In all my fights and all my gambles at the poker table, the stakes were never so high, so important. This is the most crucial fight of my life. I'll win. I won't let you or Kendall down. You two are my world now."

She'd never been anyone's world. And she'd never had real forgiveness and understanding like Linc had given her. They'd fought, made mistakes and worked through it together. Her chest ached with the thick, warm sensation of their love. So powerful. He came to the Underworld for her, willing to fight.

Her breath caught at the full realization of what he was going to do, what he was truly risking, hit her. Shifting to her knees, she said, "Wait, you're supposed to get in a cage with Archer? He'll kill you! No, you have to go back!" She gripped his arm, panic pounding through her. "Linc, please. If you lose, you'll be dead, and Kendall will be at the mercy of demons."

His eyes darkened, and his shoulders swelled. "You're at the mercy of demons."

"They'll kill you. At least this way, I'll know you and Kendall are alive. That she has a chance. I can't watch you die too. I can't."

"I'm not going to die. I'm going to win your freedom." He slid something off his little finger and onto her thumb.

She recognized the feel of the ring that held her witch book, but she kept her stare on Linc.

"Why did you leave it with me? You love this ring. Darcy gave it to you."

Tears filled her eyes at his understanding that she'd valued that ring because it signified her friendship with other witches. He never tried to isolate her in the controlling way her father had isolated her mother. Instead, he'd supported those friendships because they were important to her. "That's why, Linc. I love the ring, but I love you more. If you couldn't save me, and I knew you'd try, but if you couldn't—I wanted you to have something of me. I hoped you'd feel my love in it."

He pulled her across his lap, his warm arms wrapping around her as his mouth crashed down onto hers. *My brave witch, I love you. I'm going to win and take us home.*

Desire surged into her magic, both from his touch, and the intimacy of his voice in her head. This special connection was theirs alone, and strong enough that she'd heard him even while trapped in the soul screams. Part of her wanted to hold onto this moment and stay here safe in Linc's arms. Except they weren't safe, and she needed more information. Risa eased back, staring into his eyes. "How will you win against Archer?"

Confidence brimmed in his gaze. "You. You're my secret weapon. We're going to fight together. Cage bars can't separate us."

She loved hearing him say that. Linc truly valued her. "I'll be able to use magic?"

"Yep. Look at your ring."

Risa lowered her gaze and gasped. The smooth silver had been reformed into two intricate wings circling her thumb. Running her finger over it, she caught the scent. "It smells like metal and flowers."

"Wing Slayer. He marked my knife and your ring, claiming us both. He'll make sure you can use your magic, and he gave me the ability to kill Archer in my knife." Cupping her face, he added, "It'll still be a battle, Risa. The god gave us all he could. Now it's up to us. And the demons will use any trick they can to torture and break us." His gaze burned into hers. "You can't push me away to protect me, no matter what happens. We do this together, or we lose everything."

Before she could answer, the door clanged open, and two males with red leathery skin, curved horns like a ram, and cloven feet entered. But it wasn't the grotesque creatures that got her attention.

No, she honed in on the thick metal collar, wristbands and chains they dragged.

Linc tensed, and Risa leapt to her feet. "You aren't chaining him!"

They shoved her aside and tackled Linc to the floor.

"Risa!" Linc's bellow bounced off the walls.

Two more demons rushed in to yank her up. "I'm okay!" She shouted it, but Linc was already gone.

The remaining demons dragged Risa out into a hallway. Tortured screams rent the air, and her stomach heaved. The long gray stone walls were covered in claw marks, dried blood and gore. The smell...like rotting garbage and dead animals baking in the sun.

A low, menacing growl raised the hairs on her neck. The skin over her spine prickled. What was that? Where? She twisted her head to look behind her. Long empty hallway, the walls dotted with thick bars indicating cells.

Another snarl.

Adrenaline shot into her bloodstream. It came from up ahead. The walls ended, and the walkway kept going into open air. Terror took hold. She struggled with the two seven-foot giants holding her arms.

Mercilessly the demons dragged her forward toward the sickening sounds of ripping flesh and snapping jaws. *Don't look.*

But she did. Straight down into a pit of frenzied creatures—misshapen animals. A lion's head on a gorilla body. Another that had an alligator tail on a horse's frame. The things fought over what looked like chunks of flesh.

"We feed the losers to the hellbeasts. Some are dead, some wish they were," one of the demon's said in stilted English.

She'd landed in a nightmare. Would Linc be able to get them out?

≫ 25 ≪

IT TOOK ALL LINC'S SELF-CONTROL not to fight the chains. He stood, stripped down to shorts and his knife holstered on his thigh, facing to colossal iron doors that matched the iron clamped around his neck, wrists and ankles. The demons held the chains attached to his shackles.

He couldn't lose this fight and his anxiety spiked. He'd been in countless deathmatches with his own life at stake and had felt nothing but adrenaline and fury.

But now he risked Risa and Kendall. The two who gave him a reason to live, and to kill. Protecting them mattered more than all his wealth, his life or even his soul. He had to win.

Raw determination thumped with each heartbeat as he waited, mentally preparing. He expected tricks, but he couldn't react or let his fear of what would happen to Risa and Kendall if he lost get into his head space. Fear could cause him to make a fatal mistake. He had to stay clear and focused.

The doors began to swing open with an ominous creaking of hinges. Linc steeled himself, blanking his expression and icing his emotions. He faced an oval-shaped arena roughly the size of a football field.

Demons of every shape and size filled the seats stretched around the field.

The demons pulled on his chains, forcing Linc to follow them through the doors. He ignored the clapping, thumping and bellowing to focus on the massive cage structure that covered a third of the arena. Real bars stretched up with no end in sight, enclosing the fighting ring. Behind that roared a wall of flames.

Hellfire. The smell and screams coming from that were bad enough. The distorted, melting faces flashing on the surfaces of the flames, forever locked into a mask of agony, touched off bone-deep resistance that nearly caused him to stumble. The demons yanked on the chains, knocking him off balance. He dropped to his knees two dozen feet from the cage and the wall of hellfire behind it.

The iron around his neck tightened as they held him on his knees.

"Ready to die, Feral?"

Linc turned his head toward the voice, and swear to Wing Slayer his skin crawled at the sight of Asmodeus to the right of the cage. The demon had three heads—a ram, a bull and a monster. He sat on a throne with his massive cloven hooves twitching on the footrest. Fluttering around him were three strangely lovely creatures, females no more than four feet in height, with delicate wings in jewel colors outlined in black. They had antenna-like protrusions coming from their foreheads.

Forget the women. He returned his attention to Asmodeus. Despite Linc's submissive position, he said, "I'm not the one who will die. We kicked your son's ass off of Earth and sent him back here. Where is he?" Linc glanced around, looking for the spawn. "Hiding?"

The roar of the flames amplified, and the wall of

hellfire shot up two hundred feet into the bleak sky, then split apart all the way down to the ground, like the water parting for Moses. Archer stood in the unearthly glow of the flames, leathery wings lifted high, arms spread wide.

The demons in the stands surged to their feet, shouting and clapping in thunderous adulation. In a blink, Archer vanished from the curtain of flames, appearing before Asmodeus's throne. "Father, I bring you a gift."

A trio of silvery spotlights snapped on from somewhere, illuminating the floor a dozen feet in front of Linc. A large round section of the surface vanished, leaving a gaping black hole.

Linc's icy calm cracked as the top of Risa's head appeared, rising from somewhere beneath in a slow reveal. Her hair was styled into dark, shiny curls around her face, eyes rimmed with blue liner, lips painted a luscious, shiny red, and diamonds dripped from her ears.

The dais she stood on lifted her higher. Bared shoulders gleamed beneath the lights. She wore a designer halter dress in seductive red, which cupped her breasts, slid over her hips and down her legs. A slit to the top of one thigh showed too damned much. Silver sandals adorned her feet, exposing red toenails.

The dais slowly turned, and the crowd roared their lust over her long, slender back bared down to her ass. The smell of pheromones saturated the place.

She was being displayed. A thing to use just as her father had done to her.

Linc lunged against his chains, desperate to get to her, to yank her against him to protect her and shield her from being displayed like a whore.

"The witch who dared to steal my daughter, your granddaughter," Archer announced. "She used her sex appeal and lies to lure witches and hunters to help her."

"A beautiful traitor," Asmodeus's ram head said.

The bull turned its eyes on Linc. "She's lured you as she's lured so many others. You will die as they did."

Risa's face was frozen, her chin held high in defiance. He could barely feel her magic. Her power was trying to protect her as it had when he'd first met her. But she had nothing to be ashamed of, no reason to hide. He mentally reached through their bond. *Don't look at them, look at me. They are nothing to us. They might see your body, but I see the beauty of your soul.*

Her eyes came to his. *They won't break us.*

There she was, his warrior witch shining out of that seductress costume. Pride in her filled his chest and his wings surged out, slamming into a half-dozen demons on either side of him.

The furious males jumped up, ready to attack.

"Enough."

Linc recognized the voice. Wing Slayer stood on his left, opposite of Asmodeus. The god moved his hand and Risa vanished from the dais and instantly reappeared in a chair close to Wing Slayer. A second later, Linc's chains broke off, and a force yanked him from the aisle to inside the cage.

Automatically, he locked his gaze on Risa, relieved that Wing Slayer would watch over her.

Risa stared back as she raised her hands, pulling gossamer threads of her magic from her witch shimmer and weaving them into a shield. His wings lifted high as her power flowed into them. *Go kick some demon ass.*

Her voice bushed his mind, reaffirming her belief and trust in him. Before he could respond, the cage door clanged shut, the reverberation ringing in his head and sharpening his awareness. Whipping out his knife, he turned. Where was Archer?

A hissing noise raised his guard.

Linc spun as a flaming arrow streaked from above. Cinnamon magic flooded him, and he blocked with his wing.

Another arrow fired, and Archer soared down, his face contorted in fury.

Linc blocked the arrow and leapt, grabbing the spawn's calf and slashing his blade into the leathery skin.

An arrow rocketed toward his face. Linc had to pull back, releasing Archer. The shaft missed his cheek but singed a path of hellfire across his deltoid. He smelled his own flesh burning. He focused on Archer, losing track of time as he fought, slashed, blocked and searched for an opening to kill the spawn.

"Where is the child?" the bull head of Asmodeus suddenly bellowed.

Don't get distracted. Linc kept his full attention on Archer, blocking another arrow as he somersaulted in the air, trying to get behind the spawn.

"She's in the astral plane, awaiting the outcome," Wing Slayer answered.

"We demand the child!" all three heads decreed. "You issued the *Provocatio.* We answered by bringing the witch. You will produce the child now or your hunter forfeits."

Worry gnawed at Linc, but he lunged, plunging his knife deep into Archer's side.

The demon spawn screamed and shot a volley of arrows so fast, Linc could barely track them to block them with his wings.

"We insist the child be present. That was the agreed terms." All three heads nodded.

"Hold the fight until I return," Wing Slayer commanded.

Wait, what? No, he didn't want Wing Slayer leaving Risa. "It's a trick!" Linc shouted.

"No choice, hunter." Wing Slayer vanished.

"We demand a penalty for this duplicity," Asmodeus decreed.

Icy dread kicked Linc's stomach. Before he could think what to do, two demons grabbed Risa from the chair, dragging her to the front of the cage and forcing her to her knees in the same place where she'd risen from beneath the floor.

The doors that Linc had entered the arena through blew open, and a huge demon came in wearing thick gloves and holding a long pole with...

Oh, fuck, a branding iron! A bellow tore from his soul, and Linc threw himself at the bars. "No!"

Risa raised her face to his, tears streaming down her cheeks as her hands continued moving fluidly to weave her magic into his wings. *Don't look. They want you to hurt yourself before Wing Slayer returns and the fight resumes. They're trying to break you.*

"Brand the witch a Harlot! Brand the witch a Harlot!" demon voices shouted.

The brand glowed a sizzling, violent red.

"Brand me!" Linc shouted, wrapping his hands around the bars, his knife clanging as he fought to get out. He couldn't endure it, couldn't let this happen. Every cell screamed, his muscles jerking with insane agony.

The demon raised the brand, and Linc's vision turned scarlet. "Don't fucking touch her!"

The bird screeched in his head, wings beating against the bars with Linc. Wild desperation jacked his heart rate when he honed in on her hands, which were still moving in that weaving motion. *Risa, use your shield!*

Can't. Archer'll kill you if I pull back my shield from your wings.

The brand closed in, only a foot away from her back.

Use your fucking shield! He couldn't bear it.

Archer's behind you! Fight or this is for nothing.

The brand edged in, sizzling inches from her skin.

"Stop!" Wing Slayer roared, appearing next to Risa. The god shoved the demon holding the brand across the arena with one hand while carefully cradling Kendall in the other.

Through it all, Risa kept weaving. She would have let them brand her to keep feeding him magic. He gripped the cage bars, panting and unable to believe it.

She lifted her gaze to his, her eyes blazing fierceness through her tears.

His heart kicked. She'd been terrified, scared, but his mate hadn't run. Hadn't left him, not even emotionally. *You're my warrior witch.* He needed her to know and tried to project more when a voice interrupted him.

"You killed my mother," Archer said above him.

With Risa safe, Linc pivoted. Time to end this fight. He had to free the woman he loved no matter what the cost to him.

The spawn hovered fifteen feet off the floor with his back to the bars, hellfire leaping around him. "I gave up my humanity to save her from the flames. She spent four months being tortured with hellfire. I could only get her out by spawning and grabbing that kid so she could be raised to want to spawn." Archer's eyes filled with fire.

"Dude, I'm not your therapist or priest." Seriously, did this look like soul confession time? Linc eyed the way the flames appeared to be feeding the spawn energy or fire. Not good. Deciding to keep the bastard talking while he figured out a way to attack, he said, "Your mother chose to serve a demon master and saddled you with him as a father. She deserved to die. But I could understand wanting to save your mom despite that." Linc gripped his knife, looking for some weakness, but the flames protected Archer. "But then you had a daughter."

Red rage smoldered in his eyes. "Told the bitch to get rid of it."

Risa's pain slammed into him, hot, bubbling anger and grief for her friend and outrage for Kendall.

He's going to pay, love. Focused on Archer, he said, "That's what makes you a flaming asshole. When Asmodeus demanded the child, forcing you to choose between your mother or kid, you should have chosen Kendall. She's the innocent. You should have refused to spawn and taken her and Blythe and gone anywhere you could to be safe. Instead, you chose your mother who'd made a deal with a demon."

"He tricked her!"

"Bullshit." Linc pushed harder. "How do you suppose your mom got so rich? Her business so successful? She negotiated everything she wanted in exchange for having a demon brat and promising to raise him to spawn. She didn't protect you." Maybe. Linc had no fucking idea.

"Shut up! My mother loved me!" Yanking an arrow from the quiver on his back, he slammed it into the bow and released.

Linc shot up, snapping his wings out to block.

Too slow. The arrow dodged the wing, angled down and tore into his calf and through the bone with fast and deadly force thanks to the hit of hellfire energy. Fuck, that burned. Flames hissed and snarled, hungrily tearing his flesh.

The hellfire rushed inside him. Hot. Raging. Killing him. No time. He had to kill Archer. As long as Archer died before Linc, Risa and the baby would be freed. He shot forward, wings pumping. Flames raced up his thigh.

Archer shoved away from the bars, his wings flapping, another arrow nocked. "You're dead, hunter."

Risa's power bloomed, lighting up his entire being.

The flames on his leg sputtered and choked, then died. *Together. We fight together,* Risa said through their link, her presence in his mind a source of strength. *Let me worry about the hellfire. You kill Archer.*

His warrior witch filled him with pride. Linc thrust his wings faster, stronger. "Hey, dumbass, you forgot something." He crashed into Archer, slamming him back to the side of the cage a few feet away from the hellfire.

The arrow between them hacked into Linc's side, the fire eating at his organs. *Ignore it.* If possible, Risa would heal it. He shoved the knife into Archer's chest, slicing through skin and ribs. The tip of the blade pierced the spawn's heart, but not deep enough to kill him.

Archer screamed and wrapped both hands around Linc's wrist, stopping his progress. Black-edged flames burst out of the demon's fingers. Agony bit into Linc's nerves. The skin bubbled and blackened, peeling off in strips.

He blocked it out, determined to hold the knife and push it far enough into the heart to kill Archer. Didn't care if the hellfire burned through to his bones, he'd keep his grip on that damned knife to save Risa. She was worth any torture. "Want to know what you forgot?"

Archer's crimson eyes faded to a pinkish white. "You have to die!"

"No, I don't. You forgot the real threat here." The fire around his wrist snapped and hissed, wrestling Risa's beautiful magic. "My witch. Risa fights at my side. That's her magic kicking the shit out of your hellfire." Leaning in, he made sure Linc's eyes would be the last thing Archer saw before he died. "And my knife killing you. No one threatens my mate or my child." Linc tightened his grasp and shoved, using his body weight and love to drive the blade straight through the demon's heart.

The wall of hellfire flames rushed over Archer, yanked him away and receded. Yet it didn't touch Linc.

Blinking, Linc dropped to the mat. Agony shot up his leg. He didn't care. The arrow that had been embedded there had vanished, either from Risa's magic or it had disappeared when the hellfire pulled the spawn to his death. Spinning around, Linc noted the throne and viewing stands were empty. All the demons had left too.

The cage door swung open.

He raced out, fell to his knees, pulled Risa into his arms and kissed her. Finally he lifted his head and looked at his god. "Thank you."

Wing Slayer nodded, shifted the baby and touched Linc's fire-ravaged hand, wrist and arm. Heat flashed and then receded, leaving the limb healed. His leg healed in the next instant.

"Better." Wing Slayer held out the baby. "Now for your daughter. You have claimed her, hunter. She belongs to you and your witch until she is thirty, at which time she will choose to remain human or spawn."

Kendall stared at Linc for a second, then held out her pudgy arms.

Linc gathered her to his chest, and one of his wings folded around her. Kendall giggled, petting the feathers. He looped his free arm around Risa.

Her gorgeous eyes glittered with unshed tears. "You trusted me. Believed that I could fight the hellfire."

A huge grin split his face. "Just like you believed I'd come for you here in the Underworld." He'd fought with his fellow hunters and trusted them with his life. But Risa? He trusted her with his heart and soul. "Told you, little warrior, I will never doubt you again. Never pull away." He brushed her face with his fingertips. "Together."

"Always."

"Rise," Wing Slayer commanded.

They stood, Linc cradling Kendall. The god loomed over them. "I cannot grant you immortality until the souls are released from your magic, Risa."

Linc felt her distress and rubbed her shoulder. "The soul screams are unbearable for her. How can she release the souls?"

The god looked at Risa. "You need to ask your Ancestors. They can assist you."

Before they could respond, they were sent back to Earth.

Risa watched as Linc laid the sleeping baby down in the crib shielded by a screen made of wings. They were on the rooftop, the one where Linc had made love to her. "Where did this come from?" The crib and screen hadn't been there before.

"Since Wing Slayer sent us here, it had to be him." He took her hand.

She let him pull her toward the glass overlooking the city. Linc wore shoes, jeans riding low on his hips and the bird inked over the brand. Risa had on the yoga pants and tank top she'd been wearing before being pulled into the Underworld.

Thankfully, that dress was gone.

Her eyes were drawn to his back, and she reached out to skim her fingers over the bird.

Linc stopped, his muscles tensing.

"I want to look at the brand that marks you as the man who fought to free me. I heard you scream at the demons to brand you instead. I'd rather they hurt me than you." He'd been hurt enough already. "Please. May I ask the bird to step aside?"

Linc looked over his shoulder. "The bird is yours. You don't have to ask."

Risa wanted him to understand. She'd never abuse the trust Linc gave her. "I had no choice in the Underworld. I had to wear that dress and was displayed as a creature who used her beauty and sexuality to hurt others. That dress was like a scarlet letter proclaiming me as the evil seductress my father turned me into. The thing I hated in myself."

His eyes filled with rage. "I know, baby. But that's not who you are."

His love swelled in her, a healing balm that helped her let go of the past. She wanted to do the same for him. Stroking the bird, she said, "This brand exposes a part of you that you sometimes hate. I'll respect your choice if you don't want me to see."

Linc spun, tugging her into his arms, his mouth claiming her in a hot, wet kiss. Possessive heat sizzled between them. His hand squeezed her hip as he pressed his erection against her belly.

No. He was saying no. Risa fought a wave of disappointment, but she understood. In time, he'd trust her enough.

Linc pulled back, and his nostrils flared. "I'm on the edge of losing control. They held a fucking branding iron close to your back. I need to strip you bare and turn you to see your back. To kiss every inch of that flesh those animals threatened. And while I do that, I'll be inside you, claiming you."

The fierce heat of Linc plowed into her veins, yanking open her magic to spill out. An ache bloomed deep in her womb, one only he could fill.

He released her, pivoted and sank to his knees.

Confused, she stared at his massive shoulders covered in bronzed skin and ink. What was he doing? "Linc?"

"I don't hide from you, love. Ask the bird to move. He'll do it for you."

Shivers danced over her skin, raising a million tiny

bumps of emotion. Her heart swelled, and tears filled her eyes. He was giving her this gift—a trust so deep, he'd let her see his brand. "Falcon." Her voice quivered. "Will you show me?"

The bird slid down to Linc's lower back. Across his shoulders, burned into his flesh, was the word *Feral*.

A huge wave of emotion surged into her chest. He'd made a choice, choosing this mark over hurting a woman. To her, this brand represented a man who strove to do the right thing no matter the cost to him, and she loved and admired him for it. Risa dropped to her knees and kissed each letter.

Linc pulled her around in front of him, his mouth hungry for hers. She held nothing back, kissing him with the passion that belonged to him. Only him. Her magic rose, stripping them of their clothes.

Then Linc did as he'd promised, turning her to kiss her back while sliding his cock into her body.

Branding her as his.

≈ *26* ≈

LINC WALKED OUT ON THE balcony of the suite. Kendall wiggled in a brightly colored baby-bouncer contraption. Going over to her, he crouched down and caught sight of the words blazed across the bib covering her sleeper.

My Daddy Has Wings.

His chest ached. *His daughter.* Once he hadn't thought he wanted this, then he'd lost Risa and learned just how far he'd go for his mate and child.

To hell and back.

He and Kendall were still getting to know each other. But Linc looked into her sweet face and experienced a growingly familiar wash of protective emotion—love. Yeah, she was his.

"So what do you think of my new friend?" He held up the stuffed dragon toy he'd bought today.

The baby's eyes lit up, and she held out her arms.

Linc helped her hold the toy, which she immediately put in her mouth. Laughing, he got up and turned.

Risa stood against the railing, watching him.

She took his breath away. With the moonlight gleaming off her dark hair, her magic shimmered the lightest blue on the skin of her shoulders and arms. She wore a black tank top and a white skirt down to bare feet.

Drawn to her, he crossed the balcony and slid his arms around her. "I like this outfit."

She leaned her head back. "Carla said I should wear a dress for the spell. Close-to-the-earth kind of thing." She lifted her chin.

So she'd chosen something that suited her and that she felt comfortable in, not exposed and displayed. After they'd arrived back at the academy, she'd gotten to work with the girls, figuring out how to reach the Ancestors to release Nola's soul to them. While seeing Nola had been a figment of Risa's desperation, loneliness and cracking mind, the baby's soul was as real as all the others in Risa's magic. Taking Nola's soul to the Ancestors in Summerland would give Risa the closure she needed. And while there, Risa would ask how to free the remaining mortal souls to go on to their afterlife.

He drew a finger down her slender throat. "I'm told spell work requires you feel your desire." Axel had filled him in, warning him to be prepared.

"Will that embarrass you?"

Linc wrapped an arm around her waist, pulling her to him. "Never. Your magic and desire are part of you. It's real and honest." He studied her face. "Have you been worrying about that?"

"A little."

"Why? We're going to be out there with our friends who understand magic."

"I don't want to embarrass you. In the Underworld, I was painted up as something—"

"That enraged me for you, but it didn't embarrass me." Had she thought him ashamed of her? Demons and their fucking tricks. Mindful of Kendall right by them, he kept his voice gentle. "Don't let those demons do this, Risa. Don't let them make you doubt yourself. Last night I was proud of you. When they displayed you that way, you refused to cower and kept your eyes on me." He leaned down to kiss her. "Only me."

"Because you saw the real me."

"Damn right." Oops. He had to remember not to swear in front of the baby. "I saw my courageous witch willing to sacrifice herself for Kendall and me." She'd pushed him away so he wouldn't be dragged into the Underworld with her. And she'd been willing to let those demons brand her to keep feeding him magic. That kind of selfless bravery was a pure love that Linc hadn't believed in—until Risa.

She relaxed a bit.

"You're going to succeed tonight." She had to. Linc needed her free of the soul screams and to have peace.

She nodded. "I hope so. I can open my third eye, but it's up to the Ancestors if they wish to talk to me or help me." Her gaze filled with vulnerability. "If they forgive me for failing so many souls. I'll beg them, Linc. Not for me, but for the souls. They've suffered enough."

"You've suffered." Didn't she get this? "You never deserved this."

"I don't think it's about deserving it. Growing up, I was spoiled and vain. I wasn't mean or awful, but I had everything handed to me. I think my journey was to understand magic is a gift that has responsibilities. I've carried some of these souls for years. I understand the costs to actions that maybe I wouldn't have learned otherwise." She looked up at him. "I could have been my mother. She willingly helped my father kill. I love her for the moments we had, especially with music. But I don't like that about her. She turned her back on what it means to be an earth witch."

"They will accept you." How could they not? A

woman who understood herself so well? Risa didn't hate those souls in her magic who tormented her, who had cracked her mind repeatedly. She cared for them, protected them. "Are you ready to let Nola go?"

"I am. Her soul lodged in my magic when I miscarried her, and she deserves the chance to either stay in Summerland or reincarnate." She laid her head against his chest. "I know she wasn't real when I saw her, but to me, she was, and I will always love that she was with me then."

Linc remembered his own moments when he'd seen his mother in his cage. Not the druggie she'd become, but the flashes of a loving mom he'd occasionally seen as a kid. It'd been real to him too. "She was your angel when you needed her. Now it's time for her to go home, perhaps to be someone else's angel."

"I like that. It's how I'm going to think of her." She turned to the railing.

Linc tugged her back against him, both of them watching as the night deepened and the moon rose higher. "It's a mess out there. The town has been torn apart by Archer's destruction, and fear is running high, especially after Lake Mead dried up."

"And?"

She knew him, understood he was working up to something. "Baron has asked me to stay and help him and what's left of his crew get control and kill off the rogues. But if you don't want to stay here, we'll go back to Glassbreakers. I have a home there. If you don't like it, we can get something else. You'll have your friends, Darcy and Carla, and you'll love Roxy and Ailish too." He wanted her to know she had options and that her needs came first.

"We can't leave here. I mean, if you have to be in California for Wing Slayer Hunter business, that's fine, I'd love to visit. But Vegas is where our home needs to be."

Stunned, he moved to her side to look into her eyes. "I thought you hated Vegas." She'd never said it, but she'd moved away after her father went to prison. He'd gotten the impression that the town held too many bad memories for her.

"Once, yeah. But now..." She turned to look at Kendall.

The baby chewed on her dragon.

Risa shifted her gaze back to him. "This is home. Hilary is here, and she's Kendall's grandmother." She took his hand, threading their fingers. "I know she's not your biological mother, but she saved you and loved you exactly the way you needed. Kendall needs a woman like her in her life. And Hilary is already in love with the baby. You need Hilary too. And Baron. I only met him last night when he helped me, but he's impressive. He didn't hesitate when I told him the plan."

Linc saw it again, Baron and Risa on that motorcycle, flying across the grass toward Archer. How the witches cooked up that scheme he'd never know.

Risa went on, "He helped you figure out what being a witch hunter means, right?"

"Yes, and to manage the rage of the feral creature in me."

"Both Hilary and Baron did, and Kendall will need that kind of support too. At some point, she will feel her demon side. Like you feel the feral side of you. Kendall will need all of us to help her."

When he'd met Risa, she'd been in a cage wearing a shock collar and facing death. Prickly and scared, not letting anyone close to her. Now? She had embraced the people in his life. "So you want Hilary, a former educator and hardass as her grandmother, and Baron, who runs an outlaw motorcycle club and illegal prostitution ring, as her grandfather?"

"Yes."

Damn, that was one lucky baby.

"And also, I think you should rebuild your house, but it's your money, so whatever." She shrugged. "Hilary said we can live with her in the meantime."

He laughed, joy welling in him. "We'll rebuild if that's what you want. Something that's ours with a music room so you can teach our girl to play piano."

She leaned into him for a minute. "It's time to do the spell." After kissing him, she went to Kendall and lifted the baby from the bouncer.

He pulled in a breath. This had to work. He couldn't bear Risa getting dragged into any more soul screams.

The night fell velvety quiet around the athletic field of the L.C. Academy. White candles burned on an altar draped with silk. Risa stood in the center, Carla to her left, Darcy on her right.

Linc's hands were warm and steady on her hips, his breath stirring her hair. She could feel him merged into her mind, the wings of his falcon in her magic, corralling that power while singing to the souls.

Ginny stood two yards away, holding Kendall and flanked by Eli and Ram. Hilary had gone back to her home, saying she had a ton to do to get it ready to have a baby there.

More magic flowed from Risa's chakras, filling her pores and heightening awareness of everything around her. The cool grass beneath her feet, Kendall's soft chatter, the flames on the candles and the scent of the wax.

The pressure in her head increased.

"Your third eye," Carla said. "Come, Risa." She held out her hand.

"Where?" She trusted the witch but wasn't sure what she was supposed to do.

"I'm going with you to take your daughter home."

Linc's thumbs tucked beneath her shirt to stroke the bare skin over her hipbones. *I have you. Go with Carla, love, and take Nola home.*

Linc's words in her mind dissolved the last shred of her uncertainty. Trust welled in her, and the second her fingers joined Carla's, her mind flew out of her body. Her third eye opened to a million pops of light. It was astonishing, like being in the middle of a starburst.

"Ancestors," Carla said. "They've met us to welcome Nola, and you may ask them how to free the remaining souls."

The souls glittered and glided, mesmerizing her with their breathtaking splendor. Struggling to find her voice, she managed to get out, "It's an honor, thank you for seeing me."

"We've been waiting for you, Risa. Are you ready?" a thousand voices asked her in the sweetest sound.

Carla's hand gently squeezed hers in a reminder to answer.

Risa pulled herself together. The Ancestors had granted her this audience, and she didn't want to disappoint them, or fail the souls. "I'm ready."

"Cup your hands."

Releasing Carla's fingers, she lifted her hands as if holding a baby bird. As she waited, a light appeared there, so tiny and fragile, it brought tears to her eyes. "Nola. My little bell. I love you."

"Release her," the voices said as warmth spread around her, a wave of welcoming.

Risa stared at the soul for another minute, drinking her in. Then, like opening wings, she parted her hands.

Nola floated away into the embrace of the starburst.

Her heart ached for what might have been had she

not miscarried, and yet the beauty of the moment soothed her and gave her the courage to say, "May I ask how I can free the other souls in my magic so that they will go to their afterlife?"

The lights shifted and moved. "You must call an angel of the mortal realm to coax them from your magic and shepherd them home."

Like the Ancestors did with Nola, she thought. But what spell?

"Be at peace, Risa. You will see Nola again one day." The stars burst open, spilling out words that formed into the spell to call an angel. The text hovered just long enough for Risa to read them, then faded away into the silky night.

When she opened her eyes, she was back in her body with the candles glowing in front of her. Linc's arms circled her, holding her against him. The comfort eased the lingering grief in her heart. Gazing down at her fingers twined with Carla's, she pulled the witch's hand between both of hers and lifted her eyes to the woman. "Thank you."

She smiled. "I had to take my sister to Summerland. I wanted to be there with you. Know that your baby is safe and loved."

Tears ran down her face. How did one ever repay a gift like that? "I do."

Linc said nothing, his heart thumping a slow, steady beat against her back. He supported her, aided her, but didn't interfere in the moment that was going to be a special bond between her and Carla.

Finally she released Carla's hand and turned to Linc. "The Ancestors showed me how to send the souls home. It's a spell. I'm not sure what will happen, but I want to do it before I forget. And while I still feel the Ancestors with me. They were amazing, Linc."

"This is your show, love." Leaning down, he brushed his lips over hers. "Every time you unleash your magic, I'm awed and proud. Let's free those souls."

Smiling, Risa turned back to the altar. Everyone did their spell work differently. For Risa, the altar gave her a sense of reverence. Confidence surged in her. The Ancestors had showed her how to do this.

Linc resettled his hands on her hips, and her magic resumed the pulsing power, rising and pushing. Risa pulled every strand as if she were going to weave a shield.

But instead of using her hands, she harnessed the magic into her voice.

Hand of an Angel,
I call you this night.
The souls are trapped,
With no place to rest.
Weary and frightened,
No hand to hold.

Wings of an Angel,
Hear my call tonight.
The souls seek freedom,
To move on from here.
Peace will not find them,
Without wings that soar.

She took a deep breath, raising her arms and holding out her hands in a plea.

Heart of an Angel,
We beseech you this night.
Call your souls home,
To be lost no more.

The candle flames flared six feet in the air, the individual blazes joining together as light flooded the field.

Risa closed her eyes, the illumination piercing her retinas and stabbing her brain. Yet even with her eyes closed, the brightness blazed against her lids.

Linc said in her head, *What is that? I can't open my eyes.*

An angel.

"I am Vigilance."

"Your father!" Ram roared. "Run, Ginny!"

"Silence." The angel's voice blared out like a trumpet.

What? Panic slammed into Risa. Snapping open her eyes, she pivoted. Ginny held Kendall, but her eyes were on the being glowing beyond the altar. What's more, she glowed with a matching brilliant light, her eyes jewel green, and her dark hair shimmered. Plain Ginny had morphed into a stunningly beautiful woman.

An angel. Ginny was an angel. And Risa had inadvertently summoned her father.

Ram and Eli each held a hand around her arms, but no one moved. Kendall buried her head in Ginny's shoulder.

"I have answered your call, witch. You may cast your eyes on me. I have dimmed the angel fire."

No one spoke or moved. The power radiating from the being on the other side of the altar thrummed in the air. Had he frozen them or merely stunned them? Slowly, she turned her gaze from Ginny to the angel.

Magnificent. He had wings so stunning she could barely look at them. The feathers were the color of the moon reflecting on water—white diamond with veins of blue and gray. He shone as if he had internal spotlights. Even dimmed as he claimed to be, he was difficult to focus on directly.

Regaining a fraction of her wits, she said, "You're Ginny's sire." The one Ginny had said wanted to take her from Ram. She turned to the woman. "I'm sorry. I didn't know."

Ginny couldn't answer. Whatever the angel had done, everyone remained silenced.

Vigilance moved forward, *through* the altar as if it wasn't there. More light spilled over Risa, flooding her cells. "There they are. So deep in your magic, yet their souls live. You have done well."

The angel's power was inside her, which was...well, not creepy, but not comfortable. Then he stepped back and held out his hands.

Risa's magic swelled up like a wave in the ocean. A sudden ache in her head warned her an instant before her third eye opened. The bird soared in, singing his soothing tune. One by one, he gently gathered each soul in his claws and ferried them to the angel, laying them in the being's hands, before flying back to retrieve another. Until he came to the last soul, the one that clung to her magic with such longing it filled Risa's throat. Without permission, she turned from the angel and walked to Ginny. Linc went with her, his hand staying on her hip.

When she reached Ginny, she eased Kendall from the woman's frozen hold. The baby came to her easily.

In that second, Blythe's soul released her hold on Risa's magic. Through her third eye, Risa saw the small light slide around Kendall, touching her cheek, stroking her hand.

The tenderness wrenched Risa's heart. "I'm sorry, Blythe. So sorry. But I swear to love and protect her."

The light glided to Risa and touched her face.

"It is time."

Risa jumped, not having heard the angel move up to her left side.

Vigilance lifted his hand, and Blythe settled there then vanished.

"So now you leave?" Risa was grateful that Vigilance had helped her and the souls, but Ram's reaction worried her.

"With my daughter." He reached past Risa.

"No," a thunderous voice said.

Risa whipped her head around to see Wing Slayer appear behind Ginny, both his massive hands clamped on her biceps.

"Wing Slayer," Vigilance trumpeted.

"Vigilance," the god responded. "I claim Ginny."

"You cannot!" The ground shook, the candles spitting fire.

Linc yanked Risa aside, his wings popping out and wrapping around her and Kendall.

"You stole my hunter," Wing Slayer shot back. "Your daughter is marked by the wings of my protection." He lifted his hands, and two bronze bands shaped like wings surrounded Ginny's biceps. "You will not force her to ascend unless she removes the bands, or you free my hunter."

Risa opened her mouth, but her throat didn't work. She couldn't move.

The angel froze us all. Axel, Sutton and I can fight it, but the others can't, Linc said in her head.

I was talking earlier. So much was happening, Risa couldn't keep track of it all.

Because he wanted you to.

This is crazy. Ginny's father is an angel?

So it would seem.

"You dare much," Vigilance said to Wing Slayer.

Thunder boiled below the ground. "Eli Stone is mine. Release him, and I will lift my mark from your daughter."

"This is not finished, Wing Slayer." The angel shot up into the sky and vanished.

The god stepped around Ginny, Ram and Eli.

Axel, Darcy, Sutton and Carla all knelt. Darcy's necklace and Carla's armband glowed, but the god passed by them.

Risa started to kneel when the god reached out his hand. "Come."

But what about Ginny, Eli and Ram? Risa couldn't get her head around all that had happened once Vigilance, and then Wing Slayer, had arrived. She glanced over to see that Eli, Ginny and Ram were still frozen in place.

"I have done all I can for them this night," Wing Slayer said.

Startled, she returned her gaze to the god, realizing he'd heard her thoughts. Or maybe saw her looking at Ginny and the two hunters and guessed her question.

"They will be released from the freeze in a moment, and as safe as I can arrange for now," he added. "No more questions."

She glanced up at Linc. Did he think her an idiot for silently challenging his god?

He gripped her fingers. *No. We both care about our friends, love. We'll be there for them when they need us, just as they've been for us. It's all we can do.*

Reassured, she held Kendall tighter. Together, she and Linc placed their hands in the god's outstretched one. In seconds, they knelt on the roof of the L.C. Family Recover Center. But Risa's arms were empty, sparking her panic. "Kendall!"

"Peace, witch, she's here."

Risa looked up to see the powerful, scary god holding Kendall. The baby lay in one enormous arm, watching the god's wings with rapt fascination.

"Hunter, your knife." He held out his other hand.

Linc slid his knife free and handed it to the god.

Kendall reached for the shiny blade.

Risa reacted instinctively, catching the baby's arm. "Would you like me to hold her?"

Wing Slayer raised his eyebrows, his wings twitching. "Do you think I'd allow harm to come to this child?" As he spoke, the knife moved from the god's hand to rest on the air well out of Kendall's reach.

Embarrassment heated her face. Wasn't it bad enough that in her concern about Ram, Ginny and Eli, she'd hesitated when Wing Slayer held out his hand to them? Now she questioned his care of Kendall? "No. It was automatic. I... She's a baby and fast. She'll grab anything." Risa squeezed her eyes shut. He was a god. He could easily keep Kendall from getting the knife.

Easy, love, he's not angry, Linc said gently in her head. *When he's pissed, his demon side shows. Two horn things protrude in his forehead, and the red in his wings pulses. Fucking scary to see.*

"I can hear you," the god sighed. "Risa, you have no reason to fear my demon side. Nor that I will allow harm to befall Kendall." Wing Slayer gazed down at the baby, his harsh face softening and his wings brightened.

All her earlier confusion and worries slid away at the sight. Wing Slayer wasn't just a god, but half demon as well. He'd protected Kendall, even knowing she was the child of his enemy. "I don't fear your demon side," she whispered, her throat going tight. "Having met you, felt your protection, is an honor. Seeing Kendall in your arms is... I have no words. People may say that Kendall is marked by demon blood, but I look at you with your demon blood and see hope for our daughter. She is part demon, and I won't ever deny that. Instead I will point to you to show her the standard of what her demon side should represent."

A wave of fierce pride flooded into her from Linc, and he squeezed her hand. But Risa hadn't said those things to impress anyone. They were the truth.

The god smiled at Kendall. "You've chosen your mothers well, little one. Both your birth mother and your adoptive one." When he returned his attention to

Risa and Linc, he grew solemn. "Lincoln Dillinger, Risa Faden, you have proved yourself worthy. Raise your joined hands."

Once they obeyed, Wing Slayer's hand settled over theirs. "Look around you, Risa, your Ancestors are here."

Her breath caught at the stunning sight. Each Ancestor looked like a unique and dazzling star in a velvety night.

I see them. Linc's voice echoed in her head. *You're showing me through our link. They're magical.*

Risa couldn't think of a better word to describe them.

With their minds joined, the touch of the god seared through them right down to their cells. Risa clung to Linc's hand as their life forces twined together, weaving and reshaping. Winds blew and time spun. Through it all, she hung on to Linc mentally, emotionally and with their laced fingers. The full scope of the moment settled over her.

Lifting his hand, Wing Slayer said, "You bear the mark of immortality."

"How?" She gazed at the healed white rings circling the base of their thumbs. "You didn't have the knife in your hand. I didn't feel a cut."

Linc laughed. "He sliced it, but he moved so fast you couldn't track it. I felt the cut for both of us before he healed it."

"Exactly as he should," Wing Slayer said. He laid the baby in Risa's arms, spread his wings and lifted off into the night. "Care for them well, hunter."

Linc sat back on his butt, pulling Risa and Kendall into his arms. "You're mine now."

Worry edged into her happiness. Everything had happened so quickly. "Are you sure this is what you want? Being a dad? And a mate? Forever?" She closed her eyes, holding Kendall close. Love for Linc swamped her. This man was special, extraordinary, and she desperately wanted him to be hers.

But he'd been caged too long and in too many ways. And she loved him enough to put his happiness first. "Linc, you're finally free. Truly. No captors, no bloodlust. You don't have to do this. If you aren't really ready to be a mate or father, or you ever feel trapped, I won't hold you back. I'll never hold you back," she said fiercely, her love nearly choking her.

His eyes glinted in the moonlight. "Risa, baby, don't you know?"

"What?"

He cupped her cheek in the palm. "I escaped my cage years ago, but since then I've been searching. I've won millions. I've bought houses, cars, built schools. I became a Wing Slayer Hunter and saved countless lives, fought the evil of demon witches and rogues, but nothing I did ever eased the gaping, aching hole that left me hurting and wanting."

Her heart swelled with hope as bright as any angel and as powerful as any god. "Linc." The word was torn from her heart.

He leaned his forehead against hers. "Until you, my warrior witch. You are my happiness, Risa. I love you and our baby girl."

Tears filled her eyes. She'd never been anyone's happiness. "I love you too. It feels like I've been alone all my life, until you rescued me and showed me that love is the real magic."

The End

Dear Readers,

Thank you for reading Caged Magic! I hope you enjoyed Linc and Risa's story, and catching up with all the characters from the series.

I wanted to take a second to express my heartfelt thanks to all the Wing Slayer Hunter fans for being so patient and never losing faith in me, or in the characters. For various reasons, it took a long time to write this book, but I know one thing for sure—it would never have happened without you. So thank you from the bottom of my heart.

My future plans consist of at least two more books—*Primal Magic* which will be Eli's story, and then *Fallen Magic* which will be Ram and Ginny's story. And I always have more stories brewing as I love the Wing Slayer Hunter world!

In the meantime, if you haven't checked out my sexy contemporary series, The Plus One Chronicles, you can get the first book, *The Proposition* for free in digital format.

Happy Reading!

~Jen

Other Books By Jennifer Lyon

The Wing Slayer Hunter Series

Blood Magic (Book #1)
Soul Magic (Book #2)
Night Magic (Book #3)
Sinful Magic (Book #4)
Forbidden Magic (Book #4.5 a novella)
Caged Magic (Book #5)

The Plus One Chronicles Trilogy

The Proposition (Book #1)
Possession (Book #2)
Obsession (Book #3)
The Plus One Chronicles Boxed Set

Anthology

The Beast Within Anthology
with Erin McCarthy and Bianca D'Arc

WRITING AS JENNIFER APODACA

ONCE A MARINE SERIES

The Baby Bargain (Book #1)
Her Temporary Hero (Book #2)
Exposing The Heiress (Book #3)

THE SAMANTHA SHAW MYSTERY SERIES

Dating Can Be Murder (Book #1)
Dying To Meet You (Book #2)
Ninja Soccer Moms (Book #3)
Batteries Required (Book #4)
Thrilled To Death (Book #5)

SINGLE TITLE NOVELS

The Sex On The Beach Book Club
Extremely Hot

ANTHOLOGIES

Wicked Women Whodunit Anthology
with Mary Janice Davidson, Amy Garvey & Nancy J. Cohen
Sun, Sand, Sex Anthology
with Linda Lael Miller and Shelly Laurenstron

About the Author

Bestselling author Jennifer Lyon lives in Southern California where she continually plots ways to convince her husband that they should get a dog. So far, she has failed in her doggy endeavor. She consoles herself by pouring her passion into writing books. To date, Jen has published more than fifteen books, including a fun and sexy mystery series and a variety of contemporary romances under the name Jennifer Apodaca, and a dark, sizzling paranormal series as Jennifer Lyon. She's won awards and had her books translated into multiple languages, but she still hasn't come up with a way to persuade her husband that they need a dog.

Jen loves connecting with fans. Visit her website at www.jenniferlyonbooks.com or follow her at https://www.facebook.com/jenniferlyonbooks.

CPSIA information can be obtained
at www.ICGtesting.com
Printed in the USA
LVOW07s2127041217
558590LV00004B/1038/P